NH₃

STANLEY SALMONS

RICKSHAW PUBLISHING

NH₃

STANLEY SALMONS

RICKSHAW
PUBLISHING

Rickshaw paperback

First published in Great Britain in 2013 by Rickshaw Publishing Ltd,
102 Fulham Palace Road, London W6 9PL

www.rickshawpublishing.co.uk

A CIP catalogue record for this book is available from the British
Library.

ISBN 978-0-9565368-6-0

Printed and bound in Great Britain for Rickshaw Publishing Ltd by
CPI Group (UK) Ltd, Croydon, CR0 4YY

RICKSHAW
PUBLISHING

This hasn't happened – yet

PROLOGUE

The river flowed slowly, smooth as glass, deep brown fading to the colour of tea at the margins. Under the trees on the opposite bank it was all reflections, a tangle of inverted grey limbs. A curled brown leaf glided slowly through them like a miniature galleon, the only evidence of movement.

He scanned the water, shifting his gaze to the left, following the flow. A submerged rock scarred the surface with a long V and in a few more yards the water was criss-crossed with oyster-shell patterns across its width as it encountered a bed of shingle. The wavelets became more agitated, cresting with white foam as they splashed over the pebbles. Then the river gathered its skirts and flowed on down towards the village.

One September a lovely trout rose to his floating fly here, ambushed as it slipped quietly under overhanging branches, then heavy with foliage. No chance of that tomorrow; with the leaves just breaking it was too early in the season to rely on surface activity. He'd have to sink the flies – but without snagging a hook on the stony river bed. That was one reason the Welsh Rivercast Competition was such a challenge.

The late afternoon sun cast his shadow along the bank, long and thin. The shadow withdrew towards him as he lowered himself to the grass and sat, cradling his knees in his arms, savouring the tranquillity, looking forward to the next day.

He frowned. Something was wrong.

For a long time he sat there, looking and listening.

The river burbled across the shallows; the trees sighed, stirred by a breath of wind.

Then it dawned on him.

Where were the birds? No crows arguing in the topmost branches; no clucking of ducks as they sculled around the bend; no feathery flutter from a curious robin; no clatter of alarm from a blackbird; no raucous rattle of a magpie.

Even in April the surface of the river should have been dimpled by the touch of dancing midges; geese should be flying home; squirrels should be looping across the ground and spiralling up the trees.

Everything was unnaturally still.

For a moment he closed his eyes, straining to heighten his awareness. There were the expected scents of the countryside: a faint whiff of cow dung; the sweet, wine-soaked smell of silage; the cold, metallic air that rises near to fast-running water. But something else was there, too, something that did not belong. It was hard to place.

He shook his head, got up from the river bank, and walked briskly back to where he'd left the car at the side of the road. He strode past it, up to the old bridge. It spanned the river at its narrowest point, where the flow funnelled into a rock-strewn ravine. The tightly fitting stones blushed orange in the setting sun and a shaft of light strayed inside the mossy arch, its path a rectangle of vivid green.

The banks on either side were steep. He edged down a short way and watched the rushing water as it tumbled noisily over the rocks and hurried under the bridge. Something silver caught his eye, in a foaming eddy at the foot of the opposite bank. It was a small fish, floating on its side, rocking gently. Dead.

The smell was more pungent here than it had been on the bank further upstream.

Ammonia!

Ammonia?

Ammonia. A colorless, pungent, suffocating, highly water-soluble, gaseous compound with the formula NH_3. B.p. -33.5°C. Forms salts with most acids. Employed in refrigeration and in the synthesis of pharmaceuticals and commercial chemicals, including fertilizers and explosives. Although widely used, ammonia is caustic and hazardous to health.

Stoddard's Technical Dictionary, 2007

CHAPTER 1

Dr. Terry McKinley returned to his car and drove across the bridge towards the village. A few minutes later the road became the High Street, Stryd y Fawr. Normally there'd be a banner stretched from side to side of the street to welcome visitors to the competition and people would be strolling or chatting on the pavements, but there were neither banners nor posters and the village seemed strangely deserted. He pulled into a small cobbled courtyard at the side of the Black Lion, an old-fashioned, privately owned inn with two or three rooms that were small but cheap, and comfortable enough for a few nights' stay. He'd been here often enough to get a friendly reception.

Daffydd Morris came out as Terry was opening the boot.

"Hallo, Doctor, welcome back!" They shook hands. "Here, let me take that for you."

He lifted Terry's suitcase out and led the way to the rear entrance. Their shoes echoed on the wooden staircase, blackened over the years by successive layers of polish. There was a faint odour of lavender. Daffydd opened a door off the uncarpeted landing and ushered him into his room. He put the case down on a threadbare rug in the middle of the floor and turned to him. He was a good deal shorter than Terry, and broad in the chest and arms, but his waist had thickened in recent years and he was breathing heavily.

"It's good to see you again, Doctor. I suppose you came here for the competition, then?"

"I did indeed, Daffydd, but I just took a look at the river. Seems to me to be in very poor shape."

The man shook his great head sadly.

"Terrible, terrible. I would have said something about it when you booked but Ewan kept saying 'No, you mustn't do anything to discourage our visitors, Daffydd, not yet, not while we still have a chance.' You remember Ewan Maddock, do you? He's organizing this year." He sighed. "They had to cancel in the end, all the same."

"Cancelled? What, altogether?"

"Ay, afraid so. The river's dead, you see."

"Oh for God's sake. It would have been nice if somebody had told me. What happened?"

"Best if he tells you himself. Maybe you could pop round there in the morning?"

Terry felt the heat rising to his face. "Actually, I think I'll head over there right now."

Terry knew the Maddock farm; it was off a narrow road that branched away from the high street at the other end of the village. He was angry when he emerged from the Black Lion but as he walked he began to take a broader perspective. The Welsh Rivercast Competition was the one time of year when the village filled up with visitors: competitors, onlookers and press. All the bed-and-breakfast accommodation in the village was fully booked. The sandwich bars and the two tackle shops did a roaring trade during the day and the two pubs were in full swing every night. For many of the villagers it was a significant outside source of income. Cancellation was disappointing for him; it would be financially disastrous for them.

Terry opened the gate, walked up a short path, and knocked on the door of Maddock's cottage. It was answered by Ewan's wife. She was a dumpy, busy woman, well-known to the visitors for running a virtual conveyor belt of tea and refreshments during the competitions. There was a brief light of recognition in her eyes as she wiped her hands on her apron.

"You'll be wanting Ewan, I expect," she said.

"Is he around?"

"He's just moving the cows to another field. Come and sit down – won't you? – he'll only be a minute."

He followed her into the kitchen and she indicated a bench alongside the table, which was almost white with constant, daily scrubbing. As he sat down she said:

"Can I get you a cup of tea?"

"No, I'm all right, thanks." He didn't feel like accepting hospitality.

"I'll just get on, then," she said, turning back to the big stone sink. "I was in the middle of something."

He looked around the kitchen. The quarry tiled floor and heavy oak furniture probably hadn't changed since the small cottage was built a few centuries before. It was not unlike the cottage in Northumberland where he'd grown up.

There was a heavy thump of boots being discarded in the porch and Ewan entered the room. He was a big, red-faced man with surprisingly blue eyes. He was still wearing his cap and a high-necked wool jersey under his jacket which was full of holes.

"Visitor for you, Ewan," his wife announced.

He extended a powerful hand.

Terry shook it without warmth. "Terry McKinley," he said, and added pointedly, "I *was* here for the competition."

"Oh, Mr. McKinley, you had a wasted journey! I'm sorry, didn't you hear? We had to cancel the competition."

"Yeah, I know that now. Why didn't you contact me?"

"I tried – left several messages for you on your answering machine."

"Answering machine? Not voicemail?"

He shook his head. "Answering machine. I recognised your voice."

Terry winced. They'd been phoning his flat and he'd been at a conference in Cardiff for four days. He had a mobile phone but they probably didn't have the number.

Ewan's wife broke in.

"I'll put the kettle on, shall I?"

"Please, *cariad*. You'll join us in a cup of tea, Mr. McKinley?"

"Er, yes. Thanks." It seemed churlish to refuse now.

Ewan lowered himself to the bench opposite Terry, gripping the edge of the table with fingers like fat red sausages.

"I've been down to the river," Terry said. "I smelled ammonia. What was it, some sort of spill?"

"Must have been. We had the water people down and they checked the river and they said it wasn't from the factory but nobody believes that, do they? There isn't another factory for miles. Accidents do happen but they should have been made to clean it up – and pay proper compensation. If you ask me there's been a bit of the old..." He gave Terry a meaningful look and rubbed finger and thumb together.

River inspectors on the take?

"What about the Salmon and Trout Association – did someone alert them?"

"Yes, and they flagged it up with the Environment Agency Wales. They said they were already looking into it. Not a word since."

"When did all this happen?"

"October last, just at the end of the season."

Terry looked at him in surprise. "As long ago as that?"

"Yes. Someone saw a couple of dead fish washed up by the bank. But that was only the start of it – a few weeks later the place was littered with them. Stank to high heaven, it did. We went down there and scooped them up and I buried the lot in the field out there." He jerked a thumb behind him at the window. "Might as well use it for fertilizer, I thought, but it broke my heart to do it, all the same. Some lovely fish, there were."

Mrs. Maddock served the tea in an earthenware cup and saucer for Terry and a large mug for her husband.

"Would you like some biscuits?" she asked.

"Not for me, thanks," Terry replied.

Ewan gulped down a mouthful of tea. "It was a good competition last year. You missed it, didn't you?"

"Yes, too busy unfortunately. I would have missed this year's too, but I thought I could fit it in on my way back from Cardiff." He paused to take a sip of his tea. It was hot and strong. "So what happened after the fish died?"

"Ah well, we didn't panic," he said. "We had six months for the river to come back. To be honest, I still don't understand why it hasn't. Two weeks ago the committee met. We'd have done anything not to cancel. We agreed to put in some stock fish – took every penny we had in the competition coffers." He leaned forward, placing a hand flat on the table, and dropped his voice. "Died, every last one of them." He sat back again. "We had to give up then. You can't have a fishing competition where there's no fish, can you?"

Back at the Black Lion Terry hung up his jacket, tossed his suitcase on the bed, and opened it. Pushing aside the dirty washing that had accumulated while he was in Cardiff, he took out his toiletries bag and some casual clothes and set them out on the chest of drawers. He had a quick wash, dressed, and went downstairs.

There were already a few regulars in the bar. They stopped talking as he entered and he stood for a few moments in the heat of their stares. Out of the corner of his eye he saw one of them half rise, only to be pulled back by restraining hands. You didn't have to understand Welsh to hear the truculence in his voice and the placatory noises from the others. It was understandable. A stranger like himself was quite possibly a water inspector or an employee from the factory and neither one would be welcome here at the moment.

Daffydd Morris appeared behind the bar and Terry walked over. Daffyd indicated the menu chalked on a small blackboard at the side of the bar.

"Now, what can we get you, Doctor?'

"I'll just have a pint of bitter and a packet of salt and vinegar crisps, thanks Daffydd."

"Are you sure? Got some lovely pie fresh out of the oven."

"Thanks, but I'm not actually that hungry."

"Fair enough."

Daffydd poured his drink and got his crisps from a box behind the bar. Terry thanked him and took them upstairs, away from the disgruntled regulars.

He perched on the side of the bed but got up again almost immediately and paced the room.

Ewan had said the pollution started six months ago. To have continued this long it had to be more than an accidental spill: there must be an ongoing leak. Why hadn't it been identified and stopped? Had there really been collusion?

Local people always referred to that place as "the factory". He'd seen it often enough: the shabby Victorian block fronted on the river about a mile upstream from the main road. There was a small metal pedestrian bridge, presumably erected by the current owners, but he'd never ventured across it, deterred by the sound of dogs barking in the distance. Most anglers avoided that stretch of the river, preferring to fish upstream or on the prime run down towards the old stone bridge. So far as he knew it wasn't an unproductive spot, merely unattractive, and they viewed with suspicion the large-diameter, aluminium-clad pipe work that emerged from the brick wall and disappeared under the surface of the water.

He paused at the window. The small, uneven panes gave a distorted view of the courtyard where he'd parked his car but it barely registered. He continued to stare sightlessly, taking an occasional pull at his beer, drifting back twenty-two years to his first visit to the village.

It had been "Hugh" and "Marjorie" for as long as he could remember. "Uncle" and "Aunt" seemed somehow too formal and they wouldn't have been comfortable with "Dad" and "Mum".

They weren't churchgoers but Marjorie was a strong believer in Providence. It was Providence, she used to say, that Terry was pulled, unmarked, from the wreckage of the car in which both his parents had been killed. Her own marriage had been childless, and for her it was an unexpected blessing to be entrusted with her late sister's baby.

Hugh and Marjorie. The only family he'd ever known.

The idea for the fishing trip had taken shape when Hugh was

rummaging in what they called the stock room, looking for a motor to power their latest Meccano model. In a trunk he found a fishing satchel, and Terry, watching him from the door, heard him muttering, "Well, well, well." A further hunt uncovered a green linen bag, which he declined to open, saying it was all going to be a surprise. He and Marjorie were already planning a touring trip of Wales in his small Rover. It required just a small diversion to incorporate a few days in a village recommended by one of his retired architect friends.

They'd left Marjorie selecting wool and knitting patterns in the tiny but well-stocked craft centre, a short walk down the High Street from the bed-and-breakfast where they were staying. Hugh stopped off at the Post Office to get a licence and a permit, and then, at last, they were heading down to the river. The time had come to undo the ribbon ties on the green rod bag. Hugh unsheathed two shiny black carbon sections and fitted them together. Terry's excitement gave way to consternation as he looked into the fishing bag. There seemed to be an awful lot missing.

"Um, Hugh, aren't you supposed to have coloured floats and maggots and stuff like that?"

Hugh smiled. "This is a different sort of fishing, Terry. This is what we use."

He opened a tin box, revealing row upon row of tiny hooks, tied with feathers and fluff so as to resemble flies. Many of the hooks were rusty.

Hugh clucked his tongue. "Haven't used these for a while." He poked around with a finger. "This one looks okay, let's tie it on."

Hugh wasn't much of a fly fisherman but once he'd explained the rudiments Terry began to cast tolerably well. It was a source of wonder to him that a fluffy confection not much more substantial than a dandelion seed could be delivered for yards across the water. That day he caught a small trout and it wasn't just the fish that was hooked…

In the courtyard outside the window the light was fading. Terry smiled sadly into the gloom.

It was just like Hugh to do something as brilliant as that; to bring him here, to this perfect river, to show him how to cast a fly. If ever he had a son, he'd want to do exactly the same thing. Thirteen would be about the right age. He could visualise a younger version of himself: tall and spare, hazel eyes, curly brown hair.

He'd try to give the boy a childhood as happy as his own. They were always busy, always into new "projects". He could picture the ever-expanding mural on the wall he'd painted with Hugh along a whitewashed passage outside the kitchen. Then there were wildlife walks, jigsaws, model aeroplanes, Meccano models. The kitchen windowsill was lined with runner beans in jam jars, carrots in saucers, even – very briefly – a formicarium, although Marjorie directed that one firmly outside, saying she didn't intend to be picking ants out of the sugar bowl.

In the end, though, what had really captivated him was the night sky. Removed as they were from major towns there was no light pollution and on cloudless nights Terry would be out there in the garden with Hugh's old binoculars, gazing at the moon and planets. Before long he'd started to devour books on astronomy. On one particular night Saturn, Jupiter, Mars, and Venus were all up there, strung out in a line across the sky, and he had a vivid mental picture of the whirling disc of dust and gas from which the whole solar system had condensed. That, more than anything, had set him on the path of his present career.

He looked down into the foam-laced bottom of his glass, remembering how proud Hugh and Marjorie had been when he was awarded his Physics degree. Barely six months later Hugh had died of cancer. By that time Terry had moved nearer, to Newcastle University, for his doctoral studies. A frail Marjorie saw him get his Ph.D. in Astrophysics before she, too, was taken from him. Parenthood had come too late in life for Hugh and Marjorie.

For Terry this was much more than a fishing destination; it was a place of pilgrimage. To defile it in this way was like kicking over their gravestones.

He took a deep breath and turned away from the window. In the morning he would go the factory himself and get some answers.

CHAPTER 2

It was only a faint cry and at first he thought it was a lamb. He heard it again, coming from somewhere up ahead, but the river curved to the right and his view was obscured by the bank. He quickened his pace, listening carefully, and rounded the bend. There was something at the water's edge. It looked like a bundle of clothes, swelling and subsiding as each slow ripple washed up on the bank. Then he saw the hand.

He hurried forward, a tightness in his chest. But as he got closer the fingers of that outstretched hand curled and opened again. A low moan issued from the bundle.

The man was lying on his side in a foetal position. He was wearing thigh waders, which were covered in mud, and his jacket had come up around his head, which was why the heap had looked so formless. Terry dropped to his knees, drew the collar down and winced. The face was badly bruised. There was a lump on the forehead on which the skin had split; it was bleeding, but not too much. One eye was closing rapidly; the other was fixed on him in terror.

"It's all right; I'm going to help you. I'll phone for an ambulance."

He straightened up, took out his phone, then muttered a curse; there was no reception here. The man was trying to say something.

"Get back... factory."

Terry frowned. It wasn't a good idea to move an injured man but he had been lying partly in the water and he was soaking. He wasn't young, either; he needed to be taken to somewhere warm and dry where he could get treatment quickly. Moving could be the best thing for him.

The man resolved his dilemma by making a painful attempt to get to his hands and knees. Terry stepped in. "Hang on," he said. "Just lie back a moment while I get these off."

Gently he removed the thigh waders then helped the man slowly to his feet. He was holding his ribs and his teeth had started to chatter. He pointed with a shaking hand to a small crate lying on its side on the bank. There were several small bottles in it, some of them smashed. He must have been taking samples just downstream of the factory.

"Never mind that," Terry said crisply. "Let's get you sorted."

He hooked an arm around him, feeling the cold damp of his clothes and the shivers running in waves through his body. The village had to be the best part of a mile back; the factory would certainly be closer. They faced up-river and began to hobble along the bank.

The small metal bridge came into view. They struggled over it and along the side of a high wire fence. Looking to see where the gate might be, Terry realized there was more to the factory than you could see from the river. The building had been extended at the back so that it formed three sides of a square with a central yard, presumably for loading and unloading. Evidently they'd been spotted because one of the gates to this area opened and two security men hurried out. Dogs barked from somewhere inside the compound.

"It's Mr. Loomis!" one shouted to the other. And then to Terry, "What happened?"

"I don't know. I found him by the river."

"Michael, phone Dr. Saunders. And get Jenny Davies down here right away. Jenny's the First Aid," he said to Terry.

"I think he may need more than that."

"We'll see in a moment."

They assisted the injured man to a glass-walled security office at the side of the yard, where they settled him into a chair. The man called Michael returned, putting his radio back into a holster on his belt.

"Jenny's coming." He turned to Terry. "Thank you for bringing him in, sir. There's no need for you to hang around. We can look after him now."

"Who's Dr. Saunders?" Terry asked.

"He's Mr. Loomis's supervisor."

"Well, if it's all the same to you I'll hang on here and have a word with him."

The man shrugged. "As you wish. He's on his way now."

A large woman – presumably Jenny, the First Aid Officer – came bustling into the office. Terry stepped outside to give them more room. A few moments later a tall man wearing a white coat came out of the old section of the building, hurried across the yard, and stood in the doorway. Terry listened to the conversation.

"Good heavens! Look what they've done to him! Have you called an ambulance?"

"Not yet, sir. We were waiting for you."

"What do you think, Jenny?"

"Definitely. He needs to be looked at properly."

"I'll call them, Dr. Saunders."

"Thank you, Michael."

"By the way, sir, there's somebody outside waiting to see you. He was the one brought him in."

The man emerged and saw Terry, apparently for the first time. He extended a hand.

"Trevor Saunders," he said. "And you are…?"

Terry gripped the hand briefly. "Terry McKinley."

In the office the woman was saying, "Take it easy now, Mr. Loomis. Ambulance is on its way. You're going to be all right."

"I gather you brought Henry in?"

"Yes, he wasn't all that far from here. I found him half in and half out of the river."

Saunders cocked his head slightly. "You don't sound like a local man to me."

Terry fished in his wallet and handed over his university ID card. Saunders studied it, then handed it back.

"Department of Physics, University of Liverpool," he said. "So what are you doing in these parts, Dr. McKinley?"

"I was on my way back from a conference at Cardiff. Came down to have a look at the river."

"I see. Well, we're most grateful to you. I do hope this hasn't spoiled your day."

Terry ignored the note of finality.

"What do you think happened to Mr. Loomis?"

"I don't know, we'll have to wait until he can tell us. We'll inform the police, of course."

"Dr. Saunders, let's be frank. I know this river well; it's one of the loveliest natural brown trout rivers in the whole of Wales. I come here straight from the conference and when I get here I find everything's dead. The annual fishing competition's been cancelled because there are no fish to catch. And why? Because there's so much ammonia in this river you can smell it from the bank. You're the only factory within miles and you have a man out collecting water samples so it's not hard to guess who's responsible. Now I may only be an outsider but I'd still like to know how you can stand by and let something like that happen."

For several seconds they held each other's gaze. Then Saunders said, "Come with me." He turned to one of the security men. "We'll be in my office. I'll bring him down when we've finished."

Terry looked around him as he followed Saunders up a flight of stairs and along a short corridor. The interior seemed quite modern; evidently these people had only preserved the shell of the original building. Saunders opened a door, on which a small black-on-white plaque read "Environmental Control Officer", and they entered the room. It was filled with natural light from a large window behind the desk. Saunders indicated a chair but before sitting down himself he drew a large ledger off a shelf. He cradled it in his hands as he dropped into a leather swivel chair behind the desk.

"Dr. McKinley, you brought Mr. Loomis in, so you deserve some answers. But you're wrong about what's happened. You're a physicist, I'm a chemist; we're both used to looking at data and drawing conclusions. That's all I'm going to ask you to do now."

Terry nodded cautiously. "Alright."

Saunders placed the ledger on the desk and flicked over a few pages, then turned it around for Terry to see.

"We had an Anti-Pollution Officer here from the Environment Agency. I'm going to show you what I showed him. It's part of my job to keep detailed records of everything we discharge from this factory. The analysis is done on a daily basis."

Terry looked at a tabular print-out. Down the left-hand side was a long list of substances: elements, like aluminium, calcium, magnesium, silver, antimony, arsenic, mercury, nickel; salts, such as sulphates, fluorides, nitrates, nitrites; and organic compounds that he wasn't familiar with, like tetrachloromethane, trihalomethanes, atrazine, and bromacil. His eyes wandered to the columns, where a series of figures appeared to list the measured levels and the permissible levels.

Saunders reached into a desk drawer and brought out a thin sheaf of papers.

"Now this is the analysis performed on samples collected from the river by the Anti-Pollution Officer." He ran a finger down the columns. "Let me draw your attention to the figures for ammonia. In the river they measured 50 milligrams per litre. That is a grossly polluting level and explains the state of the river. But look at the figures for ammonia in our effluent. They're less than one hundredth of that level. You can turn to any date you like: since this factory was established we have never exceeded permissible levels."

Terry lifted an eyebrow. "Well, something's done it."

"Indeed it has. The obvious candidate would be sewage, but look at the BOD." He placed a finger on the Environment Agency report.

"What's BOD?"

"Biochemical Oxygen Demand. It's a way of measuring material that removes oxygen from the water as it's broken down. Sewage is one such material, so if there is a lot of sewage present then we would expect a high BOD. But these figures show that the BOD was pretty well within normal limits, so whatever caused the ammonia to rise, it wasn't dumping of sewage." Saunders sat back in his chair. "What we put into the river," he gestured at the factory analysis, "is perfectly compatible with aquatic life. What's in there, most definitely isn't, but it's not coming from us. The Environment Agency reached the same conclusion." He detached a sheet of paper from the sheaf he'd taken from the drawer and pushed it towards Terry. "This is their report. They gave us a clean bill of health."

Terry scanned the letter. It looked genuine enough. Examining the figures had drawn him into scientific mode, and his anger and indignation had abated. He studied the man who was facing him calmly across the desk. The fact remained: ammonia was an industrial pollutant and this was the only factory for miles. He must be missing something.

"What do you make here, Dr. Saunders?"

"Circuit boards. Specialised ones for extreme conditions: high temperature, high humidity, that sort of thing. Mainly for industrial control systems."

"And you use ammonia in the processing?"

"Yes, in some of the cleaning cycles. That's why we have to be so careful about waste treatment."

"But the Environment Agency has to rely on your figures for what's in the effluent, doesn't it?"

Saunders' eyes narrowed fractionally

"No, it doesn't. Agency staff made an independent analysis of our effluent. Their results agreed with ours."

Terry sat back and for a while they contemplated each other. Saunders broke the silence.

"We know very well how it looks. We're confident of our processing but people still think we're responsible. Why do you think poor old Loomis was attacked out there? Feelings are running high locally, particularly about the loss of the competition."

"What I can't understand is why anyone allowed a factory to be set up here in the first place. It's such an environmentally sensitive site."

"Oh, the Council welcomed it, so did the Environment Agency. There was a factory here before we came, you know. The building was derelict and the soil was seriously polluted with heavy metals. In time all that would have leached into the river. They couldn't afford to clean up the site. We did it for them. It was part of the deal."

"But it would only take one spill from you..."

"It just can't happen. The analyses you see here," Saunders tapped a finger on the big ledger, "are performed on the water in holding tanks, prior to any discharge from them. If we ever found that the water wasn't up to spec it wouldn't be discharged. Our treatment is state-of-the-art so that's never happened." He leaned forward. "I could dip a beaker into those tanks and drink it. You haven't been cleared by security or I'd take you down there and do it for you now."

Terry gave a non-committal grunt. "Tell me, did the Environment Agency analyse the water upstream of the factory?"

"Of course. The analysis was very similar upstream and downstream. And as you said before, there aren't any other factories upstream of here."

"So if your factory isn't responsible, what was your man – your Mr. Loomis – doing out on the river today?"

"Dr. McKinley, environmental control is my job. None of us are happy about what's happened to that river, least of all me. I asked the Environment Agency to look into it but they're fairly stretched and frankly I'm not expecting miracles. I sent Loomis out so we could make a few measurements of our own."

"Who do you think attacked him?"

He opened his hands. "Who knows? People in the village are upset and some of them may be tempted to have a go. So far as they're concerned any member of our staff is fair game. It could have been the Anti-Pollution Officer from the Environment Agency out there this morning and they'd have targeted him too, because they think we're all in cahoots. They may not even be from the village. Word travels fast. That sort of rent-a-mob will turn up wherever there's a prospect of violence – football riots, animal rights, it's all the same to them."

The brief two-tone blast of a siren floated up to them.

"Sounds like the ambulance," Saunders said. "Henry will be in good hands now."

"Well, I hope he'll be okay." Terry got up.

Saunders stood too. "I'll see you out."

"Just one more thing. How would you feel if I collected some samples of my own – from the river, I mean? I may get an opinion from some of my contacts in the university."

"You're a free agent, Dr. McKinley; you don't need permission from me. Watch out for those lunatics, that's all."

CHAPTER 3

Terry returned to the river that afternoon. Swinging from one hand was a pair of green thigh waders. He hadn't brought his own because the local rivers were always fished from the bank, but Daffydd had found these for him. In the other hand he carried an old milk crate in which nine of the twelve compartments were occupied by small glass bottles. They were empties from various mixers, which had been consumed at the bar and were awaiting collection. He'd rinsed them out and peeled off the glossy top surface of the labels. Each bottle had a tightly fitting screw cap, which made them ideal for his purposes. The bottles clinked musically as he strode along the bank.

He would start upstream of the factory. It wasn't a wide river but it varied greatly in both depth and speed of flow from one place to another. He didn't know if this would affect its composition so to be on the safe side he'd take three equally spaced samples across its full width. Then he'd do the same at the factory and finish up with another set of three downstream from that. Analysing those should reveal exactly what this factory was doing to the river.

Fifteen minutes later he was sitting on the bank, pulling on the thigh waders. He took three of the bottles and entered the water. Almost immediately he sensed the cold, even through the waders. He trod carefully, feeling for rocks. It was deeper than it looked and before long he was up to mid-thigh, the air in the waders buoying him up, the flow heavy against his legs. As he moved he scanned the width of the river until he judged he was in the right place. He unscrewed the cap on the first bottle, rinsed it in the river and took a sample. Then he shook his head, emptied the bottle and took the sample again, this time upstream to avoid the clouds of silt he was stirring up with every step. Using a ballpoint he wrote "U" on the remaining traces of label: "U" for upstream.

He sloshed back and took a further sample in the middle and another nearer to the bank. Moments later the three samples labelled "U" were stowed safely in the milk crate.

He kept the waders on and clumped along the bank. At the factory he stood for a moment looking at the pipe work. Why was there such a lot of it? Did they use river water for cooling purposes, too? Effluent would certainly be discharged into the river through one of those pipes and it would be lovely to get a concentrated sample, but it was impossible to know which one. He selected a position just downstream, close to the metal bridge. This wasn't far from where Loomis was attacked so he looked warily about him but there was no one in sight. Soon he had three more samples, labelled "F" for factory. He set off again.

The final site would be further downstream, approaching the road. Still wearing the clumsy thigh waders he passed the place where he'd paused the previous evening, crouching on the bank, trying to interpret the unnatural stillness of the scene. The stone bridge came into view. Now the banks were high and the river deeper and more turbulent. He set the crate down and contemplated the water. People had been borne away and drowned in a flow like that. He gritted his teeth, took the last three bottles and descended into the river.

The sheer pressure of the current took him by surprise. Each time he lifted a leg the water pulled at it as if it were hell-bent on turning him over. He felt his way carefully; the river bed was strewn with rocks and it would be easy to get a foot trapped. He decided to take his samples on the way in rather than on the way out. As soon as he'd filled the first bottle he capped it then lobbed it into the short grass on the bank. He edged forward, the water pressing even harder, foaming noisily all around him. The second sample landed on the bank and he went further in. Now the water was nearing the tops of his thighs. With the next step his foot contacted – nothing. For one unnerving moment the leg was weightless, taken by the powerful current as if it were no longer part of him. He resisted, dragging it back against the pressure, and found his footing again. Evidently a deeper channel had been scoured out in the middle. It was too dangerous to go on. He took one more sample, tossed the bottle to the bank, and splashed his way back to the shallows and out of the river. As he retrieved each bottle from the grass he checked the cap was screwed down tightly, labelled it "D" for downstream, and put it in the crate. Nine in all: he was done. Going up the bank wasn't easy with waders on, but it was the quickest route back to the village.

He saw them as soon as he straightened up at the top: four young men, heading his way. One of them must have spotted him earlier. He sat down immediately to take off the waders. That wasn't easy because they were tight and slippery from the water. He tugged hard at the right one, felt it loosen; it came off and he stood up. There was no time for the second – they were less than thirty yards away. The youth in front was carrying what looked like a pick-axe handle, the one behind him a baseball bat, and they were coming on at a deliberate pace. There was little doubt about their intentions and the sight of a somewhat rangy academic would be the last thing to deter them.

An image flashed into Terry's brain of Loomis's battered features. His stomach contracted.

To run – with one wader on and one off – was out of the question.

Twenty yards.

He was still holding the other wader by the straps. He swung it lightly, then thought better of it and dropped it to the ground.

Ten yards.

His breathing quickened and his heart thudded in his chest.

The youth in the lead gave an animal roar and charged in, lifting the pick-axe handle high in the air. Terry didn't have to think about it. He caught the wrist before the weapon could fall and used his opponent's momentum to carry him over his head in a stomach throw. With three more coming on he had to make sure of this one so he let go of the wrist and straightened his leg hard, sending the youth sailing out over the bank. The cry and the crunch of a bad landing registered somewhere in the back of Terry's mind as he backward rolled and rose to face the next man. Then he spotted the pick-axe handle on the top of the bank where the youth had dropped it. He snatched it up and hefted it. It was shorter and heavier than the *shinai*, the bamboo sword he'd used in *kendo* practice, but it would do.

The one now running towards him was short and powerfully built. He was swinging the baseball bat, his features distorted by derision and hatred. Terry lifted into a block, rolled his wrists to deliver a short, chopping blow to the forearm, turned the weapon again to strike the middle of the upper arm, and finished with a hard thrust to the torso. The man doubled over. His mouth opened wide in pain and astonishment but no sound came out. The baseball bat had dropped from his fingers, the arm was rigid, the hand clawed.

An agonized howl floated up from the other side of the bank. The other two ground to an uncertain halt.

Terry remained in the fighting stance, the pick-axe handle pointing directly at them. He fixed them with an unwavering glare.

They eyed him. Everything had gone very still apart from the antics of the second man, who was trying to coax some feeling back into his paralyzed arm. Then another wail rose from the other side of the bank.

"For fuck's sake…!"

One of the men muttered sideways, "We better see to him." And then to Terry, "You, we ain't finished with you, mate."

Terry watched the two men go down the bank then dropped the pick-axe handle at his feet. He took several deep breaths and sat down to pull off the second wader. Then he rose, picked up his things, and set off quickly for the village.

As he walked he replayed the encounter in his mind. He'd practised moves like that so often they had sunk to the level of pure reflexes, like a tennis serve. It was reassuring to know it was all still there, even though it was a good twelve years since his last inter-university judo match.

The bottles clinked in the crate as he swung it in his left hand. The thigh waders were hanging over his right arm. In the right hand he still had the pick-axe handle.

CHAPTER 4

It was Tuesday afternoon before he had a chance to take the samples over to Dr. Maggie Ferris. From the Physics Block it was just a short walk through the campus to the much newer Biological Sciences Building. Up to two years ago he didn't know anyone in that building. Then the head of Biology had talked to the former head of Physics and they agreed to run a joint course for Second Year Biology undergraduates. Staff from Physics would explain the principles underlying different types of measurement and for each technique the biologists would give examples of the way it was applied in the lab and in the field. Such a course required two organizers: Terry was asked to take care of the Physics side of things and Maggie accepted the task for Biology.

Maggie was about eight years his junior. This was her first permanent university post and the first time she'd organized a course. He enjoyed working with her; what she lacked in experience she made up for in energy and enthusiasm. Analyzing what was in these bottles wasn't really in her line but she probably knew someone who could do it.

He forged a way through a noisy gaggle of undergraduates who'd congregated in the foyer, took the stairs to the second floor, and tried her lab. He knew that other people were sometimes in there, and she had her back to him, but the mass of black curls over the white coat was all he needed.

"Hi Maggie."

She turned and came over as he placed the crate with the samples on a bench. She watched with a bemused expression and her dark eyes travelled from the samples back to him, one slender eyebrow arched.

"River water," he explained. "From my trip."

"Well that's very kind of you, but flowers would be nicer next time."

He smiled. "Hey, I risked life and limb to get those samples."

"What for?"

"The river's dead, polluted. I took those samples last Saturday. I'd like to know what's in them."

"I'm a molecular biologist, Terry, not an analytical chemist."

He shrugged. "I know, but I thought you could point me to someone who could help with it."

She withdrew one of the bottles from the crate and surveyed it dubiously. It was labelled "U", one of the three samples he'd taken upstream of the factory. "You might do better over at Chemistry – "

She'd been absent-mindedly unscrewing the cap as she spoke. There was a sharp hiss of escaping gas.

"What have you brought me here, Terry? Tonic water?" Then she screwed up her eyes and waved a hand in front of her nose. "Ugh Ammonia!"

Terry picked up another sample bottle with interest and unscrewed the cap. It hissed in the same way and he saw bubbles rising in the water. He looked at it for a moment, sniffed at the neck of the bottle and jerked back, coughing.

"God," he said, "it smelled a bit down at the river, but nothing like that. How did that happen?"

"What was in the bottles before?"

"Oh, various things, but I washed them out thoroughly."

"In tap water?"

"Yes, but I rinsed each of them in the river before I took the sample."

"Well, I don't know. It must be contaminated somehow. Look I'll give some of it a low-speed spin and we'll see what comes down. It'll only take a few minutes."

He watched her use a chunky automatic pipette to transfer a measured sample from the bottle into a tiny plastic vial. She changed the pipette tip and did the same with the bottle that Terry had unscrewed. Then she went over to a small bench centrifuge, popped the vials into holes on opposite sides of the rotor, and closed the lid. She dialled something and pressed the button. He heard an ascending whine as the motor wound up to speed.

"Now, Terry, it's a good thing you're here. There's a timetable clash and we're going to have to rejig the lecture schedule. Do you want to come through?"

As they crossed the corridor she said, "How was Cardiff?"

"Pretty hectic. Lot of stuff on exoplanets. Funny – isn't it? – a few years ago just finding one was a big event; now there are so many it's not new anymore. People are more interested in composition and atmosphere."

"Lucky old you."

"Yes, lucky me."

She opened the door of her office and they went in.

Fifteen minutes later they returned to the lab. Maggie lifted the lid of the centrifuge, withdrew a vial, and held it up to the light. Then she did the same with the other vial.

"I was half expecting to see some mineral content," she said, "but there isn't a well-defined pellet."

The bottles she'd taken the samples from were still standing on the bench. She unscrewed the cap of the nearest one and started at the sound of escaping gas. It wasn't as loud as before but it was unmistakable.

She looked up at him, frowning. "It's still producing it," she said.

He blinked. "Can't be."

She lifted the vial again.

"Terry, there is something there. Was the water clear when you sampled it?"

"Yes, more or less. Clear enough that I could see the silt stirred up by my waders and it went on for yards."

Her eyes sparkled. "My, you really did risk life and limb, didn't you?"

"You don't know the half of it."

"Hang on."

She attached a rubber bulb to a slim glass pipette and lowered the tip into the cloudy layer she'd noticed at the bottom of the vial. Then she pulled open a drawer, removed a glass slide from a box and put a couple of drops on it. She covered it with a thin slip of glass, carried it across the lab, and sat down at a microscope. It took her just a few moments to manoeuvre the sample around on the stage, twiddling the focus knob and moving lenses in and out, and then he heard her murmur, "Ah, that's better."

"Have a look," she said, as she got up. "That cloudy material is filamentous."

He squinted down the microscope and adjusted the focus. What he saw was a mass of fine threads. As he moved through the plane of focus a subtle cross-banding came and went. It made each thread look like a fine watch bracelet. He looked up at her.

"What is this stuff?"

"I'm not sure. Some sort of algae, I think. But there are people I can ask. I'll give you a ring tomorrow, all right?"

"Thanks, Maggie."

Terry thought about it while he was shaving the next morning. Those river samples were becoming a bit of a mystery. They'd reeked of ammonia, even the ones he'd collected upstream of the factory, so maybe

Saunders was being straight with him after all. If the factory wasn't responsible, what was? Was his river the only one affected?

On his way to the university he stopped by the public lending library and started to leaf through back issues of *Trout and Salmon*. When the river was polluted in October it had wiped out all the fish. If the same thing had happened to other rivers it should show up in the fishing reports.

In the October issue he read: "In spite of the weather, Mr. Thompson had ten fish in the first week of September, including a fine two-pounder..." Then he realized this wasn't going to be so simple. Fisheries took pride in their catch returns. They wouldn't fabricate records but would they report pollution or zero catches? It seemed more likely they'd just wait for the problem to pass, preferring not to report at all. He went back along the shelf and pulled out the issues for September and October of the previous year. Then he quickly ran a finger through the report pages, comparing them side-by-side with the same months in the current year.

In Wales there seemed to be reports missing for the Mawddach, Dysynni, Rheidol, Gwendraeth Fawr, and Loughor. The Camel in Cornwall was also absent. On the other hand reports from fisheries on the North Sea coast were as robust as usual so it looked as if the affected rivers were ones that drained to the Atlantic coast, although by no means all of them. He glanced at his watch and decided there was no time to look at Ireland as well. He was just returning the magazines to their shelves when he paused, his hand resting on them. Wales and Cornwall? That didn't make sense. If it was some sort of local problem, like a factory chimney belching out pollutants, you'd expect it to poison everything within reach. But the Camel and the Welsh rivers were miles apart. Even within Wales the affected rivers weren't all together; the ones in between seemed to be fishing normally. He shook his head. Maybe he was on the wrong track.

When he arrived at work his postgraduate student put her head round the door of the lab.

"Thought I heard you, Terry. Maggie phoned. She wanted to talk to you."

"Thanks, Maria," he shouted back. He was punching in the number before he'd sat down. It was picked up on the first ring. "Hi Maggie, it's Terry."

There was a moment of silence.

"Terry, I think you ought to get over here."

When he came into the lab she took off her white coat and hung it on the back of the door. They crossed the corridor to her office, where she sat down behind her desk and brushed her hands briefly through her hair, fluffing out the black curls.

"This material," she said. "I showed it to one of my colleagues, Jake Brewer. Jake's a freshwater biologist. Cyanobacteria, he said. What used to be known as blue-green algae. You get it all over the place, on soil, moist rocks, and in lakes and rivers. It should be familiar enough to a fisherman like you. Any time you've ever slipped on a stone you've found some."

"Right."

"Jake's an expert. He gave me a mini-tutorial on types of cyanobacteria. Some, like *Anabaena*, can thrive in both salt water and fresh water. He's fairly sure this one is a freshwater species of the genus *Nostoc*."

"Okay. Go on."

"I asked Jake if it was easy enough to grow it in the laboratory and he said it was, so long as you added the right elements and nutrients. He already had some suitable solution in his fridge and he let me have some. I washed some of your algae by centrifuging it and re-suspending it in clean water several times. Then I dropped it in the nutrient solution and left it overnight."

"Why did you want to do that?"

"I'll show you why."

She led him back into the lab and over to a bench where she held up a plastic flask. He looked carefully and frowned. The solution inside had an emerald green tinge.

"Was it that colour when you started?"

"No, I'd only added a small amount of the algae so the solution was still clear. But it isn't any more. That stuff has been growing hand over fist."

"All right, you've proved you can grow it. What's the point?"

"The point is: I'd washed the sample, so the only thing that had been added to the solution was clean algae. When I started, that solution was odourless. By this morning it was smelling of ammonia."

He looked at her. "The… algae… is what's producing the ammonia?"

"Yes. There's nothing else it could be."

He shook his head, as if to clear it. "Sorry, I've been a bit slow here. I mean, there was so much gas in my sample bottles it escaped under pressure. I never expected a biological organism to do anything like that."

"You're right: no *normal* organism would do that. That's why I called you over. This organism isn't normal, Terry; it must be some sort of mutation. And ammonia is a serious pollutant. Has the Environment Agency been informed?"

"Oh yes."

"Well how come they haven't picked it up?"

He thought for a moment.

"You know, they probably dealt with their samples straight away – just put them through a standard analysis routine. They didn't notice the organism because it was only present in tiny amounts. My samples stayed in the bottles for several days before I brought them here so that gave the stuff a chance to multiply and produce the gas. You could well be ahead of them on this."

"I think you should contact them right away."

He glanced at his watch. "I can't do it now; I have my appraisal in ten minutes. I'll do it first thing this afternoon."

At the door he paused and turned. "Did you say anything to Jake – about the ammonia, I mean?"

"Of course not – I'd have looked a right idiot!" She shrugged. "Well, I didn't believe it myself at that stage. All I said was I'd found it in a river sample a friend brought in."

"I'd keep it that way for the moment."

"Why?"

He chewed his lip. "I don't know. Talk to you later."

CHAPTER 5

Professor Brian Harthill, Head of the Department of Physics, bent over the stapled set of sheets on the desk in front of him. Terry waited patiently, vaguely noting the way the window light reflected from the man's scalp through the thinning hair. He'd completed that appraisal form before leaving for the conference in Cardiff. It was an annual chore. He had a lot of sympathy for Brian: the administrative burden of the headship had wiped him out as a researcher. The poor chap would have to repeat this exercise with every member of staff in the Department. All over the university, other heads of department would be doing the same thing. Terry let his mind wander.

Before I take it to the Environment Agency I need to find some other way of checking those rivers…

"Grants?" Harthill asked.

Terry quickly gathered his thoughts. "My European Commission grant is still current, Brian. It's worth 8.9 million Euros."

"Yes, but you're just one participant and it only has two more years to run." He looked up. "You know, Terry, it would be in your interest to have something in your own name. At this stage you're probably thinking about promotion. I've got to have some ammunition if I'm going to put your case forward to Faculty – and that's just the first hurdle. There'll only be a few Senior Lectureships awarded and you'll be in competition with other staff from all over the university. I'd say you need a personal grant."

"All right, I'll think about it."

The Salmon and Trout Association. They'd know something about those rivers…

"What about publications? Anything this year?"

"Um, there'll be a good paper coming out of Maria's work."

Harthill pointed to the form. "You mention a review article here. That's the sort of thing, you know. Establishes you as an international scholar. Have you started to write it yet?"

"Not yet."

Brian scratched at the short grey beard that looked not so much intentional as the result of having forgotten to shave for a week. He made a few notes then put down his glasses. "Try to make a start on that review, Terry. It'll be good for you and good for us. We've got to make sure of the

Department's rating in the next round."

He sighed. "I'll try, but it's a question of time. I have a pretty heavy teaching load."

"You do quite a bit in another department, don't you? This Instrumentation course in Biology."

"They need to know how to measure things too, Brian. The Department gets credited for the time spent. Anyway that's not the problem. I'm still running Electricity and Magnetism for First and Second Year Physics. That's the real killer. It's a mammoth course."

"Yes, I know. It got starred in the Teaching Quality Assessment. Well done."

"The TQA was horrendous – it generated paperwork a mile high. I've been teaching that course for five years now. Any chance of offloading it onto someone else?"

It was a fair question. Formally the performance appraisal was intended to be "enabling", designed to ensure that people achieved their potential. In actuality, of course, it was just another way of cracking the whip.

"I'll look at it, but we're short staffed as it is."

It was the answer he'd expected. It was no good blaming Brian; it wasn't his fault. He was probably under pressure from the Dean, and no doubt the Dean was under pressure from the Vice-Chancellor, who in his turn needed good departmental ratings to increase the research allocation to the university. It was the dead hand of managerialism, which the government laid on the universities and the universities in their turn laid on their staff.

When he got back to his room he found a manuscript on his desk. It was the first draft of the paper Maria had prepared on the work she'd presented at the conference. He glanced at the first couple of pages then put it in his brief case to deal with at home.

He turned to his computer and typed "Salmon and Trout Association" into Google. It was a good web site, giving him access to a range of fisheries and water companies. He started to make phone calls.

An hour later he sat back and looked at his scribbled notes. It seemed he'd been on the right track after all. Of the suspect rivers he'd picked up from the magazine reports, the Rheidol was actually all right; the correspondent had died and they hadn't yet found anyone to replace him which was why the reports were missing. The others, the Mawddach,

Dysynni, Gwendraeth Fawr, Loughor and the Camel, all had problems.

He checked his watch. He needed to contact the Environment Agency.

The man he spoke to was polite at first but when Terry pressed him harder he almost sighed.

"Yes, thank you very much. As I said, we're aware of the problem and we have it under review."

"Look, I'm sorry, but I'm not sure you fully appreciate the scale of the pollution this could cause."

"We deal with this sort of thing all the time, Mr. McCarthy."

Terry's patience was beginning to wear thin. "It's McKinley. *Dr.* McKinley."

"May I ask if you've looked at our website?"

"Yes I have, but it only tells me who you've prosecuted successfully for pollution. It doesn't tell me what I want to know."

"Which is...?"

Terry ran his fingers through his hair. "Which is: what's the full extent of the problem in these rivers and how much staff time are you allocating to it?"

There was a pause. Then the man said, "I've said a number of times, Mr. MacInroy, that we do have the problem under review. Now, we appreciate your concern but I think it would be best if you let us tackle it in our own way." And he rang off.

Terry slammed the receiver down and glared at the phone. Then he started as it rang. He picked it up and almost barked:

"McKinley!"

"Oh. Terry? Is this a bad time?"

"Sorry, Maggie, what's up?"

"I was wondering if you'd spoken to the Environment Agency yet."

"Yes, I just got off the phone from them." He glanced at his watch. "Tell you what – I'll come over. Could you put some coffee on?"

Maggie had a small room adjacent to her lab where her research students could work and make coffee. She poured a mug for Terry and one for herself and they carried them across the corridor to her office. She placed the mug on her desk and settled into a chair, fluffing her hair in that habitual way which he found himself beginning to like, even if it didn't achieve anything noticeable.

"So how did you get on?"

"Not too well, I'm afraid. He kept laying platitudes on me. When I pushed him harder he rang off."

Her lips twisted. "Pity. Did he say how far it's spread?"

"I don't think he had a clue, but actually I have. I've looked up local fishing reports for England and Wales and checked them with the Salmon and Trout Association."

Her eyebrows lifted. "Good thinking. What did you find out?"

"They've got the problem in four Welsh rivers and one in Cornwall. Nothing on the North Sea side; all the affected rivers drain into the Atlantic."

"Wales and Cornwall? So it's not confined to one area?"

"No. That was true within Wales too. You'd get a couple of polluted rivers and the ones in between were okay. Weird, isn't it?"

She was looking at him intently, her eyes even darker than usual.

"What?"

She drew a deep breath.

"Look, Terry, we've got a strange organism here, something that produces ammonia hand over fist. What are the chances that it popped up spontaneously in half a dozen places at the same time?"

"Small."

She looked at him.

"OK, tiny."

"Right, so it must have arisen in one place and spread to the others."

"Seems so."

"Then how does it come to be in rivers miles apart and yet not in the ones in between?"

"That's what I was wondering. Any ideas?"

"There's only one explanation I can think of. This problem didn't start here."

CHAPTER 6

When Terry got back to his office he sat with his chin in his hands, turning it over in his mind. There was nothing wrong with Maggie's reasoning; if he hadn't been so hung up on factory pollution earlier he might have reached the same conclusion himself. The organism had to have a common source and if the affected rivers were some distance apart it had to be somewhere out in the Atlantic Ocean. But no sooner had he accepted that as the solution than Maggie had come up with an even bigger problem.

Some organisms lived in fresh water and some in sea water. A few could live in both, but *Nostoc* wasn't one of them. So they had a freshwater organism producing ammonia in the river, yet everything pointed to a source out at sea. Something was missing – but what?

He'd left her to think about it and he would try to follow up on the source, but there wasn't a lot to go on.

Whatever it is, it's somewhere out in the Atlantic Ocean, presumably some sort of organism. It could be concentrated in one place or spread more thinly. It could be producing ammonia, but it wouldn't have to be: that might happen only after the transfer to a freshwater environment.

He shook his head; too many possibilities. What he needed to do was generate a few hypotheses and test them. He could start with the most likely scenario: a patch of the stuff somewhere in the ocean, producing ammonia.

Would something like that show up from space? Almost certainly. Remote sensing of ammonia was possible over very large distances – he was familiar with the technology through his own research. The Cassini-Huygens spacecraft had measured the abundance of ammonia in Jupiter's atmosphere while on its way to Saturn, so traces in Earth's own atmosphere would surely have been mapped by NASA's surveillance satellites.

He accessed the NASA web site. The only satellite photographs of any relevance were ones showing algal blooms off the Californian coast and off the Atlantic coast of the United States. It was nice to know that the algae could multiply and aggregate on a scale visible from orbit, but such phenomena had been known for centuries, and there was nothing to indicate that these particular ones were producing ammonia. He'd have to look elsewhere for answers.

He decided to phone someone in Geography. He punched in the number he found in the university directory and asked the Departmental Secretary if he could speak to a member of staff involved in Ocean Sciences. After a pause the secretary said, "I'll put you through to Dr. Craig Liddle."

The number rang briefly.

"Liddle."

"Hi, this is Terry McKinley, Physics. Sorry to bother you. Would you happen to know where I could find surveys of marine microorganisms?"

"What sort of surveys?"

"Well, analysis of samples taken by research vessels, mainly in the open Atlantic."

"Not really my thing. I'm more interested in the interaction between the ocean and the weather. If you're talking about the Atlantic, that's a hell of a lot of ocean. I shouldn't think there's much systematic sampling away from coastal waters."

"What about Institutes of Oceanography? Do they do that sort of thing?"

"What, like Scripps and Woods Hole? Yeah, they do but it would be targeted research. They'll be studying a specific organism – maybe in the lab – or they'll be looking at it in relation to commercial fisheries. Again it's mostly coastal waters. If you're thinking about open ocean, Bermuda may have some information about the waters off their shores."

"Bermuda? I hadn't thought of that. It's kind of in the middle, isn't it?"

"Nearer to the States than here, but it's a major focus for marine life."

"Right, I'll follow it up. Thanks a lot."

"No problem."

Terry found the official Bermuda government web site and started to surf it. It was extensive but he couldn't seem to find anything specific on water quality or cyanobacteria. He wondered what it would be under. Out of a combination of curiosity and desperation he clicked on "Transport". That opened another menu and he began to work through the choices. When he selected "Bermuda Radio" he found, to his surprise, a site for Bermuda's Maritime Operations Centre. This seemed more like it. There was a tab marked "marine incidents", and he worked backwards, scanning the brief reports for each month. When he reached the previous April he stopped, blinked a couple of times, then reached for the phone.

Maggie sat down, still wearing her short coat. She was out of breath.

"I came as fast as I could," she said. "What is it?"

He turned the screen towards her. "This is a list of marine incidents at Bermuda. Look at this one from last year."

17th April: 11:35 a.m. Bermuda Harbour Radio advised by USCG RCC Norfolk that New York Air Traffic Control have received a report from commercial airliner of possible oil pollution approximately 90 NM north-east of Fort George. Bermuda Radio requests in/out bound aircraft to overfly the area and report further. At 12.55 inbound Delta flight confirms no oil pollution but a large patch of weed with vessel apparently stranded in it. Incoming merchant vessel "Wichita" asked to divert. "Wichita" finds missing 32-foot powerboat "Fair Wind" with five people on board, four dead and one in critical condition. Crew report foul choking smell in area. "Fair Wind" towed in, met by Police Marine Launch "Cormorant 3". Sole survivor has breathing difficulties and dies before reaching port. "Fair Wind" taken to boatyard for detailed examination.

"Five dead, Maggie, and at least one of them had breathing difficulties before they died."

"It only says 'foul, choking smell', Terry. It doesn't mean – "

"Wait, you haven't seen all of it yet. While I was waiting for you I found a follow-up article in The Royal Gazette, Bermuda's daily newspaper."

He brought it up on the screen and waited while she read it.

MYSTERY TRAGEDY AT SEA CLAIMS FIVE LIVES

The Bermuda Police Service has confirmed that the vessel discovered stranded in a mat of floating weed some 90 nautical miles north east of Fort George was the missing powerboat "Fair Wind". There were no survivors. The two crew members have been named as Joseph Hedley, the owner of the vessel, and Axel Thorsen. The names of the three holidaymakers with them, two men and a woman, have not yet been released, but they were understood to be from Florida. The cause of the tragedy remains a mystery. The crew were very experienced and the sea was calm. There was no damage to the craft and there was fuel in the tanks.

Brian Morrissey, captain of merchant vessel "Wichita", says they were making good time into port when they were asked to divert. They launched a rescue boat when they were within range, got a line on the powerboat and pulled it clear. Michael Muldoon, one of the crew members on the rescue boat, said there were rods out on "Fair Wind" so maybe someone had a fish on and they didn't see the weed in time to stop it fouling the screws. "Four of them were dead, and the fifth was in a bad way, struggling to breathe. That was no surprise – all of us were coughing, and we were only there a few minutes. The air was really irritating. There was a smell like something between decaying fish and stale urine. It was kind of quiet, too. As a rule we have a lot of sea birds following the "Wichita" but they'd all gone – not one in sight. I can tell you, we were glad to put that place behind us; fair gave us the creeps."

Dr. Alan Watkins, a marine expert, said that all the evidence pointed to the "Fair Wind" getting caught in a very large algal mat. "The most likely explanation is that a bubble of gas, from decaying vegetation trapped beneath the mat, broke to the surface and asphyxiated the crew as they were trying to break free. I understand that post mortems are being carried out, and we may know more about the cause of death after that."

She straightened up, unbuttoning her collar.

"Sorry," he said jumping up. "Let me take your coat."

He hung the coat over his own, on the back of the door. When he turned she was looking around her. For him an office was an office, but now he saw it through her eyes. It was dingy compared to her light, modern room. Of the two windows, one was painted shut and the catch on the other jammed so frequently he tended to leave it open in summer and closed in winter. There were bookshelves on one wall and four filing cabinets lined up against the other. The remaining floor space was just big enough to accommodate his desk and a couple of chairs.

"So what do you think?" he asked, as he returned to his desk.

"Ammonia doesn't smell like decaying fish."

"No, but it is irritating and it does smell like stale piss. And any fish living amongst the weed would have died so that would account for the rest of the stink. Also the remark about sea birds. It was almost the first thing I noticed when I went down to that Welsh river: it was unnaturally quiet, and there was no bird life."

"Let's not get too excited, Terry," she said gently. "Their expert could well be right. It could have been a pocket of methane or something from decaying vegetation."

He grimaced. "I suppose so. It looked like a really good lead, that's all."

"What made you look at Bermuda?"

"I spoke to someone in the university. He said Bermuda is a major focus for marine life."

"He's right. That area of ocean is known as the Sargasso Sea. Now I'm thinking about it, it is exactly the sort of place you might expect a mutation like this to arise – very rich environment, full of algae and marine life of every sort. When did you say this incident was again?"

"Last April. Almost exactly a year ago."

"Well just suppose that is the source of the organism, how did it get into your rivers by October?"

"No idea."

Terry pulled a World Atlas off the shelf and busied himself with a ruler. Then he accessed an on-line encyclopaedia for some data and started to tap figures into a calculator.

"Let's see. It's about five and a half thousand kilometres from Bermuda to Wales. The Gulf Stream comes from there and up to our shores as the North Atlantic Drift. It travels at a maximum of two metres a second at the surface. If bits of the organism travelled in the surface current they could arrive here in just over a month. Plenty of time."

She smiled. "You physicists and your numbers."

"What else is there?"

"There are vectors."

"Vectors are numbers too. They just have direction as well as magnitude."

She laughed. "Not that sort of vector. Biological vectors. Animals or insects that carry disease. For example, the *Anopheles* mosquito carries the malarial parasite. It's an insect vector."

"Right..."

"So the organism wouldn't have to be dependent on the vagaries of an ocean current. It could have been carried here."

"Carried by what?"

"Birds? Manx Shearwaters travel those distances, and they nest on cliffs down the west coast. The organism could have been trapped in their feathers."

"There weren't any birds around that weed mat."

"Well, all right, migrating fish – of course, why didn't I think of it before? Eels!" She leant forward excitedly.

He scratched his head. "Eels?"

"Yes. Eels go to the Sargasso Sea in their millions to spawn."

He turned back to the computer. The encyclopaedia was still online. "It says here the larvae of the European freshwater eel hatch in the Sargasso Sea and then they travel back to their rivers of origin in Western Europe."

"There you are," she said triumphantly. "And during that time they could be carrying the organism in their gills."

"That would explain a lot, wouldn't it? Eels don't just come up to the estuary; they come right up the rivers. According to this, though, it takes them about two and half years. That doesn't fit."

"Perhaps the organism came on ocean currents, like you said, and the eels picked it up in the estuary. If they return to their rivers of origin it explains why some rivers are affected and others aren't."

"Yes, that's right!" He felt a sudden surge of excitement. There was a brief silence. A fleeting frown crossed her face and he realized he'd been gazing intently at her. To cover his confusion he said:

"How did you know all that about eels?"

She raised an eyebrow. "Come on, Terry. I am a biologist."

"Well if they are carrying this stuff it could be all over Western Europe. Not just rivers, either. Eels wriggle across fields so it could have reached other bodies of fresh water – lakes, reservoirs. And you said it can survive in soil, too. This whole thing's much bigger than I thought."

Her face fell. "What are we going to do?"

"I don't know. We've got to do something, though. Right now everyone's treating it as factory pollution. The real culprit's under their feet."

CHAPTER 7

It was just before lunch the next day when Terry gave Maria's draft paper back to her. She thumbed through a few pages and looked at him in dismay.

"Blimey, Terry, I'll have to get you a new red pen. Sorry, I knew it was rubbish."

"It's not rubbish – it's very good for a first draft. I've marked the bits where I thought there are gaps in the logical flow and I've pointed out some relevant literature you haven't cited. I think you could make a bit more of the spectroscopic data. Put the detailed maths in an Appendix. I've written it all down. Remember, anyone who heard you at the conference will want to read the full paper. You have to make it worth their while."

She looked again at the manuscript and back up at Terry, and screwed up her face. He smiled and added gently:

"Don't worry. It's an excellent start."

She sighed. "Okay. Thanks, Terry."

He went back to his office and sat there, thinking. Had he skimped on that? Not really. It needed a broad brush approach at this stage and he was too distracted to do more than that at the moment. They could pick up the details – matters of style and English – on the next draft.

He wanted to discuss things with Maggie again but he was supervising a practical class that afternoon and he knew she was trying to beat the deadline for a grant application. Perhaps he could suggest meeting over dinner tonight. It seemed like a good idea but he was hesitant to suggest it. Theirs was a working relationship and he didn't even know if she had a partner.

He took a deep breath and picked up the phone.

After letting him stumble around for what seemed like an age, Maggie put him out of his misery.

"I think it would be very nice to have dinner together, Terry. And if you're trying to ask me if there's anyone around who might object, the answer is 'No'. Where would you like to eat?"

They settled for The Village, an inexpensive restaurant close to the university which served a variety of vaguely South American dishes.

They walked there together. Neither of them had had a chance to go home and change, and that was a relief to Terry, who wanted the whole thing to be as casual as possible. When they got to the restaurant he helped her off with her short coat and she hung it on the back of the chair. She was wearing tight blue jeans and a dark V-neck sweater.

"The Village" was popular with staff and students. Too popular, as it turned out: it was crowded, and there was a group of boisterous students on the next table.

Maggie said she'd prefer to skip the starter and just order a main course. Terry said he'd do the same. The waiter, a slim-hipped young man in tight black trousers and a short waistcoat, took the menu cards and went away with the order, leaving them looking at one another across the table.

Terry said, "Did you get your grant application away?"

"Yes, I should just about make the deadline. God, what a lot of work."

"Well I hope you get it. At least it'll make all that effort seem worthwhile."

"To be honest, I had a job concentrating," she said. "I couldn't stop thinking about that organism."

"I know what you mean. The guys at the EA clearly haven't grasped what they're dealing with. Really I'd like to take the whole thing to a higher level – when we're more certain of our ground."

The waiter arrived with a couple of beers which he poured far too quickly, leaving them with the bottles and two glasses half full of foam.

"Are you all right to talk about it now?" he asked.

"Of course."

"Well, let's sum up where we are. We have a Welsh river that's polluted by ammonia. We have solid evidence that the culprit is a freshwater organism – a species of cyanobacteria – that's undergone some sort of mutation. It seems pretty likely that other rivers in Wales and Cornwall have been affected in the same way, but they aren't next to each other so the origin has to be somewhere out in the Atlantic. All right so far?"

"Yep, Go on."

"We have a candidate location for that origin in Bermuda waters – "

"Though that's pretty speculative at this stage."

"All right, but consider the evidence in favour." He began to count on his fingers. "One, the deaths. A boatful of people die with breathing difficulties, the air is described as irritating and smelling of stale urine, and there are no sea birds – all consistent with ammonia. Two, you said it yourself: the Sargasso Sea is just the sort of rich environment where you'd expect a mutation like that to arise. Three, it explains why only selected rivers are affected. Eels migrate to the Sargasso to spawn, pick up the organism, and carry it back to their home rivers." He opened his hands. "I'd say that's pretty persuasive."

She pursed her lips and nodded. "Okay. Then what?"

"Then it all falls apart. The polluting organism is a freshwater species, not a saltwater one. So how could it have survived in the ocean? Somewhere along the line we've gone wrong."

They looked up as the waiter arrived with their meals, which he placed without ceremony in front of them. For a while they ate in silence.

He noticed that she was only picking at her meal. His wasn't much good either. He tried the beer. It was all froth and no flavour. He wondered why the place was so damned popular.

She put down her fork. "Something just occurred to me. Cyanobacteria are actually made up of thousands of individuals."

He had to crane forward to hear her. The students at the next table had presumably had a few beers by now and they'd become very noisy.

"Individual what?"

"Individual bacteria."

"Right …?"

She was silent for a while lost in thought.

"Well?" said Terry prompting her.

"Well... Maybe that gives us a route for the mutation to pass from a saltwater to a freshwater organism."

"You mean we could be on the right track after all?" He had to raise his voice to make himself heard.

"Yes, there are mechanisms…"

Now he could only pick out phrases between the gales of laughter from the next table.

"…horizontal gene transfer… plasmid exchange…"

"A plasmid isn't the only possibility," she said, during a brief interlude. "It could be a transposon."

"Did you say transposon?"

"Yes. They're very similar but a plasmid would stay as a separate entity whereas a transposon would incorporate itself into the chromosomal DNA. It would be much harder to find…" The laughter and shouting started up again and she glanced towards the next table. "Oh, let's get out of here."

"My place isn't far. I can rustle up some coffee. Sorry, I'm not trying to..."

She smiled. "Thank you, Terry. That would be fine."

He lived in a late nineteenth century terraced house which had been converted into two self-contained flats. His was the one on the ground floor. There was no intercom at the entrance, just two bell-pushes marked "A" and "B", and whichever occupant was summoned had to come to the front door to open it. He used his key and led Maggie through a narrow hallway into the sitting-room.

"Make yourself at home. I'll get the coffee on."

He retreated quickly to the flat's kitchen-dining area. He hadn't expected to bring her back here and now he was having second thoughts. The place was reasonably tidy but he was suddenly aware of things that would normally have passed him by: the cheap paper lampshade, the worn carpet, the shine on the armrests of the second-hand sofa. He didn't have to live like a student; he could afford better now. It was just that replacing the furniture would require a lot of searching and comparing fabrics and styles and prices. There was always something else to do, something more urgent.

He filled the kettle and switched it on. Then he opened a cupboard and out of sheer habit picked up a couple of mugs. He looked at them, replaced them, and went to the shelf above. The metal tray started to fill up: cups, saucers, teaspoons, cafetière, a jug of milk, a bowl of sugar – Terry didn't take milk or sugar himself but he thought Maggie might.

The kettle boiled. He rinsed the cafetière with the boiling water and put in two carefully measured scoops of ground coffee. Then he filled it to one of the lines he'd scribed on the glass with a spirit marker.

He looked at the tray for a moment. It wasn't very elegant but he hoped it would do.

Maggie was sitting in an armchair, waiting quietly. She got up as he came in.

"No, you're all right, stay where you are if you're comfortable there."

He placed the tray on a coffee table, plunged the cafetière, and poured the first cup.

"Milk?"

"That smells good – no, I'll have it black, thanks. I do put milk in the lousy 'instant' we have at the lab. It helps, but it still tastes like mud. I really ought to get a decent coffee maker."

He poured his own coffee and sat down on the sofa, self-consciously placing his hand so as to cover the shiny patch on the armrest.

With his other hand he vaguely indicated the room. "Sorry, it's not very fancy, this place..."

"It's quiet and it's comfortable, Terry, and that's perfect."

"Okay, can we start again? – I couldn't hear you properly over that racket. What was it you were saying about plasmids and transposons, and where do they fit in?"

She sipped the coffee. "I'd remembered something. Those strands we were looking at under the microscope? They actually consist of bacteria – thousands of them, strung together in long chains."

"Yes, I got that much."

"Well, bacteria have some interesting quirks." She paused to take another sip of coffee. "Think about super bugs."

"Like MRSA, you mean? Resistant to a number of antibiotics. Big problem in hospitals."

"That's right. Do you know how antibiotic resistance spreads?"

"I thought it was a kind of natural selection: most are killed by the antibiotic, but if any are resistant they continue to divide."

She nodded. "That's right, but there's another process as well. The bacteria that have the gene for survival can transfer it to other bacteria. They pass it in a small package of DNA called a plasmid."

"Clever. So you think that could be how this mutation is travelling?"

"I can't be sure, but it's a distinct possibility. And if that *is* what's happening it explains the way it's spread. The freshwater organism in your rivers could have picked it up from a saltwater species that was carried into the estuary."

He put his cup on the table. "Hang on, let me understand this. This plasmid thing passes the mutation from a saltwater species to a freshwater species? Then presumably there's nothing to stop the freshwater species passing it to another freshwater species."

"I suppose that's right. Shit."

"Quite. An innocent lump of slime in a pool or on a rock suddenly starts generating ammonia. And then that one passes the mutation on in turn. It's a chain reaction. It's worse than the bloody eels."

She bit her lip. "I can't be sure that's the mechanism, Terry. I just haven't been able to think of anything else."

"All the same, we've got do something before the situation gets completely out of hand."

"What was it you said in the restaurant – about taking it to a higher level?"

"Seems to me there's no choice; we have to tell someone. We can't rely on anybody else flagging it up. If I can arrange something will you come with me?"

"Of course. But who are you going to see? And are you sure they'll want to see you?"

He scratched the back of his neck. "Good point. I don't know, actually, I've never done anything like this before – I'm not a political animal, never have been. I suppose I could start in the university, talk to someone with the right connections…"

"The Vice-Chancellor?"

"It's a possibility. I'm not happy about that, though. He's a Chaucer scholar, isn't he? Mention *The Miller's Wife* and he'll give you chapter and verse. But say 'cyanobacteria' or 'plasmid' and the shutters will come down. I'd sooner approach a scientist in the first instance."

"What about CaSE – the Campaign for Science and Engineering? They lobby the Government all the time."

"Do we know anyone on the Committee?"

"Isn't Professor Barlow on it?"

"Hugh Barlow? Chemistry? That's more like it: a chemist would see the point. I'll give him a ring tomorrow. Nice thinking, Maggie."

She smiled and sat back. Suddenly the immediate business was over, and a silence settled on them. Terry broke it before it became oppressive.

"More coffee?"

"Thanks."

"You know, if Prof. Barlow does take it on board and arranges a meeting at some Ministry or other we'd probably have to go down to London, and I shouldn't think we'll get much choice about the time. Is that all right with you?"

"I suppose so. If it clashes I'll just have to reschedule my teaching."

The silence fell again. She sipped her coffee.

"Um, where do you live, Maggie?"

"Actually I'm a warden at Eden Hall – you know, it's one of the Halls of Residence."

"Sounds good. What's the accommodation like? A lot nicer than this, I bet."

"Not really. More modern, of course, but a bit austere. You put a few pictures up and it still looks like a very plain room with just a few pictures in it. But it's cheap and it's walking distance from the Department so I don't need a car. The duties aren't onerous. I've been thinking of getting my own place, just the same. The kids are all right but I feel like I'm never off duty."

Terry nodded.

"I suppose I should run you back there, then," he asked, a little awkwardly.

"Thanks," she said. Was that a fractional hesitation on her part? It was too late, he'd said it now and she was standing up.

There was no further conversation in the car. Perhaps he'd been a little too correct but he wasn't used to this sort of thing. Right now what he needed was her help. What he didn't need was to make a fool of himself with misguided romantic advances.

He swung into the drive leading down to Eden Hall, stopped near the entrance, and switched off the engine. She turned to him.

"Thanks for dinner, Terry – and coffee."

"My pleasure. I'll let you know what's happening when I've spoken to Professor Barlow."

"What are you going to say?"

"I'll tell it like it is. We have a common organism with a seriously polluting mutation. We have a good idea where it arose, and plausible mechanisms for how it's spread. And I'll emphasize the urgency. That algal mat didn't simply pop up in Bermuda waters last April. It could have been growing for months or even years, drifting around on currents, passing the plasmid to other bacteria – what?"

Maggie had put her fingers to her mouth.

"Oh my God," she said. "Why didn't I see it before?"

"See what?"

"What you just said, about passing the plasmid to other bacteria in the ocean." She drew in her breath. "Most phytoplankton consist of cyanobacteria."

He frowned. "I'm not sure I understand what…"

"Terry, the oceans are full of phytoplankton. They produce up to half of the oxygen in the Earth's atmosphere!"

The concern on her face started to seep into him. He leaned forward. "You're saying if this plasmid was passed to the phytoplankton they'd stop making oxygen?"

"Worse than that…"

As she spoke her voice rose and there was a tension in it he'd never heard before. Before he could respond she made a small sound in her throat, little more than a tiny groan, and pushed open the passenger door. She got out quickly, closed the door, and hurried off. He was poised in a state of indecision, his own door half-open, wondering whether or not to go after her. He could hear the tap-tap of her shoes across the tiled vestibule. Then the moment had passed. She was already inside.

He dropped back in the driver's seat but made no attempt to move off or even to close the door. He stared ahead in stunned disbelief, struggling to absorb what she'd just said.

"If the phytoplankton are affected they might produce ammonia instead of oxygen. They could eventually fill the entire atmosphere with pure ammonia! This isn't just a pollution problem we're dealing with, Terry. It's a potential global disaster."

CHAPTER 8

Someone was already with the Minister so Maggie and Terry waited in the outer office. The room was comfortable and quiet; the only sound the faint clatter of keyboards in the secretaries' office next door. They sat together on a soft leather sofa, ignoring the artistically overlapped copies of *The Field*, *Country Life*, and *Homes and Gardens* on the glass coffee table in front of them. There was no way of knowing how much time the Minister was going to give them so it had been agreed in advance: Terry would do the talking and Maggie would respond if there were specific questions on the biology. They'd discussed the issues between themselves enough to know what needed to be said; for now they were content to wait in silence.

Terry remembered when he was about to be interviewed for his lectureship. The situation was utterly different then, yet the flutter of nervous anticipation was the same. He tried to occupy his mind.

"You could go several ways with this," Barlow had said. "One way would be to present it to the House of Commons Science and Technology Committee. But to get any action it would have to go a stage or two further, and you might well find yourself out of the loop. I'd recommend going to a Minister: Brady at Science or Monteith at Environment, Food and Rural Affairs. Not a lot to choose between them. They're both classics trained – like most of these people. But I think Giles Monteith would be quicker to see the point. And the big advantage there is you have a first-class scientific adviser, Sir Ashley Gibbs. If he comes on side he'd be a good intermediary."

Terry had sent Sir Ashley a summary of their findings and concerns. It was brief: just one side of a sheet of A4; that way, Terry thought, it was more likely to be read. It was read. Sir Ashley had telephoned and listened to him carefully. His verdict was not encouraging.

"Let's be brutally honest: what you've told me is, at best, suggestive. I think you're right to be concerned but you need more hard facts if you want other people to share that concern with you."

Terry had agreed. But, as he pointed out, getting those facts would require resources. If the Minister recognized the potential danger and the scale and urgency of the problem wouldn't he make those resources available?

Sir Ashley had considered that for a moment. "All right, this is what I suggest. I meet regularly with the Minister. As it happens I'm seeing him first thing next week. I have quite a lot to discuss with him but I can arrange for you to come in at an early stage so that you can present your case. I wouldn't push too hard: it could be counterproductive. When the interview's over you'll have to take your cue and leave me to go through my own agenda. I'll copy this summary of yours to the Minister so that he knows what it's about."

A buzzer sounded in the next room, followed by a low murmur of conversation. On the opposite side of the outer office a door opened and an urbane-looking man passed through. Terry thought it must be the previous appointment. Moments later a secretary came up to them.

"Mr. Monteith will see you now," she said.

She conducted them down a short corridor to a large oak-panelled door, knocked lightly, opened it, and stood aside.

Monteith was sitting at a desk that dominated the room. In front of it were two large upright chairs covered with green leather. To one side was another chair, this one occupied by Sir Ashley Gibbs. He stood immediately and Terry was struck by how immaculately formal the man appeared. Everything from his grey hair to his dark suit screamed civil service. He wondered whether his own clothes screamed academic.

"Hello, nice to put a face to the voice," he said, shaking hands.

The Minister had come round from behind the desk. He extended a hand to each of them in turn.

"Dr. McKinley, Dr. Ferris. Thank you for coming. Do take a seat."

He returned to the desk. On the tooled leather pad at its centre was a single sheet of paper, which Terry recognized. Some key phrases in his summary glowed yellow, the work of a highlighter pen.

The man they'd come to see looked to be in his forties – clean-shaven, dark brown hair neatly parted. He wore a well cut navy suit, a finely striped shirt, and a club tie. He was younger and fitter than Terry had imagined he would be, and the way he was sitting forward suggested someone who was ready to do business.

Sir Ashley broke the ice.

"As I explained earlier, Minister, Dr. McKinley and Dr. Ferris have some interesting information. I thought it would be worth your hearing it from them first hand."

Monteith nodded briskly at Sir Ashley and glanced down at the summary sheet. Then he looked at Terry.

"I read your briefing. Very much to the point. Anything you'd like to add?"

"There isn't a whole lot to add, Sir, actually. Cyanobacteria are found everywhere in Nature. It's deeply disturbing to find a species with a dangerous mutation. It's already killing all the life in at least five river systems I know of and it has the potential to spread a whole lot further."

The Minister took a fountain pen from an inside pocket, unscrewed the cap, and scribbled a note in the margin of the briefing sheet. He looked up, pen still poised.

"You've informed the Environment Agency, I suppose?"

"They already know about the rivers, and they've taken samples from at least one of them. But they're treating these as isolated incidents of pollution. They haven't seen the pattern and they don't seem to be aware of what's causing it. Frankly, they weren't very helpful. In any case, the problem isn't confined to these shores."

"You're referring to a possible origin in Bermuda waters. To be honest, this isn't a field I'm familiar with. Do you get plasmid exchange with cyanobacteria?"

Terry's spirits lifted. This man had at least been well briefed.

"The evidence is indirect," he replied. "The polluted rivers are all on the west coast but they're not clustered together. That points to a common origin somewhere out in the Atlantic. If the mutation can jump from a saltwater species to a freshwater species it can almost certainly make the smaller step to phytoplankton. And that's where the real danger lies."

"I didn't follow that part entirely. I thought the oxygen in the air we breathe came from the rain forests? 'Lungs of the planet' and all that."

Terry looked to Maggie to respond.

"That's the common view, Minister. But lungs breathe in as well as out; rain forests also consume oxygen in a big way and over long periods they're not net generators of oxygen. We're actually dependent on billions upon billions of tiny photosynthetic organisms floating in the oceans of the world, and most of them are species of cyanobacteria. If they switch to making ammonia instead of oxygen, the results would be catastrophic."

"All right," Monteith said. "Can you spell it out? Assuming it gets into phytoplankton, what's the worst-case scenario?"

Terry took a deep breath. Here it was. He'd been thinking of nothing else since Maggie had dropped that bombshell on him in the car.

"I see three major consequences. First of all, ammonia is a good deal lighter than air. You'll have large volumes of rising gas, which will behave like very warm air. This will add energy to the existing circulating cells and exaggerate all normal weather trends. For example, you'll get severe hurricanes."

"Where?"

"They'll probably follow the usual track: the Caribbean, Gulf of Mexico."

Monteith shrugged. "Well, they're pretty used to that down there, aren't they?"

"Yes, but these would be more violent and they'd occur outside the usual season."

"Ok, go on."

"Now, as I said before, the main reservoir of the organism at the moment seems to be out in the Atlantic, so the ammonia will be brought to our shores by the Westerlies. It will be stirred into the atmosphere and it'll combine there with acidic gases to form tiny crystals of ammonium sulphate, nitrate, chloride, and carbonate. These will act as condensation nuclei and they'll seed moist air rising from the ocean. Storms will batter our coast and torrential rain will cause widespread flooding. Not in the Gulf of Mexico, but here."

The Minister raised an eyebrow and glanced at Sir Ashley, but his advisor was listening impassively, hands folded on his lap. He returned to Terry.

"How long will that go on for?"

"Well, the storms won't be continuous and they may eventually die out because of other factors we needn't go into here. The point is that all the time this is happening the organism will be spreading and producing more ammonia. That leads us to the third consequence, the most devastating one of them all."

"Which is…?"

"The ammonia will increase at every level in the atmosphere. Things will be especially bad when it rolls into the towns because it'll combine with acid emissions from industry and traffic. The salts will hang in the air as a choking white smog. Mixed in with them will be the uncombined ammonia, so the air will be toxic as well as highly irritating. Thousands of people will be at immediate risk: the young, the old, heart sufferers, anyone with asthma or other breathing difficulties. Hospitals will be overwhelmed by the admissions; there'll be a lot of fatalities. Eventually the entire atmosphere will become poisonous. Every man, woman and child, every animal, bird, fish and insect on this planet will perish."

CHAPTER 9

No one moved. Outside, Big Ben struck the hour. Two o'clock.

Monteith's eyes narrowed. "That's a pretty chilling prospect, Dr. McKinley. Just how sure are you about all this?"

"If the phytoplankton are affected by the mutation, large volumes of ammonia will be entering the atmosphere. That will certainly have a major effect on the weather. If you want detailed predictions you'd need to bring in the experts, research teams who can run large-scale computer simulations. As for the smogs and the eventual poisoning of the atmosphere, it has to happen sooner or later. Precisely when, I don't know; an awful lot depends on how far the organism has spread already."

The Minister sat back and there was a short silence during which he fixed his gaze steadily on Terry.

"What exactly is your specialty, Dr. McKinley?" he asked.

"Planetary physics."

"It seems we must count ourselves lucky that it was someone of your background that stumbled across this... this phenomenon."

"I'd be nowhere with it if it wasn't for Dr. Ferris," Terry put in quickly. "She was the one who recognized that the ammonia came from a mutant organism and spotted the implications. I've been speaking for both of us."

Monteith glanced at Maggie and nodded. Then:

"All right. You've outlined a worst-case scenario. The question is: what's the likelihood of it actually happening? Any views on that, Ashley?"

"Minister – and I've said this very candidly to Dr. McKinley – the evidence is not strong at the moment. There are too many imponderables. This mutation may not spread by plasmid exchange. It may have adverse effects on the organisms themselves, in which case they may not survive or may simply stop producing ammonia. Even if ammonia levels do rise the consequences are hard to predict. The storms Dr. McKinley was talking about may wash the ammonia out of the atmosphere so the whole thing becomes self-regulating. My own view is that it's too early to say with any confidence."

Terry felt a stab of disappointment. Sir Ashley wasn't wrong, but he had hoped for a more supportive statement from him.

Monteith replaced the cap on the fountain pen and held it in both hands, turning it slowly between his fingers.

"Well, I'm glad to be aware of the possibilities. Whether or not they're going to become realities, I dare say time will tell. There are, however, some immediate implications."

He put the pen down.

"The scenario that Dr. McKinley has just described so graphically – choking white smog blanketing our towns and cities, hospitals filled to overflowing, deaths on a large scale – is an alarming one, alarming enough to cause serious unrest if it became general knowledge. It could trigger wholesale panic – roads jammed in an exodus into the countryside, marches, riots, looting, civil unrest of every kind. In other words, whether or not these fears are justified, the release of this information would be seriously prejudicial to the national interest."

He leaned forward.

"Dr. McKinley, Dr. Ferris, you do understand what I'm saying, don't you?" He tapped the briefing sheet on the desk in front of him. "I'm classifying this under the Official Secrets Act."

Terry and Maggie looked at each other. He knew the shock he saw in her face must be echoed in his own. Then her expression hardened and she turned back to the Minister.

"We're university researchers," she said, her voice no more than a rebellious little growl. "We haven't signed up to anything."

Monteith opened a desk drawer. "You don't have to, Dr. Ferris. The Official Secrets Act is part of the law of the land – we're all bound by it."

He took out a pink highlighter pen, and started to write on the briefing document.

"I just want to be sure that you're aware of your obligations. Now you are."

He held up the sheet. Scrawled diagonally across it in large letters was the word "SECRET".

"Level 4," Monteith added. "And that's how my secretary will file it. Not the highest security level, but high enough." He tapped the desk again, harder this time. This information does not go beyond the people in this room. If so much as a hint of it gets out, the culprit will be in breach of the Act. Ashley, you said Professor Barlow was consulted on this. You'll warn him, will you?"

"Yes, Minister. Barlow's very sound. That won't be a problem."

"Good," Monteith continued. "Now as I understand it, the Environment Agency is unaware of your theories at this time and it's best it stays that way."

Terry's was struggling with what he was hearing. He had to say something.

"Minister, there's a pressing need for us to find out more about this organism and how far it's gone. We need to consult phytoplankton ecologists, atmospheric chemists..."

"No, we can't allow you to do that, and for the same reason. Once that many people are in the picture it's going to get out, and we might find ourselves in serious trouble over what could be no more than a wild theory."

"Maybe Bermuda has investigated it already," Maggie said pointedly. "After all, five people *died* out there."

"Ah yes, Ashley mentioned that. I checked with the Foreign Office and they've been in touch with the Governor. Apparently those people were overcome by a bubble of gas from a mat of decaying vegetation. That's the official line and they're sticking to it. It was a year ago now and there won't be any further investigation." He placed his hands lightly on the desk, the fingers interlaced. "Bermuda is a major offshore financial centre, but tourism is their second largest industry. They would not welcome the suggestion that their beautiful ocean waters have been polluted."

Maggie's eyes once again met Terry's. She looked dumbfounded.

Terry turned back to the Minister. "What are we going to do, then?"

He sat back. "We're going to wait and see."

Monteith must have seen his expression. "That doesn't mean I'm dismissing it," he added. "If there's any suggestion that your fears are coming true, then of course we will take appropriate action."

Terry bit his lip. Sir Ashley had told him not to push it too hard but he had to try once more.

"Sir, we're dealing with planetary phenomena. The distances, the areas, the volumes of air and seawater involved, are all on a huge scale. The climate changes and the other consequences I've described won't happen until this organism is really well established. By that time it will be too late."

"I can't help that. At the moment there just isn't enough to go on. Of course if the two of you want to conduct a little private research, that's fine so long as you maintain strict confidentiality."

Maggie spoke up again.

"Molecular biology is an expensive business, Minister. There's no way I can do it without proper support, and I can't ethically use grant money that was awarded for other purposes. Isn't there some way you could make funding available?"

Monteith thought for a moment, then shook his head. "No, I can only free up contingency funding like that to deal with a catastrophic situation, and right now I'd have a job convincing anybody that there is one. If things change I'll reconsider it. Right, that's the position. I'm grateful to you both for bringing this to our attention."

Terry glanced at Maggie, who half-closed her eyes in a gesture of weary acquiescence. They stood.

"Well, thank you for your time, Minister, Sir Ashley."

CHAPTER 10

"Well that didn't go as well as I'd hoped," said Terry, holding the door open for Maggie, then following her onto the pavement.

"How can those idiots sit there and do nothing?" she said angrily. "We could be dealing with a global disaster and they wouldn't even investigate it! What's wrong with them?"

They took a taxi to their hotel. Terry had guessed there wouldn't be time to catch a train back after the meeting with the Minister, so he'd booked them into a hotel in Half Moon Street, off Piccadilly.

The cab pulled up outside their hotel and they went inside. "Come on, I need a drink," Maggie said, heading for the hotel's Cocktail Bar. She ordered a gin and tonic and a double whisky before Terry had even reached the bar.

"Good choice," he said and they flopped down into a couple of arm chairs. He sighed. "I guess we just weren't persuasive enough."

"Rubbish. You laid everything out perfectly. Only a moron could misunderstand you. These bureaucrats make me so angry."

"I know what you mean and I suppose I should feel angry too, but I just feel… well, deflated. As things stand I've made matters worse, not better. Now we're in a Catch-22 situation: we can't get support without evidence and we can't gather evidence without support. Monteith and Gibbs probably think I'm a nutcase and a doom-monger. They can't believe anything disastrous is going to happen – oh, correction: they believe it's just enough of a possibility to slap the Official Secrets Act on the whole thing."

"Can they really do something like that?"

"I don't know. He might have been bluffing, but I'm not sure I want to find out the hard way."

"Christ, Terry, there's got to be something we can do."

"You heard the Minister; they've tied our hands."

"Officially, maybe. But as he said, they can't stop us acting in a private capacity, can they?"

He looked at her. "What do you mean?"

"What's the weakest link in our case?"

Terry paused, but it seemed Maggie meant the question to be rhetorical and continued.

"It seems to me the key is what's going on in the Sargasso Sea. The best possible scenario is that there's only one mutant organism in those waters, and it's the same as the one we found in the river."

"Right, which would mean it hasn't been spreading from one type of organism to another. But didn't your colleague say that what was in the river was a freshwater organism?"

"*Nostoc*, yes. But you know the differences between those organisms are subtle. Maybe the mutation also brings about a slight change in appearance so that it only looks like *Nostoc*. Or maybe there was a mixture of algae in that sample; Jake identified *Nostoc* correctly, but another species in there was actually generating the ammonia." She shrugged. "These are remote possibilities, but plasmid exchange is a crucial issue so we need to be certain of our ground."

"How could we settle it?"

"Well, if there are multiple organisms, all producing ammonia, and they're different again to the one in the river, that's strong evidence for transfer between species."

"The doomsday scenario."

She swallowed. "Yes. The doomsday scenario."

"Could that be established fairly easily?"

"Yes, if we went to Bermuda and got a sample of their waters."

He gulped on his drink and coughed. "You're not serious?"

"Why not? An economy flight to Bermuda, a couple of rooms at a bed-and-breakfast and the hire of a boat, and we'd have the answer."

"Just like that?"

"Just like that. Remember what's at stake here. Come on Terry, we'd only need a few days, a week at most. We can leave this weekend. I bet we're both owed loads of leave from the university and we can get others to cover for us if necessary. If we meet any resistance from the higher ups we'll just tell them it's top secret government stuff."

She laughed and he joined in.

"Okay," he said. "You're on."

CHAPTER 11

Bessie Johnson presided over her tiny dining-room like a benevolent mountain.

"Now what would you dear people like for breakfast? You can have waffles or pancakes with maple syrup. Or scrambled eggs with bacon and sausages and tomatoes…"

The trip had been easier to organise than Terry had thought, despite the fact that a few mistruths were required to comply with the Official Secrets Act.

Terry noticed Maggie's sickly expression. "I think I'll just have coffee, thanks," she said.

"Jus' coffee? That ain't enough to keep a termite alive!"

"Maybe some toast?" Maggie ventured.

"Ah right, and what you want on that? Scrambled eggs and …"

"I don't suppose you have any marmalade, do you?"

Bessie's eyes lit up. "I sure do. And none of your shop-bought garbage, either. This was made by my own fair hands."

She held up two pink palms, the only inch of her that wasn't a deep nut brown. Then she seemed to catch herself, and the three of them dissolved into laughter. When they'd recovered, Terry added:

"I'd love some toast and marmalade, too."

Terry soon realised Bessie wasn't exaggerating. It was the most delicious marmalade he could ever remember tasting. Even then they couldn't do justice to the mound of toast that was placed in front of them.

"My Mum used to make marmalade," Maggie said. "When I was little I'd help her cut up the peel."

Terry smiled. He had a mental picture of a little Maggie perched on a stool at the counter-top, legs swinging, tongue protruding from one corner of her mouth, cutting up oranges and fluffing up her dark curly hair from time to time with sticky hands. He wiped his own fingers on a paper napkin.

Bessie came to the table again. "You had enough?"

"We have, thank you," said Terry. "That was great."

She beamed. "And where you off to this fine morning?"

Terry said, "We thought we'd go down to St. George's Harbour and look around."

"Aaron can take you. He's going to town."

"I wouldn't want to put him to any trouble."

"What trouble? It's on his way and he like the company."

Bessie's husband dropped them off at the harbour, where they hoped to find a boat that would take them out to collect their samples. They waved goodbye, then turned around. In front of them was a great crescent of intensely blue-green water. White sails flashed in succession as yachts came about to leave the harbour.

Maggie shook her head. "You know, when we were coming in to land I thought it was tinted by the cabin windows or maybe a trick of the light. But the water really is that colour."

"Amazing, isn't it? I suppose it has something to do with the pink sand."

All along the harbour, vessels rocked gently at their moorings. A stiff breeze from the Atlantic set in motion the irregular music of halyards chiming against masts. Behind them on the quayside, and rising in tiers beyond that, were buildings painted in white and pastel shades of pink, red, yellow, green, and blue, each capped with a low white roof. Sunlight reflected back at them from every surface.

"This place reminds me of the Amalfi coast," said Maggie putting on a large pair of sunglasses that Terry though looked uncharacteristically modern and expensive. "A present from a wealthy Aunt," she added as if reading his mind. Terry put on his own pair of worn and scratched aviators that he'd found in his classroom one day and nobody had ever claimed.

Maggie grinned at him. "Cool prof. Present too?"

"Sort of," he replied smiling back at her.

He turned and looked out to sea, breathing in air laden with salt, seaweed, fish, diesel fuel, tar... everything, it seemed, but ammonia.

"It's hard to believe there's a problem somewhere out there, isn't it?"

Maggie nodded. She looked up and down the harbour. "Where do we start?"

"Let's divide our efforts." He pointed to the left, where a towering cruise ship had berthed. "You start down there and I'll take this side. We'll meet..." He looked round, then pointed to a café with some tables and chairs outside. "We can meet there about twelve-thirty. Sound good?"

"Sounds good. See you later."

There was no shade outside the café where Terry waited but the inshore breeze was cool and he was comfortable enough in his cotton T-shirt and jeans. When Maggie arrived she was carrying her lightweight jacket and her face was flushed. He smiled and held the door open for her.

It was warm inside and there was a heavy smell of cooked fish. The lady behind the counter was, however, happy to make them coffee and a couple of sandwiches. They took the tray to one of the tables outside. Maggie drained the glass of iced water in front of her and sighed.

"That's better."

"How did you get on?" Terry asked.

"Not great. They're happy to take you out for diving or fishing or just a cruise, but the moment you say where you want to go they suddenly lose interest."

"Same here. You told them we have respirator masks?"

"It made no difference. It's the weed. There's a risk of getting caught in it and fouling the engines. Apparently there's quite a bit floating in the water even away from the big mats."

"But that's the stuff we want to sample, isn't it?"

She nodded, her lips tight. "The trouble is, if they take us as close as that they have to spend the next day cleaning it all off before it's safe for them to go out again. Just not worth their while. At least that's what they say."

She turned her attention to the sandwiches, which were generously filled and decorated with crisps, coleslaw, and salad. "Wow. Next time I think we'd better order one for both of us. How did you get on?"

"Pretty much the same as you. I got fed up in the end – went down to the quays and just walked along, chatting to any crewmen I could find. It did give me one lead."

"Oh?"

"Yeah. There's a guy here called Max Gibson. They say he knows these waters better than anyone. If he won't do it, then nobody will."

"Did they say where we can find him?"

"Should be on his boat. Up that way." He pointed. "It's called *Cleaver II*. Worth a try."

The commercial boats they'd seen already were gleaming white-and-chrome, multi-deck affairs, festooned with aerials. Expecting something similar, they walked right past *Cleaver II* and had to ask and double back before they eventually found it. It was a no-frills fishing vessel, drab but well-scrubbed, with a wheelhouse up front and an afterdeck and not much more. They glanced at each other. Terry shrugged.

"As long as it's seaworthy, I suppose." They stepped onto the wooden jetty that ran alongside and he raised his voice to speak to a figure moving around on deck. "Hello there. I'm looking for a Captain Max Gibson."

The man straightened up. The peak of a battered white cap cast a dark shadow across his face. "An' now you found him," he called back, in a voice as deep as the Caribbean Sea.

"All right to come aboard?" Terry asked.

"I'll come to you," he replied. He walked along the afterdeck, hopped onto a bulwark, and down onto the jetty.

Terry looked into a face the colour and texture of dark brown leather splintered from exposure to salt wind and sun. He in turn was surveyed by liquid, dark brown eyes with bloodshot whites.

"You wantin' me?"

Terry began carefully. "People round here say there aren't many who know these waters better than Captain Max Gibson."

Max's eyebrows made the briefest of excursions. "I guess people say right. 'Xcept people round here call me Max. Where you wanna go?"

"About ninety nautical miles north-east of here."

Max frowned, then a faraway look entered his eyes. "Been a long while," he said. "Used to go up there, crewin' on a fishin' boat when I was a kid. Get a lot of eels."

It was just what Terry wanted to hear. "Would those be the English eels that go out there to spawn?"

"Yeah. American eels, too. Come out from the East Coast. You wanna fish for eels?"

"Not exactly. My friend Maggie here is a biologist. She'd like to take some samples from the ocean out there." He took the plunge. "Near the place where a powerboat called 'Fair Wind' got stuck about a year back."

Max's face clouded. He dropped his voice. "Nobody go out there now, mon. Too dangerous. Full of weed. Foul you up before you know."

"We don't have to go right up to the weed mats, just near enough to get some samples."

Something between a grunt and a laugh escaped from Max's throat. "That stoff don't stand still for you, mon, it move around. And people *died* on that boat."

"We know, but we've got top quality respirator masks with us, so if we run into some foul air we won't be at risk. It'll only take a few minutes to get the samples and then we can clear out."

Terry could almost see the man's mind working. It was still quite early in the tourist season and demand would easily be satisfied by the luxury vessels further up the quay. A boat like this wouldn't attract a lot of business right now. It was better to take it out than keep it in harbour, even if there was a small element of risk.

Max shook his head slowly from one side to the other. Then he swung a hand around, pointing to the cloudless blue sky and the incredible green water. "Look at this place, mon. We can go cruise round the islands, or I can take you fishin', scuba divin', anythin' you like. Now why you want to go to a God-forsaken place like that?"

Before Terry could reply, Maggie said:

"I know it sounds strange, Max, but there's some really interesting stuff in the water out there and I just set my heart on getting hold of some of it." She smiled up at him and Terry could see Max's eyes soften.

"Straight out, and straight back?"

"Yes."

He pursed his lips, then shrugged. "Right now I got some work to do on the boat. Tomorrow mornin', though."

Maggie's face lit up. "That would be wonderful."

"Need to make an early start. Which hotel you stayin' at?"

Terry answered. "It's not a hotel. We're staying at the Johnson's guest house. It's – "

"I know where it's at." His expression lightened. "Bessie and Aaron. Good. Josiah Smith can crew for me tomorrow. He lives close by – he'll give you a lift in. Be ready for him 'bout seven-thirty."

"Brilliant. Thanks very much."

He pointed. "You go on up to the office now and make the bookin'." He withdrew a cell phone from a pocket. "I'll tell them to give you a special price, otherwise they gonna charge you for a full day's fishin'."

Maggie reached out and gave the man's forearm a little squeeze. "Thanks again, Max. See you tomorrow."

As they walked towards the office Terry said, "You certainly worked your charm on him."

"I think he took us for a honeymoon couple. Better not push it too far. He knows the Johnsons. He could find out we're booked into separate rooms."

"See, I told you we should have booked a double."

"Behave yourself, Terry."

Terry glanced at his watch. It was after two o'clock. They had risen at six and left harbour shortly after seven that morning. Lulled by the rhythmic rocking of *Cleaver II* and the incessant throb of her twin motors, Maggie had dozed off and Terry was feeling his own eyelids drooping. He got up and went out onto the open afterdeck, turning his face into the refreshingly cold breeze. Some sea spray prickled his cheeks and he felt alive and alert. He stood, hands on hips, swaying with the motion of the boat, scanning the ocean. Out here the water looked very different from the harbour; it had taken on the deep grey of the open Atlantic and the waves were flecked with white. He bent over the gunwale and looked down. The waves were rising high enough against the hull for him to reach out and plunge his hand below the surface. Viewed through the water, the skin took on a sickly hue. He withdrew his hand and as the breeze dried it the shine of the water receded, leaving behind a greenish powder. He frowned, then brushed his hands together to dust it off.

He looked round sharply as the engines changed note. Maggie jerked awake and rubbed her eyes. Max was staring intently at the horizon and Josiah Smith had his head around the side of the wheelhouse, straining in the same direction. Maggie joined Terry on the afterdeck, both of them following Max's gaze. At first they could see nothing unusual. Now that the boat was moving forward more slowly it was pitching and screwing, making it hard to get a clear view of what lay in front. Then Terry pointed.

"What?" Maggie shouted over the engines. "I can't see anything."

"The waves. They're flatter out there."

She narrowed her eyes and compared the ocean ahead and behind them. "I see what you mean."

Max shouted to them over his shoulder, "Weed up ahead," and dropped the engines to an idle.

Terry was back in the wheelhouse in a few strides. He pulled out the box with the respirator masks. "Let's get these on."

He helped Maggie fit one first, adjusting the straps carefully. She gave him a thumbs-up and pointed vigorously at him.

"Max and Josiah first," he said.

Max accepted the procedure with some reluctance, but Josiah waved it away. "Don' need that stoff."

"I think you do, Josiah."

Max intervened, and while they were arguing Terry put his own mask on. Then Max looked up.

"We gettin' too close," he called, and began to turn the boat.

With the change of direction a breeze crossed the deck, carrying with it a pungent smell of urine. Josiah doubled over, coughing violently.

Terry shouted, "Quick, get a respirator on him."

There was a flurry of activity as they put on the mask. Terry tightened the straps, ignoring Josiah's hands clawing at it. The man's chest was rising and falling in great jerks. After several minutes the spasms became less frequent and he settled into a bout of violent coughing. Terry lowered him so that he could sit propped against a bulwark. He turned to Max, his voice muffled by the mask.

"Sorry about that, Max."

He shook his head dismissively. "Get your samples quick as you can."

As they opened the box to take out the sampling equipment Maggie murmured through her mask, "Well one thing's settled already. It's producing ammonia all right."

She'd brought a dozen culture flasks to take the samples and Terry had rigged up a wire contraption on a length of fishing line so they could throw them out and tow them back through the water. The motors puttered and the side of the boat swung up and down as they pulled the first bottle in. Maggie capped it tightly, held it up to the light and pointed. The water was greenish and there were strands floating inside. She tucked it into a cool box with some gel packs they'd left overnight in Bessie's freezer. They repeated the process several times, working as quickly as they could.

"We've got six," Terry said. "That's enough."

He looked round. Josiah was coughing less violently now but his chest still made paroxysmal heaves from time to time.

"Josiah, we'll take your mask off as soon as we get clear. All right?" The man rolled his eyes and nodded.

"Okay, Max. We can go."

Max reached for the twin throttles and the engine note rose as they set course for the harbour.

"I'd like to go out again."

Terry looked up from his seafood platter. They'd found this place in a narrow alley that curved through the town of St. George, and decided to eat before going back.

"Why? We've got what we came for."

"I've been thinking about it. All the evidence points to the problem starting here and moving north-east, either on ocean currents or carried by eels, right?"

"Right…"

"Well, then the water to the south-west should be all right. If we sample it there I can get some normal organisms to compare the mutant ones with."

He put his knife and fork together on the empty plate. "Okay. We'll see Max about it tomorrow, but I'm not sure he'll be too keen to take us anywhere."

"I'm sure we can talk him round," she said with a winning smile.

"Well maybe you can."

"Ha. Only not so damn early this time. I barely got any sleep last night."

"The tree frogs?"

"Yes! I couldn't think what it was to start with. Sounded like a steel band starting up outside my window."

"I found it quite soothing after a while."

She pushed her plate away, yawned and covered her mouth. "Oh dear, look at me. And I've done nothing but stare at the ocean all day long."

"It's all that healthy sea air," he said with a smile.

Max shook his head from side to side, and this time he was adamant.

"There's no risk. It's in the opposite direction," Terry explained. "Just an hour out should be enough."

"It ain't that, mon. Hurricane comin' through tomorrow."

Terry looked at him in astonishment. "A hurricane? Bit early in the year for that, isn't it?"

"Very, leastways for one this big."

"Will it do a lot of damage?"

"Maybe, maybe not. Be stronger by the time it hits the Gulf. But there'll be high winds, for sure. Wouldn't be safe."

Maggie closed her eyes. Max seemed to register her disappointment.

"Should have passed through by Friday. I could take you then."

"No good. We're flying back on Friday."

"Jus' as well it ain't tomorrow. My guess is they'll ground all flights."

Terry sighed. "What about half an hour, Max? We could be out and back before the hurricane hits."

Again the man shook his head firmly.

"No way. Wouldn't go out on my own, let alone with tourists."

Maggie shrugged and touched Terry's arm.

"Okay, thanks anyway, Max. Some other time perhaps."

"Sure."

Max shook hands with each of them.

"You take care, now."

"You too."

They walked away from the harbour.

"An unseasonal hurricane," Maggie said morosely.

Terry glanced at her.

Was it really bad luck? Or was this the beginning?

CHAPTER 12

Apparently the rain had started in the UK soon after they left for Bermuda. Since then it hadn't stopped. The streets were running with water; in some places it was bubbling out of the drains. Unwary pedestrians were drenched twice: once by what was coming from the darkened skies overhead, and again by the spray and bow waves set up by passing cars. Apparently it was the same up and down the country, and worse the nearer you got to the Atlantic coast.

At mid-morning on Tuesday Terry stood watching the rain stream down the windows of his office, then decided he couldn't wait any longer. He put on his raincoat, turned up the collar, and hurried over to the Biological Sciences Building.

Maggie laughed when she saw the state of him. She hung up his coat, then tore some sheets of tissue off a roll in the lab so that he could rub his hair dry. They went into her office.

"I thought you might have got something from the samples," he said.

She nodded. "I got Jake to look at them with me. There's certainly more than one type of organism present. Some form filaments, others are free-living. Some are similar to the one in your river samples, but even they could be different strains or even different species."

"That's what you wanted to know, isn't it?"

"Not quite. We don't know yet which ones are producing ammonia. Is it a single species, or several, or all of them? If it's a single species it's unlikely the mutation is spreading by plasmid transfer and maybe we can breathe again."

"I see what you mean. So what's next?"

"I don't know, I'll have to think about it." She registered his disappointment. "I'm sorry; I wish I had more answers for you."

He shrugged and grinned. "I guess I'll just have to be patient while you figure out if the world's going to end sometime next week."

Terry tried to focus on his other work. He cleared the immediate backlog and put the final touches to the manuscript he was preparing with Maria, which they submitted to the *International Journal of Planetary Physics*. He even made a tentative start on his long overdue review paper.

Every few minutes he found himself surfing the web for any sign that his predictions might be coming true. Initially most of the news was dominated by the aftermath of Hurricane Ailsa. They had witnessed its noisy passage close to Bermuda, which was impressive but left behind it little more than blown litter and some broken palm fronds. The system then tracked down through the Gulf of Mexico, gathering energy all the time, and it had caused billions of dollars worth of damage to oil rigs in the Gulf, and to houses and infrastructure in the cities of Port Arthur and Galveston. The authorities had been caught on the hop and there were political, as well as economic, repercussions. The clean-up had just begun when a second hurricane began to form over the Atlantic. It was watched anxiously but this one petered out over Mississippi. Both had occurred unusually early in the year.

It was hard to believe that the unusual weather events were linked to the organism: those were long-term effects, something that could only be the result of a really substantial build-up of ammonia in the atmosphere. It was probably a coincidence; there'd been early hurricanes before, and it wasn't exactly the first time it had rained long and hard in the UK. Experienced scientists were familiar with observational bias: if you were looking for something hard enough there was a tendency to find it.

Towards the end of the week he spotted a short article on the inside pages of the *Daily Telegraph*. A Westland Sea King returning from a search and rescue mission had reported a silvery patch of ocean about one hundred and fifty nautical miles southwest of Land's End. On closer inspection it turned out to be a huge floating raft of dead fish, which the prevailing winds were likely to drive onshore somewhere on the western coast of France or the northern coast of Spain. He looked at the article for some time. Was this a coincidence, too?

Maggie phoned on Sunday and he invited her over to dinner. As he waited for her to arrive he read a newspaper he'd bought that morning on the way to work.

On page 2, below a picture of a car crushed under the weight of a fallen tree, he was reading:

...had a lucky escape. Fierce gales caused chaos at ferry ports, and many flights from Birmingham, Stansted and Heathrow were cancelled. Power lines were down across the north east of England, leaving more than 30,000 homes without electricity. After more than a week of unprecedented storms, heavy rain and high winds, flood warnings are now in place in North Yorkshire, Cumbria and a number of towns along the River Severn. The Met

Office has been tracking another weather system across the Atlantic and this will be moving into the southern part of the country during the...

His head jerked up as another squall shook the windows, the rain rattling against the glass like a fistful of gravel. Then he heard the door bell and hurried to let Maggie in. She greeted him breathlessly.

"Hi."

"Hi, come on in."

He had to lean against the front door to close it. She shook the rain off her coat and he hung it up for her. Then she stripped off her woolly hat and stepped out of her wet shoes. She held up the sopping hat in her fingertips. He took it from her.

"I'll put this on a radiator."

"It's really wild out there." She scooped back a wet curl from her forehead as they moved into the sitting room.

"Did you read about Hurricane Ailsa?"

"Yes, we were lucky Max refused to take us out. I'll know to trust his judgment next time." Her lips tightened and for an instant their eyes met. He knew exactly what she was thinking. Unseasonal hurricanes? Severe storms? Yet neither of them could bring themselves to say it.

Maggie broke the silence. "Hey, guess what."

"What?"

She perched on an armchair. "I've been allocated a departmental technician."

"Wow, lucky you." Terry was grateful for the change of subject. "Though some people are going to be jealous."

"I don't care. Let them work as hard as I do and maybe they can have technicians."

He grinned.

"Her name's Michelle, Michelle Taylor. I think she's quite bright. She doesn't have much experience in my area but I can teach her." She clapped her hands together. "I can do so much more now."

"You hungry? I thought I'd do a Thai-style fish curry."

"Sounds great."

"Okay, make yourself comfortable and I'll get cooking."

He went into the kitchen. He wasn't a very skilled cook and he liked meals that didn't call for too much coordination – a main dish and rice was about as much as he could manage. After a short while Maggie came in. "Mmm, that smells delicious. Can I do anything?"

"You can lay the table if you like."

She found a clean tablecloth, cutlery and glasses. From the kitchen he could see her looking at the table for a few moments, head tilted to one side. Then she walked away and came back with two candles.

He uncorked the wine, sniffed it with approval, and placed it on the table as she was lighting the candles. Then he prepared the starters, slicing and stoning an avocado, setting the unpeeled halves out on plates, and tipping a little vinaigrette into each of the creamy cavities.

Twenty minutes later they sat down to eat.

During dinner they both continued to avoid the conversation hanging in the room. They cleared away the dishes and settled down in the lounge with the coffee. Maggie was still talking about all the time she would have for extra research. He sank comfortably low in his armchair, his legs stretched out in front of him, ankles crossed, offering the occasional comment but mainly enjoying her animation. He was savouring the contrast with the weeks and months and years that had gone before. Sharing things with Maggie had transformed his life. A wave of tenderness coursed through him.

She stopped talking and there was a sudden stillness in the room. Something had passed between them. He could feel as well as see her looking at him and there was such warmth in her eyes that he rose slowly from his chair…"

The phone rang in the kitchen. He lifted his eyebrows.

"I'd better get it."

As he returned to the sitting-room Maggie looked at him.

"What is it?"

He stood motionless in the doorway, his tall frame slightly stooped.

"I'd better drive you back, Maggie. We have to leave for London first thing tomorrow morning."

CHAPTER 13

They said little on the train journey to London but stared out of the window, each of them alone with their own thoughts.

At least the Minister had had the good grace to phone in person. He had told Terry he'd set up a crisis meeting. The Department of Health and the Home Office would be represented. Could they be there?

Terry couldn't help feeling a little resentful. When he and Maggie had made a case for immediate action Monteith had set it aside. Now events had overtaken him and he expected both him and Maggie to jump at his command. After a pointed silence Terry had said, "All right."

"Good," Monteith had replied. "Twelve midday, in my office. Don't worry about the logistics; my PA will handle all that. Oh, one other thing. I should bring a supply of smog masks. Surgical masks will do, but the doggie muzzle type is better. Only they're in very short supply down here at the moment."

Minutes later the phone had rung again. It was Monteith's PA.

"Dr. McKinley, I haven't booked your rail journey. Could you and Dr. Ferris come down on the first train? We'll reimburse your First Class fares, of course. I'll book your hotel for you. Do you want to stay at Flemings again?"

"That would be fine."

"Very good. A car will pick you up there at eleven-thirty sharp. Is there anything else I can do for you?"

"No, I think you've covered it."

"Very good. Thank you, doctor. We'll look forward to seeing you tomorrow."

He'd paused after replacing the phone. There was a clear change in attitude but something about the conversation bothered him. He shook his head. He couldn't put his finger on it.

The first of the fog appeared when the train was several miles north of Watford Junction. It hovered in long white drifts over the fields. It didn't seem to be going anywhere. At Watford Junction the people waiting on the platform were holding scarves or handkerchiefs to their faces. As they settled into their seats there was a good deal of coughing. The station itself had a colourless, wintry look, more as if emerging from an overnight frost than the bright May morning it should be.

Ten minutes later they arrived at Euston. They crossed the concourse and went straight downstairs to the taxi rank. It was chilly at the lower level, and the air was stale and irritating. Maggie immediately began to cough and hastily got out a mask for each of them, avoiding the envious glances of others in the queue. Then a line of taxis came in, each one ghostly in a coating of white dust broken only by two black fans where the windscreen had been cleared by the wipers.

The queue in front of them cleared quickly. Terry opened the door of the next cab and Maggie climbed in.

"Flemings Hotel, please."

"Where?"

"Flemings? Half Moon Street."

"Half Moon Street? Oh yeah, I know it, just opposite Green Park. Hop in."

As they emerged from the ramp the driver took up his monologue.

"Cleaned the cab this morning, would you believe?" he said. "Look at it now. Wouldn't normally take it out in this state – matter of pride, know what I mean? They say a freak wind picked this lot up from a soda lake in Africa or something. Never seen anything like it in all my days. I seen brown dust brought from the Sahara, though. Ever seen that? Makes a mess of the cab too, but it's once in a blue moon. And it doesn't get in your throat like this stuff. A lot of drivers off today. Can't take it, you see? I don't smoke, that's probably why my lungs are stronger. That's why I come out. Look at Piccadilly today. Along here as a rule you don't want to know."

They were only half listening; they were peering through the dusty windows at the bleak urban landscape beyond. It should have been broad daylight but it was gloomy enough to have triggered the street lamps. The thin mist seemed to be drawn to the lights, making each one bloom in a haze of orange. The same thing happened at street level, where it created a chromatic soup from the tail lights and headlights of the cars, the neon signs and illuminated shop windows. Green Park was drained of colour: the leaves and branches draped over the railings were chalk-white; more distant trees were little more than vague grey ghosts.

"It's over there, your hotel. Be there in a tick."

The cab turned sharply into Half Moon Street and drew into the kerb. Terry paid the driver.

"Ta very much, sir. Go careful, now."

"You too."

The engine burbled into greater life and the cab moved off, leaving behind it an oppressive silence. As they crossed to the hotel entrance they felt and heard the whitened paving stones rasping on the soles of their shoes. A young man in a smart black uniform stepped out and held the door open for them and they were in the warm, clean surroundings of the reception area.

CHAPTER 14

There was barely time to go to their rooms and drop their bags before they had to return to the lobby. It was just after eleven-thirty, and a large black Jaguar was already waiting for them in the dim daylight outside the hotel. They drove directly to Whitehall, making swift progress along roads that would normally be crawling with cars, buses, and taxis. The PA got up as they entered the outer office and conducted them straight in. Four men were seated around the big desk and they stood as Terry and Maggie came through the door. Giles Monteith greeted them.

"Hello, good of you to come. You've already met my Scientific Adviser, Sir Ashley Gibbs."

Terry nodded curtly. Monteith continued:

"I expect you recognize the Home Secretary, Robert Spalding…" He paused to allow both of them to shake hands. Spalding was a familiar figure; the same height as Monteith, he looked a good deal older, partly because he was almost entirely bald. He was wearing the pale grey suit in which he was often interviewed on television.

"And Gareth Evans is here from the Department of Health."

Evans was a young man with thick, dark hair and a flushed face. His hand was hot and sweaty. Terry was standing slightly behind Maggie and noticed her wipe her palm discreetly on the back of her skirt.

Monteith waited until they had all taken their seats.

"Good, let's get started. First some facts. The white smog which has overtaken the capital is due to a cloud of ammonia – no doubt about that, you can smell it everywhere. It seemed to come in from the Atlantic when the rainstorms moved off to the north-east. It's not due to an industrial accident: anything that released a volume of gas that size would have to be on a massive scale; we've checked both here and in northern France and nothing showed up. So if it isn't due to an industrial disaster where did it come from? The reason I've asked Dr. McKinley and Dr. Ferris to join us is that they have a unique take on what may have been happening. Dr. McKinley, do you think you could give us a quick rundown on what you believe is behind this phenomenon, just to get everyone on the same footing?"

Terry had been waiting for this. He summarized their findings as he'd done before and followed up with the implications for the weather: the early hurricanes and the torrential rain. As his predictions had been borne out by events, he could do this with confidence and with a slight air of inevitability that would not be lost on Monteith and Ashley. Then he turned to what they really wanted to know.

"Ammonia gas is invisible. What you're getting in this noxious white smog is a mixture of the gas with fine crystals of ammonium salts – the sulphate, nitrate, chloride, and carbonate – formed when the gas combines with the acid emissions you get in any large city." Then, addressing Monteith and Ashley directly, he said:

"In short, the sequence of events has been pretty much what I laid out in this office about three weeks ago. The only surprise is how quickly it's all happened. That's the major concern. It suggests that these organisms are already well established in the environment. Perhaps if you'd taken us more seriously before we could have been better prepared." Monteith's mouth was opening to reply but Terry turned quickly to Maggie. "Dr. Ferris, anything you want to add?"

"Just this." Maggie's voice had a steely edge. "As Dr. McKinley and I were unable to convince Mr. Monteith and Sir Ashley that we were facing a serious potential threat, we had to follow it up privately and at our own expense. We now have samples of the ocean in the Sargasso Sea area, taken near the algal mats where the organism may have arisen. We can confirm that the ammonia-producing organism, or organisms, is present there. I'm afraid we can't say more than that at the moment because," she fixed her eyes on Monteith, "we were given neither the opportunity nor the resources to mount a proper investigation."

Monteith's face was slightly flushed. "Thank you, thank you very much. Let's be clear: the situation facing us before was purely hypothetical. Now it's a reality and we have to deal with it. Yes, Mr. Evans?"

The Junior Health Minister said, "Thank you, Minister." He tugged nervously at his shirt cuffs, and Terry caught a flash of inappropriately large cufflinks. "First of all, the Minister of Health sends her apologies. As you can imagine, she's extremely busy with the current crisis. Now, if I may... Dr. McKinley. Our immediate problem, as I see it, is this smog. The hospitals and general practitioners are working at full stretch now. People are already dying. How long do you think it's going to last?"

"That's hard to say. If you're lucky, this is just a pocket of ammonia that's been blown in by an unfavourable wind. In that case it should clear in a day or two. But that won't be for long. The organism has obviously been spreading unchecked for many months. Fogs like this one are going to become more frequent. Eventually the air will become too toxic to breathe, and not just in the towns."

Monteith came back. "Well, what can we do about it? Could we spray something on these algal mats? Dr. Ferris? Would that be a useful place to start?"

"Not without knowing which ones are affected. We could end up killing the good phytoplankton and making things worse. Also the plankton are at the bottom of tremendously important marine food chains. You can't go about disrupting things in that untargeted way, even if it were feasible."

"Well, do you have any other suggestions?"

Maggie sighed. "We're dealing with a mutant organism. The only sure way to combat a mutation like this is first to find out what it is. That means identifying the DNA sequence responsible. What you need is a team of experts – as we suggested before – and they'd have to be adequately resourced. It will take time and even after they've succeeded they'll have to work out a way of neutralizing it, and that will take more time. All the while the smogs will be getting worse. Sorry, I'm afraid there are no easy answers."

"Giles, may I?"

"Of course, Home Secretary."

"Dr. McKinley and Dr. Ferris, we're deeply indebted to you for the remarkable work you've done. Without your insights we would be at a total loss to understand what's going on.

"The PM's in the States at the moment, having talks with the President. The visit was prearranged and in some ways the timing hasn't been ideal. President Kinghorn has his hands full right now, dealing with the legacy of Hurricane Ailsa. It left a dreadful trail of destruction and now they're faced with the challenge of restoring services, rehousing the homeless, repairing highways, and so on. Needless to say, the cost of all that is a major headache for the present administration. With me so far?"

"Yes…"

"In the circumstances you wouldn't expect him to be unduly exercised by the news that London's been afflicted by a white smog. However, when this crisis arose yesterday Giles briefed the PM on your previous conversations, and the PM's passed it on. He's told the President that there's a possible causal connection between a white smog on our side of the Atlantic and an unusually severe and unseasonally early hurricane on theirs. The President's interested. If nothing else he wants to be better informed so that he can make appropriate provision – that way he might avoid some of the political backlash he suffered this time around. One of us will be speaking to the PM again after this meeting and if you agree I will be suggesting that you, Dr. McKinley, and you, Dr. Ferris, go out to the States to share your knowledge and expertise with their people."

Maggie frowned. "We just happened to be the ones who came across this organism. There must be lots of people better qualified than us. It seems to me you're just using the first scientists you come across."

"Not at all, Dr. Ferris. You're losing sight of one thing: it's still absolutely vital to keep this entire business secret. If the truth got out, there would be serious public disorder – Giles was right about that. Now if we did as you suggest, and started to trawl around for suitable scientists, why, the whole thing would get out in no time at all! The fact is, we've been rather fortunate: the people who've brought this to our attention, and who are already in the picture, are also very suitably qualified."

Terry's eyes narrowed. "You're placing a lot of reliance on Dr. Ferris and myself."

"Oh, I think that's justified, don't you? You've discovered the problem and already begun to do the necessary research. And there don't seem to be any difficulties from a security point of view. You haven't got criminal records. You both belong to a trade union but you're not especially active. You're not members of any political party – in fact politics probably doesn't interest either of you in the slightest – "

" – well, you've got that right."

"You've done as Giles instructed and kept this to yourselves. You're not seriously in debt…"

Terry sat up, a tingling sensation in his palms. "Wait a minute, how do you know all this?"

The Home Secretary smiled: "Don't be offended Dr. McKinley, we have to take precautions."

Terry wasn't sure whether to be flattered or furious. He knew now why he'd felt uneasy about that phone call. This was how they knew which hotel they'd stayed in before and how to contact him at home. But they also knew a lot more.

"We stay together?"

"Of course, unless you yourselves choose to act independently. All expenses will be met for both of you, of course, here and in the States."

"What about our day jobs? We do work, you know. We've got teaching, research, we sit on committees…"

"I'll have a word with your Vice-Chancellor. I'm sure he'll be amenable to treating it as a Leave of Absence. We'll fund a couple of temporary lecturers if it helps."

Terry looked at Maggie and back at the Home Secretary.

"Sir, would you mind if we have a moment to discuss this in private?"

"Not at all, but please bear in mind that all of us here have busy schedules."

They walked down the corridor to the outer office. Fortunately it was empty, but they kept their voices down to avoid being overheard by the secretaries in the adjacent room.

"What do you think, Terry?"

"I think they're being cheap. They wouldn't give us the resources to investigate the problem before. Now they see the need for it, but they still won't do what's needed. They've had a better idea: they'll use us to pass the bill to the Americans."

"It's better than doing nothing, surely?"

"I guess so. I can't help but feel they don't want anyone to point the finger at them. If we succeed they'll take all the credit. If we fail it's our tough luck; they'll say they did everything possible and we let them down. They'll hang us out to dry."

"You're probably right but right now there's nothing else on offer. This way at least we'd get the chance to do something."

He nodded. "That's true."

"So, are you up for it?"

"Off we go again."

"Time to save the world, Dr. McKinley."

"After you, Dr. Ferris."

CHAPTER 15

By the time Terry and Maggie's plane took off for Washington a few days later the situation in London had eased: a strengthening wind had dissipated the smog, driving the last traces out to the North Sea, and life was returning to normal for all but the unfortunate few still confined to hospital. Gazing out of the window at the retreating landscape Terry had the distinct feeling that they, too, were being blown away from UK shores, and the problem with them.

The Headquarters Building of the National Science Foundation was a massive W-shaped block on Wilson Boulevard in Arlington, Virginia. The car dropped them off and they stood outside for a few moments, gazing up at the sheer size of it.

At the reception desk they were greeted by a young woman in a black uniform carrying the NSF logo and a Security Officer tab. Terry handed over their passports and she tapped at a keyboard, consulted the computer screen, then picked up the phone. After a quick exchange she turned back to them.

"Wait here, sir, someone will be down for you."

A couple of minutes later a woman came around the corner and walked straight over to them. She was wearing a burgundy trouser suit and her hand was already outstretched.

"Hi, I'm Tricia Lawton, the Director's PA. Please come with me."

As they followed her to the elevators Terry was thinking of the hundreds of offices that must be contained in this huge building, the number of personnel in those offices, and the hierarchy of organization needed to run it.

Once in the lift Tricia placed her ID card in a slot and pressed a button for the top floor.

The PA's office was thickly carpeted, the walls lined with bookshelves carrying box files and bound volumes. In addition to her desk there were two polished wood tables, on which piles of coloured booklets and other papers were stacked. The faint sound of tapping came from beyond an unmarked door, which Terry presumed led to the secretariat. The PA knocked lightly on another door, marked "Director", and ushered them into an office that was similar in size to her own but more sparsely furnished. The Director rose from behind his desk as they came in. He was tall, his height subtly emphasized by the cut of his suit. He wore a striped shirt and a blue tie. Beyond him was a large window, through which they could just make out the distant tops of high-rise buildings.

"Thank you, Trish," the Director said, as his PA withdrew. He shook hands with them in turn. "Chris Walmesley. Welcome to Washington. Please have a seat."

He returned to the office armchair behind his desk. With his clean-shaven appearance and dark hair he seemed young to be in such a senior post, but the corded skin of his throat suggested he was older than he looked. He fixed them with keen grey eyes, then sat forward, his forearms on the leather desktop, hands clasped.

"Now, I have instructions to assist you folks in pretty much whatever way I can."

"Instructions?" Terry said, with interest. "May I ask from whom?"

"From the President, of course. Right now his prime concern is the havoc created by Hurricane Ailsa. We're all hoping this is a freak event. If that's not the case – if it's part of some new pattern – he wants to be the first to know. At the same time he's anxious to avoid public alarm, so there's no one else in the loop. I hope that's understood."

They nodded and Walmesley continued:

"All I know is that you have some kind of explanation for these unseasonal hurricanes, and you're saying we could be due for more of them. Would you like to take it from there?"

Terry had presented their case twice before but now the responsibility weighed more heavily on him. This could well be their last chance to get something done. He had to strike the right tone: persuasive, without indulging in overstatement.

"With respect, it would be helpful if I knew what level to pitch this at."

"You pitch it as high as you like. I'll tell you if I don't understand something."

"All right."

Terry gave him the story: the ammonia-producing organism, its likely source, the possibility that it had spread to other species, and the consequences if quantities of ammonia were being liberated into the atmosphere. Walmesley listened without interrupting. Terry concluded:

"This is what I told the UK Minister for the Environment, Food and Rural Affairs less than a month ago. What I didn't realize at the time was how far the organism had spread already. Because of that, things have happened sooner than anticipated. Otherwise the picture is consistent with expectations: unseasonal hurricanes on your side of the water, storms and torrential rain on ours. So far as I'm concerned, the final confirmation was the choking white smog that rolled into London earlier this week."

When he'd finished Walmesley blinked a couple of times, then got up and went over to stand facing the window. They waited for several minutes, watching his silhouette. He returned to the desk.

"It's all very interesting stuff, Dr. McKinley, but I have to say I'm not totally convinced."

Terry almost sagged with disappointment. "You're not?"

"Not based on what you've just told me, it's circumstantial at best. Let's get down to brass tacks guys. Here at the NSF we've been funding, through our Geosciences Directorate, several long-term programs. These are designed to provide more precise data on the prevalence of greenhouse gases in the atmosphere and they involve analysing air samples at high altitudes. The evidence we have is unequivocal: it supports global warming. Now I'm sure I don't have to tell you how difficult long-range forecasting can be, but it seems more likely that this, or simply a random fluctuation of climate, is what's behind these hurricanes."

"It doesn't explain the white smog that hit London, though does it?" Said Maggie, quickly.

"That's assuming the two things are connected."

"Fair point," she continued "but surely that's what we're here to find out. And if we are right about this we need to do it now, before things really get out of hand."

"What exactly are you saying?"

"I'm saying we should put together a team of experts – phytoplankton ecologists and molecular biologists, atmospheric chemists, oceanographers – to investigate the organism and the effects it's having on the atmosphere. Then we can assess the scale of the threat and figure out how the hell we can fix it."

Walmesley shook his head. "Out of the question."

"Why?" said Terry.

"For one thing the President would never allow it. Look, the American public sees unseasonal hurricanes as an Act of God: devastating – certainly; unusual – certainly; but no more sinister than that. You put together a high-powered group like that and it'd be as good as announcing on national television that we're facing the end of the world. At best it would cause unease; at worst, panic and disorder – and maybe all for nothing."

"So you don't think there is a global threat?" asked Maggie, her voice rising with exasperation.

"Right now? – no, I don't. A long-term threat, maybe, from global warming, but not an immediate one."

"What about an organism that produces ammonia? Is that a threat or isn't it?"

"That I can't say. But I'd regard it as an epiphenomenon, unconnected with the hurricanes."

"And the white smog?"

"An unreported industrial accident. Or a one-off, a local accumulation of ammonia driven to low altitude by freak atmospheric conditions."

Maggie sat back and threw up her arms. "Well it's going to happen a hell of a lot more if the ammonia levels continue to rise."

"That too is a long ways from being certain. Ammonia's a light gas; it could escape from Earth's gravity or be driven out by the solar wind. Atmospheric chemistry's complex: it could react with free radicals in the upper atmosphere. The storms may wash the ammonia out. It doesn't have to rise. The levels could plateau; they may even drop again."

Terry could feel his own frustration growing as Maggie continued. "So what are we supposed to do? Go back to the UK and tell the government that the Americans aren't interested?"

"Now don't mistake me. I am interested. I think what you've found is worth investigating further, but I can't authorize funding just like that. You'd have to go through the normal channels, a grant proposal, peer review – "

"That'll take far too long," said Terry.

"Dr. McKinley, you have to see it from where I'm sitting. My Directorates consider more than forty thousand research proposals a year. Some get funded; most are rejected. We don't have an inexhaustible supply of cash here. There's only so much we can do. I understand the President wants this looked at but you haven't convinced me it deserves immediate prioritisation."

Maggie sighed loudly and lowered her voice to a gentler tone:

"Dr. Walmesley, may I ask you something? What would cause you to change your mind?"

"What would change my mind? Evidence that it wasn't a purely local issue. Something that showed ammonia levels were rising globally, unchecked."

Terry raised his eyebrows. "Well surely you have that information already – from your atmospheric analysis. It would include ammonia levels, wouldn't it?"

"Ye-es, it would, but ammonia's only present at trace levels in the atmosphere so I guess no one's looked at it."

"It's not at trace levels any more. Could I extract that data and process it?"

"That's a complex task."

"I'm a planetary physicist; I think I can handle it."

Something new entered Walmesley's eyes. "A planetary physicist? That's interesting. They told me you were couple of biologists."

"Maggie is, I'm not."

"I see. I did wonder when you started to talk about atmospheric movements. Seems we speak the same language, then. I was in Geophysics. I headed up the Geosciences Directorate for some years before I took overall charge of the Foundation."

Terry detected a slight softening of the Director's attitude.

"So you'll let me have the data?"

He grimaced. "No, I can't do that. The Foundation supports the project but we don't have our own research staff or labs; the monitoring is done by a consortium of universities. It's a lot of work to collect material like that and the data is theirs to interpret."

Maggie drew a breath. "Couldn't you be more helpful than that? I mean, you did say you were instructed to assist us."

Walmesley sat back slowly. "You're twisting my arm now, are you?" He smothered a smile. "Well, as the funding body it would be legitimate for us to request a copy of the data collected so far. I could get someone to extract what we need and pass me the raw data…" He placed a hand on the desk. "Okay, look, I'll do that. And bearing in mind the security aspect I'll analyse it myself. It'll make a welcome change to pushing all this Goddamned paper around."

"Great. Thanks very much."

"I'll try to deal with it over the weekend." He pressed a button on an intercom. A voice said "Yes, Chris?"

"Trish, do I have a slot on Monday or Tuesday to get together with Drs. McKinley and Ferris again?"

There was a slight pause. "Not Tuesday. But on Monday if you leave the Advisory Committee before the end you could see them between three-thirty and four-thirty."

"Perfect, put it in the diary, would you?" He turned to them. "Monday afternoon, three-thirty. With a bit of luck we should have something by then."

He pushed his chair back and got up. They followed suit.

"This your first time in Washington?"

Terry answered, "Yes, actually – for both of us."

"You should use the weekend to take a look around the city. There's plenty on offer: the White House, the Monument, the Memorials, the Library of Congress, the Smithsonian... A lot of it's within walking distance of your hotel. Should keep you busy." They shook hands. "We'll meet again on Monday. One way or another we're going to see if there's anything in this theory of yours."

CHAPTER 16

They spent the Saturday trying to take Walmesley's advice, but soon discovered it was impossible to concentrate on sight-seeing with so much going on inside their heads. They gave up in the early afternoon and returned to the hotel to go over once more what they knew so far. Maggie got Terry to go over the climate changes again and how much of it could be explained by global warming, as Walmesley seemed to believe. Terry asked her how the ammonia mutation could have arisen, and she spent some time drawing out DNA base sequences and describing the various mechanisms.

Terry's phone rang just as they were considering where to go for dinner and he answered it. He sat forward in his seat, listening intently before saying: "Ok, we'll be right over."

"That was Walmesley," he said excitedly. "He wants to meet us in his office right away. Sounds like he's onto something."

As it was Saturday the NSF building was largely deserted. Security staff showed them up to Walmesley's office and they waited for him outside the door by his assistant's desk. Walmesley came in a few minutes later, a little breathless.

"Sorry about this." He dumped a thick folder on his PA's desk. "Come through, come through."

He hung his jacket over the office chair and sat down. "Okay. I got the data on the composition of atmospheric samples late on Friday. I analysed most of it straight away."

He paused, eyeing them.

"And…?" Terry asked.

"Levels grossly elevated everywhere I looked. They're not just up: they're rising more rapidly." He placed his hands on the desk. "You know, at first I couldn't believe it – I thought I'd made a mistake. So I analyzed the data again, checked the calibration, everything. Same result. What you gave me on Friday was interesting, but your evidence was circumstantial. Not anymore it's not. This is hard data. Usually I don't mind being proved wrong, but I gotta be honest, in this particular case I wish I had been right."

Terry gave him a grim smile. "Me too. So where do we go from here?"

"Well, I tried to speak to the President, but he's in Texas, touring the areas damaged by the hurricane. He left word for me to liaise with Herbert Kramer."

"Herbert Kramer?"

"Dr. Kramer is Director of the Office of Science and Technology Policy. When it comes to science policy the President depends heavily on his counsel."

Something about the way he said it, the merest hint of sarcasm, suggested to Terry that the arrangement was not one that had Walmesley's wholehearted approval.

"And what did Dr. Kramer say?"

Walmesley's lips tightened. "Herbert Kramer is a stickler for protocol. To be frank, we've never seen eye to eye and now he's pissed because the President bypassed him and sent the two of you to me. I explained that the President had seen it as a geosciences problem and dropped it in my lap." He shrugged. "He seemed to find that hard to accept. It was uphill from then on in."

"You gave him the data on ammonia levels?"

"Of course. He asked whether I had incontrovertible proof that this was the cause of the unseasonal hurricanes. I said of course I didn't, but the issue was clearly more far-reaching than just changes in weather patterns. I asked him to advise the President to set up a task force immediately to investigate it fully. He wouldn't do that. He said the President was far too occupied with an actual disaster to concern himself with some hypothetical future threat. As for my concerns, since it was 'a geosciences problem' I should identify funding through the usual NSF channels. I think he enjoyed saying that."

"But we've been over that ground before. It would take months!"

"I know. Look, I'm prepared to take this to the President myself but first we need more evidence. Kramer has a point: Hurricane Ailsa was one of the most violent storms in recent years, and the damage was very severe. The President's been heavily criticized for not responding quickly enough to the situation down there. I think that was unfair, but it hasn't stopped his political opponents – they've had a field day. Now the President's fighting back and the reconstruction effort is his top priority. If we're to convince him that this issue is even more important we've got to be on very solid ground. We'll have to strengthen the case."

"Strengthen it how?" said Maggie.

"I'd like to have some more independent verification. And it would be good to make a stronger link between this organism of yours and the rise in ammonia levels."

"I don't see how we can do that without knowing exactly when the mutation occurred."

"True, but if it arose in Bermuda, as you said, the distribution of ammonia may reflect that. There could be more data in the system, some of it going back several years. Terry, if I gave you access to other governmental bodies, like the US Geological Survey and NOAA – that's the US National Oceanic and Atmospheric Administration – do you think you could take a look at it?"

"Yes, I could do that. But the trouble with atmospheric sampling is it only gives us data at discrete sites. It would be more useful to have an overall picture of ammonia distribution, the sort of thing you get from Earth surveillance satellites. I'd have thought NASA has that data for Earth's atmosphere but I'm damned if I can find it. Would you have access to information like that?"

"Sure, that's not a problem; we work closely with NASA. If they have data on ammonia I can get it put on a DVD for you. There's probably specialized software for displaying the images. I'll have them download that as well. Look, this is what we'll do. I'll set you up with an office in this building with access to the internal network. You can work on whatever atmospheric data is available while I'm getting those disks from NASA."

"Great. Thanks."

"Dr. Walmesley?" Maggie said. "What about the organism? Couldn't we make some progress on that, too? We have samples."

The grey eyes narrowed. "You have?"

"Yes. Terry took freshwater samples from a river that was affected, and we collected ocean samples in the Sargasso Sea, close to an algal mat that was producing a lot of ammonia."

"And they're here?"

"Not here, no, in Liverpool. A colleague is looking after them for us. But he can send some over. I could have them here on Monday."

Walmesley nodded slowly.

"We have no lab facilities here and we can't let this get into the public domain. But if you can keep it to yourself I may be able to get you some lab space at the National Institutes of Health. I can speak to Elaine Zanuck – she's the Director."

"Thank you."

"The NIH is at Bethesda. It's only six or seven miles from here so you could keep your room in the hotel and commute by cab." He sat back.

"Now, is that everything?"

Terry looked at Maggie and, sensing agreement, said, "Yes, I believe it is."

"Good." He scribbled on a piece of paper and handed it over. "If you need to reach me, this is my cell phone. I'll try to contact you before the end of the day."

Terry glanced at it, then put it in his pocket. They all got up and Walmesley saw them to the door.

"By the way," he said. "Just a basic security precaution: first names only on the phone. In any case, since we're colleagues now I think it would be appropriate, don't you?"

Terry extended his hand. "Chris."

"Terry, Maggie," said Chris shaking his hand and then Maggie's.

CHAPTER 17

Maggie was allotted space in one corner of a large, fourth-floor lab in the National Institutes of Health building on Monday morning, with access to the microscope room down the corridor. One of the technicians seemed happy enough to help her find the equipment and materials she needed without being too curious about what she was up to.

In the early afternoon she took a cab to the air freight terminal, armed with the print-out of an Air Waybill that Jake Brewer had emailed to her. She asked the driver to wait for her. Twenty minutes later she re-emerged and he drove her back to Bethesda. She paid the fare, added a generous tip, then hurried into the building with her precious package.

Back in her corner of the lab she found a scalpel and cut through the wide tape securing the lid of the carton. Jake had done a good job. Under a heap of expanded polystyrene pellets and inside several layers of bubble plastic she found two flasks in close company with a couple of cold gel packs. As she'd requested, he'd sent one of Terry's river samples and one of the Bermuda samples. She picked up some slides, cover slips and a micropipette from a drawer, and took them along to the microscope room.

She and Terry had dinner that evening in the hotel's Avenue Grill, choosing a table at some distance from the other diners.

"So," he said as she sat down. "Did the samples arrive?"

"Yes, they look fine, one from the river and one from the ocean."

"What are you going to do with them?"

"Well, we already know the Bermuda samples contain a lot of different organisms. The crucial issue is whether only one type of organism produces ammonia. If they're all producing ammonia, that's strong evidence for plasmid transfer."

He nodded so she continued.

"I thought of a couple of ways it might be done. One would be to separate the different types and grow them up individually. I spent several hours today sucking single organisms into a micropipette and putting each one in its own culture dish."

"Sounds tricky."

"It was. I managed to isolate a few but I don't know whether they'll survive. So I'm trying something else. I've plated out a sample on a nutrient gel. Not an ordinary gel; I put a pH indicator in it. Normally it's yellow but if alkali is present it'll go red. Ammonia is alkaline, so any organisms producing it should have a red halo around them. That's the theory, anyway."

"Genius. Seriously, it's a great idea, Maggie."

She smiled and Terry though he detected a slight colouring of her cheeks. "See if it works before you say that. What about you? How are you getting on with the atmospheric sampling?"

Terry pushed his plate aside. "Okay so far. Chris has me accredited with all the important organizations now. NOAA definitely has useful data. Trouble is, I'm surrounded by office bods in that building. When it comes to accessing databases I'm on my own and it's taking longer than I'd like. Do you want coffee?"

"No, I'm fine." She hesitated, then leaned a little closer and dropped to a whisper. "Terry, weren't we supposed to report back to the Home Secretary, tell him what's happening?"

"Oops, I'd forgotten about that." He sighed. "Suppose I'd better. He gave me a number to call."

"Is it wise to use the phone?"

"He said it'd be safe enough from a cell phone but I shouldn't say 'organism', 'cyanobacteria', or 'ammonia'. I'll do it in the morning."

"What time?"

"Seven-ish probably."

"Mind if I listen in."

"If you like." He glanced at his watch, then pushed his chair back. "Early start, then. Let's get back."

At a few minutes past seven Terry tapped on the communicating door between the rooms.

"You ready?"

The door opened and Maggie came in. She looked like she had just showered. Her hair was still damp and Terry caught the fruity scent of her shampoo.

"Put it on loudspeaker," she said. "So I can listen."

He punched in the number and waited.

"Home Office."

"This is Dr. McKinley. Could I speak to the Home Secretary?"

"Dr. McKinley. We've were wondering when you'd update us. Why haven't you called before now?"

Terry's mouth set. "We've been busy. Who is this?"

"This is Adrian Spencer-Talbot."

"I was told to contact the Home Secretary."

"Mr. Spalding's very busy. You can talk to me."

"Sorry, I've been told to treat this matter as confidential. You're expecting me to talk to someone I don't know and I've never seen."

"You've been patched through to a special number, Dr. McKinley. It's who have to trust you."

"Oh, really? Well I'm sorry, but if the Home Secretary is too busy to take this call himself right now I'm going to hang up."

There was an audible sigh. *"I'll try his extension."*

Several seconds passed. Then: *"Spalding."*

"This is Dr. McKinley."

"Dr. McKinley, I don't have a great deal of time at the moment, but rest assured Adrian is fully briefed and ready to deal with you. Now, there's a Cabinet meeting tomorrow and I intend to report on what progress you've made. Please give your report to Adrian. I'll pass you back to him. Please do be sure to update us regularly."

The line buzzed. A flush of anger had risen to Terry's cheeks.

"Adrian Spencer-Talbot."

Was there a note of triumph in that voice? He took a deep breath. "All right, here's the situation."

He gave a brief account of the two meetings with Chris Walmesley. He and Dr. Ferris had been given facilities and were now in the process of strengthening the case in preparation for taking it to the President.

"That's it, is it?"

Terry delivered the answer between clenched teeth.

"Yes, that's it."

"All right. I'll pass that on to Mr. Spalding. And from now on, Dr. McKinley it would be helpful if you could report daily – "

"Sorry, can't hear you, connection's breaking up." Terry clicked off.

Maggie smirked. "Hanging up on the British government. Anarchy."

"These people. For weeks we couldn't beg them to listen to us and now we're not talking to them enough." He looked at the phone, then back at her. "Maybe I'll get myself another mobile and next time we cross the Potomac accidentally drop this one over the side."

Maggie laughed. "I'd better get to the lab. I'll meet you back here this evening?"

"Sounds like a plan," Terry answered. "I'm going to work from here today. No one to help me in the NSF building anyway."

She smiled again and kissed him on the cheek before heading out.

CHAPTER 18

That afternoon Terry sat at the small desk in his hotel room, staring at the sheets containing the ammonia data he'd extracted from the NOAA records. Different flight paths and different sites to the NSF data but it was the same story all over again.

It seems to be rising everywhere.

There was a knock at the door. He went and opened it and saw one of the hotel porters standing there with a small brown parcel in his hand.

"Delivery, sir."

"Thanks," said Terry and took it from him. He started to open it when he noticed the porter was still standing there looking at him expectantly. He stared at him for a moment and the porter gave a little cough.

"Oh, right" said Terry quickly and pulled out some crimpled bills from his pocket. He selected a five dollar note and handed it to the man.

"Thank you, sir," he said, and quickly turned and walked away.

Terry closed the door and opened the parcel. Inside were two disks. Both had NASA stickers on them and someone had scrawled "Software" on one and "Data" on the other with a spirit pen. This would be the spectroscopy data from the NASA satellites that would show the concentration of ammonia in the atmosphere and the software that would let him decode it and build up a visual picture.

He booted up his laptop and installed the software, then the data. His fingers moved rapidly over the keys and from time to time he'd mutter to himself: "So why can't I…?" Eventually he got the hang of it. He paused for a moment.

Where and when to look first?

He glanced down at the papers on his desk and his eyes rested on one of his briefing documents outlining the evidence they'd collected from Bermuda.

As good a place as any. He pressed a key combination. A dialog box appeared and he typed in the coordinates for Bermuda. He paused, then entered the dates for April the year before, knowing there was a pocket of ammonia around there at that time. The screen displayed a fuzzy purple image.

Is that it?

This couldn't be right. He didn't expect very high resolution but what was on the screen in front of him was absolutely featureless.

The colour wasn't a problem; it was just a way of displaying the level of ammonia. The colour purple would be assigned to the lowest concentration, blue to the next step up, and then through the spectrum to green, yellow, orange, red, and finally white, for the highest concentrations. But at these coordinates he expected to see at least some sign of the Islands, and what he was looking at was just a purple fog. He couldn't get anything from this.

He clicked on an icon which switched the view to optical wavelengths, showing what it looked like in the visible spectrum.

The screen changed to a conventional satellite view of the Atlantic Ocean with a small streak of land in the middle. He zoomed in. The streak expanded and revealed itself as the Bermuda Islands. It looked sharp enough.

He slapped his forehead.

Idiot. By April last year the ammonia had already risen into the stratosphere. The satellite's picking up a thin layer of atmospheric ammonia which is masking what's going on underneath.

He switched the view to the ammonia spectrum again and started to tap an arrow key, stepping back through the data a month at a time. The picture remained fuzzy. He continued to tap. Then, when he'd gone back a further seventeen months, the screen cleared abruptly. The diffuse purple had gone, to be replaced by a clear purple and blue patch the shape of a tadpole, with a green centre to the body.

He returned to the optical view. At this altitude he could see the whole coastline of Bermuda. He switched back to the ammonia spectrum, then alternated between the two. He concentrated on the green circle. It appeared to be exactly where the weed mats had been. He paused again, looking at the tadpole's tail.

What the hell?

It looked like it was moving westwards.

He frowned. It couldn't be. The Gulf Stream flowed to the east. This didn't make sense.

Just then there was another knock at his door. He went and opened it and saw Maggie standing in the corridor. She rushed in past him and sat down on the bed, her head lowered.

"Maggie? What's wrong?"

She took a deep breath. "It's spreading Terry, in the worst possible way. It's plasmid transfer. There's no doubt about it."

They both sat in silence for some time on the large hotel bed. Terry was leaning up against the headboard. Maggie was still where she had sat when she first came in, but now had her knees drawn up to under her chin with her arms hugging her legs to her chest.

Finally she spoke.

"I spent all morning tracking down the stuff for a cell viability assay, then most of the afternoon using it on my cultures. Dead, the lot of them. I was a bit surprised none survived but then lab work can be like that; obviously I didn't hit on the right growing conditions. Then I had a look at my indicator gels."

She paused.

"There's already a little red halo round each and every one. All those different organisms are producing ammonia. There's no doubt about it any more, Terry. It's plasmid transfer, all right."

Terry grimaced. "The worst possible outcome."

He stood up and fixed them both a drink from the mini-bar. They sat in silence again for a while, sipping their drinks, before Terry spoke.

"You're a biologist. Tell me: how does Nature come to play such a lousy trick on us? It makes no sense. Those mutant organisms could wipe out all life on the planet."

"But they won't be wiped out themselves – and that's the point, isn't it? Organisms like this don't know anything about planets; they're looking after their own interests and they're doing it brilliantly. You know how evolution works, Terry. Without chance mutations that give individuals an edge, life wouldn't have got as far as the dinosaurs, let alone us."

"And the more favourable the mutation, the bigger the competitive advantage, so the quicker it spreads."

"Exactly. It's not the organism's problem; it's ours." She drained her glass and got up to make another. "Any progress at your end?"

He looked at her for a moment, before realising what she was referring too. With her news he'd completely forgotten what he had been doing.

"Oh, yes. I did find something weird in the ammonia data NASA sent over."

He showed her the laptop screen and explained what he had found.

"Maybe it's coming from another patch of weed further to the west. You'd better take a look."

He brought up the dialog box with the coordinates and tapped repeatedly, moving the image progressively to the west to see where the purple tadpole tail ended. The only sound in the room was the soft tapping of the keys as he tracked the tail further and further west. Then, to their surprise, it sent another branch up to the north and stopped.

"Now what?" said Terry. "Let's see where we are." He switched to the conventional satellite view. It displayed a coastline. "Just a minute, I'll change to a wider view." He typed a number in and the picture changed to display a much longer stretch of the coastline. Now it was unmistakable: the Eastern seaboard of the United States. Terry just stared at the screen.

"Jesus," exclaimed Maggie. "It's here?"

Suddenly she clutched his arm.

"Shit, Terry, why didn't I think of it before? You remember what Max Gibson said about American eels? There's a species of eel that migrates from the Eastern seaboard each year to spawn in the Sargasso Sea. They probably picked up strands of the stuff in their gills and took them back home."

Terry stayed silent, still staring. "Unless…"

"Unless what?"

"Unless they were transporting the stuff in the opposite direction."

She looked at him and blinked a couple of times. "I suppose that's possible. But there's no way of knowing that, is there?"

"Yes, there is. This picture is from last April. I can go further back in time and see which end it started from."

He brought up the ammonia display again. On this scale they could see the purple branch extending north and the long tail ending in the patch at Bermuda. He selected the date dialog box and pressed the arrow key several times, stepping back one month, two months, three… At Bermuda the patch was changing: first the green disappeared, then the blue, then the purple tail retracted away from Bermuda altogether. He kept tapping. All that was left now were two shorter purple tails and these shrank and merged into a single patch which blossomed blue and green, then disappeared entirely. He looked up at her.

"We were totally wrong about Bermuda," she said slowly. "It started in the States!"

He nodded. "The American eels picked it up there and took it to the Sargasso. It's so rich in phytoplankton it was as good as an incubator! No wonder it looked like the problem came from there!"

Maggie nodded. "Well it did, for us. English eels spawn in the

Sargasso too, so they carried phytoplankton with them when they migrated back across the ocean and up UK rivers. Now we know. Our organisms have succeeded in hitching a ride right across the Atlantic and they're passing the mutation on wherever they go. No wonder atmospheric levels of ammonia are rising!"

He bit his lip. "Maggie, I've had a thought. The purple branch we saw going up to the north. Eels are only part of the story: this stuff will be carried on ocean currents, too. And they don't just go eastwards towards Bermuda; they flow up the coast from Florida to Cape Cod. America has a lot more to worry about than hurricanes. This problem's right on their doorstep!"

Terry's phone rang.

"Terry? It's Chris."

"Chris. I was just about to call you. You won't believe what we've found."

"Well I hope it's something helpful. You watching the news?"

"No."

"Switch to CNN."

Terry went over to the TV and switched it on. He grabbed the remote and scrolled till he found CNN. There was a view of high-rise buildings peeking out of the top of a continuous white cloud.

"...*familiar view of downtown Pittsburgh, except there's nothing familiar about it. Normally from here you'd have a clear view of the Golden Triangle, where the Monongahela and the Allegheny come together as the Ohio River. It's somewhere under that white smog.*" The reporter coughed. "*Excuse me. The air's pretty bad even up here on Mount Washington, but it's a lot worse in town. A couple of hours ago we received this footage taken on cell phones.*"

The blurry, unsteady pictures showed people hurrying down the streets coughing and trying to cover their mouths and noses. Another view showed an almost deserted Central Business District; a thin white veil covering cars, buildings, and roads. There followed an interview with a spokesman from the Allegheny General Hospital.

"*We're advising people to stay indoors right now. We've been admitting people all day and at this time there's a Code Red in operation.*"

"*Does that mean you're turning patients away?*"

"*It just means we have to direct them to other hospitals. But there's pressure on services in the whole region so we ask that you don't contact the hospital or the ambulance service unless it's a genuine emergency.*"

"Is this a return to the bad old days, Dave?"

"Well, Lee, we're told this is a pretty freaky weather situation, and it should pass over soon. People haven't seen smog like this here in Pittsburgh for sixty years or more. I wasn't around back then, but of course in those days it was black smog from the steel mills. This stuff may be white but I'd say it's every bit as choking. That's why we're advising people, particularly if you're elderly, don't go outside until this thing blows through. And keep young children indoors; they're vulnerable, too."

"Thanks, Dave. Back to you, Rick."

The picture returned to the newscaster. *"As yet there are no official casualty figures, but it's estimated that at least six thousand people have been admitted to hospitals all over the city, and some of them are in a critical condition. As we said earlier, things appear to be just as bad in Baltimore and Cleveland..."*

"Terry? You still there?" Walmesley's voice jolted him back into the room.

"Yeah, Chris. I'm here."

"The President's called an emergency meeting tomorrow at the White House. He wants you both there."

CHAPTER 19

They saw only one person in the outer office when they arrived at their meeting inside 1600 Pennsylvania Avenue, the worlds' most famous address. He was an avuncular looking man with ginger hair, whitening at the temples, a ruddy complexion, and a large moustache. He wore a fawn check suit. "That's Robert Cabot, Director of National Intelligence. He's one of the President's closest advisers" Murmured Walmesley. "I'll introduce you."

"Dr. McKinley, Dr. Ferris," Cabot said, as he shook hands with both of them. He had a deep, velvety voice. "I hear you've had first-hand experience of these white smogs."

"Yes, sir," said Terry, "we were summoned to London when it was hit by one a few weeks ago."

"Terry predicted it but nobody believed us," Maggie added quickly.

Cabot's keen eyes searched her, before returning to Terry. "And you think the same thing is behind these unseasonal hurricanes?"

"It's a distinct possibility."

Cabot looked up as another man walked in. "Ah, here's James. James, come and meet Dr. McKinley and Dr. Ferris. James Brierley is the Secretary for Homeland Security," he added.

Brierley was tall and slim, almost delicate, but his hair was clipped close above the ears and neck, suggesting a military background. He took Maggie's hand first with a slight bow and said, "Dr. Ferris." As he moved to Terry he pointed and said to Cabot:

"Are these the scientists from – ?"

"They are."

Maggie glanced at Terry. At least these people knew who they were.

Two more arrived: Richard Pevensey, the Secretary of Defense and Dr. Elaine Zanuck, the Director of the National Institutes of Health. Maggie was particularly interested to meet Elaine Zanuck. She turned out to be a heavily built, rather motherly-looking woman in her late fifties, wearing a well-cut trouser suit. She scanned the room with the air of someone who, Maggie surmised, allowed little to pass her by.

"It was very good of you to give me lab space, Dr. Zanuck," Maggie said as they shook hands lightly.

Zanuck shot a quick glance at Walmesley and smiled. "No problem. You have everything you need?"

"For the moment, yes, thank you. People have been most helpful."

"Good. You let me know if there's anything more we can do." Her gaze strayed. "Excuse me one moment." She moved off to join Cabot and Brierley.

Maggie leaned towards Walmesley and Terry and said quietly: "High-powered gathering. Who suggested these people?"

"I did. It has to be at this level because of the confidentiality issue." Walmesley scanned the room and checked his watch. "We're all here now. I wanted the Director of NASA as well, but he's out of the country right now. So's the Vice-President. Kramer was asked but for some reason he's not coming."

The President's Secretary appeared and the group followed her in.

Terry felt a sharp jolt of excitement as he passed through the doorway. This was it, the famous Oval Office. He felt diminished by the volume of the room and the opulence of the furnishings. This administration had chosen a decorative theme based on burgundy, cream and gold. Burgundy was the dominant colour of the elliptical rug, woven with the Presidential crest, and it was echoed in broad stripes on the chairs and soft furniture. His eyes wandered up to the high arch of the ceiling where the Presidential crest was repeated as an oval medallion. He had to suppress an urge to run around touching things: the famous ornately carved *Resolute* desk with the two tall flags behind it, the sumptuous golden drapes framing the floor-to-ceiling windows, the long-case clock, the Remington sculptures of horses and cowboys... As the others dispersed to their places he saw President Harry Kinghorn greeting each one by name, shaking hands, indicating the two four-seat sofas, arranged facing each other in the centre of the room. At the far end he expected to see the fireplace and the two high-backed chairs in which the President was often photographed with prominent visitors. Much of the fireplace was now obscured, however, by a large flat-screen monitor with a computer on a shelf below it. Clearly, Walmesley had requested this for the presentations.

The President smiled as he caught sight of her and Terry.

"You must be Dr. Ferris and Dr. McKinley. Thank you for coming. Would you like to sit over there?"

When everyone was settled in their places the President took a chair at the desk end of the room so that he could speak to people on the sofas on either side and still view the screen beyond.

Maggie stole a look in his direction. He was older than any recent

President. The forehead was high, the grey hair a mere stubble above his ears, and age had slackened the flesh over a once craggy jaw, but there was still a contained energy about him that seemed to permeate even a room of this size. She felt a little overawed. She glanced at Terry, who was seated on her left. He caught her eye and gave her a reassuring wink.

"Right," the President said. "You know why we're here. Shall we get on with it? Dr. McKinley, do you want to lead off?"

"If you don't mind, Mr. President, I think everyone should see the data Dr. Walmesley has to show us first."

Walmesley walked over to the screen and brought it to life with a remote control. He faced the room.

"In May an unseasonally early hurricane, Hurricane Ailsa, came in from the Gulf of Mexico. There's no need for me to remind you of the extensive damage it caused. A couple of weeks later a choking white smog rolled over London, England, resulting in a ton of casualties and major disruption. Drs. McKinley and Ferris came over from England last week. They had some evidence that an increase in atmospheric ammonia might be responsible for both these events. Dr. McKinley persuaded me to examine data from our environmental sampling program, data on the levels of ammonia in our atmosphere. I did so. What came out of the analysis shocked the hell out of me. In fact at first I thought there'd been some mistake. Since then Dr. McKinley has checked the data from my own NSF-funded surveys against a data set collected independently by NOAA. I can tell you now that there ain't no mistake. I'll show you a typical record."

A graph flashed onto the screen.

"Notice the date on the axis; we can go back five years. There's always some ammonia around but it's normally just a trace, in fact it barely registers on this scale. But look what's been happening over the last three years or so. The level of ammonia has been rising like a rat up a drainpipe. And you can see that the curve is getting steeper and steeper."

Terry heard a low murmur and noticed the others exchanging glances. Pevensey was pointing. "What in God's name made it go up like that?"

"We'll get to that," answered Walmesley.

"Is it increasing exponentially?" Cabot asked.

"Yup, you probably could fit that curve with a rising exponential. Some of the ammonia is removed by rain and some falls out as ammonium salts but those losses aren't sufficient to make the curve flatten out to any noticeable extent. Okay, now let me show you just a sample of the data we've recorded from other locations."

The screen changed to white, and a series of smaller graphs started to go up. Each one was labelled with coordinates and an approximate location: Ohio, Pennsylvania, South Carolina, Bermuda… Every single graph showed the same upward trend.

Walmesley faced his audience.

"What we're seeing here is an alarming increase in atmospheric ammonia. Ammonia is a light gas. As it rises it adds energy to weather systems and this could sure as heck explain the unseasonal hurricanes." He pointed to the screen. "These samples were taken in the stratosphere, but there's little doubt that it's around in the troposphere too – that's the weather-forming lower level of the atmosphere. When local concentrations are blown into the air over a city, the ammonia combines with acidic gases from vehicle exhausts and factories and creates the white smog – like what's just kicked our asses in Baltimore, Pittsburgh, and Cleveland."

The President raised a finger. "But the levels are increasing. So you're saying these white smogs are going to get more frequent?"

"Yes, sir. More frequent and longer lasting."

"This is a disaster. I mean, quite apart from the horrific loss of life, the economic consequences would be incalculable. And Baltimore's no distance at all. If it had happened here, to the nation's capital, we'd have been paralysed. The country would have been vulnerable to every tinpot nation that wished us harm."

"I'm afraid it's even worse than that, sir. If the ammonia continues to rise at its present rate it won't be long before the air becomes too poisonous to breathe. When that point is reached neither we nor any other form of animal life will survive."

"Good God! Well what sort of timescale are we talking about here? Decades?" He paused. "Years?"

Terry held his breath as Walmesley answered, "It's hard to be precise because a lot depends on mixing in the lower reaches of the atmosphere. But all the current indications are that in many places levels incompatible with life will be reached within six months."

CHAPTER 20

Someone whistled and there was a burst of conversation. The President looked grim.

"That doesn't exactly give us a whole lot of time, does it? How has this happened?"

"I'll hand you back to Dr. McKinley, sir. He's best placed to answer that question."

Terry got to his feet and Walmesley passed him the remote as he returned to the sofa. He took another deep breath and began.

"Dr. Walmesley showed you evidence of a widespread increase in ammonia," he said. "I'll show you first where it's coming from."

He put up a conventional satellite view. "You'll probably recognize this; it's the Eastern seaboard of the United States as viewed from space. Now here is the same view, processed to show ammonia. We'll step forward, one month at a time."

At first the screen was blank, then coloured rings developed and expanded, starting with purple and adding blue, green and yellow. As the levels increased the rings became distorted and highly elongated.

"We're looking at the western and southern boundaries of the Sargasso Sea. We have a distribution of ammonia that travels north along the Eastern seaboard and another branch that's reaching eastwards towards Bermuda. It's my guess that your white smogs derived from the northerly branch."

"Where's it coming from?" Cabot asked. "Industrial pollution?"

"No. Believe it or not we're dealing with tiny organisms called cyanobacteria – you may know them as blue-green algae. They're a normal part of our environment and we're used to them undergoing seasonal expansions, such as algal blooms and mats. But this is different. One of these organisms has mutated. It's processing nitrogen from our atmosphere and releasing it as ammonia. Because it's enriching its own environment it grows without limit. It's even worse than that. Dr. Ferris has evidence that it also passes the modification to other species, by a process called plasmid transfer. When it does so it makes them produce ammonia, too. As I said, the organisms are tiny but there are trillions of them, so they're producing large volumes of ammonia."

James Brierley pointed at the screen. "If the problem's confined to those sites how do you explain the smogs in Pittsburgh and Cleveland?"

"I'm afraid it's not confined to these sites. For technical reasons I've had to show you the situation about two-and-a-half years ago Since then it's had ample time to spread much further. We believe London's white smog was the result of the organisms being carried from the Eastern seaboard to Bermuda and from there to the UK. The cyanobacteria tend to build up in rivers, lakes, and oceans – that's probably why the white smogs here have affected cities located near to large bodies of water: Chesapeake Bay in the case of Baltimore, a junction of major rivers in Pittsburgh, Lake Erie in Cleveland. But by now there's so much ammonia up there it could be stirred into our weather systems almost anywhere. So that's our problem. For millions of years, organisms of this type have pumped oxygen into our atmosphere. Now, they're progressively poisoning it with ammonia."

"There's got to be a fairly simple solution," said Cabot. "Some sort of algicide, maybe? The kind of thing we put in garden ponds and aquaria."

"Come on, Bob," the President replied. "You know how much you need for a tiny job like that. Look at the quantities you'd need to tip into the ocean!"

"An oil spill, then?" Richard Pevensey said. "Smother the stuff. Sink a tanker where it started, pretend it was an accident."

"I hope you're not serious, Dick," the President said heavily. "I have enough environmental problems down in the Gulf without adding pollution of every beach up and down the East Coast. In any case, the way I understand it, these organisms have spread all over the Atlantic. You wouldn't be going near the problem." He glanced at Terry, who nodded his agreement.

Pevensey looked at the others, shrugged, and said, "Well, I don't know. What else is there?"

The President's gaze went round the table and settled on Maggie. "Dr. Ferris, Chris tells me you had a suggestion."

Terry tensed. Maggie had come up with her idea only that morning and she'd come running into his room to share her excitement. This was her chance to set it out for the others but she'd had very little time to prepare...

He needn't have worried; she sounded relaxed and confident.

"Terry mentioned plasmid transfer – it's the process responsible for some of the antibiotic resistance you see in hospitals. That's why this ammonia mutation has spread so rapidly: it's been passing from organism to organism in a chain reaction. But..." she held up a finger, "that also suggests a way of fighting it. The affected organisms would be receptive to another plasmid, one that we could introduce, one designed to turn off ammonia production. If we could do that it would spread in the same way as the rogue organisms and go wherever they've gone. In my view, that's the way to defeat it – assemble a team of experts to design, produce and distribute our plasmid across the globe."

There was a murmur of interest around the table.

"Elaine?" The President turned to Dr. Elaine Zanuck, Director of the National Institutes of Health. "What do you think of that idea?"

She nodded. "Sounds feasible. The sequencing could be done fairly quickly; there are platforms around that can sequence an entire genome in a matter of days. They're mostly set up for human genomes so they'd have to be adapted for this type of organism. But in a way that's the easy part. Then you have to find out what the plasmid is coding for and how to switch it off. And then you need to construct another plasmid that would do the job, put it into another organism and distribute it. Like Dr. Ferris said, it would solve the delivery problem because it would spread in the same way. I think it's a great idea, but it won't be easy."

"But you think it can be done?"

"I think so, sir."

"Elaine, could you accommodate an expert group like that at the NIH?"

Zanuck thought for a moment. "I believe we can. Right now one of the older buildings is being refurbished to house the new Center for Integrative and Systems Biology. There'll be lab accommodation on all four floors."

"We can't wait, Elaine."

"No, you won't have to. When I last looked the top two floors were finished. There are three or four good-sized labs in there. They were working on the rest."

"All right. Throw the workmen out and we'll base the operation there."

"Why do we have to set up a separate expert group?" Robert Cabot's voice was a growl. "We have all the expertise we need at NBACC."

"Sorry," Terry said. "En Back?"

"NBACC, the National Biodefense Analysis and Countermeasures Center out at Fort Detrick."

Terry caught his breath. A development like this could leave Maggie on the periphery of the research or, worse still, excluded altogether. It was

Zanuck who spoke up.

"Bob, with respect, I think our way is better. I have a high regard for the work going on up there, but we don't have the time for conventional solutions. We need top drawer people, guys who can think out of the box, cut corners, work fast."

Richard Pevensey raised a hand. "Sir, the DoD has a lot of experience with contract research, and despite our best efforts it often goes over time and over budget. What worries me is, we don't have that luxury in this case."

"Good point," the President said. "This project will have to be monitored very closely. That's another good reason for setting it up in the Washington area. I want to keep things tight. We can't afford to overshoot."

"Sir?"

"Yes, Dr. McKinley?"

"There's one possibility we shouldn't ignore. The NASA data shows the mutation originated here, on the Eastern seaboard. Because of that atmospheric ammonia is elevated in the Western hemisphere. There's no reason why it should hang around here. I would expect it to mix in the upper atmosphere, and that would spread it around the world and dilute it. I'm not sure why this hasn't happened yet, but when it does the levels should drop. It may give us more time, possibly as much as another six months."

The President sighed. "Well now, that's the first good news we've had today. We need to keep a close eye on that situation."

"Sir," Walmesley said, "I've set Dr. McKinley up with an office in my building. He has access to data from NSF, NOAA, and the US Geological Survey. We'd have no difficulty setting up contact with our counterparts elsewhere – the British Atmospheric Data Centre, for example. If he's happy to continue he's in pole position to monitor the atmospheric levels."

"All right with you, Dr. McKinley? Do you need any help with that?"

"I can handle most of it at the moment, sir. I'd like some help with climate modelling, though, and I'd like to expand the scope of the sampling effort: more sites, more frequent flights."

The President nodded. "Work through Chris and we'll see if we can't organize something." He sat back.

"So, we need a crack group of scientists on the job and we need them yesterday. Dr. Ferris, exactly who is it we are going to be hauling out of bed and putting on a plane?"

Maggie smiled. "I was hoping that would be your response, sir. I have a list of the most important names. We can add more as we go along and require additional expertise. First up is Pieter van der Rijt and his colleague Ulrich Lunsdorfer from Enschede, the world's foremost experts on cyanobacteria and algal blooms. Next is Matt Oakley from New York; leading scientist in the human genome project. Then we have Silvia Mussini, an expert in gene silencing from California. We'll start with them and their teams and build from there."

"Do we have accommodation for them, Elaine?"

"There are hotels in Bethesda we use for guests."

"Good. Take one over. Book every room for six months. We have to minimize outside contact. Elaine, get your team to start working the phones. I want all these people here within 24 hrs. Don't give them all the info, but don't take no for an answer!"

CHAPTER 21

Pieter van der Rijt was the first to arrive. Maggie met him in the hotel lobby.

She knew Pieter was in his late thirties but he looked a lot younger. He had a full head of blond hair, a small blond beard, and a high, somewhat orange complexion. It was the kind of face that easily broke into a smile and she warmed to him almost instantly.

"Good journey, Pieter?" she asked.

"Yes, fine. I have not flown Business Class before; this was very nice. And thank you for sending the limousine to the airport."

She smiled. "All part of the service. Is your room okay?"

"Yes, it's very fine for me."

"Good. I can show you the labs if you like, but you must be tired."

"Well, I am still on European time, of course. But I would like to see the labs. It is best when I go to bed at a normal time. I need to change my body clock."

"All right, I'll take you over. We can walk – it's not far."

As they set off he asked: "Am I the first to arrive?"

"Yes, you are. But most of the others should be arriving later today."

He eyed her speculatively.

"Big rush. The President must be very concerned about white smogs?"

Maggie flushed a little and turned her face to hide it. "Well, yes. It is becoming a big problem."

Pieter continued.

"Well, I thought I could look at the facilities and see if there is more we need. Ulrich had a few things to tidy up in Enschede. He will also be here later today."

Maggie nodded. Ulrich Lunsdorfer was his colleague. Ulrich was a more traditional biologist; Pieter was an expert in modelling the growth kinetics of the organisms. Their joint expertise would be invaluable.

They turned left.

"It's not your first time in the States, is it, Pieter?"

"No, I was a year working at Woods Hole. It was a very good time for me."

"Right, here we are. Sorry about the mess."

They faced a plain four-storey building. It was evident that work here had stopped abruptly. To the right of the glass-fronted entrance was a large skip, overflowing with rubble, splintered planks of wood, pieces of pipework, and coils of old cable. A line of paving stopped short on a path of compacted sand. The rest of the slabs could be seen stacked in bundles on the back of a nearby truck, a built-in grab poised over them, motionless, jaws open wide, like a predator frozen at the instant of the kill. The whole area was criss-crossed with heavy tyre tracks.

Maggie used her key to let them in. The foyer had been swept but a fine layer of dust had resettled, and they left a print with each footfall.

"We're on the third floor," she said, leading the way to the stairs.

On the third floor she pushed open a couple of doors and they entered a large laboratory. There was a strong smell of fresh paint. Daylight flooded in from a row of large windows, supplemented by fluorescent panels in the ceiling. The left-hand wall was occupied by glass-fronted cabinets and a fume hood. A bench ran the length of the room under the windows and three shorter benches projected from it across the width of the room. All the benches were topped with white laminate and the under bench cupboards and drawer fronts were dark green. Everything was brand new; one or two of the cupboards still had labels attached.

Pieter went over to take a closer look at the taps set into the bench tops.

"Hot and cold mains water, distilled water, gas, and compressed air," he said. "Are all the services working?"

"Yes, everything's connected here and on the floor above. They still need to decorate and install lab furniture on the bottom two floors but there's nothing going on there at the moment."

She walked on, pointing to a recessed area containing a granite table set on solid brick supports. "Weighing room, for a microbalance and maybe a top pan balance." They went inside a small annex at the far end of the room. "Glassware washing and autoclave," she said.

He nodded. "It is well equipped."

"Still, there must be a lot of things you need that aren't here."

"Oh yes. I have brought a list with me. I see already fridges, freezers, incubators, centrifuges, and water baths. I will cross these off. I do not see any reagents on the shelves."

"I only ordered standard buffers for calibrating the pH meters. I left it up to you guys to say what you needed."

"I have a print-out of the list we use for safety purposes. I'm afraid there are several sheets."

"Give them to me. We have people who'll take care of it."

"Glassware? Sterile plastic ware?"

"Just list whatever you need."

He raised an eyebrow. "Within reason?"

She smiled. "Reason doesn't enter into it, Pieter. If you need it, we'll get it."

He smiled in return. "Very good. Of course much depends on what we are going to do here. All I know, it is to tackle the business of the white smogs, but it is not clear how we can help with that."

Maggie indicated some lab stools and they sat down at a bench. She had thought carefully about what she was going to say, not only to Pieter but also to the others when they arrived. "The white smogs are a serious problem, Pieter. The death toll in Baltimore was fifteen hundred; in Pittsburgh it was more than seven hundred. The smog didn't last as long in Cleveland but it was still responsible for nearly a thousand deaths. The hospitals were overwhelmed – some long-term patients had to be sent home to free up beds. In total, nearly thirty thousand people were hospitalized."

"This I heard. It was in the news. What is the cause?"

"The smog develops when ammonia combines with acid gases from traffic and industry. We asked you to join us because the ammonia is coming from local blooms of cyanobacteria."

His eyebrows shot up. "These cyanobacteria are producing ammonia?"

"Yes. And our job is to find a way of stopping them."

"I see." He tipped his head to one side. "Some cyanobacteria fix nitrogen. But to produce ammonia in such quantity…"

"I've been assuming it started with a mutation. It crossed my mind that it could be an existing species that somehow got transported to a more favourable environment. What do you think?"

He shook his head. "I do not know of any species that behaves in this way – it must be a mutation. How far has it spread?"

"The smog in Cleveland suggests that these cyanobacteria have already reached the Great Lakes. That's bad: it means a number of other large cities could be at risk: cities like Detroit, Chicago, Milwaukee, Toronto. I've done some rough calculations, based on city centre populations. If the casualties occur at a similar rate to, say, Pittsburgh, we could expect at least twenty thousand deaths and as many as two hundred thousand hospital admissions. Add in cities up the St. Lawrence and you could increase those figures by fifty per cent. Those figures are unacceptable. Someone has to prevent it all from happening. The US Administration has given the job to us."

"I see." Pieter nodded slowly. "And what about London? There was a smog there also."

Maggie thought quickly. "Ah, yes, well, London may be different. There's a big concentration of this stuff north-east of Bermuda. A freak wind could have brought a pocket of ammonia in from there."

"Bermuda? The Sargasso Sea?"

"Yes."

"I was there a while ago. We took some samples."

Maggie's pulse quickened. "When was this, Pieter?"

"Oh, perhaps five or six years ago."

Maggie thought about it. That was before the problem arose, but it could serve as a good baseline for comparison.

"Do you still have some samples?"

"I don't think so. But we made a record of the organisms and their relative abundance. This may be useful. Which species is carrying the mutation?"

"It's not just one species, Pieter. Here, let me show you."

She crossed to a refrigerator and brought out one of her culture dishes.

"I've been working in one of the other labs but I put this in here on my way over to your hotel. It's a smear of organisms taken from that area off Bermuda. I grew them on an indicator gel. There are several different species in there, but you see the red rings around each colony? They're all producing ammonia."

He frowned. "The mutation is being shared by horizontal gene transfer?"

"Exactly. It's probably being passed on by a plasmid."

She replaced the dish and they returned to the stools.

"So," he said. "How do you plan to deal with this?"

She took a deep breath. "The idea is to design a plasmid of our own, something that would switch off the ammonia production. We introduce it inside some normal cyanobacteria and they go wherever the rogue organisms have gone."

He was silent for several moments. Then he nodded. "So, you have a problem." She gave him a puzzled smile. "The rogue organisms, as you call them, are very well established," he said. "They will out-compete anything you put with them. Yes, that *is* a problem." He got up. "Shall we look at the other labs on this floor?" He made for the door.

For the moment she was unable to move. It seemed like alarm bells had gone off all over her body.

Of course, he was right. How could she not have considered this? There's no way her plan could work.

She managed to follow him, but suddenly she felt like she was moving in a daze.

The next lab was similar in design but a good deal smaller.

"We do not need a big lab," he said. "This one is very fine for us."

"Oh good. Well, we must get back, mustn't we? I'll come for those lists tomorrow, shall I? Perhaps we could meet for lunch at the hotel."

"Yes, okay. By then I will have them for you."

Terry sat in his office at the NSF, thinking. He had been speaking to a former colleague from the UK, Dr. John Gilchrist, who had just arrived. John was a first-class climate scientist and an expert in climate modelling. He would be a real asset when it came to tracking atmospheric movements.

The sampling flights had started and were already bringing back data on ammonia concentrations at high altitudes. Terry had also sifted through data collected from balloons. The balloons sampled the air from the moment of release and transmitted information as they soared skywards. The data from some of those releases suggested that ammonia was accumulating at lower altitudes.

Up to now it had been assumed that white smogs developed when weather systems stirred the atmosphere, gathering up clouds of ammonia in the process and sending them down tens of thousands of feet to ground level. That could still be true, but smogs would become a lot more frequent if ammonia was already present low in the atmosphere. The data he had was sparse and he was wondering how to supplement it.

Then he thought about wildlife. People suffered when the white smogs rolled into cities; the deaths in Baltimore, Pittsburgh and Cleveland illustrated that well enough. But fish and birds and wild animals would suffer, too, and huge numbers of them lived well away from heavily populated areas, in places where white smogs would never develop.

He contacted the US Geological Survey National Wildlife Health Center and several conservation movements, requesting copies of their reports and asking to be placed on their email list for updates.

Knowing Maggie's sensitivity when it came to animals he decided to say nothing about it to her when he returned to their hotel that afternoon. As it happened, her concerns were very much elsewhere.

She paced around Terry's room.

"He saw it straight away, Terry! I'm just an amateur among professionals. I feel terrible. I misled all those people about how we could solve the problem. The President's set up the group we always wanted and spent all that money and now look." She ran the fingers of both hands repeatedly through her hair. "We already know it won't work and we haven't even started!"

He guided her to a sofa and sat her down. "Now don't be so hard on yourself, Maggie. There were some pretty bright people in that room and this didn't occur to any of them either. I certainly didn't think of it."

"But I'm supposed to be the expert! I feel so stupid! What on earth am I going to do?"

"Come on, Maggie. You're upset, and it's been a long day, and neither of us is thinking very clearly at the moment. We're too close to the problem right now; we need to take a longer perspective. Talk me through it again. What Pieter said was that the rogue organisms are too well established; they'll out-compete any organism we try to put with them?"

"Yes," she said, in a small voice.

"All right, let's think about it. There's nothing wrong with the basic idea, is there? All you need is something to level the playing field, load the dice in favour of your organism." He fell silent, thinking hard, but aware of Maggie's eyes on him. "Can you make your organism more robust in some way? Have it grow more quickly than the other one, divide faster, something like that?"

She shook her head. "We have to use an existing organism, and it'll be subject to all the normal limitations. The rogue organisms are there in heavy numbers. They'll consume all the nutrients around and our organism will just starve."

He nodded. "Well, what about growing up your organism in huge quantities first?"

"You mean in a bioreactor of some sort?"

"Yes."

Again she shook her head. "It's the scale of the thing, Terry. The whole idea was to put in a small amount here and there and let it spread by itself. If we have to put in an overwhelming quantity everywhere we go the problem gets out of hand. You've got the whole of the Atlantic Ocean to treat, all the rivers, the Great Lakes – it's beyond us."

He took a deep breath. "All right, let's look at it the other way round. Is there something we can do to put the rogue organisms at a disadvantage?" He rubbed his jaw and spoke, almost to himself. "We've ruled out algicides. They don't get diseases like we do…"

Her eyes widened and she jumped to her feet. "That's it! You've got it!"

He frowned and looked up at her. "What…?"

"We'll give them a disease, we'll use a bacteriophage!"

"A which-what?"

"A bacteriophage. People usually call them phages. They're very tiny – you can only see them under an electron microscope. They infect bacteria, a bit like germs infect us. Then they multiply inside the bacteria and the bacteria die and that releases a lot more phages, which can go on to infect other bacteria. It's just like an epidemic." She leaped up, took his face in her hands and gave him a brief, hard kiss on the lips. "Thanks, Terry."

He blushed and looked at her in bewilderment. "But I didn't – "

"Yes you did. I should have more confidence in myself. This is great. I need to think it through."

And she opened the communicating door and disappeared into her room. Terry put his hand up and touched his lips lightly as she left.

CHAPTER 22

Ulrich Lunsdorfer arrived later that day. He came with an experienced postdoc, Jos Wentink, and a technician.

Next to arrive, from New York, was Matt Oakley, then Silvia Mussini flew in from California, with a postgraduate student, Sara Tennant. Maggie briefed each of them in the same way she'd done for Pieter, allotted lab space, and made a note of everything they needed.

She tracked down Pieter that evening, who was having dinner in the hotel.

"Do you know anything about bacteriophages, Pieter?"

"Phages? A little. Why?"

"I was thinking that when we introduce the organism with our plasmid we could introduce a phage at the same time, something that targeted the rogue organisms. Then they wouldn't out-compete ours."

He put down his knife and fork and stared into the distance. Then he came back to her and nodded slowly. "It is an interesting idea. But you know the Russians have been working on phages for years. They are looking for something different to antibiotics to fight bacteria. To find a phage that attacks only your ammonia organisms would be like, well to look for the needle…"

"In a haystack," Maggie finished for him. "Yes, I know. But I was thinking about doing it the other way round. We introduce our new organism together with a phage that's lethal to all organisms of this kind. Of course we'd make sure our own organism is resistant the phage. Then wherever they're in competition our organism will have a selective advantage."

He frowned. "Maggie, there are hundreds of different phages in the oceans. Why do you think any bacteria survive?"

She blinked. "I suppose they reach some sort of balance. A bit like foxes and rabbits."

"Yes, this perhaps, but there is something else. Bacteria have a defence against phages. It is in effect a genetic memory. It gives them a sort of immunity against phages they have seen in the past."

"All right, we'll look for a bacteriophage they haven't encountered before."

"It would not last. They would acquire resistance."

"Yes, but by then it would be too late. The phage will go in together with our own organism. By the time the rogues develop resistance our guys would have swapped plasmids into them and turned off ammonia production."

Maggie watched him anxiously. Then he nodded and smiled as he picked up his knife and fork again. "Yes, it is a neat solution. I can do some searches, but really you need a phage expert on this."

"Any suggestions? I can recruit other experts to the group. Who's the best in the field?"

"Well, Sergei Kolesnikov is the world authority, of course. Jose-Luis Guerrero is good, too, but Kolesnikov is best. Also you should have an expert on interference pathways in bacteria – this is the mechanism for resistance. I like very much the work from Rajiv Gupta's group. Rajiv is a nice guy. I met him at a conference in Delhi."

Maggie fumbled in her handbag and brought out a small notebook and a ballpoint. "Kolesnikov is where, Pieter?"

"Moscow. Russian Academy of Sciences. At least I think he is still there."

"And Gupta?"

"Calcutta University."

"Excellent, Pieter. Thanks very much."

Over the next few days the research progressed rapidly. The molecular biologists were setting up in the larger of the two labs, while the cyanobacteria experts made their preparations in the smaller one. At the moment there was no need to expand into the labs on the floor above.

Maggie spent nearly all her time ordering more lab supplies and coordinating the installation of equipment. There was a confident bustle about the group, and she was anxious not to hold them up. She made a habit of joining them in the hotel for lunch, when they continued to discuss strategy and she made notes of anything that was lacking. The incubators in the small lab were already full of culture flasks, as Pieter and his colleagues tried to establish the best conditions for growing on the Bermuda sample. The sequencing equipment was on its way, and Maggie had already ordered a range of DNA standards for Matt's group so that they could check that everything was working properly as soon as it was in place.

Terry found that Maggie's high spirits were rubbing off on him. The latest flights had gone out and they'd be coming back with the next set of atmospheric sampling data in a couple of days. Meanwhile he was analyzing another batch of balloon measurements.

Some wildlife updates came in and his mood became more subdued. There were disturbing reports of rafts of dead fish washed up on beaches in the Canary Islands and Cape Verde.

Then the spreadsheets from the atmospheric sampling flights arrived. He looked at them straight away, printed out the key information, and arranged all the charts on the desk in front of him. Once again every chart showed a rising curve for the level of ammonia. None of the curves showed any evidence of flattening off, in fact ammonia was increasing even more rapidly than before.

Strictly speaking, atmospheric science wasn't his forte. All the same he'd expected some mixing to have occurred by now. He planned to go over it again with John later that day.

"You should have seen them at lunch today!" said Maggie, as she and Terry were having dinner that evening. "They're totally focused on the problem – they talk about nothing else. A lot of it's over my head – stuff about genes and transacting factors I've never heard of. Of course Matt and Silvia are more familiar with mammalian genomes but Pieter puts them right from time to time. They want to recruit someone else: Alain Laroche. He's a Professor at the Institut Pasteur in Paris and he can help when it comes to synthesizing our plasmid. I'll invite him; it makes a lot of sense for the team to include top biochemists like Laroche." She pushed her dish aside. "Sergei hasn't arrived yet. Any news on him?"

"I spoke to Bob Cabot. I think he'll iron it out."

"What was the problem?"

"I don't know. Something in his background. Could have been student protests years ago. The cold war may be over but since 9/11 they're touchy."

"You can't blame them. What about you? How are you getting on?"

"We're doing okay." He lowered his voice. "The President's set up a national emergency fund. He did it for the hurricane disaster in the Southern States so nobody will raise an eyebrow about having another. But this one will fund your group. And Chris has managed to get some of it piped into the NSF. It's gone via the Director's Reserve of the National Center for Atmospheric Research, but it's earmarked for me. It's separate from their normal funding so it can bypass their committee structure. I'm commissioning additional flights, covering a larger geographical area and a whole range of altitudes." He gave her a quick smile.

"You'll be able to get a more detailed picture."

"Yes, but not only that. When you and your fellow geniuses drop your magic potion into the waters we'll be able to monitor exactly what effect it's having."

"Wonderful." She looked up as the handsome, dark-skinned waiter came over to collect their empty appetizer dishes and waited until he'd gone, although there was enough music and noise in the Latin-American restaurant to cover their conversation. Then she reached across the table and took Terry's hands in hers.

"It's all coming together now, isn't it? We're really going to beat this thing."

CHAPTER 23

On Sunday evening Maggie phoned to say she'd be delayed and Terry should eat without her. He replaced the receiver and looked at it for a few moments, frowning. Then he shrugged, went downstairs for a quick snack, and returned to his room to work. By nine o'clock he was glancing at his watch, finding it increasingly hard to concentrate. Finally he heard sounds of movement from her room and moments later there was a light knock and she came through the communicating door.

She dropped onto the sofa.

"You look beat. What's the matter?"

She sighed. "We spent the whole day working on a schedule – all of us." She leaned right back, gazing at the ceiling, one hand on her forehead. "We looked at every stage, estimated how long it would take, and then Matt and I drew out the entire project."

"Right…"

She straightened up and looked at him.

"It told us we'll have a solution – in one year."

He blinked. "As long as that? Surely not."

She closed her eyes. "Terry, these people are experienced; they know what's involved." She opened her eyes and seemed to register what was on his face. "I know. I made them go over it again and again, but unless we have a lucky break that's the way it comes out. The trouble is, there are a lot of unknowns, so we have to work through it one step at a time, each step building on the result of the previous one."

"A whole year?"

"I'm afraid so. And that's just how long it'll take to reach a solution in the lab; after that it still has to be produced in bulk and distributed."

"Well, we should throw more money at it, more people."

She shook her head. "That'll help at the production stage but it won't help with the research. The chart looks like a goods train with a series of wagons. Adding a train to the track each side won't make it any shorter. " She lowered her head into her hands. "Oh, I'll never get to sleep. My brain's red-hot with it all."

"I think you need a drink."

A few moments later he placed a glass of brandy on a small table at the side of the sofa and she picked it up. He clinked his own glass against hers.

"Cheers."

"Cheers." She took a good mouthful, savoured it, then swallowed. She looked up at him. "You don't seem all that bothered."

"About the timescale? Not really."

"Why?"

"Well, two reasons. First, your project management chart is only as good as the data you're putting into it. You have a bunch of world-class people in that lab. It's hard to believe they won't find the odd short cut here and there, and that will shave weeks, maybe months, off your timescale."

She sighed. "Oh God, I hope so." She took another mouthful of brandy. "What's the second reason?"

"You're forgetting the mixing in the atmosphere. It's taking a while but when it starts the ammonia levels are bound to go down. That should give us extra time. I'm not saying it won't be a close-run thing, but I still think we'll make it all right."

She reached out and gripped his hand. "I feel better already. You're a good man, Terry McKinley." Then she looked into the empty glass. "Either that or it's the brandy."

He smiled. "It's probably the brandy."

CHAPTER 24

Next morning Maggie was in the main lab when Pieter came in.

"Yes, Pieter?"

"Maggie, while we are waiting for the cultures Ulrich and I want to search the literature on line, just in case any new sequences have been published. Does Matt have bioinformatics software here?"

Outside there was a distant sound of police sirens; it was part of the background noise out here, and they paid no attention to it.

"I'm sure he does. Let's ask him – "

She stopped short. Sara Tennant, Silvia's postgrad, was standing there

"Excuse me, Maggie," she said. "I think we have visitors."

She walked over to the window and Maggie went with her. A small motorcade had pulled up in the road outside, a black sedan about a hundred yards in front of a black limousine, with a second black sedan about the same distance behind it. The cars at the front and rear each disgorged two men wearing suits and dark glasses who scanned up and down the road and over the building. Then a chauffeur opened the rear door of the limousine and a man emerged. He stood there for a moment adjusting a silk pocket handkerchief. A woman came out and joined him and they took the path leading up to the research Center. Maggie narrowed her eyes, then hurried down the stairs to the foyer to let them in.

"Well," she said, as she opened the door to Robert Cabot and Elaine Zanuck. "This is a surprise."

"We apologize for the intrusion, Dr. Ferris," Cabot said. "The President asked us to drop by. You know Dr. Zanuck, of course."

"Of course. Do come in, you're most welcome," Maggie said. "Would you like to see the labs?"

"Yes, if it's not too inconvenient. The President is pretty tied up with the hurricane business right now, but he's anxious to know how things are going."

Maggie led the way to the stairs. "I'm afraid the lifts – er, elevators – aren't working. We're on the third floor."

The research staff looked up with interest as the visitors came in.

"People," Maggie said. "This is the Director of National Intelligence, Mr. Robert Cabot, and the Director of the National Institutes of Health, Dr. Elaine Zanuck. They're here to take a look at what we're doing."

She began to show them around, introducing them to each member of the team. When they met Matt Oakley, Zanuck pointed at the equipment.

"Is this sequencer okay for you?" she asked.

Maggie noticed that she didn't need to be told what the equipment was.

"Yeah, actually it's a more recent model than the one I left behind in New York State. Real nice. It'll do the job."

"Do you have any results yet?" Cabot asked.

Maggie held her breath. Matt had a tendency to speak his mind, and in language other people would find a little too colourful.

Matt's eyebrows shot up briefly, then he recovered. "Ah no, we're only just operational. Any case we can't start sequencing the cyanobacteria until we've extracted the DNA; they're working on that next door. Meanwhile we're running standards, just making sure everything's working properly."

Cabot nodded, and Maggie experienced the mental equivalent of a sigh of relief. Zanuck went over to the chart on the wall and examined it. "What's this?"

"It's a project management chart," Maggie explained, "so we can all keep an eye on where the work's got to."

"It's pretty linear."

"I'm afraid so. As Matt just said, he can't start sequencing until we've grown up more organisms and extracted the DNA. And Silvia Mussini can't work on gene silencing until we know the sequence, and so on. Shall we go next door?"

In the lab next door Maggie introduced Pieter van der Rijt and Ulrich Lunsdorfer, and they showed the visitors the culture facilities where they were trying to grow up the cyanobacteria.

Cabot turned to Zanuck. "All right, Elaine, seen enough?"

"Yes, I think so."

They went down the stairs and paused in the foyer.

Zanuck said, "The timeline on that chart: it looked like you'll need a full year to get to the solution."

Maggie swallowed, then nodded. "That's right. We may be able to shave some time off with short cuts, though. Of course that's hard to predict at this stage."

"I thought we only had six months."

"Do you remember Terry – Dr. McKinley – mentioned mixing in the upper atmosphere? We're counting on that to give us more time."

"I see. Your team's smaller than I expected. Could you use more people?"

"Not really – right now they'd be hanging around with nothing to do. Once things get under way we can expand the operation. We'll be getting a very good biochemistry group from France, led by Professeur Alain Laroche. And there's Sergei Kolesnikov – Mr. Cabot, has there been any progress on his transfer?"

"The checks are still going on. I don't think there's anything major; it's more a question of gaps in what we know about him. If we can get some assurances on one or two issues we can issue a temporary visa."

"I understand there are procedures in place for this sort of thing, but I can't stress how important it is that we get him here as soon as we can. Sergei and his expertise are vital to this project."

He nodded. "I'll try to hurry things along as best I can. So you have everything you need right now? Equipment, personnel? Barring Kolesnikov, that is."

"Yes, thank you. It's all here. It's just a matter of getting on with the job."

He smiled. "Very good. We'll tell the President. And you be sure to let us know if anything's holding you up."

"Thank you, sir."

She opened the door and they walked briskly down the path to where the chauffeur was already holding open the door of the black limousine. The suited men were still looking up and down the road. She watched them all get into their cars and drive off. Then there was the sound of motorbikes starting up, followed by police sirens, and a cruiser came past. She realized that the road must have been closed temporarily at both ends. She returned to the lab.

Back at the hotel she knocked lightly on the adjoining door and entered Terry's room. They both started to speak at once.

"Hi! Guess what?"

They laughed.

"You first," he said.

"We had a visit this morning – from Robert Cabot and Elaine Zanuck."

"That's interesting, he visited me, too."

"Really? With Dr. Zanuck?"

"No, with a guy called Noel Harrison. He's only the Director of NASA."

"My, we are moving in elevated circles these days!"

"Come and sit down. What's it to be tonight: juice or brandy?"

"Oh, juice would be fine."

She took a seat on the sofa. While he was getting out the glasses she unrolled the Washington Post, a copy of which was hung on the door in a plastic bag every morning.

He poured a glass of orange juice and set it on the low table. Then he poured one for himself and sat in the chair by the writing desk. He sipped the juice. "So what was your visit about?"

"Oh, they just wanted to look over the labs. They met the people and saw the equipment and the cultures. I think they were satisfied. They seemed to expect a bigger operation but it's just not realistic at the moment. Zanuck spotted the wall chart and I had to explain why it's going to take longer than we thought. I asked Cabot about Kolesnikov and he thought there wouldn't be a major problem. I stressed how important it is that we get him here ASAP and then they took off. What about you?"

"I think Harrison mainly wanted a rundown on what's been happening, because he missed the White House meeting. I showed him NASA's own images and our latest results. He asked me if I needed more staff and I told him I was expecting a few more climate people soon, and otherwise we had what we needed."

"What's this all about, Terry? Are they being supportive or checking up on us?"

"Both, I imagine. The President did say he wanted to monitor the whole thing closely."

"Well, he's using some pretty high level people to do it."

"He's got no choice, has he? Not if he wants to keep a tight lid on the whole thing."

She sipped her juice and began to flick over the pages of the newspaper.

"And why didn't Kramer put in an appearance?" she asked. "You'd have thought he'd at least be around for visits like that."

"No idea. He seems to be leaving everything to us. Maybe he sees his job as just keeping an eye on the budget."

She'd been flicking the pages as she spoke but now she stopped, set the glass down and sat forward.

"Hey, Terry, look at this."

He came over. She was pointing to a single column: the brief round-up of international news. The short item was headed "Mystery smog hits Bangkok." They read it together.

"It's a white smog," she said.

"In Bangkok? Can't be."

"White dust, pungent, choking fumes, hundreds in hospital with breathing difficulties... It certainly sounds like it."

He read the article again, frowning.

"Shall we see if there's any more on the internet?"

He straightened up. "I've got a better idea. You remember when I used the NASA program and stepped it back in time so we could see when and where the organism escaped?"

"Yes, of course."

"Well, I only ever looked at Bermuda and the Eastern seaboard of the U.S.A. It never occurred to me to look at the rest of the world."

She blinked. "That's right. But there was no reason why – "

"I'm going to have a look now."

He picked up his laptop from the desk and sat back down on the sofa next to her. He clicked to start the program, then took the NASA data disk from his brief case and fed it in. Maggie was at his shoulder now, watching. He looked up at her. "The most recent pictures won't tell us anything; we'll just get that purple haze from the ammonia in the stratosphere. But that's not relevant anyway: you'd only expect to get a white smog where the organisms are well established. It can't be any earlier than we were looking at before so we'll start two-and-a-half years ago."

The program came up on screen and he set the date. Then he entered coordinates for Bangkok, made sure the land mass they were looking at was Thailand, and switched to the ammonia spectrum. There was nothing. He stepped forward one month, two months... Broad concentric circles of purple, blue, and green expanded. His jaw dropped.

"Good grief!" He switched back to the conventional view. The rings were centred in Central Thailand.

Maggie craned forward. "That's not Bangkok," she said.

"No, it's north of Bangkok but if the stuff was well established there it wouldn't take long before it was washed down the rivers to the sea. That's where it would really thrive and Bangkok would get the ammonia with any good on-shore breeze." He ran his fingers through his hair. "I don't believe this! Two-and-a-half years ago that stuff appears on the Eastern seaboard. A month or two later it's on the other side of the world. Could migrating birds have taken it there?"

"From North America to Thailand? Not that I know of."

"We'd better widen the search."

He switched back to the conventional view and changed the scale until it extended from India to Eastern China. Then he returned to the ammonia view. On this scale the rings in Thailand had shrunk in size. But now circular bands of purple, blue, and green showed up in north-east India and purple, blue, green, and yellow in China's northern provinces. It was as if a handful of stones had been thrown into a pond.

She gasped. "It's all over the place! Terry...?"

He barely heard her. He was staring at the screen, a feeling of cold dread crawling through his body and coalescing in the pit of his stomach.

He rose slowly to his feet and faced her. "I'm sorry, Maggie. Looks like we won't be getting that extra time after all."

"What do you mean? We have to! You thought..."

He ran his tongue round his lips. "Yes, I know; I thought mixing up there in the atmosphere would give us an extension. I'm afraid that's not going to happen. Mixing may go on – for all I know it's going on right now – but it won't make a blind bit of difference. The atmosphere's as thick with ammonia on the other side of the world as it on this."

Her face fell. "Well how long have we actually got? Chris said six months. That's worst case, right?"

He shook his head. "Ammonia's accumulating fast. To judge from the reports I'm seeing now, six months is optimistic, if anything. You need to get back to your schedule, find the corners and cut them fast. There's no way you have twelve months?"

"Terry, we've already considered the best possible scenario. If we got all the right breaks we could shorten it to eight or nine months."

He winced. "It's too long. By then the air everywhere will be too toxic to breathe."

She stared at him in shocked silence. Seconds ticked by.

He lifted his hands in a small, helpless gesture. "We're going to run out of time."

She continued to look at him, lips slightly parted. She blinked once, twice. Then her jaw tightened.

"That's it, then – it's over. All that work, all our efforts to get the problem recognized and dealt with – it was doomed from the start, wasn't it?" She gestured at the lap top. "There's the truth, right there on your screen! Two-and-a-half years ago that stuff was so well established the effects were visible from space, for God's sake! Two-and-a-half years, and it's had all that time to grow and spread..." She faltered, then her shoulders went slack and the tension in her face and throat slipped away. Her voice descended to something like a sob. "We tried, Terry. We tried so very hard. We were just... too... late."

He hesitated, then reached out and she fell into his arms. They sank back into the sofa and he felt the weight of her head against his chest. He closed his eyes and rested his cheek against her hair. They stayed that way for a long time and eventually fell asleep in each other's arms.

CHAPTER 25

High in the stratosphere, crystals of ammonium salts scattered away the sunlight and the countryside beneath was bathed in an eerie orange glow. Snow fell thickly and never melted. With each passing day the air became more difficult to breathe.

They walked out into the snow until their leaden limbs could carry them no further and then folded to the ground, freezing and exhausted. She reached for him and he took her in his arms.

Their words escaped in small plumes of frozen breath.

"This is it, Terry. The end of the world."

"Of our world, yes. Earth will go on. Who knows? Maybe in time... intelligent life... will evolve here again."

He could feel her body weakening, sagging within his embrace. Her voice was faint.

"I keep wondering... Could we have done more to stop it?"

"It had gone too far. We needed more time."

Her eyes closed.

"Goodbye, Terry darling."

"Maggie..."

Their cold lips met for the last time and he held her until she stopped shivering. Snow continued to fall, the pretty crystals lodging in her thick eyelashes and in the curls of black hair that had escaped from her hood. He cradled her head in his hands, pressed his cheek to hers, feeling its softness against his skin, and his body erupted into great wracking sobs...

Terry jerked up in bed, breathing hard.

"Terry, what's the matter? It's all right. You've been dreaming..."

He wiped tears from his eyes with the heel of his hand and looked wildly at her.

"I've got it" he said hoarsely. "Jesus Christ, I've got it!"

CHAPTER 26

Only a week ago, Terry had found it hard to believe that they were actually meeting in the Oval Office with the heads of the NSF and NIH, several Secretaries of State, and the President of the United States. Now, those feelings had been replaced by a grim foreboding. The Vice-President was still abroad but they were joined this time by the Director of NASA and Herbert Kramer. Kramer was tall and cadaverously thin, so much so that his clothes – white shirt, grey tie, dark grey suit – appeared too large for him. His straight grey hair was neatly parted, his pallid features a mass of hollows. Without acknowledging either Terry or Maggie he took the matching armchair which had been placed next to the two four-seat sofas. As before, a computer and flat-screen monitor had been set up at the end of the room.

"Well," the President said. "I apologise for bringing you all here again so soon. Dr. Walmesley tells me there are important new developments and he assures me these are serious enough to warrant another meeting. I must say I'm keen to know what these new developments are. Who's going to start?"

Chris gestured towards Maggie. "I think Dr. Ferris should start, sir."

She cleared her throat. "Sir, following the last meeting we recruited our experts, accommodated them, and equipped a lab for them, just as we'd agreed. Every one of these people is at the forefront of their field. They're focused, they're motivated, and it's safe to say we couldn't have brought together a better qualified team. But this is a complex problem. We're dealing with an unknown plasmid and organisms that are largely uncharacterized, particularly in terms of genome sequence, so we're venturing into new territory. That means the existing body of scientific knowledge won't necessarily help us and there's limited scope for short cuts. At our last meeting Dr. Zanuck said it wouldn't be easy. She was absolutely right. We have to find out what's in the plasmid, find some way of neutralizing its effect, select an organism to deliver it, manufacture enough to be effective, and spread it around the world. Even that won't work unless it can compete successfully with the ammonia-generating organisms, which are already well established. I won't go into detail about how we propose to deal with that one, but it complicates things still further. We've now mapped out a timescale, which Dr. Zanuck and Mr. Cabot have seen during their visit. It can all be done, but it's going to take longer than we thought."

"How much longer?" the President demanded.

"A realistic estimate is one year. If we're optimistic, eight or nine months. And that's just to reach a solution in the laboratory."

Several seconds passed.

"The way I understood it," Richard Pevensey said slowly, "we only had six months."

Bob Cabot raised a hand and spoke at the same time. "Yes, but we were going to get an extension to that, something to do with mixing in the atmosphere. Am I right?"

She turned to Terry. "I think Dr. McKinley should answer that."

Terry picked up the remote control and went to stand next to the blank monitor screen.

"As Mr. Cabot just said, we were hoping that mixing in the atmosphere would dilute ammonia from its present levels and give us more time. Since then we've made an unpleasant discovery. Let me just remind you of the satellite views I showed you last time. The data for these came from NASA."

He nodded to acknowledge Noel Harrison, Director of NASA, then activated the monitor screen.

"On the left you'll recognize a conventional view of the Eastern seaboard as seen from space. On the right is the same view taken in the ammonia spectrum. These rings," he pointed to the concentric rings of purple, blue, green, and yellow, "show the density of ammonia at that time, two-and-a-half years ago. What I did *not* know was that barely two months later we also had this."

He showed a similar pair of satellite views for north-east India.

"Where is that?" the President asked.

"This is north-east India, sir. And this," he changed the slide, "is central Thailand. And this," he changed the slide again, "is northern China."

A murmur went around the table.

"How the hell – ?" Cabot started to say.

"Please don't ask me how the organisms got into all these places – I don't know. But the fact of the matter is, ammonia is rising as fast as ever and we can't expect it to decline or even level off because it's just as bad on the other side of the planet as it is on this. If we needed further proof, Bangkok has just suffered a white smog."

They all began to speak at once and the President had to hold up a hand.

"Let me get this absolutely clear. Dr. Ferris, you are saying your group needs more time to develop the solution?"

"Yes, sir."

"And you, Dr. McKinley, are saying we haven't got it?"

"That's right, sir." He sighed and gestured at the screen. "Two years ago these ammonia-generating organisms were already well established right around the world. They've been releasing ammonia into the atmosphere ever since – enriching their own environment at the same time – so they've grown more and more rapidly and spread more and more effectively. Now we can understand why the atmospheric levels are increasing so rapidly. The conclusion is inescapable. Over the coming months, in cities here and elsewhere, white smogs will become more frequent, more widespread, and longer-lasting. Outside the cities, raw, uncombined ammonia will make the air just as unbreathable. I'm sorry."

He used the remote control to return the screen to black.

The President had paled visibly. He wagged a finger back and forth between Maggie and Terry. "You're not giving up, are you?"

"No, sir. But we wanted you all to know we're in a race we can't win. Unfortunately we entered it about two years too late."

The others watched Terry return to his seat next to Maggie.

Pevensey rubbed the back of his neck. "I don't believe this!"

"Dammitall," Cabot growled. "Does this mean we have to let these mutant bacteria wipe out all of humankind?"

"Dr. Ferris," Elaine Zanuck said. "Are you sure you can't identify some short cuts, or tighten up that schedule somewhat – anything to shorten that timeline?"

"We'll try, Dr. Zanuck, of course we will. But right now it's difficult to see where the short cuts could come from. As I said before, every member of the group is an international expert in their research area, and all of them were involved in generating that chart. Even if things go absolutely according to plan, eight or nine months looks like the bare minimum."

The President took a deep breath. "Ideas? Suggestions? Anyone?" He looked around the table, and his voice rose. "Anything? Anything at all?"

Chris Walmesley and Noel Harrison exchanged grim looks. James Brierley chewed his lip. Richard Pevensey frowned and continued to rub the back of his neck. Herbert Kramer's face was a grey mask. Elaine Zanuck's lips had set tightly. Robert Cabot was bent forward, his head in his hands. No one spoke. An ornate clock on the mantelshelf behind the screen struck the hour. They listened to every chime.

"Mr. President?"

"Yes, Dr. McKinley?"

Terry knew he was about to tread a tightrope. If he sounded too shrill, what he was about to say would be treated as the ravings of a lunatic; if he failed to push hard enough, their last chance would fade away. He did his best to keep his voice quiet and controlled.

"Sir, if Dr. Ferris and her colleagues continue to pursue the biological approach they'll succeed in the long run – I don't doubt that. The big problem is the timescale. A year is too long – even eight months is too long – we'll all be dead by then. What we need is a way of delaying the build-up of ammonia. If we could do that, it would give us the time to develop the biological solution and implement it."

"Yes, well, all right, I see that. Do you have something in mind, something to slow it down?"

"Yes, sir, I have. I've thought about this over and over and I believe we have only one possible course of action. I'm afraid it will shock you, all of you. But the situation is desperate, and desperate times call for desperate measures."

"Come on, then, out with it."

"The organisms are distributed over our entire planet. Any measure we take has to be on the same, planetary scale." He paused and looked around the room. "I want you to wake up the Yellowstone Supervolcano."

CHAPTER 27

There was a long silence, then everyone started to talk at once. The President held up his hand. His eyes were squeezed tight shut.

"Let me understand this. You want to trigger a massive volcanic eruption. And just how do you propose to do that?"

"A bunker-penetrating missile with a nuclear warhead. It needs to be big – you have to get this right first time. As you know, there's a colossal magma chamber under Yellowstone Park and it's full of dissolved gas under pressure. You deliver your missile to the point where the Earth's crust overlying the magma is thinnest. Offhand, I believe that's the area around Norris. You breach the crust and in the decompression that follows the magma boils. Nothing will withstand that pressure. The supervolcano will blow."

Again there was a babble of voices and the President had to raise his voice to restore order. He turned back to Terry.

"Dr. McKinley. You and Dr. Ferris have shown a good deal of resourcefulness since you've been with us, otherwise I wouldn't even dignify this idea with a discussion. I'm not entirely ignorant of what that supervolcano could do. I understand it would blanket much of the United States in ash, kill tens of thousands of Americans, and bring our economy down to the level of a third world country. Now why in God's name would I want to trigger a catastrophe like that?"

"Hear me out, sir. If it erupts, the supervolcano will eject hundreds of cubic miles of ash and lava into the air. It will also fill the upper atmosphere with sulphuric acid, about two thousand million tonnes of it. In a matter of weeks that will travel all around the planet, combining with the ammonia that's already up there to form tiny crystals of ammonium sulphate. The crystals and the ash will filter down to lower levels where they'll act as nucleation sites. That will generate torrential rain, which will wash a lot of the remaining ammonia out of the atmosphere. These two things on their own – the chemical combination and the rain – will purge our atmosphere of much of the free ammonia that's up there at the moment."

Terry looked at the faces around the table. They were completely focused on him. Maggie, sitting by his side, was very still; he could sense the tension in her. He opened his hands.

"*Now* you have the time."

Everyone seemed too shocked to speak. Then the Secretary of Defense leaned forward.

"You can't be serious about using a nuclear weapon. You could trigger a war."

"I don't think so, Mr. Pevensey. A hit on your own soil isn't going to prompt a retaliatory strike. You'd have to make sure your own military didn't respond, of course. But I'm not sure if any seismometer could distinguish the initial nuclear explosion from the eruption itself."

The Secretary for Homeland Security tentatively raised a hand. "Does it really have to be the supervolcano?" he asked. "Couldn't we trigger a smaller one, maybe in South America or Indonesia?"

"No, Mr. Brierley," Terry said. "You can't catch an elephant with a mouse trap. It's got to be on that scale."

"All right," Brierley persisted, "it has to be a supervolcano. Aren't there others besides Yellowstone?"

"There are suspected sites elsewhere in the world but they're hard to pinpoint. And if you hit one and it doesn't go up, then it's like Mr. Pevensey says – you'll probably trigger a nuclear war. Yellowstone's the only option."

Elaine Zanuck ran her fingers through her short grey hair. "Maybe Dr. Ferris's group is being too conservative. After all, they're right at the beginning of this project; things could look more hopeful in a month or two. Then we wouldn't have to think about this."

"Even if they could cut the development time to six months, Dr. Zanuck," Terry replied, "you're still left with the problem of delivery. You've got to produce it in quantity, then you've got to distribute it around the world, load it onto aircraft, and spray it on large bodies of water all over the planet. You can't do those things overnight."

Pevensey shook his head. "We'd have a major problem persuading every country in the world that it has to be overflown and sprayed by low-level aircraft. Can you imagine Russia agreeing to that, or China or Iran or North Korea? It would make getting agreement on nuclear arms or climate change look like child's play."

"We'd just supply the stuff, Bob," the President responded. "Let them do their own damned spraying. But they'll still accuse us of a Western plot to poison their water and make the population infertile, or some other such nonsense. We couldn't force them to accept it. It would be one hell of a job to get world coverage."

"Excuse me, sir, I didn't mean to imply that we need comprehensive world coverage," Terry put in. "So long as the neutralizing organism is widely established it'll do the rest of the distribution itself. If we've built in a selective advantage – such as Dr. Ferris is planning to do – it'll continue to replace the ammonia organisms until they finally disappear. But we're never going to reach that stage unless we buy more time. And I can't think of any way of doing it other than the one I've suggested."

"An eruption like that would bring the country to its knees!" Zanuck exclaimed. "How are our experts supposed to develop a high-tech solution under those conditions?"

Terry said, "You'd have to set up a facility outside the main ash fallout area, as far south as possible. There isn't time to build one; you'd need to take over an existing centre, a university or commercial laboratory. Move the experts there in good time."

The President frowned. "What about the centre of government and the key institutions? Would they have to move too?"

"Almost certainly, sir; Washington could well be in the zone of ash fall. There will, of course, be other consequences. The ash and ammonium crystals in the atmosphere will reflect sunlight so there'll be a global drop in temperature. It would be advisable to cancel exports of foodstuffs like grain because you'll miss at least one harvest. We can get more accurate predictions by studying the computer models people have prepared for this scenario."

President Kinghorn rested his head in one hand, passing the fingers over his forehead. Then he looked up. "I can't believe we're still talking about this. Suppose you people are wrong? This whole ammonia thing could be a gigantic mistake."

Terry exchanged glances with Maggie. A strategic decision was vital; fudging the issue now would be the worst possible outcome. There was a pleading look in her dark eyes. He wasn't sure she'd perceived all the implications when he'd explained it to her, but the prospect of a solution, however remote, had roused her from her depression. Neither of them wanted that distant hope to be snatched away.

The President gestured at Chris Walmesley. "Chris, you brought this to me in the first place. Are conditions really serious enough to justify such extreme measures?"

Chris said, "Sir, I think Dr. McKinley's right. The NASA data you've been looking at was collected two-and-a-half years ago but we know what's been happening since. The NSF has the measurements we've funded through the National Center for Atmospheric Research and they agree with ones made independently by NOAA. You already have white smogs rolling across cities – Baltimore, Pittsburgh, Cleveland, London and, as we've heard, Bangkok on the other side of the world. Sooner or later we're going to get one of those smogs here in Washington. We're in a high risk area because ocean currents have driven the organisms north and they seem to have invaded every waterway. We'd be better off if we could move the centre of government south – if only for that reason. Looking further ahead, well the evidence is clear enough. I'm afraid the atmosphere is filling with ammonia. Our projections stand. On present trends we have six months, and that's at the outside."

The President switched his attention to Herbert Kramer.

"Herbert? Any views on this?"

Kramer's expression was like stone. "I would recommend taking the entire matter under advisement, Mr. President," he said stiffly.

Terry looked at the man in disbelief. He was about to say something when Bob Cabot weighed in.

"President, I disagree. A few minutes ago we heard that we entered this race two years too late. With due respect to Dr. Kramer it seems to me the last thing we should do is procrastinate further. I'd say we have all the information we need right now. Personally I'd feel better if I left this meeting knowing we at least made some sort of decision."

Kramer bristled but said nothing. The President frowned, then turned to the Director of NASA.

"Noel, we haven't heard from you yet. What's your opinion?"

Noel Harrison spoke in measured tones. "Mr. President, as Chris Walmesley said, the situation's serious and it's going to get worse – in fact I was beginning to think there was no way out. Now Dr. McKinley has pointed to a possible solution. It's as new to me as I imagine it is to everyone else, but it strikes me as highly ingenious, and I believe it could work. On the other hand, it's unbelievably drastic and I'm persuaded by Dr. Zanuck's argument that it could prove to be unnecessary. My suggestion is this: we should prepare to implement it, but only as a contingency measure. We could set up some objective criterion for taking action. If, for example, ammonia had reached a predetermined level – a threshold – and we still weren't ready with our biological fix, then we'd be obliged to adopt the Yellowstone option. If, on the other hand, our experts come up with the goods in time, then we've avoided the need for it."

The President nodded. "Sounds like a sensible way forward. That satisfy you, Bob?"

Cabot nodded. "Very good. Who's going to decide what this predetermined level should be?"

"Noel and I could do that," Chris said. "Dr. McKinley has been extending the scope of our atmospheric sampling operations. I believe they should be extended still more, so we can base any decision on a truly global picture."

"Everyone agree with that?"

There were nods.

"Dr. McKinley? Dr. Ferris?"

It was a good compromise. He glanced at Maggie and her expression told him she felt the same way.

"Yes, sir. We'd certainly go along with that."

"All right," he said. "Now it's just as well to have a plan, but as far as I'm concerned this one is a last resort. We'll make the necessary preparations, but I'm not going ahead with anything unless all the possible alternatives have been explored. I'll instruct Sarah to convene a series of meetings over the coming weeks. There will be just one item on your agenda: to discuss some other way – any other way – we can extricate ourselves from this mess. If the meeting comes up with something, bring it to me. If it doesn't, meet again. And again. And again." He stood and they all rose. "No need, I imagine, to remind you that this Yellowstone business must never be discussed outside these walls, whether or not we ever have to resort to it. I'm going to consult other senior members of the administration and assess the kind of contingency plans we should be making now." His voice dropped. "But first, ladies and gentlemen, I intend to pray for Heavenly intervention."

In the outer office the atmosphere was subdued but people seemed reluctant to disperse. All, that is, except Kramer, who had left immediately.

Terry saw Elaine Zanuck lay a hand on Maggie's shoulder and they went off to one side, where they engaged in earnest conversation.

Richard Pevensey was chatting with Bob Cabot and James Brierley. Chris Walmesley came over with Noel Harrison.

"Well, Terry," Noel said. "Yet again you've made impressive use of our satellite data."

"It's been invaluable. And thanks for suggesting the way forward. It was a good outcome."

"Terry," Chris said, "That was a pretty wild idea you came out with in there. Why the hell didn't you discuss it with us beforehand?"

"I'm sorry, Chris, I suppose I should have. You know, part of me was hoping I wouldn't need to – I thought maybe someone would come up with something better."

Chris gave him a wry smile. "Perhaps it's just as well. I might have had you committed."

Robert Pevensey dropped by.

"Got to hand it to you Brits. I wouldn't have thought of that supervolcano idea in a million years. But then it's not your country that'll be going down the tube."

"I'm sorry, Mr. Pevensey – I wish there was some other way. But make no mistake: the UK will be as badly off as you are once that volcanic winter sets in. We're all in this mess together."

CHAPTER 28

"You didn't sleep well last night, did you, Harold?" Marie Kinghorn said across the breakfast table to her husband.

He answered without looking at her. "I was up for a while."

"I thought you might be able to relax a little, away from the capital, us being on our own for a change."

"We won't be alone for much longer," he rumbled. "The Vice-President will be coming to Camp David this afternoon."

"But that's not the same at all! Chuck and Carol Anne are old friends. We're comfortable with them; it's not like entertaining guests from Russia or Japan or some other place. When did Chuck get back from the Middle East?"

"A few days ago. He could probably use a rest. I doubt he's going to get it."

She poured some coffee into a bone china cup and held up the pot to him but he shook his head. "Well," she said. "I'm glad you decided to find a moment to come here. I'd clean forgot how lovely it can be at this time of year."

"I needed some peace and quiet. Time to collect my thoughts. Solitude. Long walks."

"Well you're having those all right. I think the dogs are losing weight." She looked at him over the rim of her cup and frowned. "So are you. I'd have thought all that exercise would make you ravenously hungry. You hardly touched that lovely dinner Toni prepared for us last night."

"Guess my appetite's a bit off." For a moment he seemed preoccupied, then he shook his head. "I didn't ask for this job, you know, Marie."

"Of course you didn't, dear. The party wouldn't have put forward anyone who actually wanted the job. We'd all had enough of sleaze and self-interest with the last administration. They wanted experience, integrity. That's why you were nominated. You were the right choice for them and, as it turned out, for the people too."

He sighed. "I know. It's just that… sometimes I wonder if I'm up to it."

"You wouldn't be the man you are if you didn't have self-doubts. The country's safer in your hands."

He looked sharply up at her, and she glimpsed in those haunted eyes a look of such unfathomable pain that her heart lurched. The cup almost fell from her fingers. She hastily set it in its saucer and hurried over to sit next to him, one arm as far as it would reach around his broad shoulders.

"What is it, dear?"

His mouth moved but no sound came. Then his jaw set. He clasped his hand over hers. She looked at the two hands, resting on the tablecloth. Her fingers, smooth, slender, the unpainted nails shapely but the joints showing the first unsightly swelling of arthritis. His hand over it, broad, blunt-fingered, the skin blotched with liver spots and ridged with blue veins.

"Harold," she repeated softly, "Won't you tell me what's troubling you?"

He looked at her, and gave her a weak smile.

"Marie, you're a wonderful wife and mother and a fine First Lady. As your husband there's nothing I wouldn't share with you. But as President there are some problems I have to face alone. That's as it should be. It's enough for one of us to be burdened with these things. All I ask for is your love and your support, and God knows you've never refused me either."

Her eyes filled with tears.

"It's unfair the way they shift everything onto you. What are your advisers for?"

"My advisers give me the facts. Only I can make the decisions."

"You've had to make hard decisions before. You made the right choices then and you'll do it again."

He regarded her sadly and squeezed her hand.

"Will I?" he said. "I wonder."

In short, we recommend that the weather situation on the Florida coast should be downplayed, as there could be serious public disquiet if the true number of deaths and homeless were released to the media. However, we are also deeply concerned about other systems currently building in the Atlantic. We are advised that these could coalesce into one or more hurricanes of unprecedented ferocity that would sweep into the Gulf of Mexico, causing untold damage along the entire coastline. If we are to cope at all adequately with an emergency on this scale we will need to make preparations now. It may be necessary to take over an existing facility, such as a university campus, to house the homeless and to provide medical facilities. Insofar as it is possible, any such arrangements should be initiated discreetly in order to avoid public alarm.

The President put the memo down. As he slid it back to the Vice-President it flashed briefly in a slice of afternoon sun that had fallen across the table.

"It's good, Chuck. Who wrote it?"

"Pat Corcoran, in my office. It's credible, because we've already had some bad hurricanes. And smaller ones have been forming in the Atlantic for weeks – that part's true as well. The big one is a fiction, of course, but even the climate boys are not going to go on record to say it won't happen. We'll send it between two departments, maybe Homeland Security and Internal Affairs, and make sure it leaks. The Press will love it."

"Good, good." He pointed at the paper. "This guy Corcoran doesn't know the real reason you wanted the memo, does he?"

"Hell, no. He doesn't even know it's going to be leaked."

"That's fine. Chuck, the key thing in all of this is to put the preparations for the move in hand without anyone out there knowing the real reason." He straightened up. "I'm sorry you had to come back to all this."

"Well, I'll tell you, Harry, I didn't think there could be any problems bigger than the ones I've been trying to wrestle with, the last two weeks. Boy, was I ever wrong."

The President's lips twitched in an empathic smile. "What about the actual move?"

"Ah yes. Are you still okay about Florida?"

"It's a no-brainer, Chuck. It's about as far south as we can go. I'm not going to cross the border. That'd present a whole slew of political problems and that means delays, and we can't afford delays. We could go further west, but what the hell for? It only makes the logistics of transport from Washington harder. Has anyone looked at a site yet?"

"Yeah, they looked at several. University of Central Florida is the best. It's a two-thousand-acre spread, well served by airports. It has a lot of modern high-rise buildings, enough to accommodate a pared-down version of the main government centres. We'll tell them the entire campus has to be requisitioned for accommodation and emergency services. When this memo comes out they won't be surprised. Indignant, maybe, but not surprised."

"Okay. They can transfer staff, students, and equipment to other universities in Florida and maybe Mississippi and Texas. We'll move the police and National Guard in to concentrate their minds; the whole thing has to be done quickly. We'll give them three days to clear out. With very few exceptions, any equipment or materials remaining after that will be disposed of. That's the stick. Do we have a carrot?"

"We can offer compensation to the host universities on a per capita basis. And the University of Central Florida's been looking for funding for a Stem Cell Institute. We can drop hints to the Board that we'll find the money from government sources when the present crisis is over. Of course, they'll assume the crisis we're referring to is the hurricane season. We won't dissuade them from making that assumption."

"Okay." The President pushed his chair back. "Is there any more paperwork we need to go over? If not, we can take a walk while we discuss the rest."

"A walk would be good. It's a relief to be back in this climate after the Middle East. Damn, it was hot there."

The President got up and led the way out of the main lodge. They crossed the lawn onto a mulched path that meandered between the trees. The untroubled peace of the woodland seeped into them. The air, laden with the sweet smell of moist earth and vegetation, was cool in their lungs. For a few minutes they were content to walk in silence.

The Vice-President inhaled deeply, then frowned.

"Harry?"

"Yes, Chuck."

"If there's that much ammonia around how come we don't notice it? The air here is as pure and clean as you could wish for."

"Chris Walmesley explained it to me. Ammonia is lighter than air so the bulk of it's accumulating at high altitude. Right now it's only the larger weather systems that stir it into the lower atmosphere. It's building up all the time, though, so it'll take less and less disturbance to bring it down. Eventually it won't need anything at all: everywhere will be permanently blanketed with ammonia: town, countryside – even peaceful havens like this."

The Vice-President clucked his tongue, looking around him. One of the smaller lodges could be glimpsed between the trees.

"Hard to believe it could happen, isn't it? All this beautiful country, and not a soul left to walk in it, see it, enjoy it."

"We're not dead yet, Chuck, we're not dead yet."

They separated to walk around a thick branch brought down by recent gales. Then the President resumed.

"Let's get back to the planning. We dealt with evacuating that campus. Now we've got to make sure every key government department is ready to move into it. But no way are we going to take a convoy out of the capital – that would trigger an exodus from every major city in the country. What I want to do is set up a duplicate operation in Florida. When the time comes, we move the centre of gravity quickly and quietly from Washington to Florida."

"Another internal memorandum?"

"Yes, but restrict this one to the highest level. Head it 'White Smogs: Precautionary Action'. Then tell it like it is. There's a distinct possibility that one of these white smogs will bring the capital to a halt and we have to plan accordingly."

"It's a big job. How long do we have?"

"Let's see. We're already at the end of May. A week? Two at the very outside, so mid June. They'll say it's impossible. The message is: Make it possible."

"Okay. A lot of the record-keeping's paperless these days; that'll make it easier. We could go one step further and transfer data from servers in the Washington area to data farms in Florida."

"Good thinking, let's do that right away. These smogs seem to block up air conditioning systems; I'd feel better about it if the servers were in a low-risk area."

"Okay, I'll get started on it as soon as we get back." He glanced at the President. "I guess this isn't just about white smogs, is it? You're thinking about the Yellowstone option."

Kinghorn took a deep breath. "It's our job to be prepared for everything, Chuck. That included."

They walked on another fifty yards, alone with their thoughts. The trees thinned and sunlight striped the path. The Vice-President looked up.

"Can I ask you something, Harry? Could you really press that button?"

The President sighed.

"I honestly don't know. You know, it would be something if I could evacuate the people from that area first, but I can't. The scientists have been monitoring the supervolcano for years, day and night. There's no question an eruption is on the cards but they know full well it's not imminent. If we moved the population as a precaution it would expose the whole damned thing."

"There'd be serious casualties."

"You think I don't know that?"

"So you haven't made a final decision yet?"

"Look, I've seen the evidence: things are getting worse all the time. We need that biological solution as soon as possible, so we'll move our expert groups to Florida right away and put a rocket behind them. And of course we'll make all the preparations so we can move down there ourselves. But am I actually going to explode a nuclear warhead in the heart of the Yellowstone system?" He shook his head. "How does a person take a decision like that? If I press the button, thousands, maybe millions, of our own citizens will die. If I fail to press the button, everyone on Earth will die."

"It's a helluva call, Harry. I don't know that any President's had to face one like it, except maybe the other Harry – Truman – when they asked him to drop the bomb on Hiroshima and Nagasaki."

"Yeah, and people still ask whether *he* did the right thing. Anyway, we're not there yet; I'm still hoping the biologists can come up with something in time. Have someone earmark one of those buildings on the Florida campus for the research institute. I'll get Maggie Ferris and Terry McKinley to take a look at it."

"The two Brits? Why them?"

"Because they'll know exactly what they need. They discovered this problem in the first place; they know more about it, and they've thought more about it, than anyone else. And they're the only ones who've come up with realistic strategies for dealing with it. That institute is our one hope of a permanent solution."

"Who's directing it?"

"Herbert Kramer."

"OSTP?"

"Yes. Advises me on science and technology policy – broad-brush stuff."

"He'll be busy with his own office."

"That's the idea, we only want him nominally in charge; it's years since he was at a lab bench. He can just keep an eye on things, oversee the budget, general admin. Ferris and McKinley will be Deputy Directors. They'll actually run the show."

"Sounds good."

Kinghorn grunted. "We have to move quickly on this, Chuck. Leak that hurricane memo the moment you get back and when it hits the media tell the university to clear the campus. As soon as that building's available I'll have Ferris and McKinley fly down there to size it up."

CHAPTER 29

Less than a week later, Terry and Maggie had taken two rooms next to each other in the residential accommodation on campus at the University of Central Florida and the huge transfer operation had begun. From that moment the whole place had buzzed continually with activity: a constant flux of deliveries, new arrivals, people hurrying to and fro, the drone of incoming trucks, the rattle of pallets, and the shouts of workmen as equipment and materials were unloaded by forklifts. If they looked carefully they could sometimes spot the armed members of the United States Marine Corps, two inside the entrance of every building except the Research Institute, where their teams were to be based.

The Institute was a seven-storey block, and its impressive glass frontage, which took on the colour of the blue Florida sky, was streaked with the jagged reflections of the tall palm trees that lined the avenue outside. The grass around it was littered with paper, discarded soft drink cans, and the polystyrene containers left over from fast food meals, evidence of the rapid evacuation which had just taken place.

Only part of their time was spent on the campus. They were flying back to Washington almost daily, coordinating the movement of people and equipment. Their colleagues also wanted the rest of their research teams brought in from the host institutions. The constant pressure was beginning to take its toll on both of them.

Kramer appeared only infrequently and seldom stayed for long. In contrast, his administrative assistants were permanently on site, busy liaising with suppliers and installation engineers, placing orders, and dealing with accounts.

During one of the Washington trips Terry and Maggie had a short, but helpful meeting with the Vice-President in his room at the White House.

"How's the move going?"

Terry took a deep breath. "Still a few glitches with equipment installation and testing but we're almost operational now. Aren't we, Maggie?"

She nodded.

Terry continued: "There were just a few things I wanted to raise with you."

"Go ahead."

"Okay. When the site was evacuated you decided to leave behind some key maintenance staff."

"Yes, they put the case for that and we thought it made sense."

"It does. But there's also a supercomputer on the campus. It was left operational, pending a final decision."

"You want to keep it running?"

"If we're going to do climate modelling we'll need access to something as big as that."

The Vice-President scribbled in the notebook.

"You got it. Anything else?"

"Thinking ahead a little, now. I think fuel will be in short supply. That'll be a problem for everyone, but it'll be a particular problem for us. We'll have aircraft doing the atmospheric sampling. That could take a lot of fuel."

The Vice-President looked at Terry and his eyes narrowed. "You're talking, like, six months ahead, if we have to blow the supervolcano?"

"Yes. Obviously we hope we don't have to, but we have to plan for it."

"Terry, you'll have to manage the best you can. We anticipate that most of the Texas wells and refineries will remain in operation, and we may be able to buy some in. Get your groups to decide what would be the most effective use of the resources you've got. What's next?"

"Are we going to be all right for electricity, sir? I'm thinking of the possible fuel shortages again. We can't afford to have computers and data banks going down in the middle of everything."

"I looked into that. There shouldn't be a problem. Even if we run out of coal and oil there are three nuclear power stations in Florida and there's also some hydroelectric power. We'll be sure to give the campus priority call on it."

"Fine. Well I think that's it for the moment." They got up and the Vice-President came with them as far as the door. Terry turned to him. "Most of the research staff have moved in now. We'd like to get the research under way again as soon as we can. When can we brief them?"

"Soon. But you have a bigger group with a lot of new people so there's still a potential security problem. The President will be flying down to make an inspection. He wants to be sure his entire secondary centre of government is operational. At that point he'll give the go-ahead and a cordon will be thrown around the entire campus." He smiled. "*Then* you can tell them."

They shook hands and left.

"You've got to admire how they've set this up so quickly," said Terry. "The sheer energy and resources they're putting into it. It reminds me a bit of the Manhattan Project."

"I hope we can leave the world a better legacy than the Manhattan Project."

Terry looked at her. "Right now, I'll settle for leaving a world at all."

"I don't know about you, but I am thoroughly and comprehensively pissed off."

Matt Oakley had that peculiar brand of youthfulness and energy that often characterized young, ambitious Americans. He'd grown up in a poor Bronx neighbourhood, and a prolonged stint at the Sanger Institute had neither left him with a Cambridge accent nor had refined, in any noticeable way, his speech habits. Matt, together with the other people who'd been moved out of the NIH and down to Florida, had congregated in the lounge at the Research Institute just after breakfast. His feet were on a laminate-topped table, ankles crossed, his plastic chair leaning back at an alarming angle.

Pieter van der Rijt said. "You don't like it here?"

He waved a hand. "Oh it's all very nice, Pieter, but I wasn't exactly planning on a sunshine holiday. I've got work to do."

"Why did we have to move anyway?" Jos Wentink asked.

"Something important has happened," his supervisor, Ulrich Lunsdorfer, said. "This is clear."

"But what?" Jos said. "Maggie would not tell me."

Rajiv Gupta came over with a plastic beaker of coffee and pulled up a chair. "She is saying something about a heightened security situation. I think she cannot say more at the moment."

"I don't know," Matt said. "I stop everything and fly to Washington because everyone's in a big fucking hurry. The moment we start work we're pulled out and plonked down here. To do what? Sit around drinking coffee?"

Silvia Mussini frowned. "Come on, Matt, you know how hard Maggie has worked to move the research group here. She looks really exhausted. And Terry, too."

"Yeah, well that's another thing, Silvia. This guy Terry. I gather he's a planetary physicist, f'r Chrissake. What's that got to do with the price of eggs?"

Silvia smiled. "The price of eggs? Really, Matt."

Sara Tennant, her postgraduate student, said, "We'll have to be patient, is all. They did say we'd be fully briefed once we were down here."

"Well," Matt said. "We're down here and we still know zip. They're taking forever to install my fucking sequencer and I'm bored out of my skull. I tell you, much more of this and I'm walking out of here."

"I have news for you, Matt." Matt turned his head to see Alain Laroche entering the lounge. "You will not be able to walk out. There is a cordon around the campus."

Other groups of staff in the lounge stopped talking and all heads turned towards Alain.

Matt pulled his feet off the table. "You're not fucking serious!"

"Yes, I am. Wayne and I just tried to go into town and they turned us back."

"Who? Police? National Guard? The Florida mafia?"

"Wayne recognized the uniforms. Wayne?"

"United States Marine Corps."

Everyone started to talk at once.

Matt jumped up. "Fuck this. I'm not going to be held a prisoner in my own country. Where's Terry?"

The lounge emptied as they all hurried downstairs. Terry was in his office on the ground floor and as usual the door was wide open. It was something they'd agreed upon even before the teams had arrived, the idea being to show that they were accessible at all times. Hearing the growing noise, he looked up, then strolled out to the foyer to see what it was about. The moment the scientists caught sight of him he was assailed by angry and indignant shouts, in which individual words and phrases could barely be distinguished. Matt's voice was the loudest of all.

"What's the big idea, Terry? What the fuck's going on?"

Terry pushed his way through, vaulted onto the reception desk, and held out his hands. The clamour died to a rumble.

"Okay, okay, listen. I gather the area's been cordoned off."

This was greeted by another outbreak of shouting. He held up his hands again.

"Yeah, yeah, I know. Look, it's time we had a full briefing." He glanced at his watch and tapped it with one finger. "In one hour we'll meet in the lecture theatre, here," he pointed to one set of doors at the back of the foyer. "One hour. It'll all be explained then. All right?"

He got down, crossed to the door that opened onto the corridor, and went through. As the door swung closed behind him it snuffed the voices down to an aggrieved muttering. He listened as he walked but there was no change in volume; no one was following him.

He went straight to Maggie's office. She was on her feet.

"What on earth was all that about?" she said. "I heard the row."

"Sounds like they've closed off the perimeter. Some of the staff were turned back. They're pretty mad."

"The President must be here. I didn't know."

"No, nor me. I think they might have warned us. We've got to get these people settled down now. I've brought forward our general meeting. We'll have it in one hour. All right?"

She checked her watch and shrugged. "All right. I had my bit prepared anyway."

"Okay. We'll go down together. I need to get a message to the President's office, just to make sure we have the go-ahead and let them know what's happening here. I'll run it over myself."

CHAPTER 30

The theatre was filled with noise. Terry looked up at the seats and made a rough estimate of numbers. It looked like everyone was there. He took the podium and waited for their attention. The conversations were tapering off when there was a disturbance at the door and a group of people came in. A rustle of interest passed through the audience. Voices whispered, "it's the President!"

Harry Kinghorn crossed over to Terry and Maggie and shook them warmly by the hand.

Terry murmured, "Thank you for coming, sir."

"Saw your message," he said. "Thought I'd drop by."

"That was good of you."

"No, this is important, Terry," the President replied. "Have to keep these mavericks of yours in line." He turned to Kramer, who had come in with him. "Go ahead, Herbert. You can introduce me."

Kramer stepped up to the microphone and said:

"Ladies and Gentlemen, please welcome the President of the United States."

There was a wary scattering of applause. It died to an expectant hush.

Terry eyed the audience. The faces were grim and resentful. Their rights had been trampled and things had been kept from them; they knew it and their anger was justified. At the same time few of them would ever have seen a head of state at close hand. They'd give him a hearing, at least. But would it satisfy them?

The President began. It was the voice of oration: slow, resonant and emphatic; the voice heard at political rallies, at fundraising parties, at campaign stops; the voice that had sailed out into football stadia, and into people's homes from the stately surroundings of the Oval Office; a voice that spoke of wisdom and authority.

"Ladies and gentlemen. We have brought you here from around the world because you are the outstanding scientists of this generation. We are asking you to focus your talents on a problem, the full scale of which will now be revealed to you for the first time. You have been told that it concerns the white smogs. That is the truth, but it is only part of the truth. The situation is infinitely worse than any of you can possibly imagine. The white smogs are just the beginning. Mankind is facing the gravest threat in its entire history. We have a war on, ladies and gentlemen, a war against rogue organisms. They have spread all over this planet. They have entered oceans, rivers, and lakes. They have penetrated the very soil of the land. And they are progressively replacing our breathable atmosphere with one of ammonia."

He paused as a wave of astonishment and alarm spread through the audience. There'd been a good deal of speculation, but not even the wildest rumours could match the reality. He continued:

"Now, perhaps, you can understand why we have drawn you from such diverse disciplines: molecular biology, bacteriology, marine biology, atmospheric and ocean sciences. You are our front-line troops in this conflict and you have only months," he repeated, "months, in which to achieve victory. If you prevail, we will survive. If you fail, all life on Earth will be extinguished."

He waited until the buzz of conversation died down.

"Among you there is a core group of people who had already started to work on the problem. You've been uprooted at short notice. I'm sorry, but it was necessary. The situation has deteriorated since you were brought in; ammonia is building up day by day and there is an imminent danger that Washington will be the next in line for a white smog. You could not be expected to work under such conditions so for your own health and welfare the entire operation has been transferred here to Florida."

There were murmurs from some members of the audience.

"Now, I have come here in person to pay tribute to the two people who gathered you together: Dr. Terry McKinley and Dr. Maggie Ferris. They were the first to see the true nature of this threat; without them we would have no chance – no chance whatever – of defeating it. They will be working under the Director, Dr. Herbert Kramer, who is with me here. I want you to give all of them your full support. Scientifically we know what you're capable of – it's why you were invited to join us. But this is not the moment to seek individual glory; we must all work as one. If we do not, all of us will perish."

He paused for several seconds. The theatre had gone totally quiet. He could have waited for any length of time now and the silence would not have been broken. His tone became less strident.

"Outside of this establishment the true nature of the situation has not been made known. If we allowed it to become public knowledge there could be serious disorder, here and elsewhere around the world, and that would benefit no one. For that reason it's vital that this operation is conducted in absolute secrecy. The United States Marine Corps is here, securing every part of this campus," he raised a finger and wagged it from side to side, "not to infringe your civil liberties, which I, and the people of this country, have gone to war many times to defend. They are here to protect you and to make sure you are not impeded in your vital work. Temporarily – and I say temporarily – you will be asked to pay a small price for this protection. Communication with the outside world must be restricted. Land lines and cell phones will no longer operate in this area. But understand this: the survival of mankind depends on the people in this room. We would be irresponsible if we did not take every possible measure to ensure your safety and security. When, God willing, you have completed your task, all these restrictions will be lifted and you will be free to leave, and with our blessing.

"The fate of humanity rests on your shoulders, ladies and gentlemen. If you succeed you will earn my gratitude and the gratitude of the nations of the world. The challenge that you face is immense. I am confident you will be equal to it."

He stepped back. The audience was still stunned. Some recovered and started to clap. The President shook hands with Kramer, then with Terry and Maggie, raised a hand to the auditorium and, without looking round, he left.

CHAPTER 31

As soon as the doors had closed behind the President's entourage there was a burst of excited conversation. Terry gave Maggie a look.

"Impressive" he said.

"The question is, what kind of reception are they going to give us?"

Herbert Kramer went up to the microphone and the noise died. His tone was cool.

"I've met some of you, and I think most of you have had some contact with my administrative staff along the corridor. My responsibility as Director is to ensure that things run smoothly. I won't always be around; I am still Director of the Office of Science and Technology Policy, which is now divided between this campus and Washington. Day-to-day coordination will be in the hands of Dr. McKinley and Dr. Ferris, and I think I can do no better than to hand you over to them now."

He moved away and indicated to Terry and Maggie that they had the floor. Terry went first.

"Thank you, Dr. Kramer. First Maggie and I want to apologize to you all. We couldn't give you the full story before and now I hope you can understand why. Well, that's behind us now and I can assure you that no one is happier about it than we are.

"You've been told the planet is under threat. I don't expect you to take that on trust – you'll want to see hard evidence. Let me show you some of the data. Feel free to ask questions at any time."

He dimmed the lights and projected on the screen above him a series of slides showing the NASA satellite maps and the atmospheric sampling data. Then he introduced the team of climatologists, oceanographers, and atmospheric chemists who would be monitoring ammonia levels around the globe and using computer models to predict how quickly and by how much they were going to change.

A hand was raised.

"There's a question. Gareth?"

"How are you going to do the monitoring?"

"A combination of methods. There are ongoing atmospheric research programs, and we'll have direct access to their results. NASA Earth Survey Satellites will do it spectroscopically. We'll also collect and analyse samples with balloons, and we've been allotted four research aircraft and some US Air Force personnel to carry out low stratospheric sampling."

Somebody gave a long, low whistle. Terry continued:

"Okay, like I said, we need to do this so we can make more accurate predictions. But I have to tell you what the situation is as of right now." He paused, and took a deep breath. "If current trends continue, conditions on this planet will become incompatible with life within six months."

A horrified gasp went round the auditorium. Terry understood the reaction. The President had said "months" but these people were used to hearing politicians make exaggerated claims. It was a very different matter to hear a scientist base that conclusion on hard data.

"That's a measure of how widely distributed these organisms are, and how little time we have to find a way of combating them. Now in a moment I'm going to hand over to Dr. Maggie Ferris, who will present a plan for doing just that. Before I do there's one more thing. We'll meet here, in this lecture theatre, every Friday at eleven a.m. sharp starting a week today. Be here. Don't schedule anything that can't be interrupted. We're working against the clock and our success depends on each person knowing what the others are doing. We'll be asking each team leader to present their progress during the week. If there hasn't been any, don't speak. If there has, keep it crisp. It isn't just progress we want to hear about: if you've hit a problem, bring it to the meeting. You know as well as anyone that research is full of blind alleys. If that's happening we've got to pick it up early – we can't afford to lose time going off in unproductive directions. I know all this will be coming fresh to some of you. If you have any doubts about where you fit in or what to do next, ask a member of the core team or Maggie or me. Remember, every single person in this room has a reason for being here. All right? Maggie, over to you."

Maggie went to the microphone.

"Thank you, Terry. Today I just want to outline the broad strategy. It's not set in tablets of stone. In particular if anyone spots a short cut we need to know about it. We're a multidisciplinary group here so I'll try to keep it simple.

She said nothing about the way they had discovered the problem, dealing only with the mutation that caused organisms like phytoplankton to generate ammonia, and how it was spreading. Then she outlined their strategy for defeating it with a plasmid of their own, combined with a bacteriophage that would give their carrier organism a selective advantage. As Kolesnikov had now arrived she introduced him at this point.

"Dr. Sergei Kolesnikov is a world authority on phages. He and his group are here to help us select a phage that will infect the ammonia organisms, multiply inside them, and kill them. Rajiv Gupta will modify our own organism so that it's resistant to the phage. That's what will give it the selective advantage. Sergei?"

The big Russian pulled himself slowly to his feet. "Is complex, but is possible. Alternative is to find phage that target only organisms which carry ammonia plasmid. Would take very long time. May be impossible, even."

"Thank you, Sergei. Sergei's had some problems getting here but we're delighted he can join us at last." Maggie paused as she saw Matt Oakley rising for his turn. "Matt?"

"Maggie, you know damn well we put together a timeline for this project. It could take a year. From what you guys just said we'll all be dead by then."

The audience murmured.

Maggie took a deep breath. "I'm glad you brought that up, Matt." She looked around the audience. "Some of you weren't around when we went through this exercise. What Matt said is perfectly true: the project could take as long as a year in normal circumstances. But these aren't normal circumstances. We have six months to emerge with a solution. We can do it, but only if every one of us devotes every waking minute of every day to the problem facing us. We have to work together. We have to stay absolutely focused. Interesting side avenues must be ignored. Difficulties must be overcome. We need to work fast, cutting corners wherever the opportunity arises. I don't want you even to think about failure; failure is not an option. Any other questions? Back to you, Terry."

"Okay. That's it for now. There are already samples of the ammonia organism in the fridges for anyone who wants them. And I'd like to meet with the sampling teams now. Let's get to work."

CHAPTER 32

That afternoon Maggie appeared in the doorway of Terry's office.

"I'm just off to the airport, Terry. I asked Jake to send over some more of our samples. I have to pick them up at the freight terminal."

"Right. How's it going?"

She grinned, then came in. "We've got such a fantastic team up there. Alain Laroche can be a bit prickly but he has an outstanding intellect. You should see him and Matt striking sparks off each other! Sometimes it takes Silvia or me to get them back on track."

"Is that a problem?"

"Not really. Underneath all the rivalry they have a high regard for each other. And they've already come up with some great ideas for cutting the development time."

Terry dropped his voice. "What do you think, then, Maggie? Last week you told them you can do it inside six months. Can you? Without my fallback option?"

Maggie's smile faded. "I don't want your fallback option, Terry. As things are going we can succeed without it. We lost a few days with the transfer from NIH, but the way these guys are working – now that they know what they're really up against – it's like none of that ever happened. Matt's already got the sequencer up-and-running. That's why I need the samples. He can't wait to get started and Pieter and Ulrich are having problems growing up enough with their culture system." She glanced at her watch. "Taxi will be waiting for me outside the cordon. I'd better get going."

"Okay, safe journey. See you later."

Matt came over when he saw Maggie entering the lab with the parcel. He frowned.

"What's the problem, Maggie?"

"I don't know. It looks like it's been interfered with. Jake makes a neater job than this, and look at these strips of tape 'Sealed by US Customs'. I asked the guy at the freight counter. He just shrugged and said sometimes the wrapping gets torn."

"We'd better see what's inside." He took out a pocket knife.

Between them they removed the brown paper and tape and opened the box. The cardboard was lined, as before, with expanded polystyrene, but the lining was eroded away in several places.

"What's been going on here...?" Maggie said, as she put her hands inside. She withdrew them hurriedly. They were covered with a clear slime. "What the...?"

"Better rinse that off right away, Maggie; we don't know what the hell it is. And use gloves."

She crossed to a sink, washed and dried her hands, and donned a pair of latex gloves. Then she spread some paper towels on the bench, sat the box on them, and tried again. The source of the slimy material was soon clear. Jake had packed the samples in cold gel packs, as before. But this time every one of those packs had been slit open. The gel had spilled inside, attacking the polystyrene. The mess was dreadful.

Matt shook his head. "Customs. They must have decided you were smuggling drugs in those bags."

She was breathing fast, her face hot with anger. "The idiots! It couldn't have been clearer. Look at the manifest." She spread the sheet out on the bench and read from it. "'Valuable samples for scientific research. Refrigerate where possible. Please conduct any inspection in the presence of the recipient as they must not be allowed to thaw.' So which part of that did they not understand?"

"These people are a law to themselves, Maggie. They'll say they were just doing their job."

"Every living being on Earth is under threat and they're 'just doing their job'! I can't believe this." She drew out the flasks with the samples and wiped them off. "These aren't even remotely cold. They've been sitting in a warehouse somewhere, in God knows what kind of temperatures, without any cool bags. Put them in the fridge right away, Matt. I'll test them for viability in a moment."

"Dead, Terry! The whole lot of them! I'd like to go down to the airport to find whoever did this and wring their bloody necks!" She sat down hard.

He got up from behind his desk, pushed the door to his office to, and returned to her.

"You say they slit open the gel bags?"

"Yes, every one of them!"

"There's quite a drugs scene in Florida. Maybe Customs are tighter here. Jake didn't send all the samples, did he?"

"I'm not that stupid!" she snapped.

"Maggie..."

She buried her face in her hands. "I'm sorry. I'm upset, that's all."

"Which samples have gone?"

Her voice was muffled. "All the river samples."

"Damn."

She looked up at him, reading the expression on his face. Her voice softened. "You could say they've served their purpose, Terry. I mean, without them we would never have got as far as this. But I want Jake to send the rest of the Bermuda samples. What are we going to do if this happens again?"

His jaw tightened. "It won't happen again. Give me Jake's contact details. I'll go over to the Department of Defense building. I don't know if Dick Pevensey is on campus at the moment but they'll know how to contact him. I'll arrange a military escort for the next batch of samples."

She reached up and gripped his hand. "Terry, that's a great idea. Why didn't I think of it?"

"You have other things on your mind. Don't worry, I'll look after it. I'll come by your office when I'm done."

Forty minutes later he walked into her office. "I was in luck, Dick was there. Couldn't have been more helpful. Your samples will be picked up by the USAF and brought back on a special flight. They'll deliver them here."

It was a warm June day and the sky was hazy but cloudless, so the thick white smog that came in off Lake Ontario was totally unexpected. Multiple collisions blocked all but one lane of the Queen Elizabeth highway. The city of Toronto ground to a halt, the streets dim and curiously quiet, shadowy figures emerging from the whiteness and disappearing again as they scurried along sidewalks with scarves, sleeves, tissues – anything – across nose and mouth. The silence was disrupted only by the ambulances wailing through the intersections as they took the casualties to hospital. At the Toronto General the wards overflowed, frantic staff hurried down corridors lined with patients waiting on gurneys, and everywhere the air was filled with the sounds of coughing and wheezing. The stocks of oxygen cylinders ran out. They were on the point of shutting the doors to any more emergency admissions when the fire service came to the rescue; wearing respirators, their drivers began to ferry patients to outlying hospitals. And still the casualties kept arriving.

Three hours later a brisk wind arose from the south-west and the smog thinned and dispersed. By that time it had taken the lives of nearly two thousand people.

CHAPTER 33

The President had remained in Washington but he still wanted to be kept posted on the progress of the research. Kramer was too out of touch to do this; over the past few weeks he had rarely been seen at the Institute, and never at the Friday meetings. The responsibility therefore passed to Terry, and he had to fly to the capital every week or so. It was a distraction he could well have done without, especially at the moment, when it seemed that everything was taking ten times longer than it should. The USAF had finally made available four aircraft for the research flights but even with the help of their engineers, equipping them was a lengthy operation. Terry wanted to short-cut the whole process by appropriating four of the aircraft that NOAA and the NSF teams had been using for atmospheric sampling. That proved to be an administrative nightmare so he returned to the tedious business of modifying the aircraft they had. After that the airborne equipment had to be tested exhaustively, calibrated, and cross-checked against samples collected by balloon. It was standard scientific practice but in the present circumstances it was even more vital to have measurements that were utterly reliable. As decided at the meeting in the Oval Office, Noel Harrison and Chris Walmsley had used all the available evidence to set an upper level of ammonia, a threshold beyond which direct action could no longer be avoided. They had also identified a number of key locations representative of atmospheric ammonia around the globe. The sites would be monitored at different altitudes and at frequent intervals, and the measurements combined for comparison with the threshold level. That level was high – alarmingly high – but if it was exceeded they'd be forced to approach the President about invoking the Yellowstone option.

While the aircraft were being prepared, the climatologists, ocean and atmospheric scientists set up a data-gathering web, and information started to flow in along the threads. They put it together, then called Terry over to discuss the results. There was a tension in the room which he felt the moment he opened the door. He sat down and said lightly:

"Okay, what have you got?"

John Gilchrist acted as the group's spokesman. "Terry," he said. "I don't know what you're going to make of this. The data we have gives us an ammonia level that's already forty-nine per cent of the threshold level."

Terry blinked. "Forty-nine per cent of threshold? That's impossible, it can't be as high as that. How representative is your data?"

"Hard to say. I mean, there isn't a whole lot of it. It would only take one rogue reading to bump up the average."

"That must be what's happened." He got up. "Okay, guys – look, it was worth a try, but let's wait for the full measurement programme to get under way, shall we? Obviously we need something more solid than this to go on."

He gave them a reassuring smile as he left, and received glum nods in return.

He accompanied the sampling team on their first flight, partly to make sure that all the equipment was working, but mainly to get an idea of what was involved. With stops for refuelling and overnight stays it lasted several days. When they got back he analyzed the raw data in his office and then calculated a global average from all the specified locations and altitudes. He stared at the result in disbelief. Then he repeated all the calculations, but the answer was the same. If anything John Gilchrist's figure had been conservative; ammonia was already at fifty-three per cent of the threshold level.

He looked up, gazing into the distance.

No wonder there've been white smogs! I thought ammonia had just been pooling in pockets, but with an average level this high it could happen at any time. What else is going on out there?

A formation of migrating geese flew high over the Himalayas, making an asymmetrical V in the sky. The V became more ragged, the rhythmic beat of the wings interrupted, uncoordinated. Geese began to tumble, landing in a line of powdery explosions on the snow-laden mountain tops. Their bodies, no longer warmed by the heat generated by flight muscles, cooled rapidly in the sub-zero temperatures. The carcasses froze quickly. Stray feathers stirred gently in the icy breeze.

Maggie had a lot of time for Matt Oakley. He'd been frank with her about his frustrations when they first arrived in Florida but they'd both put that behind them. She found him easier to talk to than Laroche. In fact in many ways he was the ideal scientific colleague: as up front about failures as successes, ready to listen to another viewpoint – and totally uninhibited in expressing his own.

"Hi, Maggie."

"Hi, Matt. How's the sequencing going?"

He flicked a lock of dark hair off his forehead. "It isn't."

"What do you mean?"

"We can't do the sequencing 'cos we can't get enough of the fucking stuff to sequence."

Maggie raised her eyebrows, but not at the expletive. "Come on, Matt. You guys can get DNA from the root of a single human hair."

"Oh yeah, if you want total DNA. But we don't want total DNA; we just want the plasmid DNA. That's the problem: separating it out. I work with mammalian cells and bacteria like *E. coli*. This stuff is different. Like you said, there's a whole bunch of different organisms in these samples and a lot of them have cell walls that are thick or protected by some sort of jelly. Straight alkaline lysis isn't enough. I had to use more aggressive techniques to break it down."

"Okay, what's wrong with that?"

"What's wrong is that it louses up the genomic DNA as well. Then all the little bits of genomic DNA reform and contaminate the plasmid DNA. We can't work with a prep like that – we won't know where the hell we are. If we're less aggressive we can get pure plasmid DNA but the yield's shitty."

"Have you brought Pieter and Ulrich in on it? They're the experts on cyanobacteria."

"Yeah, we talked about it but they never did anything like this either." He sighed. "What we need is much bigger samples."

She closed her eyes. "Matt, you don't seem to appreciate what's involved. In total there are massive amounts of this stuff around but it's still distributed thinly. To get decent samples like these you've got to go to places where it's highly concentrated. Those places are dangerous. Terry and I collected the samples you're using in the Sargasso Sea. We took respirator masks and even so we were nearly caught out. One of the crew was quite badly affected. Can't you grow some on in the lab?"

"Pieter and Ulrich are still trying but it's hard to find the optimum conditions. You know the problem; what works out there in the environment doesn't work in the lab and vice versa."

Maggie recalled her failure to grow on single organisms. If the experts were having problems maybe it wasn't so surprising. On the other hand…

"I grew some up on a nutrient gel. That worked fine."

He shook his head. "We need to do it in solution to get reasonable quantities."

She sighed. "It's a pity we lost those river samples. I got those going in a day or so and I didn't have a problem…" She made a decision. "Matt, you don't have enough? Take the rest of the samples. Pool them."

He looked at her. "We haven't totally nailed down the procedure yet. If we screw up, you've lost the lot."

"We'll just have to take the chance."

"What about Sergei?"

"Sergei's got one flask. He doesn't need large quantities. He'll manage."

He shrugged. "Okay. It's your call."

At the door, she turned. "Matt?"

"Yes?"

She smiled. "You will try not to screw up, won't you?"

He gave her a mock salute. "We'll do our best, ma'am."

"Hey, Terry, come and look at this."

Phil Drummond was the youngest member of the climate team, a PhD from Princeton. Terry went over and looked where he was pointing. The 32-inch screen in front of him displayed a satellite view of the South China Sea and the adjacent Asian land mass. There was a large spiral of cloud just off the coast.

"Category 4 tropical cyclone," Phil said. "I watched it forming up yesterday. It was a Category 3 then, but it's intensifying all the time. Could even make a 5."

"Where's it going?"

"Westward. It's going to make landfall in South Vietnam."

"There are a lot of towns and villages up and down that coast."

Phil looked at him and nodded. "It's a biggie. It'll cause a lot of damage."

One evening after the other staff had left the Institute for the day, Maggie and Terry walked back to the students' residence. In the basement area of the building there were three machines that took coins and delivered snacks, soft drinks, or hot beverages. The hot chocolate was excessively sweet but it seemed to be the best of what was on offer. They took the steaming polystyrene cups up to Terry's room and sank into the armchairs in the small sitting/study area.

Maggie took a sip of the chocolate and swallowed. "Why does it all have to be so damned hard?" she sighed. "It looked like it was going to be straightforward."

Terry gave her a tired smile. "Research never is. Even Nobel Prize winners don't go in a straight line. Medawar said if he had back all the time he'd spent going up blind alleys he'd have a third of his research life over again." He frowned. "Or was it two-thirds?"

She shook her head. "Back in England I accepted it as part of the puzzle, part of the challenge. You backtracked, you found a different way, or you gave up that approach altogether. But this is different. We're up against a deadline, and we can't afford detours. We've wasted a lot of time."

"Because of the sequencing?"

"Yes, everyone's held up, waiting for it. Well, everyone except Sergei. He's getting on, quietly screening his phages against the organisms. He keeps himself to himself but at least his lot seem to be making progress."

"Is it resolved now?"

She sighed again. "Yes, thank God. I think they'll be able to start sequencing properly next week. It's a good thing we took a good batch of samples at Bermuda, though. We nearly had to go back for more." She sipped the chocolate again. "What's happening to the atmospheric levels?"

"You're not going to like this."

"Go on."

"I've just finished analysing the data from the second sampling flight." He paused. "The average is sixty-one per cent of the threshold level."

She sat up.

"You're not serious! Sixty-one per cent? Already?"

"Yes. And it's rising rapidly."

Maggie frowned. "My God. Is this just a local accumulation?"

"No, that's the whole point of taking the average at a number of sites and altitudes. There'll be some variation but we've allowed for it."

"But at that rate we'll be across the threshold in weeks not months!"

"It's beginning to look that way."

She ran her fingers through her hair. "I thought you said we had six months."

"To start with that's what it looked like, based on the trends Chris and I extracted from the NSF and NOAA data. But a lot has happened out there since. I think the weather's to blame: hurricanes in the Atlantic, cyclones in Asia – I've had reports of water spouts in the South China Sea. Those systems carry the stuff up thousands of feet and transport it far and wide. It's self-reinforcing: the organisms generate ammonia; that injects energy into the atmosphere, and the high winds spread the organisms even further. The result is, the levels are going up much faster than predicted."

"Is Chris aware of this?"

"I'm sure he is. Chris and Noel Harrison have to monitor the levels as well; we courier the reports to them every week."

She straightened up and her lips tightened. "There's time yet. We can still win."

They were washed up in their hundreds all along the coast of the Baja Peninsula in California: Pacific white-sided dolphins, beaked whales – both adults and calves, sperm whales and orcas. Local residents and wild life experts hurried to the beaches in the hope of rescuing at least some of them. They found not a single one alive.

CHAPTER 34

A few days later Terry was working in his office when he received a message from Silvia Mussini asking if he and Maggie could come to her lab urgently. He picked up Maggie and they headed straight there.

Silvia got up from the bench when she saw them come in, stripped off her latex gloves, and had a quick word with Sara Tennant. Then she led them into her office and gestured to the chairs before sitting down herself. Silvia was one of the people Maggie had said she most wanted on the team, based on the superb reputation she'd established at the University of Padua and more recently at the University of California, Berkeley. Terry had had little contact with her until now but her message had been clear: she wanted him to be in on this.

She shook back her thick, dark hair, and the sunlight from the window illuminated her fine features. She turned to them. Her expression was warm and friendly and there was a lively intelligence in those dark eyes.

"I have something to show you," she said.

She placed a sheet of paper on the desk and turned it towards them. "This is part of the sequence for the plasmid. Matt and his team thought I would like to look at it while they are working on the rest."

She ran a fingernail along some letters, which she'd underlined. "You recognise this sequence."

Terry stared at it, but it meant nothing to him. He looked at Maggie. Her jaw had gone slack.

"What is it?" he asked.

"It's the gene for GFP, Terry. Green Fluorescent Protein. It's a reporter gene."

"Okay, but what the hell is a reporter gene?"

"Terry," Silvia said. "Molecular biologists don't just pop genes into cells. It is not so simple. If we are lucky we succeed in maybe one cell in a thousand. So we have to find out which cells actually received the gene. We do that by attaching it to another gene – a special gene that makes something easy to recognize: a reporter. For example, the reporter gene may make a compound that fluoresces. Then if a cell fluoresces it means the reporter is present. If the reporter is present then so is the gene we're interested in." She stood up quickly. "Come with me."

Silvia led the way to the microscope room. Once inside she switched on the power supplies and they waited while she selected a slide and placed it on the stage of a fluorescence microscope.

"Close the door and turn off the light," she instructed and Terry complied, pulling the door to and tugging the cord suspended from the ceiling. The small room was plunged into total darkness. As his eyes accommodated he became aware of a blue glow from the light source, the angular dark outline of the microscope, and Silvia sitting in front of it, making adjustments. She stood up.

"This is one of your ocean samples. The excitation wavelength is 395 nm."

They took turns to peer into the eyepieces.

"We can have the light on again now."

Terry found the cord and blinked as the room was flooded with light again.

He said, "Every one of those organisms was glowing bright green."

"Yes." Silvia bent forward to switch off the microscope.

"So every one of them contained this reporter sequence?"

"Correct. And if an organism contains a reporter sequence it does not get there by accident." She turned to face them.

Terry stared at her, comprehension finally dawning on him.

The small room had gone so quiet he could feel the pressure on his ears.

She nodded. "Yes, Terry. This was not a spontaneous mutation at all. The plasmid is an artificial DNA construct."

He looked at Maggie and saw the shock on his own face reflected in hers. Her mouth moved, the words almost inaudible:

"Someone wanted these organisms to produce ammonia. They did this on purpose. This thing is man made."

"Jesus."

"Shall we go?" Silvia said brightly.

They followed her back and paused in the corridor outside her lab.

Terry's mind was racing. "Silvia, we need time to take this on board. We'll come back to you, okay?"

"Of course. It was a surprise for me too."

Maggie laid a hand on her arm. "Great work, Silvia."

They took the stairs down to Terry's office and he closed the door behind them. Terry waved her to a chair and sat down, his elbows on the desk and his fingertips plunged into his hair. For several minutes they said nothing. He looked up at her.

"What do you make of this?"

"You know, it's actually starting to make sense. Originally we thought the mutation arose in the Sargasso Sea. That didn't seem hugely surprising – you might expect something of the sort to happen in a rich soup like that. Then you got the NASA data and we found out it actually started on the Eastern seaboard. That's been sitting in the back of my mind ever since. I kept thinking: why there of all places?" She opened her hands. "Now we know. But, for God's sake, who made it, and why?"

Terry's eyes widened and he started to breathe fast. His voice was taut with excitement. "Maggie, somebody made it."

"I know somebody made it. That's what we just said."

"No, you're not getting it. Somebody made it! Don't you see? Whoever it was could tell us what's in the plasmid and how it works."

He leapt to his feet. "We need to take this to Washington right away. I was due to fly up there for a status meeting in a couple of days, but I'll get us on the first flight in the morning. This is huge Maggie. This could be the short cut we need."

CHAPTER 35

Tricia Lawton came into Chris Walmesley's office carrying a tray, and the room filled with the aroma of freshly brewed coffee. She left the tray on the desk with a plate of chocolate chip cookies.

A few minutes later Chris came through the door and settled behind his desk. "Ah, good. Coffee."

He poured two cups and gave one to Maggie and one to Terry. Then he poured one for himself and took a sip.

"So, what's new? Please tell me it's good news."

"Sort of, Chris," Maggie said. "We have a partial sequence for the plasmid. It tells us this wasn't a spontaneous mutation at all. The organism that caused the problem was man-made."

Chris slammed his coffee cup down. "What the hell?! Are you sure?"

"Absolutely. The plasmid contains a well-known artificial sequence. There's no doubt about it. It was genetic modification."

"I can't believe someone would do such a thing deliberately!"

"Our thoughts exactly," said Terry. "There's more. You remember when we tracked back before and saw the problem originated here in the States? Stands to the reason that whoever designed it, they did it here, Chris. In the USA."

"Jesus. You're right of course." Walmesley seemed to be in shock.

"The real issue now," continued Terry, "is we have no idea who did it, or why, and whether it got out by accident, or whether it was released on purpose. But there is an upside. Maggie?"

"You know the situation, Chris," said Maggie. "We're running out of time – fast. If we could find out who synthesized the plasmid, he could tell us what was in it and how it worked. It would drastically cut the time we need to reach a solution."

Chris nodded once and was immediately down to business. "Right. What do we need to do?"

"Well, seeing as it was made here in the States, can't we get the FBI onto it?"

They waited. Walmesley thought for a moment. "The Director of the FBI is Joseph Englehardt, and he reports to Bob Cabot. I could work through Bob, get someone assigned."

"SomeONE," exclaimed Maggie. "Chris, the world's on the brink of disaster. We should be recruiting every agent in the country."

"The president would never go for it, Maggie. There's no way we could keep an operation like that a secret. In any case until you actually had some leads to follow you couldn't use that much manpower. But all that's not really the problem."

Maggie looked at him. "Well what is?"

"An agent or agents would have the investigative skills but it's not enough in this case. They'd need direct access to specialist knowledge and expertise." He nodded towards them. "The sort of specialist knowledge and expertise really only you two could provide."

Terry blinked. "You're not suggesting *we* work with the FBI?"

"That's exactly what I am suggesting."

Maggie turned to him. "Why not, Terry, if it would speed things up?"

"Why not? It could be bloody dangerous, that's why."

"I don't see that."

"Well think about it. How did it appear on the other side of the world? It could have been the work of an extremist organization, a highly sophisticated one. We might be up against some pretty nasty people."

Walmesley said, "Terrorists usually claim responsibility for attacks. So far as I know, no one's claimed responsibility for this one. Could be an accidental release."

"All right, even if it was think about the damage and loss of life it's caused already. We're talking about millions of dollars in law suits. Billions, probably. Whoever did this might kill at the drop of a hat if it kept them from being discovered."

Maggie flushed. "All that matters is that the ammonia's on the verge of crossing the threshold level. If we don't come up with a solution soon that countdown is going to start and tens of thousands of people are going to lose their lives. I don't know about you, but I wouldn't like to have that on my conscience when I could have avoided it by taking a small risk myself."

"Okay, Okay," said Terry holding up his hands. He sighed. "All right, Chris, looks like we're in."

CHAPTER 36

The next morning they waited together in Terry's room. He jerked when the telephone rang but picked it up quickly.

"Good morning, sir. Reception. Your tour is here."

Terry opened his mouth to say "We didn't order a tour," then thought better of it. He picked up his brief case and they went down to the lobby.

A man was waiting for them. He was tall and strongly built. His grey suit needed pressing and although he wore a shirt and tie the top button of his collar was unfastened, as if he couldn't bear the restriction. His hair was short, a little less extreme than the haircuts Terry had seen on US Marines, but not by much. He greeted them by name and took them out to a blue sedan. There was no FBI shield on the door and Terry couldn't see one on the windscreen. He hesitated but the man pointedly held the rear door open for them and they got in. He shut the door and got into the driver's seat. He looked over his shoulder.

"Name's Sam Milner, FBI," he said showing them his badge. "And in the future, if a guy you've never met ushers you into an unmarked car, best to ask him who he is before you get in."

Then he held out a hand, palm up. Terry looked blankly at it.

"Brief case. Routine security."

Reluctantly Terry handed over the brief case and Milner looked inside, inspecting the lap top, the NASA disks and a few printouts of data and graphs. He handed it back, threw the automatic into drive and moved off.

Terry felt uneasy. "Where are we going, Headquarters?" he asked. He knew the J. Edgar Hoover Building wasn't far away.

"Nope," came the reply.

There was an uncomfortable silence, during which the man must have realized he was being less than cordial. He glanced round and elaborated.

"I've been told all this is highly confidential and you two will be operating under cover. So just about the dumbest thing I could do right now would be to march you in full view in and out of FBI Headquarters. Okay?"

"I see. And that explains the unmarked car."

"Yeah. That explains the car."

There was no further conversation for the duration of the short ride.

Terry exchanged glances with Maggie. Evidently agent Sam Milner wasn't too happy with his latest assignment. The car stopped and Milner turned off the ignition. He pointed out of the window.

"We have an office in this building we can use."

They followed Milner through the lobby to a lift and rode it to the sixth floor, where he again led the way. Their footsteps were loud on the plastic tiled floor. He stopped at a door, to one side of which was a buzzer with a handwritten label: Palmerston Consulting Agency. He took out a bunch of keys, selected one and opened the door.

They found themselves in a corridor with rooms opening off on either side. Milner pushed open one of the glass-panelled doors and ushered them in. The air was warm and stale and carried with it a vague hint of petrol. The room was sparsely furnished: plain walls, one of which carried a framed print of an abstract painting, a large pine table, injection-moulded chairs, a plastic Venetian blind on the window. The floor was covered in a tough but cheap cord, which looked new enough to be responsible for the oily smell. A computer and printer sat on a small desk in the corner.

"You want some coffee? We got a machine here."

Terry looked at Maggie.

"I'm all right at the moment," she said.

"Me too," said Terry. "I'd like to get started."

"Okay, suit yourselves."

Milner threw a slim document case on the table and sat down heavily. He looked from one to the other. Then he said,

"Can I speak frankly?"

Terry said, "I'm sure you're going to."

"Yeah. Well, the boss said something about a weird organism that's doing a lot of damage so I'm dragged out of bed on a Sunday morning and told I'm supposed to find out who did it. Great. On top of which I'm less than thrilled to have two British boffins in tow. So now you know. I hope you aren't going to make things worse by getting under my feet."

Maggie's expression was stony. Terry feigned surprise.

"It's Sunday? Well, well, I'd quite lost track."

Milner grunted. "Okay. Suppose you start by telling me what you think is going on, and we'll take it from there."

Terry thought for a moment. Detailed explanations had obviously been left to him and Maggie. That, or the message had got garbled on the way down the line. He took a deep breath and went for shock tactics.

"All right. Here in the US you had a severe hurricane coming in from the Gulf of Mexico, outside of the normal season, doing billions of dollars' worth of damage. You've also had poisonous smogs sweeping through Baltimore, Pittsburgh, and Cleveland. More than three thousand people have died already and the hospitals are full of people who may still die because they can't breathe. We had a similar problem back in England and it almost paralyzed the capital. Toronto just had one; killed another two thousand people. None of this is a random quirk of nature. Someone has released a genetically modified organism which is filling the air with ammonia. Animal life can't survive in an atmosphere of ammonia. Unless we do something about it, every human being and every animal on this planet is going to die."

"No shit." Milner looked thoughtful. "So what am I supposed to do about it?"

"Dr. Ferris and I are part of a research team, investigating the organism. We're here to help you find out where it came from and nail the person or persons who made it. Once we know exactly what we're up against we'll be in a better position to design countermeasures."

"Suppose we can't find them?"

"We have to. If it spreads much more there'll be nothing we, or anyone else, can do to stop it."

Milner nodded slowly. "When did all this start?"

"About two-and-a-half years ago."

His eyebrows shot up. "Two-and-a-half years ago?! How come nobody picked it up earlier?"

"The problem developed gradually. As far as we know the first fatalities occurred in April last year. There was a marine incident in Bermuda waters: a boat got stuck in weed and five people died. The local authorities didn't know what to make of it. We do. We've been out there to collect samples and if we hadn't taken respirators the ammonia would have gotten us, too. The organism's there all right."

"So how does this get to be the FBI's baby? Bermuda's administered by the UK."

"We've gone back over satellite data from NASA. It shows the organism didn't come from Bermuda, it originated somewhere on the Eastern seaboard. We can only guess how it got to Bermuda, but it was probably carried there by eels."

"Well where do the eels migrate from? You got that, you got the source."

Terry said casually, "The Eastern North American eel, *Anguilla rostrata*, migrates from the whole of the Eastern seaboard."

"What, Canada too?"

"Yes, anywhere from the Gulf of Mexico to Labrador."

"Jesus. Do you guys have any idea how long that coastline is? We're talking maybe two thousand miles here."

Maggie joined in.

"Actually we shouldn't be restricting ourselves to the coast. It could well have been released further inland, into a river. Most big towns grew up around rivers; it was the easiest way of getting around before roads were built. That's a more likely source than something right on the coast."

Milner placed both hands flat on the table and sat back.

"Well, that's just dandy. They assign me to scour two thousand miles of coastline – not forgetting all the rivers draining into the Atlantic – on the off chance that I'm going to find some crazy outfit before they succeed in poisoning the entire world. And by the way they'd like a result some time tomorrow."

Terry met Maggie's eyes. He said quietly:

"That's why we're here. Maybe we can help."

Milner's eyes narrowed. "How?"

It was Maggie who responded.

"First of all, we don't think we're looking for a university or a research institute. You can't start working on genetic manipulation just like that. For one thing it's expensive. You need personnel, equipment and consumables so you'd have to apply for a grant. The grant agencies will want to be assured that you've adhered to all the safety regulations and installed any necessary containment facilities. In the UK you need the approval of GMAG, the Genetic Manipulation Advisory Group. I don't know how it works in the US but I'm sure there'll be some sort of oversight, either within the establishment or from a governmental organization. Given all those layers of supervision, it's pretty hard to believe that a genetically engineered organism could escape and no one would know anything about it – or do anything about it."

"That ain't so convincing," Milner commented sourly.

"All right, but that's just the beginning. An organism might escape into a lab but even if it did, it would still be relatively confined. We can't see how it could have got out into the environment."

"Unless the whole building blew up."

"Exactly. And if that had happened you'd have heard about it, wouldn't you?"

"Point taken."

"So we don't think this happened in a research establishment. It could have been some sort of production plant, maybe just on a pilot scale, but making sufficient quantities that an escape would be significant."

"Okay, I buy that."

Terry took up the argument. "The point is, if this is a production facility, it must have been a company making the stuff, right?"

"Right."

"Now genetic engineering is an extremely competitive industry. Any outfit that's got as far as producing even pilot quantities of a new organism is going to be anxious to protect its intellectual property."

"By taking out a patent, you mean?"

"Precisely. Which means that we should be checking for new patents and trademarks for inventions with the words 'nitrogen' or 'ammonia' in them, taken out by companies on the Eastern seaboard between about two-and-a-half and four years ago. We only need summaries at the moment. We can go into more detail if we find a few good candidates."

Milner's expression had lightened a little. "I wonder, how many would a trawl like that pick up? You think of all the industry along the East coast, it's still a long job."

"True. Fortunately we can narrow the search further. Let me show you."

Terry opened his brief case and took out the lap top. Milner waited in silence while Terry booted it up, inserted the NASA data disk and ran the program.

"Right – this is NASA data from an Earth surveillance satellite. We'll start with a conventional view in the visible spectrum: this coastline," he pointed, "is the Eastern seaboard. Now I'll switch to a different form of imaging. The colour is false; it just shows you the level of ammonia. Purple is the lowest, but that's still a good deal higher than normal. Blue is higher, and green higher still. You see how this purple area spreads up and down the coast and out to the east? This was the distribution about two-and-a-half years ago. If I go back one month," he tapped a key and the two purple branches shrank somewhat. He tapped again, and the branches retracted into an irregular purple patch, in the centre of which blue and green rings had developed, giving it a target-like appearance. "One more month," he tapped again, "and there's nothing. That's how we know when the problem first arose, and roughly where."

Milner's eyes were riveted to the screen. He switched his gaze to Terry. "Can you do that in smaller steps? Then we could get a real tight fix on where it started."

Terry nodded. "I had the same thought. This software's been set up to provide snapshots at one-month intervals. If we're trying to locate the source that's too coarse; I need to set it up for time intervals less than one month. I think the data's in there, but I need a little time to access it."

Milner nodded. "Look, see what you can do about that. Meantime we have a guy at HQ who specializes in company matters, patents, that kind of thing. I'm gonna to see if I can get him onto this."

"On a Sunday?" said Maggie.

Milner smirked. "This guy's always working." He got up. "Don't go walkies, it isn't that safe round here. And on no account let anyone in. I'll send a car or come back for you myself in a couple of hours. There's coffee-making stuff in the kitchen next door, and if you look in the jar you might find some cookies, though I can't promise they'll be any good. Okay?"

"Thanks, Mr. Milner."

"It's Sam. See you later."

Maggie turned to Terry as soon as they heard the outside door close.

"Do I detect a softening of attitude?"

"He's all right. I think he was just a bit overwhelmed by what his boss dumped on him. We've shown him it isn't impossible." He turned to his laptop. "Let's see if I can access that data."

An hour later Maggie popped out and came back a with assorted biscuits and two cups of coffee.

Terry was frowning and typing in quick bursts.

"How are you getting on?"

He crunched into a biscuit. "I think I've got it now. We'll see in a moment."

His jaw froze in mid-chew and they looked at each other. Each of them had heard it: the rattle of a key in the front door. They sat motionless, listening to the sound of footsteps, then low voices in the corridor.

The door opened, and Terry breathed out. It was Milner, back much sooner than they'd expected. With him was another man, of similar height but younger and more slightly built. His eyes were bright and alert behind steel-rimmed glasses. Milner made the introductions.

"This here is Clive Waxman, our companies expert. We started to talk it over and he thought it'd be best if the three of you could interact on this right away. Clive, these are the operatives from England, Maggie Ferris and Terry McKinley."

Waxman gave each of them a light but firm handshake.

"Well," Terry said. "You've come at a good time. I think I can access that data now."

Milner said, "No kidding. Let's take a look."

They all gathered around the small screen and Terry explained the display again for Clive's benefit.

"This was the distribution two-and-a-half years ago. Now, if I've got this right we can go back one day at a time."

He tapped a key and the two purple branches began to contract, then coalesced, forming the purple, blue, and green patch they'd seen before. He continued to tap. The green disappeared, then the blue. All the time the coloured patch was shrinking, until it was reduced to a single purple spot, which moved slightly inland then disappeared. He brought it back and alternated between conventional and ammonia views again.

"There's a large inlet there. Anyone recognize it?"

Milner said, "Can you make it any bigger?"

"Sure. There you are. Enough?"

"Chesapeake Bay, isn't it, Clive?"

"Yup."

Milner straightened up. "Is that smart, or what?" He pinched his bottom lip. "But we got rivers going off every which way from the Bay, and shitloads of industry. What do you think, Clive? Can you run a patent search on companies in that area?"

"I can try. I'll need to access a couple of databases. You stay here; I can use one of the other machines."

As Waxman left the room, Milner turned to Terry.

"Clive's real laid back, but show him a company that's not behaving itself and he sinks his teeth into it like a bulldog. Any chance you could make those intervals smaller still?"

Terry shook his head. "No, with this type of satellite you'd only get a scan at that wavelength once a day."

"Blow it up a bit more."

"I can try, but I think we're going to lose resolution, especially on the ammonia view."

They were staring at the pixelated images as Waxman reappeared.

They all looked at him expectantly.

Waxman shook his head. "Nothing."

Milner's face fell. "What, nothing at all?"

"Nope, not a thing."

CHAPTER 37

Terry rubbed the back of his neck. "I don't get it. Where did we go wrong?"

"Let me think about this," Clive replied. He walked over to the corner of the room and stood there with his hands in his pockets and his head bowed. The others waited in silence, anxious not to disturb his concentration. After two or three minutes he turned back to them.

"Suppose this production facility, or whatever, was a subsidiary of a larger company. The patent would be registered to the parent company's headquarters. That wouldn't necessarily be in the Chesapeake area."

Terry closed his eyes. "Of course, I hadn't thought of that. I suppose that makes a complete nonsense of my approach."

"I wouldn't say that. In a way it gives us another clue. It means we're looking for a company with reasonable market capitalization, so I can operate a cut-off to exclude smaller outfits. Then we can eliminate a lot more companies by product line. A factory that makes metal boxes isn't going to be engaged in genetic engineering. What sort of companies are we looking for? Biologicals, obviously. Chemicals?"

"Yes," Terry said.

"Pharmaceuticals?"

"It's a possibility."

"Any others?"

"I can't think of any," Terry said. "Maggie?"

"Well, the production facility could be a company spin-off from a university. In that case the university may hold the patent."

Clive nodded. "Okay, we'll include local universities. The people who staff these spin-offs usually remain on the faculty of the parent university, so we don't need to consider anything outside the immediate area." He looked from one to the other. "Now, is there anything else we should be considering that would narrow the focus?"

Maggie said, "It has to be close to the sea or a river."

Milner cut in. "I don't see why. Someone could just pick up a flask of this stuff, drive to a river, and tip it in."

Waxman said, "I can't search on proximity to water anyway, so that doesn't matter. All right, then. We're looking for one of two things. On the one hand it could be a company of reasonable size that makes biologicals, chemicals, or pharmaceuticals, and has a subsidiary in the Chesapeake

Bay area. On the other hand it could be a university with a spin-off company in the same area. In either case the organization holds a patent, key words 'nitrogen' or 'ammonia', taken out in the last four years, but not the last two. I'll go and run it."

When he'd left the room Terry said:

"He's good."

"You better believe it. I don't know why he works for the FBI. He could probably make a ton playing the stock market."

"Maybe he just wants to defend liberty, freedom, and the American way of life," Terry said lightly.

"Oh yeah. We're all in it for that."

Milner pointed to the desk top computer. "I'm going to use that for a moment. Sorry, but I'll have to ask you to stand over there. This is a highly classified site."

Terry moved where he couldn't see the screen, and Milner busied himself at the computer for a few minutes. Then he hit a key with an air of finality and looked up at them.

"Okay, I just checked the Department of Homeland Security for explosions or terrorist incidents in the Chesapeake Bay area at that time. *Nada*. It's beginning to look like a straightforward industrial accident. It wasn't reported because they don't want their rivals in the industry to find out they've had a problem, or because they don't want their shareholders to know, or because they're too goddamned scared of what this thing will do now it's out."

Clive Waxman returned, carrying a sheaf of papers.

"Okay, people," he said. "Here it is. During that period no university in the area took out a patent with those keywords. But I got nineteen candidate companies. I thought we could start by seeing what the patents are about. Maybe we can eliminate some of them straight away. I've printed out the full texts. This is a job for you guys."

Waxman placed the papers in front of Terry and Maggie, who immediately divided the pile in two and started to go through them. Milner beckoned to Waxman and they had a quiet word by the window while the others were at work.

Each patent was headed "US Patent and Trademark Office". This was followed by a number, a date, and the name of the applicant or applicants. Below that was a title and an abstract, followed by addresses and the detailed specification. Waxman had stapled together the pages of individual applications. They worked rapidly, setting each application aside as they eliminated it.

"A lot of these are totally irrelevant," Maggie whispered.

"I know. You only have to look at the abstract in most cases."

Terry finished first. There were no papers left in front of him. Maggie noticed and passed him a couple of hers. She seemed to be reading one in more detail. She finished and they compared notes.

"I didn't find anything," said Terry.

"Nor did I. Let's ask Clive over. Clive?"

Waxman broke off his conversation, came over, and sat down with them. Milner remained at the window, peering out between the louvres of the plastic blind.

"You found something?"

"No, nothing," Maggie replied. She drew one of the patents over. "This one was the closest to what we're looking for. It describes an expression cassette containing the gene for an oral form of insulin, for insertion into *E. coli*." She added, for Clive's benefit. "That's a bacterium."

"I've heard of it. Doesn't it cause food poisoning?"

"Certain strains do but the usual form is a normal part of our gut flora. It's become one of the basic tools of molecular biology. You can modify it in such a way that it can't survive outside the lab; then it's quite safe. The thing is, I'm not used to patent specifications, so I just wasn't expecting this amount of detail. There are pages of it. And it ends up with a complete nucleotide sequence for the DNA construct and the primers, everything."

"What are you saying?"

"Well, if for any reason a company wanted to keep a discovery like this quiet they wouldn't publish a complete specification like this, would they? I mean, with the right sort of setup anyone could make it. I suppose a rival could do it in such a way as not to infringe the patent. Or maybe they simply wouldn't bother, especially if they were in a country where the patent wasn't valid."

Terry looked at her. "You think we may be barking up the wrong tree?"

"We could be. Maybe this company relies on secrecy. They didn't reveal that they were working on this organism in the first place. When there was a serious escape they could easily cover that up too, because nobody even knew it existed."

"Well, if there's no patent on the organism," Terry said, "we're back at square one. We've ruled out university spin-offs, but aside from that all we can say is that it's a company that makes biologicals, pharmaceuticals or chemicals. It could be big or small."

Waxman thought for a moment. "No, it has to be a large company."

"Why?"

"Look, research and development takes a lot of money. It's unusual, but only a large company would be in a position to make that sort of investment in a product that wasn't protected by a patent. A young company would have to be launched with venture capital; the backers would certainly insist that they patented anything they had, so as to safeguard their investment."

Terry nodded. "That makes sense, I suppose. But if we don't have a patent how do we find out who's making the organism?"

"There must be a limited number of the right sort of companies with a subsidiary in the Chesapeake Bay area," Waxman replied. "In fact our trawl only came up with these. Let me have a look at that patent. At least it's in the right line of country."

Maggie pushed the stapled set of sheets over to Waxman. He picked it up, glanced down the first page, then replaced it on the desk and pointed.

"These names are the individuals who are making the application; they're the inventors. The first address is the patent agent who drew it all up and handled the correspondence; in this case it's an agency: Otis, Digby and Preiss. This address here is the assignee, the company that owns the patent: Vance Pharmaceuticals, of Lexington, Massachusetts. I think it's time I did some digging. I should have something by tomorrow. Can we meet up here again in the morning?"

Terry looked at Milner, who was still standing at the window but had clearly been following the entire conversation. He turned and nodded.

"Sure thing," he said. "We'll drop these two off at their hotel now and then go back to HQ."

Fifteen minutes later Milner pulled up at the hotel entrance and Maggie and Terry got out. He lowered his window.

"I'll pick the pair of you up here tomorrow morning, oh-nine-hundred sharp. I won't go in this time. Just come straight out when you see the car."

They said "Thanks, Sam," but the car was already on the move with the window rolling up.

CHAPTER 38

Next morning they gathered around the same table, in the same faintly petrol-smelling, minimally furnished room.

"Vance Pharmaceuticals," Clive Waxman announced, using his fingertips to align the edges of the small stack of sheets he'd placed in front of him. "You may have heard of them – they're one of our bigger pharmas. They have subsidiaries overseas and they have various manufacturing and research facilities here in the States – including the one in the Chesapeake Bay area. That facility's called Genon, and it's not far from Richmond, Virginia. It might interest you to know that it's also close to a river."

Terry and Maggie exchanged glances.

"Now," Clive continued, "how do big pharmas like Vance keep abreast of new technologies like genetic engineering? They buy in the expertise they need by taking over companies that already have it. Seven years back, they swallowed up a company called AB Genetics. Among other things, AB Genetics held a patent for this oral insulin thing. Obviously that's now been reassigned to Vance. Whether Vance is making the actual product down in Richmond, I wouldn't know."

Maggie shrugged. "It doesn't really matter, does it? That isn't the organism we're looking for."

"I know, but there's more. Over the next few years Vance made a series of smaller acquisitions. I had a quick look at each of them and most are irrelevant but there's just one that could be interesting. Exactly four years ago they took over a small company called Biomolecular Technologies, based in Texas."

"Four years ago," Maggie said slowly. "And the organism got out about eighteen months later."

"We talked about that, didn't we, Clive?" Milner said. "The timing fits. If Vance acquired the organism as a result of the takeover, they could have been in production with it at the time it escaped."

Terry asked, "This company they took over – what was it called again?"

"Biomolecular Technologies."

"Yes, did it have any patents?"

"Sure, that's the next question to ask. It wouldn't have come up in our original search because I restricted that to the Chesapeake Bay area and these guys were in Texas. I looked them up. Biomolecular Technologies had only been around for a couple of years when they were taken over. At that time they held two patents. Neither one had anything to do with nitrogen or ammonia. I've got them here."

He separated some of the sheets and passed them over to Maggie. They waited quietly while she perused them.

"No, you're right," she said, straightening up. "They're interesting, and they are in the right sort of area, but they're not the organism."

"But if they did have the organism, wouldn't they have patented that, too?" Terry asked.

"You'd have thought so," Waxman replied, "but they may not have been ready yet. A patent like that takes a lot of working up – you've seen the sort of thing that's required. This is our only good lead so far so I thought it was worth a closer look."

"What did you find out?" Maggie asked.

"Basically it was a start-up company, but it wasn't a university spin-off. The two prime movers were listed as a guy called Rod Hillman and another guy called Zak Gould. Hillman had an MBA, he was the CEO, and he seems to have run the business side. Gould had a PhD and he was designated the Research Director. In terms of intellectual property they probably patented the two main discoveries they had at the time they were launched. They never registered a trademark so I'm assuming they weren't ready to go to market. There certainly wasn't any money rolling in – that's confirmed by the accounts: the only revenues were the payments from their backers. Plenty of outgoings, though. There's no doubt they were in financial trouble. Vance paid next to nothing for them, in company terms."

"Impressive," Terry said. "I don't know how you come by this sort of information so quickly."

He shrugged. "You just have to know where to look. I've done some work for the SEC – that's the United States Securities and Exchange Commission. You'd be amazed at the creative accounting some of the big companies get up to, spreading losses around to hide them from shareholders, giving directors back-dated options, all that sort of thing. I've investigated outfits a lot more complicated than this."

There was a short silence then Milner spoke:

"Well, it fits pretty well with what we know about when and where this organism got out. I think it's worth following up."

"It sounds like the Research Director would be the best person to talk to," Maggie said. "Do you think the staff of Biomolecular Technologies were absorbed into the bigger company?"

"Possibly," Waxman replied, "but you can't rely on it. We're inclined to go for this Hillman guy. As CEO he would know what deal was struck and who went where."

"Can we find him?"

Milner nodded. "We think so. We have Social Security numbers, Driver's Licence details, and last known address for both Rod Hillman and Zak Gould. Hillman has moved to Boston. I'll get in touch with the Boston police this morning – we have to work together on this, otherwise they get touchy. We could pull him in and interview him at the local station but he'd probably clam up. Better if we treat him as a potential witness and interview him at his home. We can fly up this afternoon."

"Can we come too?" Maggie asked.

"That's what I meant by 'we'. Clive will be staying in Washington; we can contact him if we need more information. Once we've found this Hillman guy we'll know for sure whether or not we're on the right track."

"At last it feels like we're making some progress," said Maggie later as they sat in the hotel bar awaiting their taxi to the airport.

"Agreed," Terry responded. "Let's just hope this Hillman guy can give us some clues about the organism. Something we can use."

His phone buzzed across the table. He picked it up and looked at the caller ID.

"It's John Gilchrist, I asked him to keep me updated on the ammonia levels." He clicked open the phone.

"John? Hi, how's it going?"

Terry listened, his brow furrowing. After a few minutes he said goodbye and clicked the phone shut. He sat there quietly for a few moments.

"Well?" said Maggie. "What's going on?"

He grimaced. "Latest measurements just came in. We're at seventy-three per cent of threshold."

CHAPTER 39

A car met them at Boston's Logan Airport and they drove straight to police headquarters. Milner spent some time in the Chief's office while Terry and Maggie waited by a row of mismatched filing cabinets and other clutter in the corridor outside. He winked at them when he emerged but said nothing until they were standing outside the station.

"All fixed. Our hotel's on Tremont Street. We'll check in there first then a couple of uniforms will pick us up in 30 minutes. Okay?"

"Fine, no time to lose," said Maggie.

"How did you explain us?" asked Terry.

"No need – he wouldn't be expecting me to work on my own. I told him all we needed was information. When we get to the house he wants an officer up front. Then if the guy's cooperative, we go in."

"And if he isn't cooperative...?"

Milner gave a sardonic smile. "Off the record? We go in anyway."

The patrol sergeant who called for them was driving a van-like eight-seater from the car pool. He had his partner in the front; Milner was alone in the middle seats; Terry and Maggie sat in the back. They drove to Belmont, a suburb west of Boston, and down a street lined with chestnut trees.

The houses here were mansions, individually designed to a general plantation theme, each with a wooden veranda. Terry thought the gardens and the spaces between the houses were surprisingly small for the type of neighbourhood. Some of the properties were beautifully maintained, their lines softened by trees and shrubs. The one they stopped at was, by comparison, neglected; the garden was overgrown and the pale blue paint on the verandah was peeling.

The sergeant said "Wait here" and got out.

Terry watched him go up the path. He was overweight. This, together with the ironmongery he carried on his belt, enforced a sort of swagger, arms carried wide like a Western gunslinger. The effect was heightened by the way he unsnapped his holster before he rang the bell. They saw the front door open and there was a brief conversation. Then the sergeant came to the rail of the verandah and beckoned to them.

Milner whispered, "Okay, come on."

Milner strode up the path ahead of them and the wooden steps of the verandah creaked under his weight. By the time they'd joined him he was already introducing himself.

"Mr. Hillman?" he asked.

"Yes."

"My name's Sam Milner. I'm with the FBI."

He flashed the FBI shield. Hillman barely gave it a glance. He turned and led them to a sitting room. The policeman remained standing at the door, evidently prepared to stop anyone coming in – or out.

Rod Hillman was younger than Terry expected, in his early thirties, so far as he could judge. He looked like someone who led a sedentary life: his skin was pallid, and although he was slight the short-sleeved shirt was already smooth and taut around his abdomen. The blue trousers clearly belonged to a suit – he'd probably stripped off his jacket and tie when he returned from work. He indicated the chairs and smoothed his hair back with the palms of his hands. It was a brief, nervous gesture, but then he was entitled to feel nervous, Terry thought, with a policeman, a large FBI man, and two strangers descending on him.

Milner took in the spacious room with its high ceiling.

"Nice house," he said.

He may have intended the remark to sound conversational but it had the opposite effect, heightening the tension.

"Yes," Hillman replied. "Look, I don't know what this is about but I hope it's not going to take long. I have some guests arriving soon for dinner."

Milner smiled patiently as he sat down.

"Please relax, Mr. Hillman," he said in a tired drawl. "I want to be quite clear you're not under investigation here. We're simply making some routine enquiries into the business dealings of a large company, Vance Pharmaceuticals. We'd like to ask you a few questions about your own contacts with them. Oh, by the way, these are my associates from London; they're shadowing me on this case. I hope you don't mind."

Hillman glanced in their direction but Milner's tone had left him little choice.

He returned to Milner. "Okay. What do you want to know?"

"Well, let's see. Maybe you could tell me something about Biomolecular Technologies. You know, how you got started, that kind of thing?"

Hillman shrugged. "I was working for a management consultancy at the time. They sent me along to speak at Texas South-Western. The university was keen on technology transfer. I gave a seminar on protection of intellectual property. While I was there I met this guy, Zak Gould. We got on well. He had a lot of ideas and I thought some of them could be patented. We arranged to meet again. I was thinking of leaving the company anyway and I thought we could partner each other in a start-up."

"Presumably the university would have preferred to keep an interest."

"I didn't want that sort of deal. I looked at the intellectual property issues with Zak. He's the sort of guy who likes to do several things at once. In my view he wasn't under any legal obligation – not for the stuff that interested me. He resigned from the Faculty and I raised some venture capital. That's how we got started."

"And did it work out?"

"Frankly, no. I worked my butt off to raise money and he enjoyed himself in the lab."

"He was idle?"

"Oh no, I'm not saying that. He put in the hours, all right, but he never seemed to finish anything. He'd do a bit of this and a bit of that, and then he'd have a new idea, and he'd get all excited about that for a while, and so it went on. My backers were getting impatient. They wanted results. When I tried to tell him he'd just say 'You can't conduct research to order'. It costs plenty to run a lab. We were getting in deep but he didn't seem to care. I was the one losing sleep."

"How did you come into contact with Vance?"

"Yeah, Vance. I guess we'd been running for a couple of years by then. I was at a conference. As usual I was on the look-out for another investor. I met this big honcho, Warren Signett – CEO at Vance. I didn't think he'd talk to me but we ended up having a coffee together. He struck me as the sort of guy who knew how to make decisions. When we finished he said he didn't want to put money into the company but he might be interested in taking it over. You don't know how happy I was to hear him say that. We were really stretched by then."

"So you struck a deal?"

"Yeah. A cash payment for each of us, technically for the value of the company, even though it wasn't worth zilch. They paid off our debts, too – that was the best part. It was a good deal for us, small change for an outfit that size."

"What was their interest – do you know?"

"Seems they were expanding in the molecular genetics area. Zak had the right sort of qualifications to lead one of their teams so they took him onto their payroll too. We had a postdoc and a few research assistants but Vance wasn't interested so we had to let them go."

"And did you stay in touch with Zak, I mean, Dr. Gould?"

"No, I haven't spoken to him since the company was broken up."

Milner raised his eyebrows.

Hillman registered the look and added, "Zak was pissed off about the terms of the deal. He said I screwed him. I didn't, of course. He ended up in a job and I didn't, so I was entitled to a bigger pay-out. In any case I'd arranged all the financing, all the servicing of debts – it was a major headache, I can tell you. All he did was muck around in the lab, doing his thing."

"May I, Mr. Milner?"

Milner looked round at Maggie and said, "Sure, go ahead," but he looked wary.

"I just wondered – did 'doing his thing' happen to include work on an ammonia producing organism?" she asked.

She'd slipped the question in beautifully. Terry held his breath, waiting.

Hillman frowned.

"Oh, that. Yeah, it was one of his pet projects. Funnily enough Warren Signett was interested in it, too – in fact I'd say it swung the deal."

Somehow Maggie managed to maintain the casual tone.

"Can you tell us anything about it?" she asked lightly.

"Not much. It was a sideline of his; something about fertilizing the soil by fixing nitrogen from the air."

The answer dropped into the room like a grenade. For a moment or two no one spoke.

Maggie's eyes flicked to Terry. He understood. Nitrogen fixing. *Of course.*

Maggie continued breathlessly, "you don't know how he made it."

"Hell, no. I wouldn't have understood even if he'd explained it to me. He hadn't patented it or anything but Signett didn't mind – he said they could always do that later. Say, why is everyone so interested in that project?"

"No reason," Maggie replied, with a small movement of her shoulders. "Just a personal thing."

Terry saw Milner give her an approving smile, which he extinguished before turning back to Hillman.

"As far as you're concerned, everything Vance did was above board?"

"Oh, sure. They employ an army of lawyers. I couldn't fault the paperwork."

"So you completed the deal, took the money and came to Boston?"

"Yeah. I rent an office in town. I have contacts with a lot of high-tech companies around here and I do a bit of work for them. Free-lancing is okay but if the opportunity came along I wouldn't mind starting up another company. I've got a lot more experience now. If I did it again I'd know what mistakes not to make."

"Well, I think that's all we need right now," Milner said, and placed his hands on the armrests of the chair as if he were about to get up. "Say, would you happen to have a current contact address or cell phone for Dr. Gould?"

"I can give you the last contact details I had. I wouldn't know if they're current or not."

"That'd be just fine."

They waited. Hillman returned with a sheet of paper, on which he'd scribbled the address and number. Milner took it into his big hand. He gave it a glance and looked up.

"Did Dr. Gould have any family?" he asked.

Hillman shook his head. "Not that I know of. He never mentioned it."

"Friends?"

"I doubt it. Zak was always too buried in his work to have a social life."

Milner nodded and smiled. "Well, thanks very much for your time, Mr. Hillman, you've been very helpful. We apologize again for the intrusion."

"No problem. I'll see you out."

As they got to their feet Milner said, "by the way, there's no need for this conversation to go any further than this room. We're investigating unsubstantiated claims and Vance's lawyers could get real sticky if they thought we were casting doubt on the company's reputation. We wouldn't want that to happen, would we?"

"Hell no," Hillman said.

They filed out of the front door and again murmured their thanks. The cop gave Hillman a nod and followed them down the path.

The sergeant shuffled himself behind the wheel and they set off on the return journey to police HQ. Milner, again sitting on the middle bench, turned round to Terry and Maggie.

"That went well." He drew out the sheet of paper that Hillman had given him, punched the number into his cell phone, listened for a moment, then clicked off. "Like I thought. No such number."

Terry leaned forward. "Are you saying Hillman pulled a fast one?"

"Nah. It was four years ago. The guy has probably changed his phone provider and moved house a couple of times since then." He leaned forward and lowered his voice so the two cops in the front couldn't hear.

"I'll call Clive when we get back and tell him what went down with Hillman. I want him to move on Genon, that Vance production facility near Richmond. We need to know what happened there about two-and-a-half years ago. There should be an accident report. If there isn't, I want to know why."

"We need to find this Zak Gould, too," Terry said, also keeping his voice low.

"That's right," Maggie added. "He's the one who could tell us what went into that organism. That's our top priority."

"Sure. We'll track him down."

"But you said he'd probably moved."

"Yeah, I shouldn't think he's at the address Hillman gave us. The address we got from the Social Security database may not be up to date either. I figure the easiest route is to go straight to Vance Pharmaceuticals. We'll take a cab there in the morning. No need to bother the local cops about it; they already know we're operating in their territory."

"You don't want to take one of them with, then?" Terry asked.

"I could request it, but I won't. These people are usually short-staffed – at least they say they are. It was handy to have them along for the Hillman interview but I'd sooner not have the uniforms around on this one. If we can set it up I want to get a look at this CEO."

"Warren Signett," Terry supplied.

"Yeah, Warren Signett."

CHAPTER 40

The reception area at Vance Pharmaceuticals was plainly furnished and brightly lit. Apart from the reception desk itself there were two sofas, a modern painting and a couple of tall, potted plants, probably artificial. After registering their presence at the desk they went over to one of the sofas to wait. The floor was covered with some sort of plastic composite, and the acoustically tiled ceiling did little to deaden either the footsteps of people passing through or the voices of the security staff at the desk. Presently a frail looking woman in her forties appeared and came over to them.

"Mr. Milner?" she said.

Milner stood up.

"I'm Rose Fitzgerald, Mr. Signett's Personal Assistant," she said. "Mr. Signett can see you now. I'll take you up."

Seconds later they emerged from the elevator and followed the PA through a pair of swing doors into an open area. Terry glanced around. One wall was lined with filing cabinets. Opposite was a desk with a computer monitor and a small vase of flowers. Several chairs were lined up under the window. This evidently served as a waiting area as well as her office. The PA continued without a pause down a short corridor, knocked lightly on the first door, and showed them in.

They entered a large, thickly carpeted office. A massive leather-topped desk and a well-stocked bookshelf were the sole indications that this was a place where business was conducted. Warren Signett stood in the middle of the room, his hands clasped casually in front of him. He was tall and slim, his lean features clean-shaven and unlined, his dark hair only beginning to be flecked with grey. He unclasped his hands to tug gently at a shirt cuff but there was no nervousness in the gesture. Rather he exuded the relaxed air of a man at the pinnacle of his career, a man of position and influence, a man in control of a vast business empire, who was prepared to set all that aside to grant a brief audience to unexpected callers.

Milner shook hands and introduced Terry and Maggie as his associates. Signett inclined his head and gestured towards armchairs grouped around a low rosewood table.

As Terry sat down his eyes were drawn to the adjacent picture window, which extended from floor to ceiling and afforded a panoramic, if not particularly scenic, sixth-floor view of the sprawling complex of buildings that was the headquarters of Vance Pharmaceuticals. He turned and saw both Maggie and Milner staring too, both as impressed as he was.

Signett remained standing. He was clearly used to this reaction.

"The company started on this site thirty years ago," he said. "Research and Development, Production, Administration – everything was here. As business expanded, production was shifted elsewhere, mainly to our facilities overseas."

Terry thought he came close to making it sound unrehearsed, although he must have explained the vista below on countless occasions.

"All of our research is still conducted here," he continued. "The older buildings down there have been refurbished throughout to provide modern laboratory accommodation. There's still a lot of pressure on space so we've added new research blocks. The ones you can see just below were completed last year. The administration has been gathered into this tower."

He took a seat and they returned their attention to the room. His PA was waiting expectantly.

Signett said to the group, "Can I offer you anything? Coffee, tea...?"

Milner said, "Nothing for me, thanks." Terry and Maggie shook their heads.

Signett said, "All right, thank you, Rose."

The PA nodded and withdrew. Signett gave his silk pocket handkerchief a light tweak and Terry noticed a thick gold ring on the little finger of his right hand. It was set with what looked like a jade stone, carved in some sort of design.

"Now, gentlemen – sorry, lady and gentlemen – what can I do for you?"

Milner responded.

"First off, thanks for seeing us at short notice, Mr. Signett." The drawl was back, and so was the bored expression. "We're making a few inquiries about an employee of yours, a Dr. Zak Gould."

"Oh dear, has he done something wrong?"

"We don't exactly know until we talk to him."

"Ah. Well, Dr. Gould no longer works for us, Mr. Milner. Hasn't done for a couple of years or so."

"I see. Was there some sort of problem?"

"I barely recall. I seem to remember that we were very happy with his progress, then, without any warning, he failed to turn up for work. He didn't offer his resignation."

"Would you happen to know where he is at this moment?"

"No, but you could have a word with our Director of Human Resources, Cindy Westfield; she probably has the last address. I can have my PA take you down there. Anything else I can help you with?"

"Dr. Gould came to you after the takeover of Biomolecular Technologies – is that right?"

"Ah yes, that's right. It was part of the arrangement we made with them. It was a good opportunity to strengthen our research team in that area."

"What about their product lines, did you take those on too?"

"They had a couple of patents, which they transferred to us as part of the deal. But this was very much a blue skies outfit, Mr. Milner. You've clearly done your homework so you'll know we didn't pay much for them: just enough to clear their debts and give the principals a little pocket money. That was because there was so little immediate value in what they had. I must confess, though, that I was impressed with Dr. Gould. I thought that in our more enabling environment he would come up with some interesting lines. Unfortunately, as I've indicated, he turned out to be somewhat unreliable."

"That kind of leaves me wondering why you bothered to take over the company, sir. I mean, if you wanted a guy like Dr. Gould for your staff you could have headhunted him; you didn't have to take all the company baggage as well. To someone like me it seems you didn't get a whole lot for your money."

"Well at the time there was another line they had that did interest me. They hadn't patented it yet. It had to do with nitrogen fixation. But after due consideration we decided not to pursue it. We couldn't really justify the effort and it wasn't a good fit with our existing range of products."

"I see. Could I ask you about Genon?"

"Our facility in Virginia? Yes, what about it?"

"Can you tell me what you make there?"

"Certainly. It's producing human insulin, by a genetic engineering route. That came out of our takeover of AB Genetics, a much more substantial acquisition, and a potentially very profitable one. The insulin it produces is not animal-derived and it can be taken by mouth instead of by injection. I think you can envisage the size of the potential market. We're already breaking even on that one."

"Anything else being produced down there?"

"No. We're devoting the entire capacity to producing insulin."

"Okay. Well, thanks again, Mr. Signett. Perhaps we could talk to your Human Resources person now?"

"Certainly. I'll ask Rose to take you down there right away."

As they reached the door, Signett added:

"Oh, Mr. Milner, if you should discover Dr. Gould's whereabouts, we'd be grateful if you could let us know. There may have been some procedures that were never gone through when he left his employment. We like to do things by the book."

"You and me both, Mr. Signett. You and me both."

Cindy Westfield stood up behind her desk. She was a big woman with dyed blond hair. Her white shirt was heavily full, and the small indentation managed by the waistband of her navy trousers served mainly to emphasize the swell of her hips below it. Her broad, smooth features collected into an attentive expression as Milner told her who he was and what he wanted.

"Dr. Gould? Oh, I remember that one all right – must have been two years ago, maybe a little more. He stopped coming in, just like that. We thought maybe he was ill so we tried to reach him but we couldn't. He didn't respond to email or snail mail and the number for his cell phone didn't work. In the end he was in breach of contract so we had to take him off the payroll. I don't know if he ever got another job; after the way he left, no one here would have given him a good reference." She sniffed. "Pity, really – I gather he was a smart guy."

"I'd sure like to have some more background on him," Milner persisted. "His CV, last address, that sort of thing."

"I can give you a copy of the details we kept on file – for what that's worth."

"Thank you."

She pressed a buzzer. "Belinda, could you print out a copy of Dr. Zak Gould's employment file and bring it in here for me? It'll be under past employees. Yeah, you might as well print the lot, there won't be much. Thanks."

As they waited, Milner said:

"Can I ask you, ma'am, does it bother you that the paperwork on him is incomplete?"

"Not really. It's more his problem than ours."

"Did anyone think of notifying the police – you know, asking them to treat it as a missing person inquiry?"

"Well, no. Goodness me, do you think something could have happened to him? Gee, I hope not."

"You didn't contact the police, then, or send someone round to his home?"

"Oh, no, nothing like that. You know, we have to draw a line when it comes to interfering in people's private lives. He may have had some personal reason for leaving. We'd have tried to help, but only if he asked us. If he didn't, we wouldn't push it."

Terry bent forward and said quietly to Milner, "Sam, could I have a word?"

"Sure. Please excuse us a moment, Ms. Westfield."

Maggie remained seated as Terry went over to the corner of the room with Milner. There was a rapid exchange, then they returned.

"What we're wondering, Ms. Westfield, is if you could let us have a list of staff who've left the company in the last four years."

Cindy Westfield pursed scarlet lips. "Four years is a long time, Mr. Milner. Our staff turnover's probably less than the industry average, but this is a large organization. That could amount to a whole lot of people."

"I'm not talking about the shop floor; I'm talking about people of Dr. Gould's status in the company and above."

"All right, that's better. I can do a cut-off by salary. Do you just want a list, or do you want more than that?"

The question was directed at Terry. He replied:

"Just the minimum: name, contact details, position in the company, and date of departure."

A flicker of curiosity crossed her face, and Terry saw that she'd picked up on his English accent. For a moment he thought she was going to say something but instead she gave him a quick, nervous smile and started to tap at the keyboard on the desk. Soon they heard a whirring, and a series of sheets spewed from a printer on a side table.

Belinda came in with Zak Gould's papers. She was Westfield's equal for size.

"Thanks, Belinda," Westfield said. "Just leave them on the desk."

She went over to the printer, which had fallen silent, and picked up the sheaf of papers. She stacked them with Gould's papers and handed them to Milner.

"There y'are, Mr. Milner. Now, is there anything else?"

"Thanks very much, Ms. Westfield. You've been real helpful. We appreciate it."

He turned to the PA who had brought them down to Cindy Westfield's office, and who had been waiting in the background throughout the exchange.

"Well, thank you, ma'am. I guess we're all through here."

She inclined her head slightly.

"Very good, Mr. Milner," she said. "I'll show you out."

Terry's phone sounded as they were leaving the building. He glanced around him, then took it out of his pocket and put it to his ear.

"Terry? It's Chris."

"Oh, hi, Chris."

"Terry, John Gilchrist brought me the latest data on atmospheric ammonia. We're nearly at eighty-seven per cent! I can't believe it's got that high so quickly. How close are we to finding whoever made this thing?"

Terry responded quietly. "We're making progress. It was a scientist called Zak Gould. We're working with the FBI now to track him down."

"You've gotta find him fast, Terry. I had to show this data to the President and he nearly hit the roof."

"We're doing everything we can," Terry said. "I'll keep you posted."

He hung up and saw Milner eyeing him.

"People back in Washington," he said. "Reminding us the clock is ticking. As if we didn't already know."

CHAPTER 41

Terry sat on a sofa, trying to find his way around a copy of the *Boston Globe*. Maggie paced the room, paused to look out of the window, then paced some more. They'd arranged to meet Milner in the hotel restaurant for dinner, but it was still too early to go downstairs.

She sighed. "I hate to be out of the picture this long."

"Me too. Especially the way the levels are going up."

"And the president has to follow your suggestion to blow up the world," Maggie continued, with some bitterness in her voice.

"Maggie," he said in a pleading tone.

She stopped pacing and flopped onto the sofa next to him.

"I'm sorry, Terry. I know you were just doing what you think is right, but I have to say, sometimes I wish you'd never given them this idea. They might see it as too much of any easy out. Panic and take it too early." She sat up straight and looked into his eyes. "So many people will die, Terry. It can't be the only way. We need time to figure this out."

"Yes," he said quietly. "But time is just what we don't have. I wonder how the research teams are getting on without us. Maybe we could go back to Florida, at least for a few days."

The hotel lounge was almost empty. A television churned out a seemingly endless series of advertisements. Terry and Maggie settled into a couple of armchairs to wait.

Terry saw her eyes flick to the television and he turned to follow her gaze. The adverts had given way to a man reading the news:

"In Chicago, efforts are continuing to clean up the bodies of alewives, now rotting all along the shoreline."

There were blurry pictures of dark rocks covered with silvery masses. The camera panned to waves breaking against the rocks. The water was barely visible beneath undulating rafts of dead fish. The air was full of flies. She leaned towards him.

"What are alewives?"

"Small fish, a sort of freshwater herring, I think."

When she looked up again they were interviewing an irate householder.

"You seen it? You smelled what it's like? We livin' with that all day, ever' day. It ain't healthy. Why don' they get they asses down here and clean that

mess up?"

Then another interview, subtitled "Dr. Dexter Maden, biologist, University of Chicago".

"The problem's not just here in Chicago, Ted, there are tens of thousands washed up all along the shores of Lake Huron and Lake Michigan. Cleaning it all up is a major headache. The authorities have been overwhelmed."

"But this isn't a new problem, is it, Dexter?"

"No, the alewives do have seasonal die-offs, but this is bigger, much bigger. It looks like the extinction of an entire species."

"Now baseball. The Boston Red Sox..."

Maggie met Terry's eyes. "It's getting worse."

He shrugged. "May not be ammonia. You heard that biologist; could be a seasonal die-off."

"Who are you trying to convince, me or you?" She glanced towards the entrance to the lounge.

Milner came over and dropped into an armchair next to them. "Got a message for you, Terry," he said. "Just came through. FBI Headquarters asked me to pass it on. Some guy in London called Spencer Talbot. Is Spencer his first name or is it one of those English two-handled names?"

"Double-barrelled. What did he want?"

"He thinks your phone's switched off. Said the Home Secretary's expecting a report."

"Well he can go to hell. I've had it with these people. Say we're working in the field and we can't be contacted."

Maggie said, "Sam, any news from Clive?"

"He's putting his team together as we speak. The plan is to hit Genon early tomorrow morning."

"You didn't want to be with them when they go in?"

"Ah no, they know what to do."

Terry said, "We were thinking of flying back to Florida for a few days – in case we're needed by the research teams."

Sam grimaced. "I put in a request to the Bureau's Search Center, Kidnappings and Missing Persons. It'd be better if you two could stick around here, in case they locate this guy Zak Gould."

"I don't want to be at a loose end, Sam," Maggie said. "Couldn't we be following something up?"

"Maybe. What did you make of Signett?"

"I thought he was very smooth," said Maggie. "A bit too smooth."

"Yeah," said Milner. "And he told us Vance decided not to develop that nitrogen-fixing organism. That can't be true, can it? You said this organism escaped two-and-a-half years ago. It was in Vance's hands at that time so they can't have canned it."

Terry nodded. "He also told us all their research was concentrated in Lexington. If that was true what was the organism doing down in Richmond? Either they were doing research on it there or it had passed beyond the research stage into production. Either way the man has to be lying."

"But why?" asked Milner. "The guy's not a fool; he's CEO of a major company."

"He doesn't know how much we know," Maggie pointed out.

"Bothers me, all the same," Milner said. "If he thinks he can palm us off with stuff like that he must be pretty damned sure he's not going to get caught out."

"Sam," Terry said. "If they were working on the organism, maybe even producing it, why didn't we find a patent?"

Milner pursed his lips. "Could be they never took one out. Or it was taken out, but by another subsidiary, or in another country. I could ask Clive to do another search."

"Couldn't we do it?" Maggie said quickly. "Clive's busy preparing for tomorrow's raid. And he won't be able to filter the patents like we can."

"True. Terry, you have your laptop here?"

"Yes."

"Okay, I'll have him give you access to the databases you need. Some of that stuff is in the public domain, but he can probably do better than that. Meantime you've given me an idea. I'll see who I can get hold of at Otis, Digby and Preiss – you know, the agents who prepared the patent on that insulin thing. If they do all Vance's patent work this one may have passed through their hands. Look, I won't stay for dinner. We'll meet up tomorrow morning. There's a breakfast bar just a couple of doors up from the hotel. I'll see you there. Not too early, say eight-thirty – it'll give me a chance to talk to these patent guys first thing."

The air in the breakfast bar was warm and heavy with the odour of frying eggs, hash browns, and bacon. The only vacant table was close to a wall-mounted television, which added to the general noise of conversation, orders shouted from the counter to the kitchen, and the clatter of plates and cutlery. At least they wouldn't be overheard.

A waitress set down two glasses of iced water and they said they were waiting for someone before ordering. Maggie rotated the glass in front of her, which contained more ice than water. It left a widening ring on the laminated table top. Iced water was the last thing she felt like at breakfast.

Then Sam appeared at the entrance, spotted them and shuffled his chair up to the table.

"So," he said. "Anything new?"

They shook their heads. "Hit a blank everywhere." Terry said. "All we got was eye strain. What about the patent agency?"

"I couldn't push too hard, in case they started sounding the alarm with Signett. I just said the FBI was interested in a patent on a nitrogen-fixing organism, maybe pending, maybe from Vance Pharmaceuticals. The guy searched their files. Nothing."

He looked up. The waitress was standing next to him.

"You folks ready to order now?"

She took their orders and weaved her way back to the counter.

Milner's cell phone buzzed. He lifted it to his ear, listening while engaging Terry and Maggie with his eyes.

"It's Clive," he mouthed. Then, into the phone:

"Who have you got with you? Okay. Listen Clive, you know the form: it's not so important what they're manufacturing now, see if you can find out what was in production two-and-a-half years ago. Try and pull in some of the people from the shop floor who were around at that time… Great stuff… Okay… Thanks. Keep me posted."

He clicked off the phone and replaced it in the small holster on his belt.

"He's at Richmond, Virginia now with a bunch of agents. Everything's ready. He didn't let his guys in on the whole thing, just told them they were suspicious of the safety record of the facility. They'll give the place a thorough going-over."

The waitress returned with their breakfasts. Maggie winced at the pile of pancakes she placed in front of Milner.

"Maple syrup's on the table," she said. "Juice and toast?"

Maggie said, "Over here."

Terry was just having coffee.

"Anything else for you?"

They shook their heads.

"Okay, enjoy."

They unwrapped cutlery from paper napkins. The television above their heads hammered out the latest sports results.

"The urgent question now is, where is Zak Gould?" Maggie said.

Milner drizzled maple syrup onto the pancakes. "The Bureau hasn't got him listed as a missing person."

"What does that actually mean?" she asked.

"Means either the guy has gone to ground somewhere, or he's dead and no one's found the body."

"Dead?"

Milner shrugged. "Well, it's a possibility. Hillman said he didn't seem to have family or friends, so he could have died – or been killed – and no one called it in."

Maggie sighed. "Then we could be on a sodding wild goose chase."

"Won't know that until we find him – or what's left of him."

Terry said, "We may get something from the list of resignations."

"Oh, right. You know, I went along with it but why did you want that list?"

"Well, I was thinking: for a researcher like Zak Gould this was a plum job, in charge of his own lab in a major company. He'd only been in it for a year or two, so why did he leave without telling anyone? If something happened to upset him – enough to make him take off in a hurry – it may have done the same for other people. And they may be easier to trace."

"Or maybe Gould was just unstable, like Signett said," Maggie added.

"Maybe, but we already suspect Signett can be economical with the truth. It seems more likely there was a reason."

"Okay," Milner said. "I guess it was worth a shot. Did you take a look at the list?"

"Yes, we both did. There are about a dozen names on it. I guess that's not unusual for a company this size. We're not really interested in their internal problems except in relation to this case, so we thought the important thing was to focus on the period between the takeover of Biomolecular Technologies and the point at which the organism escaped."

"That makes sense," Milner mumbled with his mouth full. "How many did that leave?"

"Six. One was a straightforward retirement, and one was in packaging design. Take those out and you have four names. I wrote them down." He withdrew a piece of paper from the inside pocket of his jacket and put it on the table. "Here they are: Philip Swanson, Susan Armitage, Grant Challoner, and Joseph Avanti."

"Okay," Milner said. "We can follow up on those." He selected another pancake.

From the direction of the kitchen there was a loud crash, as if a tray had been dropped. The television blared: "*Coming up, the news headlines...*"

Milner thought for a moment. "There's something funny about this, that's for sure. Remember what Signett said as we were going out? Why was *he* so goddamned interested in catching up with Zak Gould? An employee who went AWOL two years ago? Doesn't sound like the sort of thing a CEO would normally lose sleep over. His Human Resources people weren't too bothered so why was he?"

Maggie said, "We're back to the reason why he left so suddenly, aren't we? What I was wondering was – "

Milner held up a hand. "Hold on – "

He was looking at the television.

"*A police spokesman said the body had now been formally identified as that of Dr. Grant Challoner. Dr. Challoner was an expert on environmental issues and had acted as a consultant to both government departments and industry. Now over to Gordon Jamieson at the Weather Bureau...*"

Terry looked at Maggie and then down at the piece of paper on the table in front of him. Milner reached out two fingers and twisted it towards him. He pushed the plate of unfinished pancakes away from him and stood up.

"Come on, you guys. We got work to do."

CHAPTER 42

Terry grunted his approval as the police sedan stopped at one of the road blocks that had been placed at both ends of the street. A small crowd of local reporters and a film crew were hanging around, smoking, waiting for news. They surged around the car as it drew up but Milner ignored them. Their driver had a quick word with the patrol sergeant on duty, who waved them through. As they cruised slowly down the street they could see uniformed officers going from door to door. Milner explained what was happening.

"They'll be asking the neighbours what they've seen and heard. Also they'll be warning them not to leave the street without taking some form of ID with them; otherwise they won't be able to get back in."

Their car stopped outside a house that had been taped off. From what they could see it was much less grand than Hillman's mansion but looked better cared for. In a tented area just inside the gate they each donned disposable coveralls, a hat, overshoes, a mask, and gloves before going in.

As they went through the open front door Milner looked over his shoulder and said quietly, "Don't touch anything."

An officer conducted them to a room which had evidently been Challoner's study. The forensic team was hard at work inside. Terry's gaze roamed around the room and stopped abruptly at an outline which had been chalked on the carpet. At the head end of the outline there was a pattern of brown stains. He glanced at Maggie and saw her shiver but she avoided his eyes. The room was a shambles. The floor was littered with papers and books, pens and paper clips, emptied desk drawers, upended chairs, and a smashed picture frame. The cream wallpaper was streaked with reddish-brown smears and flecks.

His eyes were drawn back again to the chalk outline. There was something chillingly eloquent about that negative space. Articulating a presence rather than an absence, it dominated the room.

Milner stood quietly for a few moments, watching the team at work. Then he went over to one of them, had a quick word, and brought the man back to meet Terry and Maggie.

Milner said, "These here are my associates. This is Detective Dominguez, the Investigating Officer."

"Eddie," he said, raising the palm of a gloved hand by way of greeting. "The Captain said you were on your way but not to hold up the investigation. Sorry, but the body's already gone to the morgue for identification and post mortem. Did you want to see it?"

"Nah, I'll wait for the report. The Medical Examiner say anything to you before they took it away?"

"Died in the early hours."

"Cause of death?"

"You know those guys – they won't commit themselves until post mortem."

"What do you say?"

"Off the record? No one lethal injury that I could see but..."

He hesitated, looking at Terry and Maggie, who were still gazing wide-eyed around the room.

"Go on," Milner prompted.

"Well, my guess would be multiple internal injuries. Victim was in his late fifties. A much younger man wouldn't have survived a beating like that."

"That bad?"

"You better believe it. I've seen some assaults in my time, but they really worked him over. Guy wasn't married but we located his sister. Even she had a job recognizing him."

"There's blood on the walls," Milner pointed out. "Any penetrating wounds?"

"No, that's just spatter. Nose was burst, lips smashed, blood all over. We're checking it, of course, in case any belongs to the perp."

"No knife, then. Another weapon?"

"No obvious indentations on the skin. Could have been something blunt. Or fists."

"How did they get in?"

"Jemmied a ground-floor window. They must have waited till he got home because no one heard the burglar alarm go off. We figure they held him captive for a couple of hours, during which time they gave him the beating that killed him."

"Who called it in?"

"Neighbour heard a lot of noise and some shouting. Dispatch thought it was a domestic – seems no one told them he lived alone. The patrol unit found the back door open. When they went in victim was already dead."

"Anyone see anything?"

"Neighbour who called in was looking out the window. He saw two guys. One was slight, maybe a hundred and ten pounds. Other was big, with a full head of hair. The light wasn't good; that's about as much as he could see. They got into a car and drove off. That's how we know for sure there were two of them, but I'd have said there was more than one just by looking at this lot."

"Any ideas about motive?" Milner asked.

"Not yet. Could be a burglary. Seems to me like they were looking for something and when they couldn't find it they tried to beat it out of him. What's the Bureau's interest in this guy, anyway?"

"Just between you and me, right?"

"Right."

Terry held his breath, but Milner was tactful.

"We're looking into possible irregularities at a company called Vance Pharmaceuticals out at Lexington. Took place two or three years ago. Around that time the victim, Grant Challoner, resigned from his post with them. We don't know why. Terry, you had the list: what did the guy do?"

"He was Head of the Division for Health, Safety, and the Environment."

"There you go: senior man. This could be a simple burglary, like you say. But there could be more to it."

The detective whistled softly. "Good lead," he said. "I think I'll pay them a visit."

"If it's all the same to you, we'd like to come with. We've been up there once but this murder kind of changes things."

"Sure, no problem. Kate?" One of the forensic technicians came over. "I have to go. Anything more come up?"

"Phil found some footprints in the mud outside. Some were made by shoes, the others by trainers. The shoes could be the victim's but there's nothing in his wardrobe that matches the trainers. In any case, they're quite a small size. We'll make casts."

"Good. Did Kent have a look at the computer?"

"Password protected. We'll take it down to the lab."

"Okay, look: we have to assume that whatever it was they were looking for, they left without finding it. Our job is to look harder than they did. Give me a call if you find anything interesting."

"Sure. Where will you be?"

"Lexington. Victim used to be a big honcho at a company up there. We'll see what they know."

At the barrier further down the street a police spokesman came over to talk to the media.

Among the reporters was a tall, heavily built man. His thick head of hair was brown and wavy and he would have been good-looking in a classic old Hollywood way had it not been for the nose, which showed all the signs of having been broken and clumsily repaired at some time in the past. He waved a notepad to gain the attention of the spokesperson.

"Who shall we say is in charge of the case?" he shouted.

"Detective Eddie – er, Edouard – Dominguez is running the investigation," the spokesman replied.

The man nodded, wrote something on his notepad. While the others continued to fire questions he slipped further back, then left unobserved .

He walked back a block to where a car was waiting. The driver, a slight man whose clothes looked too big for him, tapped his fingers on the steering wheel. His right heel bounced rhythmically on the floor, so that his thigh bobbed up and down, and his whole body seemed to be in a state of restless motion.

The door opened and the larger man got in. He unpinned the fake reporter's pass from the lapel of his jacket.

"Didja get what you wanted?" the driver asked.

"Yeah. Detective Eddie Dominguez is the one in charge."

The smaller man reached for the ignition. "Where're we going?"

The other batted his hand down. "Wait here. See if that cop car comes back."

"What didja wanna know about this Eddie Dominguez for?"

"Because, asshole, Francis Kelly doesn't pay us for cock-ups."

The driver scowled. "You shouldn't call me an asshole, Charlie."

"What else am I supposed to call you, Dave? You loused up. You thought you were going fifteen rounds with this guy and you went ten."

"It wasn't my fault," Dave protested. "He seemed tougher than he was, is all. I thought he would spill when I gave him the left under the heart, but he croaked instead. What's the difference? We'd have done him anyway."

"Not before he told us, for Christ's sake. You knew that. Now we're back where we started."

"What about the woman?"

"Fitzgerald? What about her?"

"I could smack her around a bit. See if she knows."

"She won't know. Any case, Signett won't like it if he has to find himself a new PA for no good reason. And we need to keep him happy as well as Mr. Kelly or we don't get paid."

"So how's the bloodhound – this Dominguez guy – going to help us?"

"He's in there now with the forensic techs. They got a lot more time than we had, so maybe they'll find something. If we're in luck he'll lead us to the target."

CHAPTER 43

Dominguez opted to drive the police sedan to Lexington himself.

On their way out to the car Maggie whispered to Terry: "What are we doing this for? It's Zak Gould we need to find, not Challoner's killer."

"I think we should go along with this," he whispered back. "There's been a cover-up, that's for sure. Maybe Zak Gould – and this guy Grant Challoner – threatened to expose it."

"So the company had both of them killed?"

He shrugged. "I don't know, but they left Vance at almost the same time so there has to be a connection." He paused just short of the car and Maggie stopped beside him. "That was more than two years ago, though. Why wait this long to kill Challoner? There's got to be more to it."

"Terry, an investigation like this can go on for weeks – months, years, even." She took a deep breath. "Look, I'm giving it a couple more days. If we haven't found Zak Gould by then – or found out what's happened to him – we're going back. This is a crucial time and we just can't afford to be out of the picture that long."

He nodded. "Okay."

They got into the car.

He understood what she was saying. Ammonia levels were still rising fast towards the threshold; then the countdown would start for a nuclear strike on Yellowstone Park – unavoidable, in his view, but disastrous all the same. The only thing that could prevent it now would be a major breakthrough. They'd counted on it coming from Zak Gould, but if he was dead – or couldn't be found – the breakthrough would have to come from elsewhere. Maggie would want to be back in Florida, helping to make it happen. Or at least hoping to make it happen.

He turned his attention to the conversation in the front, where Dominguez had started to talk to Milner.

"I phoned ahead. The CEO's out of town this morning. He's flying back later this afternoon and we can see him then."

"Out of town, eh?" Milner said. "I have a good idea where he's gone. I've got a squad going over their subsidiary in Richmond, Virginia this morning. He's probably heading there right now, trying to put a lid on things. He'll be sore as hell I didn't give him any warning but that was the general idea. And now he's out of position to react to the situation here. I'll bet the news of Challoner's death has gone right round the company.

We've got a fair chance of getting some genuine reactions before he gets back."

"Yeah," Dominguez added, "We don't need his say-so. This is a murder inquiry now."

Milner nodded. "Damn right. We'll get a list of divisional heads from Signett's PA – what's her name again?" He glanced over his shoulder.

Maggie leaned forward. "Rose Fitzgerald," she said. She'd obviously been listening too.

"Yeah, right, her or that big doll Cindy Westfield in Human Resources. Eddie, why don't you see Signett on your own when he gets back? If I'm there he can say he's already told me everything and you won't get nowhere. Okay, here we are." He pointed. "Take a right up ahead; there's security on the gate."

They went to Rose Fitzgerald's office first. It was empty. Milner scanned the room and seemed about ready to leave when she came in. She flushed.

"I'm so sorry," she said breathlessly. "I was just powdering my nose. I do hope you people haven't been waiting long."

She took off her cardigan and held it poised for a moment in her thin, bony fingers before hanging it over the back of the seat. Then she sat down, holding herself very straight, one hand clasped inside the other. She was wearing a white blouse, lightly embroidered and fastened high at the neck with a cameo brooch.

"Now," she said. "How may I help you?"

Dominguez spoke first. "I'm Detective Dominguez, ma'am. You remember I phoned you earlier? I'm investigating the death of Dr. Grant Challoner. What we were wondering was, do you keep a complete list of headquarters personnel here?"

"It's on the company server, Detective Dominguez. I can easily print out a copy for you. If you'd like to take a seat for a moment."

A few minutes later Rose came over to Dominguez with a stack of sheets. He thanked her and they took it to one side. Milner and Dominguez wrote their names against the various divisional heads, dividing the task between them.

"There are too many names on this list," he said to them. "We're going to run out of time." He turned to Terry. "Terry, the important division is Health, Safety and the Environment. Do you think you could work through the rank and file there while Eddie and me are talking to the divisional heads?"

"Certainly."

"And Maggie, how's about you talking to the people in the Biogenetics Division? That's your line of country isn't it?"

"Yes, all right. I just have a couple of things to do here first."

Milner raised his eyebrows but said nothing.

He handed the marked up list to the PA.

"Miss Fitzgerald, sorry to bother you again, but would you mind running off three copies of this list for us? Thanks."

She hesitated, then inclined her head briefly and took the list to the copier, which was just outside her office. Milner exchanged glances with Maggie and shrugged. He'd evidently interpreted her hesitation as reluctance to run errands for anyone but her immediate boss. But Terry sensed something more than that and it seemed clear Maggie had picked up on it too. She was putting on a brave face, but Rose Fitzgerald was very upset.

CHAPTER 44

They spent the rest of the day interviewing. At five-fifteen Dominguez received a message from Rose to say that Mr. Signett was back. The detective went off to talk to him. By that time Dominguez and Milner had seen nearly all the people on their lists. Terry and Maggie continued to talk to staff in the two divisions that had been assigned to them.

Finally Terry went to find Maggie.

"You more or less done?" he asked

"More or less. Are they ready to leave?"

"Yeah, Sam just called. He's with Eddie. We're to meet them in the lobby."

"Good."

They said little on the journey back to police headquarters. Dominguez found an empty room with a table and chairs and the four sat down together. It was their first opportunity to compare notes.

"How was Signett?" Sam asked.

"Tight as a drum," Dominguez replied. "I think he was pretty pissed off with us but he concealed it well. I tried to find out where he'd been but he dodged it. I asked him if he knew of any reason why Challoner should have been murdered. He assumed it was a straightforward burglary – wondered why we'd think it was anything else. Challoner hadn't been with them for years; he couldn't imagine why we thought he or anyone else in the company could help us."

"Did he say why Challoner resigned?"

"He said he must have had his own reasons. He was a valued employee but he had a lot of expertise in the field of safety and so on and he could probably earn more by marketing his skills as a free-lance consultant. They were sorry to lose him, he said, but it was four years ago now. As far as he was concerned it was ancient history. How did you get on with your lot, Sam?"

Milner shook his head. "From the Divisional Heads, *nada*. Either they never knew Challoner or they only knew him slightly. Nobody could say why he was killed. They assumed it was a burglary, too."

"Yeah," Dominguez said. "I got the same."

"One was more interesting, though," Milner went on. "The CFO, the Chief Financial Officer, a guy called Ansel Wyatt. He knew Challoner all right, couldn't say why he was killed. So I asked him a bit about the

Genon plant. He gave me the stock answers but I just had the feeling he was holding something back. And the way he was talking I could tell he works closely with Signett. Very closely."

Eddie frowned. "So what's new? It's normal for a CFO to work closely with the CEO."

"Yeah, I know that. I was curious, all the same. I got on the phone to the business guys at the Bureau, had them look him up. Get this. Wyatt and Signett were both in senior positions at their previous company. When the company was taken over, Signett and Wyatt moved to Vance together."

Eddie nodded. "Interesting. Doesn't tell us much about Challoner, though." He looked at Terry and Maggie. "What about the staff in those two divisions?"

Terry replied first. "All the people in Health, Safety and Environment seem to have been appointed after Challoner left. They didn't even know who he was. I tried to probe about safety but they kept deflecting me onto stupid safety-at-work legislation and how they keep up with it. I had quite enough of that back at my own department. How about you, Maggie?"

"Nothing from Biogenetics. They didn't know Challoner and they were really reluctant to say anything about their work at all. Still, they do seem to be using safe organisms, so far as I can tell. I do have something else, though. It was while I was still in the PA's office, after you'd gone off to do your interviews."

Milner and Dominguez turned to her in surprise. She smiled.

"Terry and I saw that Rose Fitzgerald was very upset so I sat down and had a chat with her. I like her a lot. She's a nice, gentle woman, and very intelligent."

Milner said, "You don't get to be PA for a top man like Signett unless you're smart."

"Well, from our conversation I got the feeling she knew Challoner quite well, but she wouldn't say much about it while we were in that office area. She kept looking around and then she said in this loud voice, 'The restroom? Certainly, I'll take you there. Is it all right if I just finish this?' I waited while she printed off some sheets. Then she took something out of a filing cabinet and she put all of it in the top right-hand drawer of her desk. There was something quite deliberate about the way she did it. She met my eyes, picked up her handbag, and we went off to the restroom together."

Dominguez said, "And...?"

"When we got there she checked to see no one was in the toilets, and then she set a tap running and we talked over the noise."

"See? Smart," Milner said. "What did I tell you?"

"What did she say?" Dominguez asked.

"It seems she and Challoner were just on friendly terms when he was with the company. But after he left they started to meet up socially. They enjoyed each other's company. They'd meet about once a week. She stressed they weren't in any sort of relationship." Maggie frowned. "Something about the way she said it made me think Challoner may have been gay."

"What did they talk about?"

"Oh, all sorts of things. They went to the theatre or concerts and sometimes they'd eat out. They mostly met in Boston or Concord; I think they didn't want to be seen together here in Lexington. The one thing they didn't talk about was work. He admired her loyalty to the company, he said, and he wouldn't want their friendship to present a conflict of interest. And then she drew herself up and said: 'But I have a loyalty to him, too.' I asked her why she thought he'd been killed. I was trying to be gentle – really I was – but her eyes filled with tears and for a while she couldn't speak. Eventually she said something like, 'He knew too much. He saw the risks, but he wouldn't run away. So they got him. They'll get the other one, too.' I asked her who 'they' and 'the other one' were but she shook her head and said slowly: 'I've already given you enough.' Then she turned the taps off and we went back to her office."

Dominguez frowned. "Given you enough? What did she mean by that? Enough information…?" He pointed a finger at her. "It's the stuff she put in that drawer! We gotta go back."

"That won't be necessary," Maggie said with a smile. She opened her handbag, withdrew some folded sheets of paper from her handbag and opened them out to reveal a small optical disk. She picked up the disk by the hub and held it out to show them a date, which had been written on one side with a fine spirit marker.

"How did you manage that?" Terry gasped.

"Well, when we got back to the office area Rose said, 'Now there's something I have to leave for Mr. Signett.' I thought she'd go for that drawer, but she didn't; she picked up some papers from the desktop and went down the corridor without a backward glance. I didn't hesitate. As soon as I heard Signett's door close behind her I dived into that drawer. I saw Challoner's name on the first sheet and that was good enough for me.

Then I heard Signett's door opening again, so I slipped it all into my handbag and got out fast."

"What's on the disk?" Milner asked.

"I don't know, do I?" Maggie said. "I haven't had the chance to look at it. I don't even know what kind of storage medium this is," she said, turning the disk over to look at one side and then the other.

"It's for a dictaphone with removable media," Dominguez supplied. "We use them when we want a permanent record of an interview. We've got machines here that'll read it for you – I'll get one right now." He stood up. "Is there anything on those papers?"

"I assume this is what she was printing off," Maggie said. She put the disk down and opened out the sheets. They were headed: "Vance Pharmaceuticals Incorporated. Minutes of the Meeting of the Board. In the Chair: Mr. Warren Signett, Chief Executive Officer." Then it listed those present.

"It must be a transcript of whatever's on the disk," she said, frowning. "But I'm sure Rose meant us to have both."

"Why?" Terry said.

Dominguez said, "We won't find out until we listen to it. Hang on, I'll get the machine."

CHAPTER 45

Before long Dominguez returned carrying a dictaphone. Terry and Maggie pulled their chairs closer so they could follow the printed version together. Milner got up and stood behind them. Dominguez loaded the disk and started to play it back. They listened attentively.

There were some shuffling sounds, then the thump of something like a large ledger being dumped on the table. The scrape of a chair. Signett's voice.

"Thank you for coming. Let's get started, shall we? Any apologies for absence, Rose?"

"No, sir."

"Good. Item 1: Minutes of the previous meeting. These were circulated. You've all had a chance to read them. Does anyone who was at the meeting have any corrections? No? Good. Item 2: Marketing Report. I have a few things to say about this and then Felix Rutter will make a short presentation."

Terry quickly took the personnel list out of his jacket pocket and pointed. Felix Rutter was the company's World Marketing Director. They continued to listen, following the transcript at the same time.

After the marketing report there came a short account of a clinical trial, followed by a progress report on a new drug, on which a decision about further development had to be reached. Then:

"Item 5. The second bioreactor at the Richmond plant. Is that operational yet, Glen?"

"Hold it. Remind me – who's Glen?" asked Milner.

Dominguez pressed the pause button while Terry ran a finger down the personnel list.

"It must be Glen Forrester, Head of Production Engineering."

"Okay, sorry, Eddie. Let's continue."

Dominguez released the pause button and the machine restarted.

"More or less. We're into final testing now but I'm not expecting any problems. It was identical to the one we built for the AB Genetics project so it was just a matter of doubling up on existing technology. It should be online in a couple of weeks."

"Excellent. And are we within budget on that, Ansel?"

Terry pointed to the second name on the personnel list: Ansel Wyatt,

Chief Financial Officer, the man Milner had interviewed.

"*Yes, Warren; so long as there are no overruns on commissioning, it'll be on target.*"

"*Thank you. Item 6. The former Biomolecular Technologies. I take it they've been absorbed satisfactorily into Biogenetics Division, Hank?*"

"*Yes, Warren. No problems.*"

"*Good. Now there's not much from their portfolio that's worth –* "

"Hold on, pause it there," Milner said. "Where's that in the transcript?"

Maggie turned the pages back and forth. "None of this is in the print-out. All it says is: 'Item 6: It was reported that Biomolecular Technologies had been absorbed satisfactorily into Biogenetics Division.' Then it goes on to Item 7 of the Agenda."

"This transcript has been edited. Okay, Eddie, let's take it carefully. Can you back-track a bit and start it again?"

Dominguez pressed a couple of buttons in quick succession. The machine squawked, then the recording picked up again.

"* – there's not much from their portfolio that's worth continuing with. There's nothing market-ready, they spread themselves too thinly. We'll wind up research on most of the projects and patent anything that's worth the trouble. You'll look into that, will you, Hank?*"

"*I'm already on it. You should have my report by the end of next week.*"

"*All right, I'll expect it then. Item 7 –* "

"*Chairman, I think there are other issues to discuss under that last Item.*"

There was a pause.

"*What issues are you referring to, Dr. Challoner?*"

"*I'm referring to the soil organism.*"

"*What about it?*"

"*For the benefit of those around this table who aren't aware of it, Biomolecular Technologies was in the process of developing a soil organism that fixes atmospheric nitrogen in a unique way. On a routine visit to our Genon subsidiary I noticed a distinct smell of ammonia. On further enquiry I discovered that this organism is being tested in a local field.*"

"*Well, so what? Dr. Gould developed this organism but he didn't have time to do anything more with it. He's busy on other projects now, so we thought we'd do it for him. It's a very limited trial, of course. When the trial's over, the field will be sprayed with algicide and that will be the end of it.*"

"Mr. Chairman, that's hardly reassuring when you learn that the new bioreactor – the one we discussed very briefly under Item 5 – has, it seems, been constructed for the express purpose of manufacturing this organism in pilot production quantities."

"No, that's incorrect. We anticipate a heavy demand for the oral insulin we acquired from AB Genetics and the new bioreactor is being installed to double our production capacity. Before it's fully commissioned we'll use it to make a pilot batch of the soil organism for testing purposes, that's all."

"Well, had I been consulted I would still have said that this project was being pursued in a reckless and hasty way."

"Dr. Challoner, this is a large company. There isn't the time or energy to consult you on every small matter, and I reject the implication that you've been deliberately bypassed. There is no secrecy about this project. I simply didn't think it merited time in the context of this meeting."

"All the same, Chairman, this meeting has been my only opportunity to express an opinion, and I feel bound to say that a project of this nature poses serious safety issues."

"You had no problem with the original bioreactor, Dr. Challoner."

"I didn't have a problem with it because the insulin-making organism was disabled."

"Sorry, can someone tell me what that means?"

It was Felix Rutter's voice. Challoner replied:

"In the AB Genetics project, Mr. Rutter, the organism was engineered to lack an enzyme for making an amino acid. That amino acid has to be added to the culture medium for it to grow. If it should ever get out into the environment it would just die. People or animals could swallow it and it wouldn't do them any harm. That's what we mean by disabled. It's a routine safeguard. The soil organism, on the other hand, is not disabled."

"Well of course it's not disabled." There was a note of exasperation in Signett's voice. "The whole point of this product is that it's almost vanishingly cheap. When it's spread on fields it starts to turn nitrogen from the air into an available form in the soil. If your peasant farmer has to sprinkle an expensive amino acid on it to keep it alive there's no advantage to him. He may as well go on buying conventional fertilizer."

"But we know nothing about the rate of growth, how it might spread to other organisms in the environment, or whether it's toxic to animals that consume it. It would be totally premature to manufacture it at this stage. Dr. Gould himself told me that it was in an early stage of development."

"And did you ask Dr. Gould how long it would take to complete the remaining development?"

"Yes. He said he'd made a start on it when we took over his company. He thought it would take about six months to a year."

"When these people say 'six months to a year'" Signett again "you can bet it's going to take two years or more. I want results a lot sooner than that, and so will our shareholders." There was a slight pause, a lowering of the voice. "Look, Dr. Challoner, this organism presents us with a significant opportunity, one we can't afford to overlook. The production costs will be minimal."

"It's not the costs that concern me, it's containing the risk. That field is open to the air. Sea birds could pick up the organism on their feet and transfer it to open water. A bad storm could wash it into the river. Or the plant could be sabotaged. A responsible company has to provide for possibilities like this."

"We're being perfectly responsible. The trial is strictly limited in both extent and duration. The equipment is being constructed to a proven design and the complex down in Richmond is secure, so sabotage isn't a serious possibility. A small batch of the stuff will be produced and then the bioreactor will be turned over to the insulin-generating organism. Right, now I'm sorry, we have spent more time than I intended on this item and there are other things on the agenda – "

"May I ask, then, what is the point of having a Division for Health, Safety and the Environment if you're not prepared to listen to advice from it?"

There was a heavy silence. Terry and Maggie looked at each other, then the machine, wondering if the track had finished. It hadn't. Signett's voice came again, deliberate and hard.

"I have listened, but at the end of the day it's my job to ensure that this company continues to be profitable and competitive. If the company goes to the wall, Dr. Challoner, there will be no Division of Health, Safety and the Environment. Now I've heard your objections and I do not consider them over-riding in this case."

"Well it's my responsibility to advise you that you are wrong."

"Your responsibility, Dr. Challoner, and the responsibility of every other section head round this table is to the company, first and foremost."

"No. First and foremost, my responsibility is to the environment."

"Well, if you see that as a conflict of interest, then perhaps you shouldn't *be here."*

"Curiously enough I had just reached the same conclusion. Be good enough to place it on record that I regard this venture as unacceptably high-risk. It has the potential to do untold harm to the environment and it poses a threat to the safety of both the workforce and the public. Good-day, ladies and gentlemen."

There was the sound of rustling papers and footsteps. The creak of a door opening. The hollow thud as it closed. There was a barely audible sigh.

"Perhaps we can move on now..."

"Pause it, Eddie."

Dominguez pressed a button. They looked at each other.

"No wonder Signett wanted this suppressed," Milner said.

"What's all this about harm to the environment and the public?" Dominguez asked. "Is there something here I should know about?"

Milner winced. "Eddie, we think there was an accident at that plant, and this potentially harmful organism escaped. The accident should have been reported but it wasn't. That's what we're looking into. As far as that other stuff is concerned, Eddie, you didn't hear it, all right?"

"Whaddaya mean? I heard it."

"You didn't hear it, Eddie. Do me a favour, now. You're just a good cop, going after a couple of murderers. Forget the rest. Believe me, you need to forget the rest, otherwise you could be in shit so deep you won't know which way is up. All right?"

Eddie shrugged. "Yeah, all right, if you say so."

"Good. Now let's see if anything more was said."

Dominguez released the pause and they listened to the rest of the recording. There was nothing more about the organism. Signett declared the meeting closed. They heard the noise of chairs shifting, papers being shuffled, the door repeatedly opening and closing.

Eddie reached for the stop button but Milner grabbed his wrist:

"Wait" he breathed. "She left it running."

Signett's voice.

"Rose, you'll be typing up the Minutes, as usual? Verbatim record and an executive summary at the end?"

"Yes, Mr. Signett."

"I don't want anything recorded under Agenda Item 6. There are issues of company security involved."

"Nothing at all, sir? I'd have to renumber the Agenda."

"Okay, just record that Biomolecular Technologies has been absorbed satisfactorily into Biogenetics Division. Nothing more."

"Very good, sir."

"Oh, and contact Human Resources. Tell them that Dr. Challoner has tendered his resignation. In the circumstances I'm prepared to waive the statutory period of notice. His employment will terminate as of today. They're to prepare his leaving documents immediately. And ask them what our legal obligations are to him, money-wise; I want the absolute minimum figure."

There was a loud click as the dictaphone was switched off.

CHAPTER 46

Dominguez pinched his bottom lip.

"Rose knows more than I thought. We need to go back and speak to her again."

Terry said, "Maggie might be the only one she'll talk to. Seems like Rose trusts her."

"And that's exactly why Maggie's not going to."

They all looked at her.

"She took a chance, telling me about this. If I try to see her again I hate to think what would happen. At best she'd lose her job. At worst – well, look what happened to Challoner."

"What makes you think she's at such high risk?" Milner asked.

"Look, this is a sensible, balanced lady. She didn't run the tap in that ladies' room because she has paranoid delusions. She must have good reason to believe she's being watched. She was seeing Challoner, after all. Signett could have found out."

"We could get her home address. You could visit her there."

"They may be watching her house. It's too risky. I'm not going to gamble with someone else's life."

"Eddie," Milner said. "Maybe there's no need. We have a window now on what happened. There's no question Signett's been lying to us. There wasn't any love lost between him and Challoner. He more or less invited the guy to resign and he couldn't accept fast enough when he did. But it's worse than that: Challoner predicted an accident down at Richmond, and he foresaw the consequences."

"It's all very well for you," Dominguez grumbled. "I can see as how it helps you guys, but I don't see it gets me ahead any. Not liking someone isn't a good reason to kill them. And if Signett wanted him dead, why did he wait all this time to do it?"

"There's an answer to that," Terry said, "and it's not very palatable. I think the fact we were around, asking questions, must have precipitated it. Anything else would be too much of a coincidence."

"Oh, God," moaned Maggie.

"You could be right there," said Milner. "The three of us went to see Signett yesterday morning. Challoner was killed last night. In my book that's no coincidence."

"So could we connect Signett to the murder?" asked Terry.

"Nah, he's too smart for that. If he hired those guys he would have worked through a third party. They call themselves 'Security Consultants' or 'Security Agencies'. You pay them a visit and they tell you how they'll sweep your office for bugs, install firewalls on your server connections and fit your place with burglar alarms. And they can do all that. But with the right introduction they can also tell you about the freelance gentlemen who can carry out the odd special assignment for you – and guarantee that no one will ever know you were involved."

Eddie said, "I don't know, though. This was no ordinary contract – it's too untidy. Normally one very careful guy tracks down the target and pops him. Why two of them? And why take the risk of breaking into his home and beating the shit out of him first?"

"He must have known something," Milner answered.

"Or had something they wanted," Dominguez added.

Maggie shook her head. "The accident was two – nearly three – years ago. Challoner could have gone public long before this. Why didn't he? It seems to me he must have been protecting someone. When Rose gave me the disk she said 'They got him. They'll get the other one too.' Maybe she was referring to this person Challoner was trying to protect." She chewed her lip. "I wonder if it was Zak Gould."

"I bet that's it," Terry said. "They were trying to make Challoner tell them where he was!"

Dominguez said, "Well, if they succeeded, that guy's life isn't worth a shit."

Milner's phone rang and he went out into the corridor to answer it. Dominguez was going back over the paper work. Maggie sidled up to Terry and whispered: "If they get to Gould it's all over, Terry. We've got to find him first."

Milner returned after a few minutes.

"That was Clive," he said. "Told me what went down at Genon."

"What did they find?" asked Terry.

"Nothing. Not a damn thing. They went over the place with a fine-toothed comb. No suspicious equipment, no accident report, in fact no paperwork of any sort, and nothing on the computers. And no one they spoke to knew anything about an accident."

Maggie said, "Did you tell him what was on the disk – the one Rose gave me? You know, about the organism being tested in a local field and the second bioreactor being used to make it?"

"Yes, I told him all that. The production people said both bioreactors were churning out that insulin stuff. They extracted samples and Clive sent them to the lab with one question: 'Is this *E. coli*?' The answer came back: 'Yes'."

"And the field?"

"Clive walked the whole area. He didn't see anything suspicious and he didn't smell ammonia."

"The ammonia organism *did* escape from that plant," she said. "Terry's NASA data shows it. And there *was* a field test down there. Challoner said as much on that disk."

Terry said, "They must have realized it was out of control and got scared. Sprayed the field. Emptied the reactor."

Milner nodded in agreement. "Yeah. There's one more thing, though. When they left Genon, Clive and one of the other agents paid a visit to Richmond Police HQ. They talked to people there and trawled through their files, looking for evidence of a break-in or sabotage or anything else out of the ordinary at the plant. Again, nothing. But around that time two of the research staff who worked at the facility were killed in a car accident. The police attended the scene. Seems the car left the road, crashed down a steep embankment. No witnesses. Tyre marks on the road and bits of plastic from a rear light suggested a collision but the other driver didn't stop."

Maggie's eyes narrowed. "Two more deaths? I wonder if they'd been working on the soil organism."

Milner shrugged "Who knows? Let's say it wouldn't surprise me."

Early that evening at the Research Institute in Florida some of the staff were taking a break in the lounge and watching the news on the big flat-screen television. Silvia and Sara met up with Matt at the coffee machine.

"Do you have any more sequence for me yet, Matt?"

"Yeah, some. I'll pass it over. I was searching the databases for sequence similarities, but there aren't any. That's the trouble with this stuff. There's so little on record."

"Well, let me have it. Perhaps I will see…"

Sara Tennant pointed at the television. "Something's happening in San Francisco, Silvia."

They hurried over to the other half of the lounge and sat down in time to hear the newscaster say:

"Now let's join our reporter in San Francisco, Craig Burdon. Craig, are you there?"

A youngish man appeared, holding a microphone. There was a large crowd in the room behind him and he had to speak over the background of conversation.

"*Yes, Don. We have permission to film here, near the top of the Transamerica Pyramid. If you look out of the windows it's like coming in to land on a cloudy day; nothing to see but a white blanket below us. With me is Matt Dryden. Matt, you were piloting a light aircraft at around the time the smog rolled in. Can you tell us what you saw?*"

The camera switched to a ruddy-faced man in his forties. "*Sure. You know, I seen cool mists rolling into the city many times, but this one was different.*"

"*In what way?*"

"*It started real close in, and it kind of creeped up the streets and between the high-rises like, sort of like fingers... no, more like tentacles. That's it, like octopus tentacles. Only white.*"

"*You could still see the tops of the buildings?*"

"*Oh sure, more'n the tops at that stage. When I came back an hour later it had thickened up. Just about all I could see then was the Transamerica Pyramid, the Bank of America Center, and the tips of the towers of the Golden Gate Bridge.*"

"*So you'd never seen a fog like this one?*"

"*No, sir. Your California fog usually forms out to sea. This seemed to form right inside the city.*"

"*Thanks very much, Matt.*"

"*Sure thing.*"

"*Craig, do you have the latest figures on fatalities there?*"

"*I'm told it's already topped eight hundred, Don. There may be more to come; the hospitals are still struggling to keep people alive.*"

"*That bad, eh?*"

"*You better believe it, Don. We're above it up here, otherwise there's no way I could speak to you. This stuff is really irritating. If you're old or sick, or have any sort of breathing difficulty it would certainly get to you. The smell is pretty bad, too; the streets down there smell like – excuse me – stale piss. Back to you, Don.*"

"*That was Craig Burdon in San Francisco. Reports are just coming in of similar smogs in Calcutta, Beijing and Seoul. More on that after the break.*"

Without a word Silvia, Sara, and Matt got up and went back to their labs.

CHAPTER 47

They rose early and made coffee in the room. Maggie was leafing through the copy of the *Boston Globe* which had been left outside the door.

She tapped the pages she was reading. "A lot here about Cyclone Amrita."

"Whereabouts?"

"It crossed the coast in Bangladesh yesterday. Damage, flooding – even worse than Vietnam last month. Ammonia organisms again?"

"More than likely. We know they're in the Bay of Bengal as well as the South China Sea."

She shook her head. "More casualties and homeless people. And Bangkok's had a second white smog." She looked up at him. "We never did discover how the organism got to Thailand."

"Or India, or China."

"You know," she said, "an accidental escape at Richmond is one thing, but having the organism pop up at almost the same time half-way round the world is quite another. What have those sites got in common?"

Terry took a sip of coffee. "Nothing. Well, they're not heavily industrialized so a lot of people will be poor, dependent on agriculture – you don't think Zak…"

"Not Zak, no," Maggie said. "It was pretty clear from that Board meeting that he wanted to complete the development first. But someone must have taken batches of the organism out there." She paused, her brow furrowing. "Terry…?"

"Yes?"

"When we saw Signett he mentioned manufacturing facilities overseas. Do you think Vance has subsidiaries in those countries?"

He met her eyes in shocked silence.

He rushed to his laptop, booted it up and started to search.

"God, you're right. Jhupar Pharmaceuticals, Mumbai; Vance Enterprises, Bangkok; Shiji Pharm, Shijiazhuang. And there's a couple more in the Philippines and Poland. Would a CEO visit his facilities abroad from time to time?"

"Most certainly. And he could have easily made a side trip during each visit. What about the timing?"

"Remember the Board meeting? The second bioreactor at Genon was due to go on line a couple of weeks later. And Signett said they were planning to test it with a pilot batch of the soil organism first. I wonder if he went on a tour of his Far Eastern subsidiaries immediately afterwards."

"We could ask Rose. She'd be the one to keep his diary and arrange his trips."

"Let's do that. And if he did go out there we should confront him with it." He glanced at his watch. "Come on, let's see if Sam's at our breakfast place yet."

"Your car is ready, Mr. Signett."

"Thank you, Rose."

Signett was at his desk, unhurriedly putting papers into a thin leather document case, material to read on the flight to Washington. He smiled to himself. One of the things his rivals in the industry envied was his ability to anticipate events. In a little over three months' time there would be a major product launch. He intended to exploit to the full the opportunity it gave him to project Vance Pharmaceuticals as a successful, expanding and forward-looking organization. He would reinforce that with the simultaneous announcement of a fresh biotech acquisition for the company. The takeover was pretty well agreed but he had to be sure of surmounting the regulatory hurdles. What could be more appropriate at this juncture than lunch with a patriot like his old friend Senator Tom McAdam?

He knew exactly what the Senator would say.

"Well, you know, Warren, in general I'm in favour of antitrust legislation, but it's getting out of hand. Who made America what it is? Entrepreneurs, wealth creators, people like you and me, Warren – not damned lawyers. The economy needs strong multinational companies, companies like yours, to stave off world competition. You know, all this openness and freedom of information business – transparency is what the management gurus like to call it – that stuff's all very well if everyone's doing the same thing. But does Russia? Does China? Or North Korea? Do they hell! How can you negotiate with these people? It's like playing poker with your cards in full view."

So would the Senator use his influence to ensure that the Federal Trade Commission didn't stop Vance from making its new acquisition? Of course he would. There'd be a quid pro quo; there always was.

"Of course," the Senator would say, "there's an election in eighteen months' time and we can't be sure the next administration will be equally sympathetic to your case."

And he would reply, "I'm aware of that, Tom. Vance will, of course, be making the usual generous contribution to party funds. And to your own personal campaign fund, naturally – in the usual fashion."

Then they would exchange smiles of understanding, shake hands, and he would fly back. It was all too easy, really.

"Did you phone Senator McAdam's PA, Rose?"

"Yes, Mr. Signett. I said you'd phone again if there was any delay. Otherwise the Senator will meet you at the restaurant at twelve-thirty."

"Fine." He stood up. "I'll be back this evening. No need to hang on here. I'll see you tomorrow."

He took the elevator down to the foyer. The top-of-the-range Lexus was already waiting outside with Graeme McKenzie, his chauffeur and bodyguard, at the wheel. Signett got into the back and put his leather document case on the seat at his side. The car swept out of the gates, turned left, and travelled about two hundred yards before it was rammed by an all-black SUV.

The doors of the other vehicle flew open and three men leapt out. Graeme drew his gun but before he could fire it the driver's side window shattered and simultaneously a red flower bloomed on the opposite window. Graeme slumped sideways onto the passenger seat, a dark entry wound in his temple.

Figures loomed all around, blotting out the sunlight. Someone smashed in the remains of the driver's window with the butt of an automatic rifle, reached in, and unlocked the doors. Signett found himself being dragged out of the car and thrust into the back of the SUV. One of his assailants got into the driver's seat, another jammed a hood over his head and fastened his wrists in front of him. He was thrown back suddenly as the car accelerated away.

He closed his eyes, trying to shut out the stifling darkness of the hood. He could feel the heat of a close presence on each side, hear their noisy breathing. He thought they were probably taking him to Boston but he had no way of knowing.

They began to talk rapidly between themselves but he couldn't understand a word. The language they were speaking was Chinese.

Maggie toyed with her coffee, swilling the liquid slowly in the cup. It was their third refill.

Terry looked at his watch again. "It's nearly ten o'clock, for God's sake! Where the hell has Sam got to?"

Some coffee spilled over the edge of her cup. She put it back in the saucer.

Terry's cell phone sounded. He caught Maggie's eye as he heard Milner's voice.

"Sam! Where have you been?"

"Sorry, shit hit the fan. Are you at the breakfast bar?"

"Yes, but we've finished – "

"Eddie and I are on our way. Come out on the sidewalk. We'll pick you up in a couple of minutes."

Several minutes later the police sedan drew up and they piled into the back. Sam turned round in the front passenger seat as Eddie drove briskly away.

"Sorry about breakfast, folks. Things have been kind of busy."

"Where are we going?" Terry asked, looking for a grab handle. Dominguez was driving fast. "We wanted to see Warren Signett again."

"You aren't the only ones."

"What do you mean?"

"Signett's been snatched – kidnapped."

"When?"

"Less than an hour ago. He was on his way to a meeting."

Terry and Maggie exchanged looks.

"Sounds like the snatch was well planned," Milner continued. "They got Signett just outside the plant; obviously they knew just when he'd be leaving. They shot the driver dead, lifted Signett, and they were gone before even the security guards at the gate could react."

"Who's responsible?" Terry said. "What do they want?"

"I don't know, but I'd say Signett won't be coming back any time soon – if at all. I was just saying to Eddie, this gives us a golden opportunity."

Terry leaned forward. "To do what?"

"Well, with Signett out of the picture I think I can get his sidekick – the CFO guy, Ansel Wyatt – to tell us what he knows. Okay with you, Eddie?"

Dominguez shrugged. "Sure, why not? I figure all this is connected somehow."

The SUV stopped and the engine died. The man on the right bundled Signett out and manhandled him, still hooded, into a building of some sort. The floor scraped under the soles of his shoes and their footsteps echoed in a larger space like a garage or warehouse. He heard a door opening and felt a shove in the small of his back. The acoustic closed in; he seemed to be standing in a room. There was another brief incomprehensible exchange and someone snatched off the hood.

He blinked at the sudden light, focused, and found himself looking at an elderly Chinese man with a leathery face and startlingly white hair. The man spoke.

"Take a seat, Mr. Signett."

A chair was pushed hard against the backs of his knees, leaving him no choice. One of the men who'd brought him in left the room. The other two remained standing, one on either side. Signett was breathing fast. He tried to steady his voice.

"This is an outrage. I demand an explanation."

"You are not in a position to demand anything, Mr. Signett," the older man replied coolly. "However, I will give you an explanation."

He placed his fingertips together and Signett waited for what seemed an age. The man started:

"Five years ago your company was expecting a major contract to manufacture and supply a low-cost generic anti-malarial to developing countries. You tendered very competitively through your Indian subsidiary, Jhupar Pharmaceuticals, in Mumbai, where the production costs are low – "

"How do you know – ?"

"Have the courtesy not to interrupt, Mr. Signett. In fact you lost that contract at the last moment – to a Chinese company. Do you know why?"

Signett's lips set in a thin line. "Perhaps you are going to tell me."

"Yes, I will tell you. There is a mole inside your company, Mr. Signett. He passed on the details of your bid and the Chinese company undercut you."

"I suspected as much."

"But you never found the mole, did you? No. He is, in fact, still in your company. He works for me."

Panic swelled inside Signett's chest. His mouth was bone dry.

"This is not all," the older man continued. "Four years ago, you acquired a company called Biomolecular Technologies. Someone there had modified an organism and arranged for it to fix nitrogen. You put it into production at your Genon plant in Richmond, Virginia."

Signett's eyes blazed. It was unbelievable how much information had leaked to this man. The mole must be very highly placed. His mind flicked through the senior management, trying to guess who it was. He was brought back by a hardening of his captor's voice.

"The northern provinces of China are home to some of our poorest rural communities. But recently they have produced record crops. They are not using fertilizers, yet the ground there is unusually rich in nitrogen and the air smells of ammonia. Our investigations show that your organism is present and it is spreading throughout the region. That was not clever of you, Mr. Signett."

"I don't know what you're talking about."

The man smiled, but his eyes were like coals.

"You are too modest, Mr. Signett. The organism you acquired is quite unique. When you are a manufacturer that is a great advantage. But when you try to deny that the organism is yours it is a great disadvantage, because we can be quite sure that you are lying. You have made a mistake, Mr. Signett, and you have displeased some very powerful people. Now you are going to suffer for it."

Signett tried to swallow.

"What do you want?"

"We want you to reverse the effects of the organism, Mr. Signett."

He licked his lips.

"It can't be done."

The man smiled patiently.

Signett blundered on. "You could spray it, from the air," he stuttered.

"Please, Mr. Signett, do not insult us. You will have to do better than that."

"I can't. I mean, I don't know how to reverse it."

"Then I hope for your sake that there is someone at your company who does. You will understand what I mean when you see the ultimatum that will be delivered to your office tomorrow." He sat back and gestured with one hand. "Mr. Signett, the men you see here are expert in keeping people alive, even under rather extreme circumstances. You may live for one week or even one month. It all depends how strong your constitution is."

The men on either side of Signett gripped his arms. One of them had produced a large knife.

CHAPTER 48

Dominguez stopped the police cruiser before they reached the entrance. Through the windscreen Terry and Maggie could see a black Lexus saloon which had partially mounted the pavement. The doors on one side were open. The whole area had been cordoned off.

A uniformed officer came over. Dominguez wound down the driver's side window and showed his badge.

"Detective Dominguez," he said. "We have an appointment in there. Where can I leave the car?"

"Best up there on the right, chief. Take it slow."

"You bet."

They edged forwards, past the Lexus, taking in the dented bodywork, the shattered window on the driver's side, the bloody mess on the window opposite. Dominguez cruised a couple of hundred yards, pulled the sedan over to the kerb and switched off the engine.

"So how do you want to play this?" He asked Milner.

"I've seen the guy before so let me lead off, okay?"

"Could I have a couple of minutes with Rose first?" Maggie asked. "There's something I wanted to ask her."

"Sure, it's on the same floor."

Dominguez, Milner, and Terry were waiting outside Wyatt's office when Maggie rejoined them. She nodded to Terry and said quietly:

"India, Thailand, and China, at just about the right time."

He frowned. "The question is, why?"

"Perhaps this man will tell us."

Milner said, "All set?" and opened the door.

The secretary looked startled as they went in.

"Here to see Mr. Wyatt," he said.

"Oh, do you have an appointment?"

"Police and FBI. We're investigating Mr. Signett's disappearance. I think he'll see us."

She got up. "Just a moment."

She went through an adjoining door and they heard a voice say, "Oh yes, Tina. Send them through."

The secretary emerged, and gestured for them to go in.

Wyatt was already on his feet. "Please come in."

Milner shook his hand. "Sam Milner, FBI. We spoke yesterday. These here are my associates, and this is Detective Dominguez, Boston P.D."

Wyatt indicated some armchairs around a low table and closed the heavy door.

His office was furnished as luxuriously as the CEO's but it had a more definite air of business about it: shelves stacked with ledgers and reference books, and a desk burdened with trays of paperwork.

Wyatt unfastened the single button on his suit jacket and sat down. He looked to be in his early fifties. The chubby face would have suggested an even younger man but his hair was peppered with grey and receding at the temples. He interlaced his fingers over the slight bulge above the waistband of his trousers and tapped his thumbs briskly together before opening the conversation.

"Before we start," he said, "there's been a new development and I think you should know about it right away."

Milner raised his eyebrows. "Oh?"

"Yes. A package was delivered by courier just a few moments ago, addressed to the 'Acting CEO'. Whoever sent it obviously knew about the kidnap so our security personnel were wary. They X-rayed it. A ring showed up, but nothing to indicate an explosive device. They asked me to join them and we took precautions when we were opening it. Inside there was a plastic bag that did indeed contain a ring. I recognized it immediately. It was the engraved jade ring that Mr. Signett normally wore on the little finger of his right hand."

"You kept the packaging, I hope?"

"Yes, we thought you'd want to see it."

"All right, so there's no doubt that they've got Mr. Signett."

"None whatsoever. Unfortunately that's not all."

He hesitated. Then he swallowed and said:

"Erm, the ring was still on Mr. Signett's finger."

Terry saw Maggie's hand fly to her mouth.

"Was there a demand with that?" asked Dominguez.

"Well, there was some sort of message. Perhaps you can help me with it."

He unfolded a sheet of paper and handed it to Dominguez. The writing was Chinese, the characters scrawled with a red pen in a vertical column, ending with a stamped symbol of a dragon clambering around a knife, also in red.

He studied it thoughtfully. "I'll fax this to a colleague of mine, Henry

Chow, at headquarters who can translate it. Can we do that?"

"Yes, of course. Tina will do it for you now if you like."

Wyatt half rose but Dominguez stopped him with a gesture, got up and opened the door to the secretary's office.

Milner spoke up: "Mr. Wyatt, while we're waiting for Detective Dominguez maybe we could pick up on the conversation we had yesterday about Grant Challoner. Do you think Dr. Challoner was in any way a threat to the company?"

Wyatt almost laughed.

"Grant? No."

"You seem very sure of that."

"I am. It's true that while he was with the company he irritated a lot of people. But that was only because he was so conscientious. Whatever else you might say of Grant Challoner he was a man of total integrity. When a man in a senior position like that leaves the company he's bound by very strict non-disclosure clauses. You can be sure he would have observed those to the letter. In fact you could say that Grant is – I mean was – even less of a threat to the company after he'd left it than when he was with it."

"So that wouldn't have been a reason to kill him?"

"My goodness, that wouldn't be a sufficient reason to kill anyone, least of all Grant Challoner."

The door opened and Dominguez came back in.

"Okay," he said, resuming his seat. "I asked him to phone me as soon as he has something."

Milner nodded, then turned back to the CFO. "Something that's been bothering me, Mr. Wyatt. How do you think those people knew Mr. Signett was going to a meeting this morning?"

"That's been bothering me, too," Wyatt said. "It suggests inside knowledge."

"We've been wondering whether this is somehow connected to the murder of Grant Challoner. Any views on that?"

"I can't see how."

Dominguez's phone sounded.

"That'll be him now," he said, and got up to take the call in a corner of the room. They waited uncomfortably while he listened, grunting now and again. Then he said, "Okay, thanks a lot, Henry. See ya later."

"All right," he said, dropping into his chair. "Henry says the dragon symbol is the sign of a triad organization in Boston with links to Hong Kong. They specialize in protection rackets and extortion. I'm afraid the message isn't pleasant, so prepare yourselves. Basically it reads: 'We will cut into another joint for each day that the organism is at large.' I'm sorry, Mr. Wyatt. It looks like your colleague is being progressively dismembered."

A look of revulsion contorted Wyatt's face. Terry glanced at Maggie. She seemed too shocked to react.

"They're clearly referring to the soil organism, Mr. Wyatt," Milner said. "The one developed by Dr. Zak Gould and put into production by your company."

Wyatt's eyebrows lifted. "You know about that?"

Milner took a deep breath. "I'd say it's high time you levelled with us, Mr. Wyatt. What do you know about that organism, and what did your company do with it? And don't leave anything out. Mr. Signett's life may depend on it."

Terry glanced at Maggie and their eyes met. He knew what she was thinking.

His and everyone else's.

CHAPTER 49

"Look," Wyatt said, "This puts me in a difficult position. I want to be open with you if it'll help Warren, but what I have to say could be damaging from a company standpoint. Can I be sure it won't be made public?"

Dominguez shrugged. "Depends what it is. The way it sounds, Mr. Signett's been taken in retaliation for something. If he was acting on his own we can try to keep the company out of it."

There was a short silence. Then:

"Very well. I'll tell you as much as I know."

He looked at each of them in turn.

"First let me say that I have the greatest respect for Warren Signett. He's been an outstanding CEO. You know, when he was appointed this was a conventional pharma, rooted in traditional research methods. Things are very different now. We've been able to maintain a good pipeline of profitable drugs and at the same time we've embraced the newer technologies, like genetic engineering. Warren achieved this by absorbing smaller, more specialized companies."

"Companies like AB Genetics?" Milner asked.

"Precisely – AB Genetics is an excellent example. We acquired a non-animal-derived insulin that could be taken orally. With the increasing prevalence of diabetes you can just imagine the size of the market. We're already having problems meeting demand – we've doubled our production capacity and we may have to expand it further."

"Nice position to be in," commented Milner. "And I guess the cash flow funds more acquisitions."

"Yes, but there we encounter a problem. You see, in recent years we've been subjected to some pretty virulent abuse because of our marketing policies in the Third World. It's grossly unfair, of course. For example, we spent one point eight billion dollars developing a drug for the treatment of TB; it was unreasonable to expect us to hand it out for next to nothing in sub-Saharan Africa. Unfortunately knocking the company became a popular political pastime. In the end Warren was called before a House Select Committee. Among other things they put it to him that the company was profiteering from underprivileged people. It can't have been a pleasant experience for him; some of these committee members can be very aggressive. I'm afraid it didn't do a lot for the company's image, either. Do you mind if I get some water?"

Milner waved a hand in acquiescence and the CFO went into his secretary's office. He returned, sipping from a plastic tumbler, which he placed on the table before taking his seat again.

"Sorry about that. I've asked Tina to get us some coffee, too, if that's all right?"

They nodded and murmured their thanks.

"As I said before," Wyatt continued, "I respect Warren, but he's not without faults: he's not a patient man, he's very stubborn, and he doesn't tolerate opposition. After a roasting like the one he got from the Select Committee the very last thing you'd expect him to do is sell drugs anywhere at knock-down prices. On the other hand we couldn't afford to ignore that lobby entirely. Some of the larger acquisitions we were planning would come up before the Federal Trade Commission. Strictly speaking, their brief is to block developments they consider anti-competitive; in practice they're bound to be influenced by their perception of a company. This is where you have to admire Warren's talents; he was thinking ahead two years or more. First, he cultivated Senators who had the ear of the Commissioners. Second, he was on the look-out for ways to improve the company's record in developing countries – short, that is, of selling drugs cheaply."

Milner nodded slowly. "And then along comes Biomolecular Technologies."

Wyatt smiled. "The company itself wasn't worth a dime, but that soil organism was something that would confound our critics – an alternative technology of the type widely applauded by the Green lobby. Warren saw its potential right away."

Terry fought the urge to say that the organism wasn't remotely ready for use or even for evaluation outside the strict confines of a lab. But Wyatt couldn't know they'd listened to Grant Challoner's warning at the Board Meeting. It had to stay that way.

Wyatt took another sip of water. "Warren had the people at Genon carry out a small-scale field test at Richmond. It looked promising so he had a batch made up in the new bioreactor. It seems you already know about that."

Milner nodded. "Was he planning to market it?"

"I believe so. He said it would cost next to nothing to produce, so we could sell it really cheaply. He obviously had in mind the good publicity and the effect of that on the Federal Trade Commission."

"So then what?"

"He was talking about a pilot project in a poor, rural area, somewhere like Northern China. I was horrified and I told him so."

There was a light knock on the door and Tina entered with a tray.

"Ah, thank you, Tina," Wyatt said.

They waited while Tina distributed the cups, poured the coffee, and set a plate of cookies on the table. Milner waited until she'd withdrawn. "Can you say why you were horrified, Mr. Wyatt?"

"Certainly." Wyatt stirred some sugar into his coffee. "You people may need a little background." He set the spoon down and faced them, clasping his hands. "Everyone knows China's growth has been phenomenal in recent years. In many respects the country's self-sufficient, and that's the way the Chinese want it. But they have four-and-a-half times the US population to feed from a cultivated area that's only three-quarters of ours, so they're forced to import grain. That bothers the regime; they'd prefer the country to be self-reliant in grain production too. Their solution is to slap grain quotas on the farmers. The farmers don't like it. They could make more money growing high-value cash crops like fruits and vegetables. They see the urban population getting more prosperous and they want part of it."

"So what?" Maggie interjected. "With a political system like theirs they can afford to ride roughshod over a few dissident farmers."

"You may think so, but actually that's not a realistic option. About two-thirds of their population earns their living from the land. That's a lot of people and revolutions have come from that quarter in the past, so they have to tread carefully. Fortunately for them there's a solution."

"Which is…?"

"The farmers can get a better return from the existing land by switching to high-yield crops and seeds, and harvesting two or three crops a season. Then they can meet the government's quotas and still grow the more profitable lines they want to. Trouble is, that sort of agriculture takes a lot out of the soil. To maintain the yield they have to use copious amounts of fertilizer."

"Right…"

"The manufacture of fertilizers starts with ammonia. There are, of course, factories all over the world. Who do you think produces the most?"

"I would have thought we did," said Milner.

"No, it's the Chinese, and by a long stretch. We have about 8 per cent of worldwide production; the Chinese have 28 per cent. Some of that's used to make polymers and dyestuffs and some is used to make explosives, but 80 per cent is used to make fertilizers. China is by far the world's biggest producer of fertilizer and they consume nearly everything they make. With me so far?"

"Yeah, go on."

"All right. Now place against that background an inexpensive organism that converts nitrogen in the air into ammonia in the soil and what have you got? The potential collapse of a very large and profitable industry. They certainly wouldn't take kindly to that. I told him China was a very unwise choice."

"And what did he say to that?"

"He just laughed, said it served them damned well right. You know, he suspected the Chinese of unfair industrial practices. We lost at least one valuable contract to them."

"So he ran the trials anyway."

Wyatt shrugged. "I suppose he must have. And this – this abduction – seems to be to punish him."

"How do you think they discovered the organism was made by Vance?" Milner asked.

"That I don't know, but the Chinese have a reputation for cyber crime, don't they?"

"You'd have defended yourselves against that, surely? Didn't the company employ an external security service?"

Terry couldn't help but admire the innocent way Milner had slipped the question in.

"Not that I know of. It's never cropped up in the books. You might ask Rose if she knows."

"I guess we should do that. Something like this, we need to follow up every security angle." Milner turned slightly so that he could catch Maggie's eye. She nodded.

"Anyway," said Dominguez, "if you're right, and the captains of China's ammonia industry decided to take their revenge on Signett, it would have been easy enough for them. They could use the triads in Hong Kong to broker the deal with the cell in Boston."

"That would explain the ultimatum, at least," Wyatt said. "But what am I supposed to do about it?"

Dominguez raised his eyebrows at Terry and Maggie.

Terry said, "Tell me, Mr. Wyatt, do you have any scientific training?"

"Me? Oh, no. My background is economics and business

management. I only have a slender grasp of these other things."

"And Mr. Signett?"

"Columbia Law and a Harvard MBA. He's very smart."

Terry shook his head. "Not as smart as you think. That organism spreads by itself. It will be well established in the environment by now. There isn't a thing you can do about it."

"Oh my God, I wish to Heaven there was."

"So, I imagine, does Mr. Signett."

Dominguez got up.

"Okay, at least we know where we are. I'll report back and we'll start searching. We'll use what informants we have but that's a tight little universe down there – people are afraid of what might happen to them if they open their mouths. And unless we find Mr. Signett soon I can't say I hold out much hope for him."

CHAPTER 50

Dominguez drove them back to Boston.

"Eddie," said Milner. "You know what he said about wanting to keep a lid on this, for the company's sake?"

"Yeah, what about it?"

"I think you should take it on board, and not just for the company's sake. The Head of the FBI briefed me in person for this assignment and he said heads would roll if anything about the organism became public. Even *he* didn't know the full story."

Dominguez glanced at him, eyebrows raised. "Goes that high, huh? Well, let's put it this way. I'm pretty sure Signett had Challoner killed. If I had the evidence I'd like to put him in the dock for it but I don't and even if I did it looks like I won't get the chance. One way and another I can't see any of this coming out. All we got from this whole business with Vance is motive. And we still don't have Challoner's killers."

Maggie leaned towards Terry and murmured, "And we still don't have Zak Gould." His lips tightened and he nodded.

Terry's phone rang.

"Hello, McKinley," he said.

"Dr. McKinley, please hold for the President."

"Yes, okay," he replied.

He covered the mouthpiece and mouthed 'President' to Maggie.

"Terry?" came the President's voice.

"Yes Mr. President."

Terry saw Dominguez's head swivel round. "You gotta be shitting me," he whispered.

"Terry, how is the investigation coming? Chris tells me you've found out who made the organism."

"Yes Sir. A scientist called Zak Gould. We're working with the FBI and local police to track him down."

"You will find him soon?"

"I hope so Sir."

"So do I, Terry. So do I." The President's voice was tight. "I've been looking at the reports on the atmospheric ammonia. At the rate it's increasing we'll be over the threshold in days. Days! I don't want to push that button Terry, but at the same time, well, you know."

Terry breathed out. "Yes Sir, I know."

There was a pause then the President spoke again. "We're all counting on you Terry. Good luck."

The call ended and Terry put the phone back in his pocket.

"Was that who I think it was?" said Dominguez incredulously.

"Don't ask, Eddie," replied Milner. "Just don't ask."

For a few minutes they travelled in silence. Then Milner said:

"This Chinese thing, Eddie. Why now?"

"I don't know. Snatched him from right under our noses, though."

"That could have been the intention," Terry said. "We've been all over that company in the last few days. Their mole certainly passed that on. Maybe they wanted to exact revenge before we could make an arrest ourselves."

"Possibly," said Dominguez. "Pity they couldn't do it before Signett ordered up Challoner's murder."

"What about Wyatt?" Milner asked. "Do you think he had a hand in that?"

"I'd say not," Dominguez replied. "I could be wrong but my feeling is, Wyatt's clean. He was clued up on the broad strategy but I don't think he had the key to the dirty tricks cabinet. Your question on security, for example. He was the one suggested we talk to Rose about it."

"Yeah, what happened about that, Maggie?" Milner asked, turning round to her.

"I asked Rose if she could show me where the ladies' room was. She got the point. She told me Signett did have a security consultant he used from time to time, a man called Francis Kelly. She didn't have any contact details because Mr. Signett insisted on handling anything to do with security himself. And then she said after we left on Tuesday she had to rearrange his appointments for almost the whole afternoon. I thanked her and left."

"What did she mean by that?" Sam asked.

"In that context? I can only assume she meant that Signett consulted Kelly at short notice on Tuesday afternoon. And I think she wanted me to know that."

"So why didn't she just say?"

"Same reason she didn't just give me that disk. I think it's a question of divided loyalties. She's a confidential secretary to Signett but she wants justice for Challoner."

Dominguez whistled softly. "And Challoner was killed that night. That just about ties it up for Signett. Thanks, Maggie. We'll be looking into the dealings of Mr. Francis Kelly. And maybe we won't be wringing our hands too much about the fate of Mr. Warren Signett."

He turned the police cruiser into the station and they followed him inside. He spoke over his shoulder.

"I just want to drop in on the Forensic Team. See if they've made any progress."

There were six people in the room, standing around a large table covered with evidence bags, taking notes and making lists. Kate, the girl they'd seen briefly at Challoner's house, came over. She was wearing a T-shirt and jeans. Without the bulky coveralls she was stick-thin.

"Hi, Eddie," she said. "We're all done at the house."

"You find anything?"

She shook her head. "Cell phone was missing. He certainly had one – Rick found the account when he was looking through the filing drawer in the desk. They could have taken it. We're monitoring the number in case someone switches it on but they're probably not that stupid."

"Damn, he probably kept his contacts on it."

"No. I don't think so. I'd say he preferred to keep a conventional appointments diary and address book." She gave the others a quick glance, then returned her attention to Dominguez. "Something like this, maybe."

She led them over to the table and picked up a sealed polythene bag. Inside was a small notebook with black, plasticized covers.

"Have forensic finished with it?"

"Yeah. Don't worry, there's nothing on it. Too textured. In any case it looks like they were wearing gloves. We haven't found a print anywhere, other than the victim's."

"Hard to believe someone gave him that beating wearing gloves."

"That's what we thought. Maybe just one of the perps was wearing gloves and he was the one going through the stuff. Meanwhile the other one was using the victim as a punching bag."

Maggie grimaced.

Dominguez pointed. "So did they miss this?"

"No, we don't think so. It was on the floor, face down and open. Like someone took a quick squint and threw it aside."

Dominguez opened the seal and took out the notebook. He leafed through it and pursed his lips.

"It's not an address book," he said. "It's not indexed. There's a few memos, shopping lists – here's some notes from one of his meetings."

He continued to turn the pages.

Kate said, "From the other examples we've seen, it's the victim's writing, for sure. Small, neat hand."

"Yeah. Oh, here's some formulas. Terry, Maggie: you're the scientists. You'd better take a look."

He passed the notebook to them, opened at a page. They saw a list of chemicals, with percentage contents written against each one.

Sulphur: 0.54%

Rhodium: 84.73%

Potassium: 0.958%

Argon: 3.3%

Oxygen: 2.81%

Zinc: 8.448%

They frowned, then looked at each other.

Kate said, "I need to get on, Eddie. Can I leave that with you?"

"Sure. Thanks, Kate." He turned to the others. "We'll use an interview room. My office is a tip."

They went down the corridor and entered a room marked "Interview Room B". It was a small, square room, furnished only with a table and four upright chairs. Terry sat down, still studying the open notebook, and Maggie took the chair next to him. Dominguez and Milner stood behind them, looking over their shoulders.

"It's weird," Terry murmured to Maggie.

"There's no way you could make up a solution from that lot," she said. "I thought for a moment it might be an analysis, but it can't be that either. Argon and oxygen are gases, and rhodium's a rare and very unreactive metal."

"The numbers don't make sense either," Terry said. "Why are some ingredients quoted to three decimal places, and others to only one?"

"He's written the elements down with their full names," she mused. "You wouldn't do that normally, not in a notebook."

"What happens if...?" He snapped his fingers.

"What?" Milner and Dominguez said simultaneously.

"I think it's a code of some sort. Replace the elements with their accepted abbreviations and what do you get? S, Rh, K, A, O, Zn."

Milner said, "That doesn't spell anything."

"Maybe it's an anagram."

Maggie was still frowning. "What about the percentages?" she asked.

Terry shook his head. "I don't think they are percentages; if they were, they'd add up to a hundred percent, and these add up to slightly more than that. Maybe the letters just give you the order, telling you how to combine them. Put them in alphabetical order, A, K, O, Rh, S, Z, and you get one long number."

"A phone number?" Milner asked.

"Too long," Dominguez said. "There's twenty digits there."

"Could be two phone numbers," said Maggie.

"True."

"But why encode them?" Dominguez asked.

"In case someone got hold of the notebook? He could be protecting the identity of the people in here. Maybe one was Rose – yes, it could be, look, Rh, O, S. I bet that's what the letters are for. There's no E but it's near enough. Rose!"

"What about the 'h'?" Milner asked.

"He couldn't help that," Maggie answered. "There isn't an element with R on its own. What does that leave, Terry?"

"K, A, Z. No, it's Z, A, K – Zak. It's Zak Gould!"

"Nice one, Terry!" Milner exclaimed.

"The 'Dr. Gould' they mentioned on the disk?" Dominguez asked. "Who exactly is this guy?"

Terry answered. "He's a scientist. He's the one who engineered the organism that escaped. He worked for Vance for a time, then just left without saying anything. We need to track him down but no one seems to know where he is. Maybe this is what Challoner's killers were looking for."

"Someone must be pretty darn anxious to get their hands on him if they'll kill just to get his phone number."

"Yeah – someone like Signett," said Milner, grimly. "Zak Gould developed the organism, knew exactly what went into it. He'd be a major threat."

Maggie pointed. "Remember what Rose said? 'They got him. They'll get the other one, too.' Zak's the other one."

Milner nodded. "That's the way it looks." He took out his own notebook. "Here, read those numbers out."

"Rose is 847-328-1954. And Zak is 844-833-5908."

"Must be cell phone numbers," Dominguez said, reaching for his belt.

"Whoa, baby!" Milner said, pushing the phone down. "Not so fast. Who are you calling?"

"Rose. It's okay, she won't be at the office at this hour. She'll be at home."

"And suppose Maggie is right? Suppose she's under surveillance?

They could have bugged her house."

Dominguez pulled a face. "Yeah okay, I'll get one of our guys to run the numbers. We'll have an answer in a few minutes."

He came back in a few minutes later with a smile on his face. "Bingo", he said. "Rose Fitzgerald".

"What about the other number?" said Milner

"No dice there, I'm afraid. One of these top up phones, not registered to anyone."

"Must be him, though," said Terry. "So do we call him now?"

"No," Milner said.

"Why the hell not?"

"Listen, if the guy was living any normal sort of life the Bureau would have tracked him down by now, and they haven't. What that says to me is, he's gone to ground. If we just phone him chances are he'll go to ground somewhere else and we'll never find him. What we have to do is trace the number. If his cell phone is switched on we should be able to find out where it is, within fifty to a thousand metres, depending on how built-up the area is. We can throw a cordon around it and then phone him and move in."

"Come on, then," Maggie said. "What are we waiting for?"

Dominguez stared at her. "Are you crazy? You've got one shot at this and you want to rush in and blow it?"

"Eddie, finding this man and talking to him is essential – it's the whole reason why we're here. If Challoner's killers are after him every minute counts."

He opened his hands. "It takes time to set something like this up! It's too late today – the whole operation has to be in daylight or he could just slip away in the dark."

Maggie turned away with a small moan. "We have to find him, we have to. Tell him, Sam."

Milner looked at her and shook his head. "Maggie, be realistic. It's Thursday, and Challoner was murdered Tuesday night. If he told his killers where Zak Gould was, the man's dead already. If he didn't, they're still looking. Better we do like Eddie says."

"Just give me the rest of the day," said Dominguez. "We'll go in first thing tomorrow."

Back in Terry's hotel room, Maggie took off her shoes and lay on the sofa. Terry took his shoes off, too, but he stood at the window, staring pensively down at the coloured ribbons of cars sliding past one another in the street below.

"So now we know what Signett was up to," Maggie said. "I still don't understand, though. One moment he's happily distributing the organism in the Far East; the next he's killing everyone who knows anything about it. What triggered the change of heart?"

Terry turned to face her. "You want to know what I think?"

"Go on."

"My feeling is, it was the escape from Richmond. Up to then Signett hadn't fully understood the risks – that or he didn't want to understand them. We know the man was stubborn; he saw it as a power struggle – he convinced himself Challoner was being over-cautious and pushed his own agenda through. But Challoner was right: testing the stuff in an open field was far too risky; the organism was probably washed into the river with the first big storm. I expect there was a massive algal bloom, the river stank of ammonia, and Signett started to have second thoughts."

Maggie frowned. "He couldn't have known how far it would spread or what it would do."

"No, but suddenly he saw the potential risk. Trouble was, by that time he'd already set up his field trials abroad. The best he could do was conceal everything to do with the organism at Richmond. That way if things went pear-shaped in China or India or Thailand the trail wouldn't lead back to his company. At the end of the day he was a business man, not a scientist. He never saw the potential consequences."

"And those two research staff who were run off the road were the first victims?"

"Yes. He'd have had Zak killed, too, but Challoner warned him and he went into hiding."

"Challoner didn't go into hiding, and he could have gone public at any time."

"Zak was the real danger. Without him, Challoner would have found it hard to prove anything – all the evidence had been destroyed. Signett must have known the two were close – perhaps very close – so he left Challoner alive in the hope he'd lead them to where Zak was hiding. Then we turned up and he realized he couldn't afford to leave it any longer, so he sent his thugs to beat it out of him."

She nodded slowly. "Signett must have thought he had everything wrapped up. Unfortunately for him the Chinese had inside information. He underestimated them."

"Yes, very badly."

She curled up on the couch. "Poor man."

"He had blood on his hands, Maggie."

"Still, no one deserves to face that."

"You may want to revise that view if his goons get to Zak Gould before us."

She sighed. "We'll know soon enough."

CHAPTER 51

Dominguez picked them up from the hotel at seven-thirty the next morning.

"The others are on their way," he said. "We'll meet there."

He turned onto Route 9.

"Where're we going?" Milner asked.

"Newton Center. Small township about ten miles outside Boston." He turned to Maggie and Terry in the back. "Bet you're glad you're here right now, not Chicago."

Maggie's face fell. "Why, what's happened?"

"You didn't see it on the news last night? Got hit by one of those white smogs. First all the dead fish, now this. Lot of fatalities – some people say five thousand, maybe more. Hospitals are bursting at the seams." He shook his head. "Big city like that. Bad place for it to happen."

Terry met Maggie's eyes. They said nothing.

The call was taken by the officer on reception at Boston police headquarters.

"This is Captain Mulhern," the voice said. "Could you take a message for Detective Dominguez? Tell him I'm running a bit late but I'm on my way right now. I should make it to our meeting in a half hour. Got that?"

"Yes, sir. I'll pass the message on when I see him, but Detective Dominguez isn't at HQ right now."

"He isn't? Well, what about our meeting?"

"I don't know anything about that, sir. He's out on a case."

"He's what! When will he be back?"

"I'm sorry, I can't say."

"Aw, hell. He must have forgotten. And I've lost his cell phone number. That's why I called you."

"I'm afraid I can't give out information like that over the phone, sir."

"No, I'm not asking you to… Shit, I can't meet him tomorrow either; I have to be back in Memphis. Maybe I can meet him where he's at now. Did he say?"

"I believe he went down to Newton Center, sir."

"Okay, I'll try my luck there."

She looked at the dead receiver for a moment, shrugged, and replaced it.

The police deployed quietly, sealing off the street at each end. A series of short service roads branched off to one side. Dominguez had parked the car opposite one of these and they sat there, waiting.

"These here ranch houses," he said, "were built after the last war for returning GIs. They've changed hands plenty of times since then, and the owners put their own mark on them, so each one is different now. Anyhow the layout's not bad from our point of view. For each house we've got a service road on one side and a sort of communal area with a path on the other. Once we've located Zak's house we can watch it front and back. The fix we got suggests it's in one of these three roads."

They watched the uniformed officers going from house to house, talking to the residents and showing them a picture of Zak Gould, extracted from the record of his driver's licence. A little more than an hour later all the officers returned to the street. "Wait here," said Dominguez, and got out of the car to speak to them. They were in a huddle for several minutes, then one of them pointed and he came back. He got in the car.

"Okay, no one recognized the guy in the picture, no answer at six of the houses. But this is a small community, people know their neighbours, so between them we can work out who lives at the houses where nobody answered. All except one: Number 25, Schott Path. They're pretty sure someone lives there, but they don't know who. The next-door neighbour knocked on the door a few times to introduce herself; never any reply. Could be our man."

The two-way radio crackled. "We're all in place, sir."

He picked up the microphone and spoke into it.

"Okay. If you see a guy making a run for it, stop him, but don't shoot. He may be scared but he won't give you any trouble. I mean that: no fireworks. Okay?"

"Affirmative."

Dominguez turned to Milner. "Are you carrying, Sam?"

"Never leave home without it. What about you?"

"Yeah, but look, there are enough sidearms on these two blocks to stop a small army. We're only talking to a scientist, for Christ's sake. Are we all set back there?"

Terry and Maggie said: "Yes."

"Good. Let's go."

Charlie wiped back his thick wavy hair with the fingers of one hand.

"There you go, Dave, Newton Center. The cop on reception said he's here somewhere. Just coast around, it's not that big."

A few minutes later Dave braked sharply. There were several police cruisers up ahead. He drew in to the kerb and switched off the engine. Charlie turned and looked the wiry little man over.

"Not bad. Clean shirt, tie. Did you put proper shoes on, like I told you?"

Dave lifted a foot to demonstrate that he wasn't wearing the usual trainers.

"Good."

Charlie opened the cubby and withdrew a semiautomatic. He screwed in a silencer, checked the safety, and chambered a round. Then he reached behind him and tucked the pistol into his trouser belt. He let the jacket fall back to cover it.

"Okay," he said. "Let's go."

Dominguez knocked again and listened. He spoke through the door.

"Police. Let us in, Zak."

A voice came from somewhere on the other side. It sounded slurred.

"Go away. Leave me alone."

"Zak, let us in. We're not going to hurt you. We're here to protect you."

"I don't need protecting. Go away."

"Zak, you sure as hell do need protecting. They got Grant Challoner and they'll get you."

There was a silence. Then the voice said:

"They got Grant?"

"For Chrissake, Zak, don't you watch the news? Grant's dead. And so will you be if you don't let us move you to somewhere safer."

Another silence.

Dominguez looked at Milner and the young uniform officer they'd brought up the path with them. Then they heard the sound of a key turning in a lock and a bolt sliding back. Another bolt. The door opened a crack, stopped by a chain. A face moved in the gap, a pair of bloodshot eyes roving from side to side, surveying them.

Dominguez had his badge ready. "I'm Detective Dominguez, Zak. This here is agent Sam Milner of the FBI."

Milner showed his shield.

"Will you let us in now?"

The door closed again. There was a rattling of links, then the door swung back. Dominguez turned to the officer.

"Stand guard here. Don't let anyone in except those two out there." He pointed. "See the guy standing in the road with the girl? When I say the word, call them over and let them through. I'll leave the door open for them. No one else."

"Yes, sir."

Dominguez turned and went into the house.

The beginning of the cordon was marked by two police cruisers, parked so as to block the road, lights flashing. The patrol officer watched two men approaching, one tall and well-built, the other small, with a curious spring in his step. When they were a little closer he challenged them.

"Sorry, buddy. You'll have to stop right there."

"It's okay, son," the bigger man said, flashing a police badge. "We're part of the operation. Is Detective Dominguez in place yet?"

"Yes, sir. He's at number 25, Schott."

"Very good. We'll join him there."

Dr. Zak Gould bore little resemblance to the bright young man in the photograph. He looked as if he hadn't shaved in days. His long hair was uncombed, his shoulders were hunched. Not just his breath but his skin and clothes exuded alcohol, which mingled with the sour odour of his unwashed body.

They stood together just inside the door.

"You've been a bit out of it, haven't you, Zak?" Dominguez said.

"Yeah, you could say that. What happened to Grant?"

"Someone beat him to death. Do you know why anyone would want to do that to him?"

Zak seemed to shrink into himself. His voice became thin, high-pitched.

"Oh shit. Poor Grant. He was such a great guy. Oh shit."

"I'm sorry, Zak." Dominguez laid a hand gently on the man's shoulder. He was inwardly cursing himself. He'd hoped to scare Zak into cooperation. He'd misjudged it.

Milner caught his eye and took over.

"Listen, Zak, there's a couple of English people outside, scientists like yourself. They'd like to meet you. Can I let them in?"

Zak uncurled slightly and gave him a bleary look. His voice dropped to a more normal pitch.

"Sure. What's the difference? Come through. Have a drink."

He shambled off. Dominguez turned and signalled to the officer to call Terry and Maggie over. Then he went inside.

When Terry entered, Milner was standing in the corridor. "He's in there," he said, pointing. "You get started, Eddie. I'm going to see if I can rustle up some strong coffee."

Dominguez headed into the living room and Terry and Maggie followed. The room was almost devoid of furniture: just a small desk with a chair, and two more chairs. Zak had probably rented the house and a few sticks of furniture to put in it. On the desk was a glass and a whisky bottle. Zak went over, lifted the bottle and held it to the light. It was empty. He said "Shit" again and dropped it into a wastepaper basket. It made a loud clink as it hit the bottles that were already there. Then he sat down heavily.

Dominguez pulled a chair up.

"Why did they kill him, Zak?"

He didn't seem to be listening.

"Why, Zak? Was it the organism?"

Zak's bloodshot eyes rolled slowly over to him and reached some sort of focus. His voice was distant.

"Th' organism. Yeah. He coulda told everyone."

"He could have done that years ago. Why didn't he?"

He frowned and refocused. "He was tryin' to protect me." He laughed a little hysterically, then slumped. "Shit. He was such a great guy."

Terry and Maggie were standing quietly at the back of the room. They exchanged glances and Terry saw her nostrils twitch. Dominguez continued.

"Did he come to see you after the Board Meeting? The one where he resigned?"

"Oh yeah. He was real angry – 'bout the organism, I mean. When he tol' me they were going into production, hell, I was angry too. We were on the same side, Grant and me, always had been. They had no right to start makin' it. I wasn' finished. Nowhere near it. Jesus."

He buried his head in his hands.

From another room there came the sound of a kettle boiling.

Zak's voice continued, slightly muffled.

"Grant said if things got out of hand I'd be in danger. Said I should hide out somewhere, helped me find this place. He shoulda done the same. But he wouldn't hide. Not Grant."

"So Grant was the only one who knew where you were."

"Tha's right." Zak's voice was a plaintive sob. "He looked after me!" He turned red-rimmed eyes on Dominguez. "I was only trying to do a bit of good in this goddamned world. You ever seen poverty? I mean, real poverty?"

"I seen poor people, yeah."

"I don't mean like we got in this country. I mean real poverty. I seen it. When I was a student, back-packing in the Far East. Poverty there all right. I'm talkin' 'bout people with a lousy piece of corrugated iron for a roof, dirt for a floor, nothing to eat but a handful of rice a day, sometimes not even that. And the damnedest thing is, these people, these people who got next to nothing, share whatever they got with you – 'cause it's a tradition with them to honour guests, see? Jeez, I said to myself, I swear if I ever get a chance to do something to help 'em I will."

"And you did…"

Milner came in, carrying a mug. The smell of coffee wafted after him, doing something to ameliorate the odours that pervaded the room. He planted the mug on the desk in front of Zak.

"Here, drink this, buddy. It'll make you feel better."

Zak sized up the mug, then reached for it. He took a swig of the coffee and swallowed noisily.

"Rod didn't like it, of course," he said.

"Rod Hillman?"

"Yeah. He said we needed to finish what we'd already started. But hell, I was working on it in my own time. It was my special project. See, these people aren't lazy; not at all. They work hard. They could grow two, three crops of rice a year, and other things too if they could only put the nitrogen back in the soil. But the soil's poor and they can't afford the goddamned fertilizer. That's why I worked on the organism. I thought I could make a difference."

He took another sip of the coffee and wiped at one eye with the back of his hand. Dominguez winced, thinking he was about to cry, but instead he suddenly looked into the mug of coffee, frowned and said, "I need a drink. A proper drink. I have to get another bottle."

Dominguez said gently, "In a moment, Zak. Have some more coffee, now. Look, there's someone here waiting to talk to you. Her name's Dr. Maggie Ferris. She's come all the way from England to meet you."

He looked up, caught Maggie's eye, and made a very slight movement of his head.

Maggie hurried over and Dominguez got up to make way for her. She pulled the chair around so that she was sitting next to Zak and laid a hand on his arm.

"Dr. Gould," she said, "it's such an honour to meet you."

He looked up at her for the first time. His expression was curious.

"It is? Why?"

"The organism you engineered. It's brilliant! How on earth did you do it?"

Zak blinked, then blinked again. He seemed to be gathering far-flung thoughts, assembling them. When he looked at her again his eyes had acquired a little more focus and the voice was a little less lazy.

"You know the hardest part?" he asked.

Maggie chewed her lip furiously. Then she took a deep breath:

"No normal organism would turn out ammonia incessantly. It would stop as soon as the local concentration got too high."

Zak brought the flat of his hand down on the desk.

"That's exactly right! You're a smart person. Okay, so what did I do? I took sequences from a nitrogen-fixing species, and put them in an organism that doesn't normally fix nitrogen. It doesn't have the feedback control, see, so it never thinks it's making too much. It just goes on and on and on, exporting ammonia. On and on and on. Better'n any species that ever existed."

"You inserted the sequences as a plasmid?"

"Yeah, 'course. A plasmid."

"Can this type of organism exchange plasmids, Zak?"

"What, like antibiotic resistance, you mean? I don't know. It was one of the things I wanted to check."

"Zak, if it could exchange plasmids that would be dangerous, wouldn't it? It wouldn't be just your soil organism that made ammonia; it would be cyanobacteria all over the world, rivers, oceans, everywhere."

"Oh shit, yeah. You wouldn't want that to happen."

"Suppose it did happen, Zak? How would you stop it?"

The young officer at the door stiffened as he saw the two men approaching. They turned up the path. The one in front was small and bounced along on the balls of his feet. He could see that the second man was larger but he didn't have a clear view of him.

He held up a hand. "Sorry, guys. No one's allowed in."

The small man smiled, and then he did a curious thing: he skipped lightly to one side.

And now the officer saw the man behind, a heavy-set man with a full head of wavy hair and a crooked nose, and there was something in his hand, and he saw the flash, and something slammed into his chest, and suddenly nothing seemed to matter anymore.

For a moment he stared uncomprehendingly at the sky. Then it darkened at the edges and shrank to nothing.

Two pairs of shoes stepped around the body, over the threshold, and into the house.

Terry stood near the door, holding his breath. This was it: the crux of the investigation. Maggie was at centre stage, yet she looked relaxed, as if she were having a casual conversation with a colleague over a cup of tea. To her right, Dominguez and Milner stood frozen so as not to provide the slightest distraction.

Zak blinked several times and shook his head. "You couldn't stop it." Then he frowned and lifted his forefinger. "'cept, maybe…"

"Yes?"

He smiled and prodded her gently on the arm with the forefinger.

"Has an Achilles' Heel," he said. "See…" he prodded her again. "It was in there already." He laughed.

"What was in there, Zak?"

Something caught the corner of Terry's eye. He looked to his right and froze. The black muzzle of a silencer was coming through the slightly open door. And it was pointing directly at Maggie.

CHAPTER 52

Before Terry could react there was a flash and a curious sound – something between a thud and a chirp – accompanied by a cry from the other side of the room. The muzzle came further through the door and there was another flash and a thud.

A tidal wave of anger surged through him. He grabbed the exposed wrist and yanked it through the doorway. He acted in the same instinctive way as he had all those weeks ago by the river in Wales. He twisted, stepped in tight, and threw the man, Aikido style, with the wrist, elbow, and shoulder locked. He felt as well as heard the sickening wrench and the man landed heavily with an agonized shout, the semiautomatic clattering onto the floor. Still gripping the wrist, Terry kicked the weapon away just as he heard Milner shout:

"Watch out!"

He looked up to see a small man coming straight at him. He threw the wrist away from him and faced the newcomer.

He didn't see where the punch came from. It shot out with the suddenness of a snake striking and sent him staggering against the wall. The man closed on him quickly, his hands a blur, throwing punches to Terry's head and body with bewildering speed. Terry ducked to one side and dived into a rolling breakfall, coming up again into a fighting stance. The man came forward again, bouncing and weaving. Two jarring hooks landed to Terry's body and another high on his cheek. Terry backed away, trying to read his next move. It came quickly, a straight left to Terry's face, but this time he was ready for it. His hand snapped around the man's wrist. He held it as he side-stepped and swept the man's legs from beneath him in an ankle throw, dumping his astonished attacker on his back. Terry moved in fast with an arm lock, his leg across the man's throat, hips lifted against the straightened arm.

Looking across the floor he could see Milner pinning the larger man face down, both arms twisted behind him. Milner shouted:

"Eddie, get the cop outside to cuff him!"

Dominguez ran for the door.

Terry yelled, "Maggie, are you hurt?"

"I'm all right, I'm all right."

Terry murmured, "Thank God." Then, louder, "What about Zak?"

"Shit, he's been hit."

Terry sighed grimly and tightened his hold. The man started to jerk up and down, trying to buck his way out of the hold. Terry raised his hips slightly, eliciting a squeal of pain.

"Keep still, or I'll break your arm," he shouted.

The bucking stopped.

Dominguez returned with a pair of handcuffs. With Milner's help he clipped the larger man's wrists behind him.

Milner snapped, "Where's the cop?"

Dominguez kept his voice low. "He's dead. The bastard shot him."

Milner's eyes flashed. "You lousy sonofabitch!" he said. He kicked the man viciously in the ribs, and the body contracted with a grunt. Then he seemed to reconsider and threw in a harder kick, prompting a howl of protest.

"Okay, that's enough," he said. "Keep him covered."

He came over to Terry, drew his revolver, and pressed the muzzle against the smaller man's ear.

"You give me any trouble, punk, and I'll be delighted to blow your fucking brains out," he said. "Got that?"

The man looked at him with wild eyes. He said nothing.

Dominguez lifted the two-way communicator in his other hand.

"Dominguez. Emergency. Everyone to the house, number 25. And we need paramedics – fast."

Minutes later they heard a stampede of footsteps and the room was full of blue uniforms. Dominguez kept the sidearm trained as Terry relinquished his hold and handed his snarling opponent over to two officers. As they put the handcuffs on, Dominguez pointed to his chafed knuckles.

"Well, well. What have we here?"

The man sneered insolently at him. "Did that just now."

"I don't think so. I think maybe you did that Tuesday night, when you were busy beating someone to death. Take him away."

Two more officers were already walking the other man through the door. Dominguez went with them.

The room suddenly seemed empty.

Terry crossed to the desk and crouched down behind it, next to Maggie. She was holding Zak's hand. A red stain was spreading across the man's shirt.

Maggie was distraught. Tears were streaming down her face as she said desperately: "You have to save him. You don't understand. He can't die."

Terry slipped an arm round her shoulders.

"Maggie" he said softly.

"We have to save him, Terry," she said, without taking her eyes off Zak. "He was just talking to me and the next thing he was flying backwards onto the floor. I didn't think, I just threw myself down, too."

"You were lucky you weren't hit too. The bastard managed to squeeze off another shot before I nailed him."

She looked round and started as she saw his face. "Terry, you're hurt!"

He ran the tip of his tongue over a split lip, then gently fingered the welt that was swelling under one eye. "He was very fast. I expect I'll be sore for a few days."

Then, seeing Zak's eyelids flicker, he said, "Hold on, there, my friend. Ambulance is on its way."

Milner came over. He looked at Zak and shook his head. Then he gripped Terry's shoulder.

"What do you think of this guy?" he announced to no one in particular. "Joe Englehardt says he's sending me a couple of British boffins and what do I get? Frigging James Bond."

Terry shrugged self consciously. "I just got lucky."

"We owe you, Terry, we owe you good. That guy was ready to take all of us out."

A murmur came from Zak. Maggie put her ear close to his mouth. He murmured again. She frowned and shook her head.

Dominguez came in. "Ambulance is here," he said. Then he saw Zak and muttered, "Oh, shit."

Maggie said, "I'm going with him"

"I'll come with you."

"No, Terry," she said. "You and Sam need to go through the house. See if he kept his lab books here. I'm sure he's trying to tell me something."

The paramedics came in at a run. They checked Zak briefly, then one put a line in and they started to transfer him to a stretcher.

Maggie got up. She said simply "I'm with him" and followed them out to the ambulance.

CHAPTER 53

As the paramedics carried Zak out of the house and down the path Maggie noticed that they had to step around something. Looking down as she followed them she realized with a shock that it was a body, covered with a blanket. At the side of the entrance a blue cap with a badge had lodged between the branches of a dead rose bush. A round-toed black shoe protruded from under the blanket. She bit her lip and swallowed, then hurried to the ambulance. Behind her the uniformed officers were already taping off the entire area.

By the time she climbed in they had Zak on some sort of gurney and the drip was on a stand. One of the paramedics was holding an oxygen mask to his face while the other went round to drive or to sit with the driver – she couldn't see which. She sat on a bench next to Zak and put her hand out to steady herself as they took off rapidly with a brief burst of the siren. She looked at Zak and then at the paramedic, who gave her a brief smile.

The ambulance slowed, sounded the siren, accelerated and turned.

Zak's eyelids flickered and her heart leapt.

"Are his lips moving?" she asked anxiously.

The man lifted the mask for a moment.

"They are," she exclaimed, "he's trying to speak to me…"

The paramedic replaced the mask.

"Lady, he needs oxygen. Chances are he's got a collapsed lung, maybe worse."

"Please, what he's trying to say, it's terribly important. Believe me, you have no idea how important it is."

He looked at her dubiously and lifted the mask. Zak's lips moved and she craned to hear.

"The Achilles' Heel…" he murmured.

At that moment the siren sounded in a long, continuous, two-note wail. She shook her head in disbelief.

"For God's sake, can't you tell him not to use that thing for a moment…?"

The man's eyebrows lifted. "Lady, we're shooting red lights as it is! Do you want to get us all killed?"

Zak's lips were still moving. The siren stopped. The paramedic promptly replaced the mask.

Maggie was about to say something, then she gave up. This man's number one priority was to keep his charges alive until they reached the hospital. It would be pointless to argue with him.

She clenched her fists until her nails bit deep into the palms, and suffered her frustration in silence.

Terry finished going through the house with Milner, then arranged to be taken to the hospital in a patrol car. The driver told him he'd wait outside.

He ran in and queued with growing impatience at the reception desk. A bored receptionist tapped at a computer and announced that she had no record of the admission but the patient would have been taken to the Emergency Department and he could ask there. Then he was bounced from pillar to post by a succession of people, all of whom seemed far too busy to help him. Eventually he was directed to a waiting area that contained nothing more than a water cooler, an overflowing waste bin, and some brown, wall-mounted, plastic-covered seats, many of them slashed.

And there was Maggie, hunched over, sitting on the end of the row. There was no one else around. The room seemed altogether too large for her.

"Maggie?" he said.

She looked up. Her eyes were red-rimmed. His heart dropped.

"When did it happen?"

"He died in the ambulance. They worked hard on him but he never recovered consciousness."

She stood and he took her in his arms. Her shoulders were quaking.

"That's three people dead," she sobbed, "and it's all our fault. They'd be alive now if it weren't for us."

"What? What are you talking about?"

She lifted her tearful gaze to him. "They got Challoner because they were afraid we'd speak to him. But first they made him say where Zak was. Or did they just follow us? I don't know. All I know is, Zak was safe enough before we came, and now he's dead too. And that poor young policeman at the door…" She buried her head in his chest.

His voice was gentle. "Maggie, stop torturing yourself. We had no choice: we had to find Zak. He thought he was helping to alleviate poverty; instead he's put the whole of mankind at risk. He didn't mean to, but that's the reality. We have to keep an eye on the bigger picture. Thousands have died already. Billions more could die if we don't stop this thing."

She responded between sobs. "I – know – I – know."

He rubbed her shoulder and after a while her body relaxed. She took a deep breath and straightened up. As she looked at him her eyes became wider and darker. She reached out, touching her fingers lightly to his bruised face. "He hurt you badly."

Her fingers were cool, their touch soothing on the inflamed skin. He tried to take the hand in his but she drew away, then searched her handbag for a tissue and blew her nose. Her voice was muffled by the tissue.

"Did you search the house?"

"Yes, it didn't take long. The house was almost bare, Maggie: no computer, not a single bookshelf or filing cabinet or chest of drawers. He kept a few clothes in a suitcase. We looked under the bed and in the kitchen cupboards, found some bread and cheese and several bottles of whisky, nothing more. There were a couple of paperbacks and some bills in the desk, not in his name. That was it. He must have been going out of his mind with boredom, a brilliant young man like that, with nothing to do except keep himself hidden. No wonder he took to drink."

"That's it, then. The end of the trail. He told us it was a plasmid and that's about all we've learned from this entire escapade."

"Didn't he say something about the organism having an Achilles' Heel?"

"Yes, he said it again in the ambulance but if it meant anything we're never going to find out now."

Terry's phone rang. He took it out and answered the call. He listened for a long moment in silence before saying: "Ok, I'll be back tonight."

He turned slowly to face her.

"That was Chris. We've crossed the threshold."

CHAPTER 54

Silvia Mussini was still in her lab when they arrived back at the Institute that evening. She led Terry and Maggie into her office and gestured to the chairs before sitting down herself. She shook back thick, dark hair and smiled. "You've been gone a while. We missed you." Then her eyes settled on the red and purple bruise high on Terry's cheek, which had by now acquired a spreading penumbra of brownish-yellow. Her smile faded. "What happened to you?"

Terry gave a small grimace. "We thought we could make a real contribution to the research effort, Silvia. We've been working with the FBI, looking for the guy who created the organism. And we found him. His name was Dr. Zak Gould."

Her eyes narrowed. "He spread the organism?"

"No, he only created it. The people responsible for spreading it wanted to silence him so he'd gone into hiding. We finally tracked him down and Maggie got him talking."

Silvia's face lit up. She turned to Maggie. "Really? What did he say?"

"He confirmed that he'd engineered the organism by introducing a plasmid. He started to tell me what was in it. Then he was shot dead."

Silvia raised fingertips to her mouth.

"They'd have killed the rest of us, too, if it hadn't been for Terry."

Silvia's voice was a whisper. "My God."

"Unfortunately," Maggie went on, "it seems it was all for nothing. He said the organism had an Achilles' Heel but he didn't tell me what it was." Her shoulders sagged. "He knew everything there was to know about that organism. I'd have brought him back here, got him to help us." Her eyes met Silvia's. "We could have been leaps ahead! Now he's dead, and we learned nothing."

Silvia placed a hand over Maggie's. "Don't be too disappointed, Maggie. You had to try."

Maggie nodded sadly, "thanks, Silvia." She straightened up. "Were you able to make any progress?"

"I have some more data from the sequencing teams." She shrugged. "I must say it would have been useful if that man was with us now. What we have is so hard to understand."

"Oh? Why?"

"Well, I have been studying the biochemical pathway for making ammonia from nitrogen. It is not simple – it takes a number of enzymes to do it. Maggie, there is nowhere near enough DNA in the construct to encode the genes needed to make those enzymes."

Maggie blinked rapidly. This was so contrary to her expectations she could scarcely absorb it. She cast her mind back to what the poor, half-drunken Zak Gould had said to her in the house. It wasn't hard; she must have gone over it a hundred times. "I took sequences from a nitrogen-fixing species, and I put them in an organism that doesn't normally fix nitrogen." That's what he'd said. She'd always assumed that meant he'd transferred all the material needed to create an ammonia pathway. Now Silvia was saying there wasn't enough material in the construct to do that. She replayed the entire conversation in her mind yet again.

And then she frowned.

"Silvia, there was something else Dr. Gould said, something I didn't understand. 'It was in there already.' Then he laughed. Does it mean anything to you?"

Silvia blinked, then turned to stare out of the window. They waited, motionless, watching her in silence. Suddenly she turned back to them. "*Ma certo!* The necessary genetic material is there already! It must be in a primitive form buried somewhere in the chromosomes. Normally it is activated only in nitrogen-fixing bacteria. So – "

She pointed to Maggie and they shouted together. "The plasmid is a switch!"

Terry looked from one to the other. "You've lost me."

Silvia's smile was enigmatic. "The basic gene sequences are already present in other cyanobacteria. This man found out how to activate them. So that is what he did. What he put in the plasmid does not encode the whole pathway; it makes some sort of regulatory factor that sets it going."

"Well I'll be damned," Terry said. "That's what Zak meant by an Achilles' Heel! His plasmid is just a switch. And switches can be turned off as well as on!"

Maggie was breathing quickly. "Silvia, that makes the job easier, doesn't it?"

"Much easier."

"Right, then. Where do we go from here?"

"We have two possible targets," Silvia said. "We can either stop the plasmid making this regulatory factor or we can stop the factor acting on the chromosomal DNA."

"Which would be quickest?"

"It's hard to say. To stop the plasmid from making the factor we need to identify the DNA construct which he has put in it. To stop the factor from acting we have to find out how or where it binds to the chromosomal DNA."

"Do you have enough people to try both approaches?"

Silvia pursed her lips. "No. But after the sequencing teams are finished they will have nothing more to do. Perhaps some of their people can come in and join us."

"Excellent. I'll tell them."

As they hurried downstairs Terry smiled to himself at the change in Maggie. She'd said next to nothing during the whole flight back but now she was positively brimming.

She turned to him. "Terry, you've got to take this to Washington. Convince them to give us more time. We can beat this."

"The threshold's been crossed, Maggie. I'm not sure I can stall them. I'm not sure I want to. Even with this new information, it'll take a long time to work up a solution."

"Please, Terry. Thousands of people don't have to die. Try to convince them."

He looked at her, then nodded. "I'll do everything I can."

CHAPTER 55

Terry took a cab straight from the airport to the NSF building. Trish picked him up from reception and Chris Walmesley was standing outside his office, waiting to greet him. Clearly he already knew about the incident in Boston. He was full of apologies.

"Terry, I am *so* sorry about what happened. Are you okay?"

"Not so bad."

"And Maggie?"

"She's fine."

"If I'd only known…"

"How did you find out?" Terry asked.

"From Bob Cabot. Your FBI agent made a glowing report to Joe Englehardt, and he passed it up the line. You're a bit of a celebrity! Well done."

"Thanks, let's hope it was worth it."

"Indeed. Noel's inside. We'll take a quick look at the data and then we'd better get over to the White House."

By the time Sarah Bethany showed them into the Oval Office, Herbert Kramer and Robert Cabot were already there with the President and Vice-President.

Cabot jumped to his feet and pumped Terry's hand. "Dr. McKinley, my congratulations! Joe Englehardt told me all about it. You're a brave man."

"News gets around."

"Good news is in short supply at the moment."

President Kinghorn patted the sofa to his right. "Have a seat, Terry."

Terry noticed that Kramer was sitting slightly apart from the others and his gaunt features looked even more strained than usual. He made no eye contact.

"We're indebted to you, Terry," the President continued. "Your action saved several lives, including your own. Great job."

"Thank you, sir."

The President scrutinized Terry's bruised face, then pointed under his own eye. "Does that hurt?"

Terry shrugged. "Only if I touch it. Looks worse than it is."

He nodded. "Well, we'd better get on with it. Originally I wanted a progress report from you, but things have moved on since then. Apparently this organism was man-made and we now know who made it."

"Dr. Zak Gould, yes. Sadly he was fatally wounded in the attack, but Maggie did get some information from him beforehand. It'll shorten the development time considerably."

"Question is, will that be enough? We're over the threshold, people. We have white smogs now in Buffalo and Detroit. The one in Detroit hasn't shifted yet. People are demanding to know what's going on. Where are we with that biological solution, Terry?"

"From the preliminary sequence data and the hints Dr. Gould gave us we now know that the plasmid he used is a kind of switch. All we have to do is design another plasmid that stops it from working. It makes the whole task easier."

"Terry," Chris said gently. "What we need to know is whether we have something right now, something we could distribute widely so as to get these ammonia levels down."

Terry took a deep breath. "Right now? No, not right now. Not exactly."

"How long's it going to take?" Cabot asked.

"The teams are working flat out. I think they're only weeks away."

"But that's just the beginning, isn't it?" Cabot said. "The way I understand it, even after they've come up with something that works we have to manufacture it in bulk and start delivering it all over the world. That means we won't be ready to take positive action for months. None of us are going to be around by then!"

Noel Harrison chimed in. "Bob's right. Chris and Terry and I have reviewed the data. The ammonia levels aren't simply above threshold; they're rising more and more steeply. We're seeing smogs in more places, covering larger areas and lasting longer. More people are dying. We can't wait."

Kramer spoke for the first time. His voice was heavy with disdain. "I know very well what all this is leading up to. It's ridiculous to have to take such a crucial decision based on one type of measurement. These data have all been collected in the same way. A good scientist checks his results by getting to them via different routes."

Chris answered stiffly: "I think we're aware of what good science is, Herbert; some of us have actually been practising it for some years."

Terry had to smother a smile but the President was not amused.

"Come on you two, cut that out, we've got enough problems here without bickering among ourselves."

Chris said, "I'm sorry, sir, but we need to be clear about this: it's not just atmospheric measurements; you can see it in other ways. You have the severe weather systems like the hurricanes and those tropical cyclones. You have the worsening white smogs. You have reports of wildlife in trouble: in India and China it's flocks of birds falling out of the sky; elsewhere it's rafts of dead fish washing up along the beaches; mammals, too – bats and whales seem to be particularly susceptible. Pretty soon people are going to start dying everywhere, not just in the major cities with the smogs. It's a consistent picture. The monitoring's necessary, but all we're doing is putting numbers on a situation we already know to exist."

The President raised his eyebrows at Kramer. "I'd say that evidence is pretty darn persuasive, wouldn't you agree, Herbert?"

Kramer's lips were taut and drained of all colour. "It tells me that ammonia levels are going up. It does not tell me they've reached a point that justifies such drastic action. Are we sitting here round the table at this moment choking on ammonia? No, we are not."

Chris sighed audibly and looked away.

Terry felt a surge of irritation. "With respect, Dr. Kramer," he said, "that is looking more and more like a lucky accident. And we're fast running out of luck."

Chris returned his gaze to Kramer. "Herbert, this ground has been trodden a number of times before. All the indications are that the situation will become incomparably worse within weeks. The international experts in the Institute – the Institute of which *you* are the Director – can't be expected to bring their research to a successful conclusion while the air they breathe is filling with ammonia. Like Bob said just now, even after they've reached a solution we still have to grow up the material in bulk. Finally we have to distribute it around the world. That requires aircraft and – as you may be aware – both internal combustion engines and jet engines are designed to burn oxygen, not ammonia. For all those reasons we have to take action *in advance of* the stage you're talking about. The idea of unleashing a supervolcano is just as appalling to us as it is to you, but the message is clear: we're either proactive about this or we're dead."

The President looked at Kramer. "Herbert?"

Kramer's pale features positively vibrated with tension. "It's your decision, Mr. President. It's not something I would wish to be a party to."

The President's jaw tightened. "No, Herbert," he growled softly. "It's not something I'd wish to be party to, either. Except I don't have a choice."

He turned to Cabot. "Bob, you and I go back a long way. What do you think?"

Cabot took a deep breath. His voice was as deep-chested and sonorous as ever. "Mr President, my feeling is we need to do something. We've already lost a lot of citizens in the big cities. People are getting really agitated. Did you see the banner headline in the *Washington Post*? – 'WHO'S NEXT?' If there's an outbreak of violence it could spread very quickly. Our options are going to become more limited if we're fighting rioters and looters on the streets." He sighed and opened his hands. "What more can I say? It's one hell of a decision but whichever way you go, I'll back you."

The President nodded slowly. "Thanks, Bob. Does anyone have anything to add?"

They shook their heads.

"And we've had no viable suggestions for alternative action?"

Again they shook their heads.

The room went quiet. Seconds passed. The President studied each of them in turn, Kramer, Terry, Chris, Noel, and Bob. No one moved or spoke. He broke the silence.

"I'm driven to the conclusion," he said heavily, "that we need to buy more time. Are we agreed? Herbert?"

Kramer set his lips tighter.

"Chris? Noel? Bob?"

Their expressions were grim. All nodded their heads.

"Chuck?"

The Vice-President nodded, too.

The President sagged slightly, as if his body were too heavy to be supported any longer. "I have already discussed this contingency with the Air Force Chief of Staff. He assured me that the operation could be carried out in total secrecy. I did not imagine then that we would ever reach the point where those preparations would be needed." He took a deep breath. "I will instruct him to commence the countdown as of midday today."

Terry closed his eyes. He was thinking of Maggie, but there was nothing more he could do or say.

CHAPTER 56

On the flight back to Florida, Terry gazed out of the window into the August sunshine, thinking about the latest encounter with Herbert Kramer. In Terry's experience you didn't have to like someone to respect them. He neither liked nor respected Kramer. Evidently Kramer felt the same way about him. He'd waited in the anteroom after the meeting in the Oval Office to buttonhole Terry.

"Why wasn't I informed about this, McKinley?"

Terry ignored the rudeness. "It wasn't a secret, Dr. Kramer. The figures are reported at the briefing every Friday morning at eleven o'clock."

The bloodless lips twitched. "I have commitments on a Friday."

"Well I'd have been happy to inform you at some other time if you'd made yourself available, but we haven't seen you down there for weeks. My hands have been pretty full lately, and I'm afraid there hasn't been time to seek you out."

"You found time to seek out Chris Walmesley this morning."

Any number of robust retorts flashed through Terry's mind and it took all his self-control to bite them back.

"Chris has data that's complementary to ours. We put it together to get a more complete picture in preparation for this meeting."

"As the President's adviser I need to know. Kindly keep me informed in future."

And he'd turned on his heel and walked out.

Kramer evidently felt his authority was being undermined, especially by Chris Walmesley. Whatever battles those two had fought in the past, this was surely a time to set aside their differences. Not, it seemed, for Kramer. The evidence was overwhelming, but as long as it was coming from Walmesley the man would go out of his way to trash it.

Unfortunately Kramer was the Director of their Institute and, formally at least, he and Maggie were answerable to him. All the signs were there before, and now it was clearer than ever: sooner or later they were going to clash head-on.

Right now that was the least of his worries. The President was about to unleash the colossal energy of a supervolcano in the north-west United States. With that prospect in view nothing else mattered. He checked his watch. About twenty-one hours to go.

How was he going to break the news to Maggie?

Maggie came running out into the corridor as Terry unlocked his office door. He turned to greet her, briefcase tucked under one arm.

"Terry, oh good, you're back!"

"Hi, Maggie." Terry pushed the door open. "What's up?"

The words tumbled out of her. "It's all hands on deck. Matt's group is still busy sequencing the plasmid but Silvia's managed to transfect the plasmid DNA into *E. coli*. She said it was easy. It's like a miniature version of that production plant at Genon! We'll be able to grow up oodles of plasmid and purify the protein switch it's making. Then we'll sequence the protein and get the structure, and – "

She frowned.

"What is it, Terry? I thought you'd be pleased."

"I am pleased. It's just… I just wish all this could have come sooner, that's all."

She looked at him, eyes narrowed. "What went on in Washington?"

"Come and sit down, Maggie." She shot him a searching glance, then went in, pulled out a chair and sat stiff-backed. He shut the door, came over, and leaned against his desk.

He met her eyes. "The countdown's started."

It was as if a chill hand had clutched inside her chest. For a moment she couldn't speak. Then: "How long have we got?"

"As of now?" He consulted his watch. "About nineteen hours."

She closed her eyes and took a deep breath. "You can't allow this to happen, you just can't. You've got to stop it."

"Sorry, Maggie, only the President can stop it now."

"Then tell him – "

"It's not for me to tell him what to do. He couldn't take advice from a non-US citizen, especially on something as sensitive as this."

His apparently calm acceptance of the situation infuriated her still more.

"This was your bright idea – you have a responsibility!" He recoiled a little, and she could see the hurt in his eyes. "At the very least you could tell him we're close to finding a solution."

When his answer came it was slow and gritty. "I have, I told him you were only weeks away. But this can't be held back on the mere expectation of success. Even if I'd gone to him with the solution in my hand it would take months to deploy it effectively." He turned his head away from her, then back again. "For God's sake, Maggie, why do I have to explain this to you? You know it as well as anyone!"

She jumped up. "This is ridiculous! You're taking a dreadful decision based on an arbitrary – a *theoretical* – condition – " she waved her hands wildly " – somewhere up there in the atmosphere."

He said nothing, just went behind his desk and booted up his computer. "Come round here, Maggie. Look for yourself."

She stood there, breathing hard. Then, lips set tightly, she went to stand behind him. He typed on the keyboard and brought up a display, a map of the world. Both Northern and Southern Hemispheres were studded with red dots.

"Every one of those dots is a city that's suffered a white smog. Some have had more than one. These are the current ones." He tapped a key and a pattern of green dots appeared. He pointed at the screen, his finger stabbing at each dot in turn. "Detroit. Dublin. Glasgow. Rotterdam. Marseilles. Athens. Istanbul. Bangkok. Beijing. Manila. The ones in Detroit, Bangkok, and Beijing show no sign of leaving soon. When they linger like that the death toll rises day after day after day. These things have already killed tens of thousands of people." He turned to her and lifted his hands, mimicking her gesture. "The problem isn't 'up there' any more. It's down here."

"Well yes, but those are major cities, with lots of industry and traffic fumes. You'd expect problems to arise there first."

"But it's happening insidiously elsewhere. Look at how wildlife's suffering."

Some of her indignation subsided and her tone became less strident. "You mean like the incidents with the birds and fish?"

"Birds and fish, and mammals, too: bats, dolphins, whales – "

"The Baja peninsula."

"Not just there: we've had reports of cetacean strandings on the Malabar coast – that's South West India. Humpback whales this time."

Human deaths, animal deaths – death everywhere they looked. She could see the strength of the evidence. But Terry had come to terms with what lay at the end of that countdown. She hadn't; her very soul rebelled against it.

"But we're so close."

"Face it, Maggie: we've run out of time."

They regarded each other in silence. She shook her head. "He won't do it. No Western head of state is going to murder hundreds of thousands of his own people! He'll have second thoughts and stop the countdown."

Terry sighed. "Well all I can say is, if he does, he'll be responsible for hundreds of millions instead."

Chris Walmesley's desk, normally clear, was a mass of papers: lists, graphs, and tables of figures. Noel Harrison sat next to him, shuffling them around. Only their advice could change things now and the burden weighed heavily on them.

In the adjacent office Trish, Walmesley's PA, was blocking all incoming calls and keeping the private line to the Oval Office free.

Noel looked at another graph, then set it down. "Dammit, Chris," he said. "I never thought it would come to this. The biologists ought to have come up with a solution before now."

"Come on, that's not fair and you know it. We gave them six months to get it done, and that was a pretty tall order. In the event they didn't even have nearly that long."

Noel sighed. "Our predictions were reasonable. The levels were going up when we first looked at the data, but not as fast as this." He gestured at the graph and shook his head. "It was those extreme weather systems; we couldn't have foreseen that."

"Noel, we're not in the blame game; we have to deal with things as they are now. And right now our chances of ever beating this thing get worse with every day that passes."

"But Yellowstone…"

"No one's come up with an alternative."

Noel extended his fingers and pushed the graph idly around. "Cabot's suggestion was best, using aircraft to seed rainclouds. That would have washed some of the ammonia out. Maybe we should have pursued it further before we committed to this."

"It was unworkable! You couldn't do it on the scale required."

Noel covered his eyes with one hand.

"Neutron bombs?" he said.

"Neutron bombs? Do we have any?"

"I don't know. Bob Cabot would know."

"All right, suppose we have them. What are you going to do with them?"

"Explode them over the ocean. In all the hot spots, the Sargasso Sea, the Bay of Bengal, the South China Sea – "

"The Great Lakes?"

"Well, maybe not the Great Lakes…"

"Noel, you're fucking crazy. You think Russia and China and North Korea and India and Pakistan are going to sit still while we explode nuclear weapons all over the planet?"

"We'd warn them. The radiation from a bomb like that would be lethal through metres of water. It'd kill the organism."

"Yeah, and it would kill everything else, too, bad organisms, good organisms, krill, fish, everything. In any case, the organism isn't just in the oceans; it's in rivers, lakes, the soil. You wouldn't be doing anything to bring atmospheric ammonia down, and the levels would carry on rising."

"Maybe not as fast."

Chris gave him a patient look. "It won't work, Noel."

Noel sat back. "All right, you think of something."

"I'm trying. Believe me, I'm trying."

Terry stirred, half sat up and looked at the clock. It was five-thirty a.m. He got out of bed and padded into the sitting area. Maggie was there. She was sitting in a chair, elbows on the table, holding her head in her hands.

"How long have you been up?"

"An hour, two hours, three – I don't know."

"What is it? The countdown?"

"Of course, what else?"

"Maggie, it's out of our hands."

"So you keep telling me." She sank her head deeper, the fingers running through the curls at the back of her neck. "There's got to be another way."

He fumbled around for something to say. "You should try to sleep. Can I get you anything?"

He hadn't meant to sound patronising but that's the way it came out.

She tossed her head irritably. "No, nothing. You go back to bed, Terry. I'm all right."

He grimaced and returned to the bedroom. He got into bed but lay awake.

Barring some last-minute change the approaching day would be like no other. In little more than six hours something catastrophic was going to occur, something which he was responsible for, yet powerless to prevent. He thought back to his comments about the Manhattan Project. Is this the way Oppenheimer and all those talented scientists and engineers felt when the bombs they'd designed were dropped on

Hiroshima and Nagasaki? Were they haunted for the rest of their lives by the hundreds of thousands of deaths – of those vaporized in the first instants of the blast, and those who died from burns or radiation poisoning over the ensuing weeks, months, and years? Is that the way he was going to feel about the people unfortunate enough to live too close to the supervolcano and those who might starve or freeze in the aftermath? Or would he think of them as martyrs whose unwitting sacrifice enabled the rest of the human race to survive? He squeezed his eyes shut. It seemed like a shameful indulgence even to think about his own feelings in the face of what could now happen.

Dawn light filtered through the curtains. Time was nearly up.

CHAPTER 57

A thousand miles to the north-west, close to the town of Knob Noster, Missouri, the doors opened on a climate-controlled hangar at Whiteman Air Force Base, home to the United States Air Force 509th Bomb Wing. At the same time six ground crew spilled out of one of the low buildings and hurried across to disappear into the shadowy depths of the hangar. Another man boarded a jeep and drove briskly away in the direction of the armoury.

A tow tractor and a refuelling truck made their way over. A man dressed in coveralls hopped down from the refuelling truck. He pulled on thick gloves and shouldered the heavy hose from the reel at the rear of the truck. As he walked away a motor automatically turned the reel, feeding the hose out behind him. He lifted a metal trap in the apron, took off a glove to fiddle with a key, and removed the cover on the pipe leading to the underground fuel reservoir. Then he uncapped the end of the hose, locked the two brass fittings together and tugged to test the security of the connection. Finally he walked to the reel at the front of the truck, operated a lever to spool out a few metres of hose, and laid it on the ground in readiness.

The jeep driver returned from the armoury. This time he was seated in a heavy articulated trolley and behind him was a twenty-foot-long, metallic pencil. He stopped and manoeuvred the AGM-129 Advanced Cruise Missile backwards into the hangar.

The door to the low building opened again. Two flight crew came out and crossed the apron.

Thirty minutes went by. Then two of the ground crew brought the tow truck in and yoked it to the nose assembly of the aircraft that was towering somewhere above them. One returned to the truck's cabin. The engine note of the vehicle rose. Slowly, from the entire width of the hangar, a giant B2 Spirit stealth bomber eased out onto the apron.

Morning light gleamed dully on its dark grey surfaces.

Noel Harrison was beginning to find it hard to stay focused.

"All right, Chris," he said. "If there isn't an alternative to Yellowstone, could we recommend a delay? I mean, it's one thing setting up a threshold when it's some months in the future; it's quite a different thing when it's on top of you."

Chris gave him a quizzical look. "The threshold was pretty extreme, Noel – so extreme we didn't think we'd be reaching it any time soon – and the level of ammonia just sailed over it. Even if we raised the threshold ten per cent it'd only give us a few days. Then we'd be in exactly the same position as we are now."

"Well okay, could we – ?"

They jumped as the phone buzzed. Chris had it on the speaker. Noel heard Trish's voice say, "Chris, Sarah has the President on the line for you."

"Okay, Trish. Put it through."

There was a pause, then the President's voice. "Chris?"

"Yes, sir."

"Noel with you?"

"Yes, sir. Both of us have been here all night."

There was a grunt. "Me too. Anything new?"

"I'm afraid not, sir."

The sigh was audible. "What about the ammonia? You sure those figures are reliable?"

"We've been over them again and again, sir. We've reanalysed them and we've graphed them every which way. We always come up with the same answer."

There was a silence. Then the voice, very quiet.

"Yes, well… It's not long now, you know."

"Yes, we know. We'll keep on it, sir."

"You'll let me know the moment you have something?"

"Of course, sir."

The line went dead.

The B-2 accelerated along the runway and rose into the air, bound for New Mexico. In one weapons bay was the cruise missile, fitted with a bunker-busting nuclear warhead set for full secondary yield. The pilot and the mission commander, both of the 394th Bomb Squadron, were not fully aware of the nature of the munition they were carrying. As far as they were concerned this was a secret rehearsal for a possible mission somewhere in Afghanistan where the terrain was similar. They weren't even aware of the final coordinates, which had been entered before the weapon was winched up into the weapons bay. The crew's task was simply to arm the warhead and deploy the missile at the assigned location.

Chris put down the phone and looked at Noel. "That poor guy. I so wish we could give him something – anything."

"What haven't we thought of?" Noel said. "The instruments themselves. Could they be faulty in some way?"

Chris shook his head. "The instruments on the NOAA flights and the NSF flights and Terry's sampling flights were all calibrated independently. Their readings still agreed."

"Can we be sure we're not looking at freak local concentrations?"

Chris slapped a hand down on the desk. "Noel, we've been over all that before."

Noel took off his glasses and rubbed his eyes with the heels of his hands. "I know, I know. We covered it by sampling at all those different sites and different altitudes. Flights, high altitude balloons – "

"That's right. Now that ammonia's built up, the levels don't vary that much around the globe."

Noel replaced his glasses. "Sorry, Chris. I guess I'm just trying to reassure myself as much as anything."

"Don't apologise, I know just how you feel. All night I've been asking myself the same question: can we really go through with this?"

"You know what worries me? Maybe we are crazy. Suppose Kramer was right?"

"You know Kramer; he'll oppose anything he didn't think of himself. And he hasn't come up with a Plan B – other than doing nothing."

"But we have no direct experience of supermassive eruptions like this! The only record is in the rocks, in the landscape. How big will it be? What sort of area will it affect? What will it do to the global climate and how long will it last? It's… it's such a gamble."

For several minutes they sat there saying nothing. Sounds from outside seeped into the silence: the muted roar of a passenger plane heading out of Dulles International Airport, the thrum of the morning Washington traffic far below, a sudden burst of laughter from further down the corridor.

"The planet's dying, Noel." Softly though Chris had spoken, his voice seemed suddenly loud in the room. "We're like doctors standing round the sick bed. We've made a decision. It's not ideal, but we're doing the best we can."

Noel sighed. "I just wonder if it's a case of curing the disease and killing the patient."

Chris's lips tightened. He looked at his watch. "Do you think the

President will go through with it?"

"I don't know, I just don't know." Noel pointed to the papers strewn on the desk and met Chris's eyes. "One thing I do know. Even with all this in front of me it's not a decision I'd care to take."

In the Oval Office the President sat staring at the red telephone. It was the moment he'd been dreading. After this there would be no turning back. The digital clock on his desk read 10:59. It was 08.59 in Colorado. One minute to launch. One hour to detonation.

Again and again he balanced the alternatives in his mind. This could be the best decision of his Presidency – or the worst. How would history judge him: saviour of the world or a trigger-happy butcher of his own people? He buried his head in his hands.

The phone rang and he jumped. He looked at it for a moment, then lifted the receiver.

A jagged V-shaped shadow raced across the open desert. It shrank as the aircraft rose to deployment altitude. The weapons bay rolled open.

Mission commander Lieutenant Colonel Scott Perry repeated the question, a note of urgency entering his voice.

Five seconds elapsed. Ten. Fifteen. The President took a deep breath. Then he said:

"That's affirmative."

His hand remained on the receiver after he'd replaced it, his head bowed.

History may never get the chance to judge him: the secret of what was about to happen would remain known to just a handful of trustworthy people. But he would know. He would always know.

His hand trembled, then the fingers contracted into a fist so tightly that the knuckles went white.

"God help me," he murmured. "God help us all."

Fifteen hundred miles away the cruise missile dropped from the B2 and its engine ignited. It flew low, hugging the foothills of the Rocky Mountains, traversing Colorado and Wyoming, on its way to Yellowstone National Park.

CHAPTER 58

Felix Rutter, World Marketing Director of Vance Pharmaceuticals, caught the early flight to Boise, Idaho. With him was Carl Neumann, the young accountant he'd brought with as his aide on this trip. It was the latest stop on a tour of Vance's manufacturing and distribution points at home and abroad. Stuart Marshall, Sales Director for the North West, had sent a car for them and the chauffeur was waiting there in the arrivals hall holding a card that bore the company logo and the word "Vance" in large letters.

For months they had been busily preparing for the announcement of their major new anti-arrhythmic drug, Rallantor. In recent weeks these efforts had escalated into frantic activity. Now, with just ten days left, Rutter was conducting a final tour of their regional offices in the States. With Carl at his side he followed the chauffeur to the big limousine and relaxed in the back for the drive into town.

In nearly twenty years with the company he'd risen from Regional Sales Director to World Marketing Director; in that time the company had had three CEOs. Things had changed yet again, since the dismembered remains of Warren's body had been found washed up on the bank of the Charles River. Now that Ansel had taken over as CEO he'd be reporting to him. That was okay. Warren had been capable, no question, but you could never be sure where you were with him. He had a reputation for firing senior staff, maybe to keep everyone on their toes or maybe because young guys were cheaper. More than once he'd thought his own job was on the line. Ansel was a lot easier to deal with.

The car stopped outside the Hyatt Place Boise/Towne Square hotel and they took the elevator up to their rooms. They had a few minutes in which to freshen up. The meeting was due to start at nine-thirty a.m.

The table in the centre of the room was furnished with the usual drinks, dishes of peppermints, notepads, and ballpoint pens. At the end was a projection screen and whiteboard, where one of the Market Analysts was completing the opening presentation. He fielded a couple of questions from Rutter, then sat down. It was one minute to ten o'clock.

They had just turned to a discussion of follow-up strategies when the building shuddered violently, rattling the windows.

Some of them got uncertainly to their feet.

Stuart Marshall held out a hand and tried to reassure them.

"Please don't be alarmed, ladies and gentlemen. The building is earthquake-proof. It's not that uncommon in this area. It'll be over in a moment."

But the aftershocks showed no sign of subsiding. The discussion lurched on but it was in no way equal to the distraction of the distant thunder in the air, the vibration of the floor under their feet, the water shivering and rocking in the glasses and jugs on the table. There was a knock at the door and a grey-faced hotel manager came in and whispered to Marshall. The others watched expectantly, saw his eyes widen, his tongue flick around his lips. He said something to the manager, who nodded and withdrew. He cleared his throat.

"Mr. Rutter, ladies and gentlemen, I'm very sorry but we'll have to break off our discussions here. I've just had word there's been a major eruption in the Yellowstone Park area. We're advised to evacuate the city."

There was a gasp of disbelief, then pandemonium broke out. A woman emitted something between a cry and a scream. Everyone was on their feet. Somebody snatched up his papers and rushed out of the door. Others fumbled for cell phones. Marshall tried to quieten things down.

"Try to stay calm," he pleaded. "There's no point in moving until we've checked the flight situation at the airport. I'm just going down to the manager's office to see for myself how things are. Please wait here. It should only take a few minutes."

Reluctantly some resumed their seats. Others remained standing, chatting nervously or looking out of the window; most were still glued to cell phones.

Rutter turned to his aide. His insides were fluttering but he managed to steady his voice.

"Damn this, Carl," he said. "I knew we should have used the company jet. See if they've fixed that engine yet. We might still get it to fly out here."

Neumann accessed the company database on his smartphone. After some searching he found the number and started to punch it in. At that point Marshall came back. He sat down and tapped a glass with his ballpoint pen. The room went quiet.

"We've been onto the airport," he said. "I'm afraid they've closed it to incoming flights. You were scheduled to leave towards the end of the afternoon on aircraft that would have arrived earlier in the day. They won't get here now so all those flights are cancelled."

"But there must be flights leaving at the moment," said a woman.

"They *are* leaving, taking off empty as fast as air traffic control will let them."

"That's disgraceful!" she said. "They couldn't care less about people. They just want to save their precious aircraft!"

"They said it wouldn't help if they waited. Right now there's some clear sky. Once the ash cloud has spread it'll be too dangerous for anything to take off. Volcanic ash and jet engines don't mix."

"Helicopters?" someone else asked.

"Commercial helicopters are being diverted as well. It's possible the National Guard will try to use their helicopters to evacuate people, but they'll be prioritizing those closer to the Yellowstone area so it could be a while before they get around to us. We had some limousines booked to take you to the airport. We're still hoping to get them here but right now we can't contact them."

"Just use a cab firm," said a heavily overweight man, mopping the perspiration off his forehead.

"We're trying, believe me. They're jammed with calls. And a lot of drivers are just putting their own families in their cabs and leaving town."

"Is it really that bad?"

"I can't honestly see the reason for panic. After all, Boise must be four hundred miles from Yellowstone so I don't think there's any immediate danger. We can extend your reservations here at the hotel," he finished lamely, "in case you'd like to wait until things quieten down."

"Stuart?" It was the Marketing Analyst who'd just finished presenting. "I have a TV plug-in for my lap top. We can see what's on the channels."

"You go ahead, Mark. I'll just see if the hotel has any shuttle buses here."

He left the room and the others crowded around the lap top. Mark scanned through the channels. He stopped abruptly at an unsteady low-resolution movie, evidently captured by a cell phone. It showed an enormous tower of black cloud, many miles across, blotting out much of the sky. From time to time it blossomed orange and red, and boiling masses would erupt from somewhere inside and surge even higher, churning the column behind them. The camera panned slowly upwards until the screen showed nothing but roiling smoke from edge to edge; then up still further to pause at the topmost reaches, where unseen forces ripped the cloud into long rags, limned with silver by the sun. It was a sight of majestic, terrifying beauty.

At the bottom of the screen was a banner with the words "Amateur film from Livingston, Montana".

"Jesus, will you look at the size of that thing!"

"How far's Livingston?"

"From Yellowstone? About a hundred miles, I guess."

"If I was the guy holding that cell phone I'd haul ass."

"Me too."

"Shh…"

The newsreader was saying:

"…erupts about every 700,000 years. The last major eruption was 640,000 years ago. Even so, this one seems to have caught the volcanologists by surprise. We'll bring you further bulletins as the news comes in. In Iowa today…"

Matt closed his lap top and they dispersed to talk quietly in small groups. Noises filtered in from the town: emergency vehicles, their sirens rising and falling as they came and went, interspersed with the strange, echoing sound of police loud hailers. It did nothing to alleviate the tension in the room.

Rutter checked his watch.

"We'll give them one hour, Carl," he said. "If they haven't come up with something by then we're leaving."

An hour later they were crossing the hotel lobby, making for the exit. Even before they'd emerged through the revolving glass doors they could hear the cacophony of horns from the street outside. The sidewalks were crowded with people in a hurry and the road was crawling with vehicles. Some of the cars had the roofs piled high with household goods. The sky to the east was already blackening.

Rutter said, "We'll start walking. If we see a cab we'll offer him five thousand dollars to take us anywhere to the south or west. If he won't take five we'll offer him ten. If we find a car showroom we'll buy a car and drive it ourselves. Once we're out of town we can charter a helicopter and arrange for it to meet us somewhere."

"Sounds good."

Others had had similar ideas, only they had no intention of paying. They smashed the windows of showrooms and either hot-wired the vehicles or broke into offices looking for the keys. In the jammed streets youths wandered amongst the cars, trying doors. One group spotted a stretch limo and surrounded it, hammering on the roof. Through the blackened glass it wasn't possible to see whether the car was full or half empty. A brick struck the window on the passenger side; it spidered but remained intact. Then it rolled down. A revolver appeared briefly and fired a single shot into the air. The youths scattered and went to look for easier targets.

Two hours later Rutter and Neumann were still walking, jackets over their arms, ties discarded and shirt collars open. Dark stains were spreading in their armpits. There'd been no opportunity to buy a car and even if they'd seen a vacant taxi there'd have been little point in flagging it down; the traffic in every direction was stationary.

Above the noise of the car engines, the shouting and the hooting, an ominous rumble emerged and grew louder and louder. Neumann stopped.

"What the hell's that?"

Rutter frowned. "I don't know. Whatever it is, it seems to be heading this way."

Neumann covered his ears. "My God…!"

Rutter grabbed his arm.

"Quick, Carl, take cover!"

They began to run. Clouds of scorching ash hundreds of feet high funnelled along the streets and smashed through buildings, blowing out windows and doors. The surge instantly incinerated every living thing in its path.

The convoy of trucks left Washington with a police motorcycle escort. The column divided, some going direct to Florida and others to Joint Base Andrews Naval Air Facility Washington, where, alongside Air Force One, cargo planes were waiting. Aircraft were being offloaded in Florida and trucks were arriving there long before ash started to darken the skies over the capital.

The speed of the operation stunned the media but it was explained to them by the White House Spokesman, Mike Grounds, in his last interview before leaving Washington. The administration had made contingency plans so that they could continue to govern the country in the event of a white smog hitting the capital. They were simply putting those same plans into effect.

In the unlikely event that he would ever need to produce evidence, Mike Grounds had an internal memo headed "White Smogs: Precautionary Action" to prove it.

The volcanic cloud spread, blotting out the sun. Ash fell heavily out of the darkness. Salt Lake City, Denver and Phoenix ground to a standstill. Outside the towns, roadside markers were buried. In every direction the landscape became a featureless grey blanket, so that rescue teams trying to bring in earth-movers became disorientated and ran off the roads. Cars skidded and sank as their spinning tyres struggled for traction in the deep, powdery surface. The stranded vehicles blocked the highways, creating queues of stationary traffic that stretched for miles. Drivers turned off their engines. Some sat in their cars, hoping for rescue. Others abandoned their vehicles and tried to continue on foot. They stumbled on with little sense of direction, handkerchiefs tied over mouth and nose in a vain attempt to filter out the choking air.

The ash continued to fall. Slowly cars and corpses disappeared from view. Everything was deadened with a cloak of unnatural silence, punctuated only by the rumbling of thunder as lightning flickered in the black cloud overhead.

Then the rain started. It fell in torrents, turning the ash into a thick sludge. In the towns that were worst affected it crawled down the streets, an unstoppable black tide that blocked sewers and drains, carried off cars and mobile homes, collapsed houses, and swallowed up people and livestock. The sulphurous air became tinged with the rancid, rotting odour of death.

CHAPTER 59

An emergency meeting had been called at the Institute.

"Okay," Terry said, when the hubbub in the lecture theatre had died down. "Now first let me say that I don't know any more than you do at this stage. We heard the reports last night and we'll have to wait for better media coverage before we have a more detailed picture of what's happening. One thing I want to make clear: so far as our own situation is concerned we won't be too badly affected. Ash has already come in but we're away from the main fallout zone and it won't get much worse than this. There will be changes in the climate; in fact, in a few weeks' time I suppose the weather here in Florida will be more like that in England, so bad luck."

There was a little uneasy laughter.

"Well," he continued. "I'm sure we can manage as far as that's concerned. What I'd like to do this morning is try to interpret this event in relation to our research effort." He paused, gathering his thoughts. "In our recent meetings you've followed the reports of the atmosphere and climate teams. What they were telling us was that ammonia was rising more rapidly than ever and at this stage we still haven't got a solution. I must say I'd started to wonder if the atmosphere would be too toxic to breathe before we had, and maybe some of you felt the same way.

"Now we have this enormous eruption in Montana and it's changed the picture dramatically. The acid gases from the volcano will fix a lot of the free atmospheric ammonia as salts, and the rain has already washed a lot of it down. At higher altitudes the ejecta and the ammonium salts will produce global cooling; that, and the reduction in sunlight, may slow the organisms down, but we can't rely on it. The net effect is that it's bought us some time. That's the good news. The bad news is that it won't last forever. Eventually generation of ammonia will overtake the declining emissions from the volcano. We have no idea how quickly that will happen. What I'm saying is: we can't afford to relax. We've got to go for that biological solution just as fast as we can.

"In view of the new situation we asked Gordon Lang to join us. I think most of you have met him by now. Gordon is a volcanologist with the US Geological Survey. He's here with his colleagues to help us follow the progress of the eruption and they'll be modelling the effects on the climate." He smiled in their direction. "The supercomputer on this campus is one of the biggest in the country, so it should be adequate even for you guys. Eruptions of the Yellowstone supervolcano aren't unprecedented but no one in history has ever had a chance to measure their effects directly. This will be an unparalleled opportunity to do just that. Gordon?"

Gordon Lang was giving him a strange look.

"Terry," he drawled, "I have to say this is a strange sort of good fortune. I was in touch with some colleagues at Yellowstone Park not so long ago. At that time they said there was no indication of an impending event. It's pretty certain that not one of them survived this eruption."

Terry's heart started to beat faster. He responded quickly. "Yes, it's taken a lot of people by surprise but there's no point in debating why. Many people have lost their lives and many more will be affected. There is no doubt this is a disaster on a scale never seen before, but it's a disaster that could save the rest of the population left on this planet. Okay, I'm going to turn this over to Maggie now, and the biologists can update us on the progress they've been making. As some of you know, there's been a major breakthrough and we should be able to speed things up."

After the meeting the staff filed out of the lecture theatre into the foyer and many of them paused to look out through the glass front of the building. Conditions had deteriorated rapidly. The clear blue hemisphere of the Florida sky had darkened to a yellowish grey haze through which the sun cruised as a sickly brown disc. A fine dust had settled over everything, coating the vegetation, the roads, the cars, and the buildings. Outside, the line of palm trees stood like petrified sentinels in the still, ash-laden air. Viewing that grey landscape, ghostly in the weak daylight, made them feel isolated and closed in. They shivered and turned away, heading for the labs.

Now that the entire administration had moved to Florida, Terry had only to walk across the campus to meet with the President the next morning. He showed his pass to the two Marines at the entrance to the building and rode the lift to the President's floor. He found the man seated with his elbows on his desk, his cheeks cupped in his hands. He released one hand to wave Terry to a chair, then laid it palm down on a sheaf of papers on his desk.

"Casualty reports from Idaho," he said. "The surge that went out over Snake River Plain." He shook his head. "My God, Terry. All the towns along that river were buried. It's Pompeii twenty times over. Big towns like Rexburg, Idaho Falls, Pocatello, Twin Falls, Nampa, Boise, and Caldwell, all gone. First estimates are at least half a million dead, and that's conservative. We're awaiting figures from Montana and Wyoming. They were hit by other surges, probably a million dead there, maybe more. And we're left with a real humanitarian crisis in that whole area. We're trying to evacuate survivors but we're short of helicopters – we're drafting them in from all over the country."

Terry looked at him, taking in the darkening of the slack flesh under the eyes, the reddened eyelids, the hunched shoulders. He pictured a mind burdened with the buried towns, the bodies in their hundreds of thousands, the stranded survivors, and he felt a wave of sympathy, mingled with guilt.

"The sheer scale of it, Terry!" he continued. "We're running the rescue missions from the West Coast but a helicopter has limited range. We have to refuel in flight so some of them can reach further. It's a slow business – too many people left behind. The best we can do is drop supplies by Hercules and hope those poor folk can keep going." He sighed. "I thought it would be bad, but not this bad."

There was nothing Terry could say.

The President dragged his gaze away from the reports, straightened up and pushed himself back from the desk. He refocused on Terry. "We've put a news embargo on this for the moment. Once we've got something positive to say about the rescue effort we'll let the media run it – we have to. I hope to God you've got something there to cheer me up."

"I believe I have, sir," Terry said quietly.

"Good, good. Let's hear it."

"It all comes down to the way the eruption was triggered. Your nuclear device sent out shock waves that weakened the crust over a very large area. When it blew, the lid came right off. The eruptive column was at least thirty miles across."

"Sweet Jesus! You're saying it was even bigger than we expected?"

"Not exactly. In terms of the volume of magma ejected it wasn't far off what we'd predicted. But the decompression was so general that it couldn't sustain the eruption. Quite early on there wasn't enough impetus to support the weight of that huge column. That's what led to the early collapse and the pyroclastic surges. The Rockies, Sierras and Cascades shielded the coastal population from the worst of it, otherwise your casualties would have been a lot higher."

"That's a crumb of comfort, I suppose. Are there going to be any more of these surges?"

"Probably not. It'll go on smoking for years but the main eruptive force dissipated in the first explosion so the whole thing won't last as long as we thought. That's the first item of good news. The second is that the release of energy in that initial eruption was enormous – it made your warhead look like a firework. The force of it carried the ejecta to a height of more than twenty-five kilometres. What that means is that the ash will be widely distributed around the planet but the really heavy fall will be restricted in extent and it'll be mainly to the east. The model suggests that by the time we get out to 1500 kilometres from the eruption the thickness won't be more than a few millimetres."

"1500 kilometres. That's what? – a thousand miles?"

"A bit less. It means your helicopter bases on the west coast shouldn't be affected and your major centres of population and industry out east won't be blanketed. The ash will be a nuisance for sure, but they should be able to function."

He grunted.

"So tell me, Terry, has all this been worth it? What's happening to the ammonia?"

"There's some good news there as well, sir. It's what I said would happen: the sulphuric acid released into the atmosphere by the volcano has combined with the ammonia to form ammonium sulphate. We're already recording a dramatic fall in the levels of free ammonia. And there's another mechanism too, one I hadn't anticipated. The ash cloud is highly charged and it's laced continually with lightning. The lightning makes oxygen and nitrogen combine directly and together with water they're forming nitric acid. That's taking more free ammonia out of the air as ammonium nitrate."

"And the rain? The rainstorms in the north-west are unprecedented. Is that part of it too?"

"Yes, I expect we'll get that here, too, sooner or later. The crystals of ammonium sulphate and nitrate and the ash have seeded the clouds and that's what brought down the rain."

"It's causing major damage out there."

"I realize that, sir, but it's also cleared the air of ammonia and the ammonium salts and a lot of ash."

The President let out a long sigh and looked wearily at Terry. "So we're winning, then?"

"No sir, I can't say we're winning."

"What do you mean?"

"We still haven't got the biological solution. Once the volcano starts to taper off it'll cease to be a serious source of acid gases. The ammonia will start to take over again."

"Oh sure, but it took years to build up to those levels before."

"It won't this time. These ammonia-generating organisms are present in far larger quantities now, and they're very widely distributed. That threshold could be reached in months, not years."

"Dammit, Terry, when that happens I won't have any bullets left to fire."

"I'm afraid that's right, sir. You won't even have a gun."

CHAPTER 60

Terry made some notes and added some papers to a pile on his desk that had been growing in the days since the eruption. Ash and gases from the volcano had spread all around the world, their research flights were bringing in an undreamed of wealth of data, and the climate modellers were beginning to make sense of it. He knew that together the team would have enough results for a lifetime of publications. It would certainly make his reputation – if they survived.

"Terry?"

Maggie came into the office. His mind was full of models and hypotheses and it took him a moment to focus properly on her. He had barely seen her since the eruption. The look on her face told him something was wrong.

"What is it, Maggie? What's the problem?"

"It's Sergei. He insists on holding the phage data close to his chest. We need Rajiv's input on the screening so we can get started on making our organism resistant to the phage. We have to work in parallel as much as we can, otherwise the whole thing will take too long. I've tried to reason nicely with him but he won't take any notice. He pretends he can't understand English. Would you talk to him?"

"Where is he? Fourth floor?"

"Yes. Do you want me to come with?"

"No, it'll seem like we're ganging up on him. It's better if I see him alone."

Sergei Daniil Kolesnikov was stubborn. His head was angled back, his bushy black beard jutting out.

"Is not problem," he said. "One team find sequence. One team switch it off. My team find bacteriophage."

"It *is* a problem, Sergei," Terry insisted. "We are running out of time. Don't you understand? I told you all at the last meeting: the ammonia levels are already starting to go up again. We need that phage, and we need it fast."

"We work as fast as we can."

"We'll make quicker progress if you can combine forces with one of the other groups."

"Not way I work. Publish findings, not one million authors."

So that was it. Terry was tempted to raise his fists to the ceiling and scream in sheer frustration. He took a deep breath and expelled it slowly.

"Sergei, when we have the phage and our engineered organism with the plasmid we've still got to grow them up in large quantities. Then we've got to start spraying it on all the areas around the world where the organisms are active. That's a huge task and it's going to take time. If we don't crack this problem soon we're going to lose the battle. There won't be any publications because there won't be any journals and there won't be anyone to read them because we'll all be dead! Do you understand?"

"Not understand."

Terry sighed.

"Okay, Sergei, do you understand this? Do you know what the temperature is in Moscow at the moment?"

Sergei's dark eyes met his. Terry held the gaze unflinchingly as he continued:

"I'll tell you. The volcanic winter is already setting in and it's minus forty degrees Celsius there. And it's going to get colder. Do you fancy going back?"

The dark eyes flashed with anger. He thrust his face close to Terry's.

"You cannot do. I am foremost expert in world with bacteriophage."

"Yes, and that's why we asked you to join us. But there are others."

The face came closer still.

"Who?"

"For a start there's Jose-Luis Guerrero, at the University of San Diego."

Guerrero had been on the reserves list. He was Kolesnikov's biggest rival. Terry knew the mention of his name would raise the Russian's blood pressure.

Kolesnikov's face reddened.

"Jose-Luis? Pah!" The words came out with such violence that Terry felt the spittle landing on his cheek. "Is pygmy, Jose-Luis!"

"Maybe, but he knows how to work in a team. Look, Sergei, you're the best in the world – you know that and so do I. Why the hell would we invite you here if you weren't? But you have to understand the rules. Here we work as one big team. Our survival depends on it. Now, are you going to help us? Because if you're not I'm going to order up that plane for Moscow right now."

Kolesnikov looked as if a thundercloud had settled on his brow.

"What you want?" he said.

"It's very simple," Terry replied evenly. "Your team is screening for the best phage. I want you to bring Rajiv Gupta's group in on it, so that he can look at resistance to the phage at the same time as you are looking at virulence and infectivity. If there's a publication you can publish together. That's all."

Kolesnikov simmered, then withdrew his face and made a conciliatory wagging movement of his head. "Not problem," he said. "Is not understand, is all. Is not problem."

CHAPTER 61

That evening Terry and Maggie joined the other staff in the leisure area, where everyone assembled to watch the main television news. Through his meetings with the President, Terry had a fair idea of the extent of the disaster caused by the Yellowstone eruption but he was obliged to keep the substance of those conversations to himself. For the others, including Maggie, the picture was far from complete. Previous reports had given them no more than views from the air: towns blanketed by ash, highways choked by lines of stationary cars, streets and homes flooded by a thick slurry of rain and ash. Tonight, for the first time, there was some news at ground level from cities destroyed by the surges.

A reporter stood at the side of the picture gesturing towards a lumpy grey landscape from which the shattered remnants of high-rise apartments jutted like broken teeth.

"What you see behind me is all that's left of Idaho Falls," he said. He winced and shifted his position. "Somewhere, maybe twenty feet below me, is one of the main arteries of this once thriving city. The death toll here is believed to be in excess of fifty thousand." He coughed and wiped his eyes. "Excuse me. The air here's full of sulphur and the ground's still almost too hot to stand on. I'm going to have to hand you back to the studio."

There were further reports, from Twin Falls, Nampa, Boise, Caldwell. The casualty figures were meaninglessly high: thirty-five thousand, seventy thousand, one hundred and ten thousand, thirty thousand... More telling were the individual images of destruction: cars carried by the surge and dumped through the second-floor windows of office buildings; rooms full of the bodies of men, women and children who had been above the surge but who had breathed the lethal cocktail of scorching hot gases and ash that came with it. A kaleidoscope of images brought it home in heart-rending detail: a shoe, a purse, a teddy bear.

Terry felt as if there were an enormous weight pressing on his chest. It was a problem he'd visualized only in global terms. He knew the numbers already but this was the reality – here, confronting him in these television pictures. Watching them he felt like a general who'd estimated the likely casualties, sent his troops into battle, and was now obliged to write to the bereaved relatives and tour wards crowded with the injured. He stared at the screen, numb and motionless.

In the studio, a sombre presenter announced that the estimated death toll in the Snake River Plain alone was upwards of half a million. Further reports, she said, would be broadcast in the days to come on the situation in towns to the east of Yellowstone.

The lounge had gone very quiet. Maggie turned and Terry saw that her eyes were full of tears. She left without a word and he followed her.

She walked quickly out of the building and towards the residence. He hurried behind her, calling her name, but she just shook her head impatiently and marched on. When they reached her room she wiped angrily at her eyes with the heel of her hand and whirled on him.

"Five hundred thousand deaths, Terry! And it's not over yet. I hope you're satisfied."

"What are you – ?"

"All those people. They didn't know what was coming. But you did, didn't you?"

"We couldn't have predicted those early surges or which way they would run!"

"You brushed it aside, that's all – the loss of life wasn't that important."

"For God's sake, of course it was important! We had no choice."

"You 'had no choice'. You turned this into a planetary disaster because it's your field; you can handle that. When all you have is a hammer, every problem looks like a nail!"

The shaft hit home. It was the same accusation he'd been levelling at himself ever since he'd put the plan forward. He gritted his teeth.

"All right, but at least I put a plan on the table. I didn't notice you or anyone else come up with an alternative. What did you expect? If we hadn't done something the whole world would have died! We knew there'd be a heavy price to pay so why are you behaving like it's all a huge surprise?"

The tears hadn't stopped flowing. Her body quivered with the force of her sobbing.

"Because *I'm* guilty, that's why! *I* failed to find a solution in time, and because of that *I* had to be a party to this decision..." She held her shaking palms out to him. "Did you see those pictures? Men, women, children, old and young, whole families – all wiped out! Hundreds of them, thousands of them! How do you think that makes me feel?"

"It wasn't your suggestion, it was mine. If anyone should feel guilty it's me."

"Well? Do you feel guilty?"

He turned his head away in exasperation.

"It's too late for that." He took a deep breath, and spoke with deliberation. "Maggie, the casualties are horrendous – I know that and the President surely knows that – but that doesn't mean we did the wrong thing. It was unavoidable. That was the scale of the problem."

She shook her head.

"It's ironic, isn't it? At one point we thought we were dealing with saboteurs or terrorists. And what do we do? We kill maybe a million people. So who are the terrorists, Terry? I've lost track, you see."

"We were in an impossible situation. It was a rational, scientific decision."

"So was Hitler's Final Solution!"

"Maggie…!"

Even through his anger he was moved by her tears. He hated to see her like this. He felt a strong urge to take her in his arms, comfort her, but he was rooted to the spot. In her present state of mind she'd recoil from any such gesture, and he couldn't face the hurt of rejection. He tried to control his voice.

"Maggie, you've got to see this through. We've unleashed terrible forces. But don't forget: all it's gained us is a little time. It isn't a long term solution – only you and your people can provide that."

She heaved an unsteady sigh and her voice descended to a growl.

"Oh, don't worry. I'll see it through. Whatever you may think of me, I am a professional."

She was gathering up her things even as she was speaking. A few moments later she left the room and slammed the door.

He sat down on the edge of the bed, staring into the carpet.

A gulf had opened up between them and he knew no way of bridging it.

CHAPTER 62

Over the weeks that followed, the temperature dropped progressively. By October a mantle of snow had settled on the Canadian provinces and the northern United States. This was followed by freezing fog. A thick layer of ice coated every surface, bringing down power cables and telephone lines. One after another, television channels went off the air. Even the major channels, like NBC, CBS, and CNN, were having problems. In the Institute the staff relied increasingly on their plenary meetings for news from the frozen regions further north but there was a limit to what Terry could tell them.

The reports were taking longer now that Maggie's teams were getting results. Alain Laroche was working with Silvia Mussini's group, designing their own plasmid. At the same time the Russian group, under Sergei Kolesnikov, was making faster progress now that he was sharing the phage work with Rajiv Gupta.

Maggie and Terry kept their personal feelings in a separate compartment. Both knew how important it was to maintain morale and they were consistently upbeat about the way the work was going. As a result, despite the dismal news from the north and north-west, the scientists tended to leave each meeting with enthusiasm and even some cautious optimism. Privately, Terry was beginning to worry that the optimism was misplaced.

Terry looked at his watch, then went to the window of his office and eyed the weather. It was time to give the President his weekly briefing on their progress. He took the umbrella that was propped up in the corner by his desk.

As he emerged from the building he paused to put the umbrella up, then started to jog across the campus. The air was chill and white with rain. The large droplets thundered on the thin silk of the umbrella and bounced in thousands of miniature upward explosions from the paths. To cross the streets he had to jump across the rivers that were flowing down the gutters. The lawns were largely submerged and his shoes splashed through the puddles that spread from side to side of the footpaths. Florida was famed for its heavy afternoon thunderstorms but it was a long time since rain had fallen incessantly like this. At least it had washed the ash off the buildings and the trees.

He turned up the path to the administration building. In the shelter of the foyer he closed and half-opened the umbrella a couple of times to jerk off the rain, then went through the door. There was barely time to flick the water from his trousers before he was accosted by the marines. They inspected his pass carefully and waved him in. They never seemed to recognize him, but then he didn't recognize them either. He rode the lift up to the outer office, watching the display flicking rapidly through the floors, regaining his breath. Close to his feet a small puddle spread from the tip of his folded umbrella. His face was flushed from the exertion but he could feel the cold damp seeping through his trousers and socks. The lift doors opened and he walked down the corridor.

Sarah Bethany was just coming out of the President's office. She gave Terry a smile and indicated that he should go in.

The President looked a little brighter. Perhaps his doctor had persuaded him to get some rest.

"Come on in, Terry," he said, as he caught sight of him. "Damned rain. Are you wet through?"

"Not too bad. It'll dry off."

They sat down. He noticed that the President was wearing a thick wool cardigan. It wasn't that warm in the building; presumably they were trying to cut down on energy consumption.

"Sir, do you mind if I ask you something before we start?"

"Go ahead."

"Well, we agreed that these briefings are between the two of us, and that's the way I've kept it. But the people back in the Institute are hungry for news, more news than they can get now on the evening bulletins. The television channels seem to be running short of first-hand accounts and we suspect they're either fabricating stories or blowing them out of proportion."

"Neither one would surprise me. In fact nothing about the media would surprise me."

"Well, you've been good enough to share some of the items that cross your desk. As we're going along I wondered if we could identify a few that I could pass on to them. It would make the meetings over at the Institute even more useful."

"Okay, we can do that. The arrangement is that everything's classified unless I specifically say so."

"Of course."

"Good. Well you can start by telling them that it's getting mighty cold. Heavy snowfalls in Chicago, Cleveland, and Boston, they tell me. And the Canadians have got it even worse. The St. Lawrence seaway is starting to freeze."

"That's going to last for a while, I'm afraid. It's the volcanic winter we talked about. We're monitoring its progress."

"Some doom-mongers are predicting a twelve degree Celsius drop in the Northern hemisphere, and more still in the south. That happens, the whole goddamned planet will be iced over."

"No, it won't be as bad as that."

"How so?"

"Well, those people are making predictions based on estimates of the release of sulphuric acid from the volcano. That's a perfectly valid approach with the information that's available to them. Unfortunately their information is incomplete: they don't know about the huge amount of ammonia that was already in the atmosphere. We released the sulphuric acid to capture the ammonia but it works the other way round, too. A lot of the sulphuric acid as well as the ammonia has come out of the atmosphere. What's left behind is mainly fine ash."

"Well if there's still ash up there, how come the FAA is allowing commercial flights again?"

"The density at cruising altitude isn't a problem now. There's enough material above that level to shield the sun, but it'll gradually get redistributed and settle out. Things will be bad, but not as bad as they say."

"That's comforting. What about the rain?"

"Well, it'll ease off once the temperature falls because there'll be less evaporation from the oceans. But there's an upside to the rain too."

"Oh, what's that?"

"You know it's been falling in parts of the country normally classed as deserts: Arizona and New Mexico, for example. And the rain is loaded with nitrogen-rich compounds – ammonium salts are your classic fertilizers. I think you'll find that'll create conditions suitable for grassland and wheat-growing. You could replace the harvests we'll be losing in the mid-West, at least until world temperatures start to rise again."

"Now that is interesting. I was beginning to wonder how we'd cope with food shortages. Trouble is, most farmers aren't going to believe you can grow crops on any useful scale so far to the south-west."

"You could offer them subsidies, couldn't you? It would cost less than having to import the stuff."

"That's true. I'll look into it." He added a note to the pad on his desk. "And presumably this isn't just happening here."

"That's right. My information is sketchy at the moment but there's been rain in the northern Sahara and the Arabian desert – I know that much. The same may be true elsewhere, even in places like the Kalahari and the Australian deserts. Areas that have been too hot and dry in the past could well support crops now. And the paddy fields and terraces in the Far East should be able to yield two crops a year. It's ironic in a way. It was just the sort of goal Zak Gould had in mind when he developed the organism."

The President shook his head and grunted. "We've certainly come to it by a strange route. Well, I hope you're right. Some of those African countries seem to have a famine every year. We ship a hell of a lot of grain to them. We won't be able to do that if our own breadbasket's running low. It'd be a relief if they could look after themselves until things get back to normal. That's assuming they ever get back to normal. I take it ammonia's still down?"

Terry's lips tightened. In the first weeks after the volcano erupted the levels had plunged. But now the picture was changing.

"It's still down, sir, but it's levelled off. And in some places the levels have started to rise. I'm afraid the race is on again."

Their eyes met. "I take it the biologists know that."

"Yes, sir. They're working as fast as they can."

"Good, because that's our last chance." He sighed and gestured towards the window. "Out there, of course, they still haven't got a clue what's really happening. In fact some of our citizens seem to regard the eruption as an opportunity created by God specifically for them to acquire worldly goods."

"You're referring to the looting, sir?"

"You know about that?"

"It was on the TV news last night. It looked to me like it was affecting towns on the fringe of the ashfall, where homes and shops aren't actually buried but emergency services are paralysed."

"Yup, dead on. Damned parasites. Well, we've got the measure of them – Terry, this is not for general consumption, right? I've imposed a form of martial law in those areas – sent the army in. We're not shooting them, though – I had a better idea. They get arrested, sentenced quickly and then put to work shovelling ash, helping to get things running again. The army's supervising the whole operation."

"Another lousy job for the army."

"Not so bad. It sure as hell beats doing the shovelling themselves."

"Did Congress give you any trouble with that?"

"Hah, now I'll tell you something, Terry," he chuckled. "You talk about upside. I've never known Congress be so accommodating. Normally they'd have given me a hell of a rough ride on a bill like that. But I guess it's what you Limeys used to call the 'Spirit of the Blitz'. People are learning to pull together, and the ones who won't are getting short shrift. All the stuff that used to clog up the system – negligence claims, libel, defamation, patent infringements, people suing for billions of dollars, that kind of thing – well, with everyone struggling just to survive, the courts are throwing it out. The old ambulance-chasers are finished. The law's becoming respectable again. Should have happened a long time ago. Now tell me, how's Maggie getting on...?"

Maggie decided she couldn't postpone the moment any longer. They were approaching the point when a field trial would be essential and that called for forward planning. Kramer had seemed studiously determined to remain inaccessible but she was going to see him anyway. For a change he was at the Friday meeting, sitting at the back and leaving quickly without taking part. She knocked on his door after he'd returned to his office.

He raised his eyebrows as she entered but indicated the chair placed, in token fashion, on the other side of his desk. There were no papers on the desk and no books on the shelves. There was a computer but the screen was blank. Maggie sat down, feeling as if she'd entered the stage set of a play that had long been cancelled. Before she had a chance to say what she wanted he opened the conversation.

"I'm glad you've come to see me at last, Dr. Ferris. I must say I'm not at all happy with the way things have been going."

She looked at him in astonishment. "You heard the reports at the meeting, Dr. Kramer. I would have thought you'd be delighted at the progress."

He waved a hand. "All this should have happened months ago." He exhaled in something approaching a sigh. "I was brought into this business far too late, I'm afraid, when decisions had already been taken. Otherwise I should have advised a totally different strategy."

She'd been tense enough in his presence; now her skin began to prickle with irritation.

"Oh? May I ask what strategy that would have been?"

He leaned back as if to study her. "Expression. That's what you people are missing. You should have been concentrating on what proteins these organisms are expressing. Where are your micro-array experts, your protein chemists? There aren't any! Instead you have Oakley with his sequencing, Mussini and her gene silencing – " his lip curled and Maggie opened her mouth to protest " – no, hear me out. This is an organism that is making an unusual protein. All you had to do was compare it with a similar organism that was unaffected and you would have identified the culprit."

She shook her head. "It's not as easy as that, Dr. Kramer. There is no one organism responsible, not any more; our samples contain a variety of species and even the ones that look similar are probably genetically distinct. A comparison such as you're suggesting would come up with hundreds – maybe thousands – of different proteins, and you'd have to sieve through the lot to find the one you're looking for."

He flicked his fingers, as if physically brushing the objection aside. "That could have been coped with if you'd brought in the right people. You've wasted valuable time. Had the President given the task to…" he treated her to a razor smile, "shall we say, more *mature* scientists, we might have avoided this senseless slaughter in the north-west."

She felt the blood rushing to her face. Why was he being so rude, so aggressive, so wise-after-the-event? His nose was badly out of joint because the President hadn't sought his advice at the outset. Now he was no doubt telling the President how much better he would have handled things. As for his so-called "strategy" it just showed how ill-informed he was and how poorly he'd thought it through. At the same time it brought to the surface the self-doubts she had every time they hit another snag, another delay. Could a different approach have been quicker, more successful? The thought that an error of judgement on her part could have been responsible for the carnage of Yellowstone was outrageous, and yet her heart thumped even at this misdirected hint of it. She swallowed and tried to collect her thoughts.

"Dr. Kramer, I think we should be dealing with the situation as it is now."

"Of course, I understand that this would suit you much better."

Her voice hardened. "It's not a question of what suits me. It's a question of survival. You've seen the atmospheric sampling data. Ammonia levels are on the rise again. Unless we act quickly we'll be back to that threshold in a matter of weeks. Now I came here to ask you something. Are you prepared to listen?"

His mouth set. "Go on."

"The biological teams are getting good results. We're approaching the point where we need to test our solution in the field. I think we should be preparing for that now."

His expression was still sour. "What do you have in mind?"

"I'll speak in general terms. To be convincing, we need to conduct our tests in an area known to be badly affected by ammonia organisms. We'll empty a canister of our material there. After a suitable interval we'll take samples at different distances to see how effective it's been and estimate the speed at which it's spreading. There are people in the group who are experienced in taking such samples, myself included."

He said nothing for a while. Then he steepled his fingers and replied with great deliberation.

"I'll speak in general terms, too. You're proposing to conduct a test of material of unknown efficacy in an area known to be badly affected. By definition, there are likely to be high levels of ammonia in such an area, and you are proposing to take a group of ordinary scientists out to do this?"

"We'd be equipped with respirator masks, of course, in case of problems."

He shook his head. "Dr. Ferris, you are being remarkably naive. Do you really think I would permit our scientists to risk their lives in this way? We pay our military to do this kind of thing for us. Servicemen are trained and equipped to deal with dangerous situations and this falls precisely into that category. It can only be conducted as a military operation."

For a moment she was too stunned to speak. Then the words began to tumble out. "They won't know what to sample or how to take the samples or how to preserve them. That's our job!"

"No, Dr. Ferris, it is not your job to get killed."

She sat back and steadied her breathing. She would try once more.

"Dr. Kramer, we're close to success now, but we have to move quickly. If we can run some convincing tests in the lab would you reconsider?"

"Of course a convincing result in the lab would be absolutely essential before we even consider going into the field. But it does not change my view about who carries out the testing. When you have the material you wish to test, we will contact the US Navy and have them undertake the procedure for you."

"They could come back with useless samples! It would be a waste of precious time!"

"When it comes to time-wasting, all I can say is that you should have thought of that earlier."

For a moment she gazed at him in disbelief, then got up and hurried out.

Back in her room, Maggie sat down at her desk. She lowered her head into her hands and ran her fingers through her hair.

The man's impossible! He's more interested in his own status than the fate of the world.

Her mind was invaded by such a variety and profusion of richly uncharitable thoughts about Kramer and his motives that it left her astonished and a little ashamed.

If things had been different she'd have told Terry straight away. He could handle it, all right – look how he dealt with Kolesnikov. He'd go to Kramer, and failing that to the President. But she couldn't go to Terry, not now.

She straightened up. There was a better way.

CHAPTER 63

Silvia, Matt, and Alain Laroche had called a lab meeting for Tuesday morning, and invited Maggie to join them. A computer screen on the bench at their side displayed a complete schematic of the plasmid Zak had used. Silvia and Matt could read the base sequences like a book.

"This part is just the vector," Matt explained. "The construct starts here – look, here's the enhancer sequence and here's the promoter sequence. Downstream you have the reporter gene – "

"The Green Fluorescent Protein."

"Yep, then there'll be sequences for DNA-binding, regulation, and of course a bit for conjugation."

"Conjugation?" Maggie said. "Remind me."

"That's the mechanism for passing the plasmid between bacteria. Some bacteria have it, cyanobacteria don't. But whoever made *this* plasmid made damned sure it encoded everything it needed to transfer itself. That's why it was so easy to transfect *E. coli* with it. We've been producing the protein hand over fist."

"All right," Maggie said. "Let's talk about that protein."

"Matt, can you get the 3D model up?" Silvia said.

"Sure. Won't take a moment. The supercomputer eats jobs like this for breakfast."

The protein molecule came up on the screen and he set it rotating slowly.

"Okay, Matt, can you stop it there?" Silvia pointed. "Look, Maggie, you see this structure here? It's called a zinc finger motif; it's a classic DNA-binding domain. Now look, here's another and here's another. Three tandem repeats, corresponding to fifteen base pairs. I'm sure this is where the switch binds to the host DNA."

Maggie leaned forward, her whole body drilling with excitement. It was like viewing a murderer at the scene of a crime, the knife poised in his hand. "So there it is," she breathed. "That's where the switch attaches to the nitrogen-fixing sequence."

Matt said, "Whoever did this must have known just where he wanted it to bind."

Alain Laroche rubbed his lower lip. "The man's a genius."

"Was," Maggie corrected.

"Was?"

"Dr. Zak Gould was responsible for developing the plasmid, and yes, actually I think he was a genius. Unfortunately he was murdered."

Laroche's eyebrows lifted and he looked slowly round at her. "Silvia said you had gone to look for him, but not that he was murdered. How did you find out?"

"How? He was sitting no further away from me than you are now when he was shot."

"Mon Dieu!"

"Was this guy working on his own?" Matt asked.

"As far as we know, yes."

Matt shook his head. "Fucking genius is right. No question. What a goddamned waste!"

Maggie nodded, her lips tight. Then she looked at the others. "So what's next?"

Laroche said, "It has been made easier for us, because the GFP tag is already present. So we cross-link all the proteins to the DNA, shear the DNA into short stretches, and use an antibody to the GFP to separate the tagged DNA sequence."

Maggie frowned. "Alain, that will tell us where in the host's DNA the switch is acting, but I'm not sure we need this information at the moment. Our priority is to block the switch. Isn't there a more direct way?"

Matt looked at Silvia. "Gene silencing? Silvia, you're the expert."

She nodded slowly. "Yes, we could design a small interfering RNA that would specifically target the construct. This we could introduce on our own plasmid. Then every strand of RNA made by the rogue plasmid would be destroyed, so the protein switch could never be manufactured."

"That sounds great, Silvia," Maggie said.

"Yes, but…" Her dark eyes narrowed thoughtfully. "Degradation of the target RNA relies on a protein complex. If it is not present in cyanobacteria we will have to add that to our plasmid. I will look into it."

"Silvia," Alain said, "if you could let me have the sequence you need for the interfering RNA my group can get started on synthesizing it right away."

Matt said, "Why don't you leave that part to me? We've got the entire sequence of Zak Gould's construct. My people can run it through the online DNA databases and make sure we're targeting a unique stretch. Shouldn't take more than an hour or two."

"Thank you, Matt," Silvia said. "And I will look into the coding for the protein complex. Alain, you should have everything you need by the end of the day."

Alain rubbed his hands together. "Excellent," he said. "Tomorrow we make a start on Maggie's plasmid."

Sarah Bethany showed him into the President's office. Harry Kinghorn looked up and smiled.

"Hallo, Herbert. Have a seat. What's on your mind?"

Herbert Kramer took the chair and sat down, back straight, his hands resting in his lap, one cupped around the other.

"I really didn't feel I could delay this any longer, Mr. President."

Kinghorn frowned. "What's the problem?"

He took a deep breath. "I'm sorry to say that your group of so-called experts has continued to squander time and resources in a most unproductive fashion. First ammonia levels were allowed to rise above this so-called threshold, and you were persuaded to take that dreadful action in the north-west. Now ammonia levels are high all over again, and I see little sign of other solutions emerging. I'm deeply concerned."

The President took a deep breath. "What's prompted this, Herbert?"

Kramer lowered his head, apparently reluctant to part with the information, then raised it again. "Ferris came to see me the other day. I won't bore you with the details but she made requests that were rash beyond reason. I regret to say the two of them have conducted this project badly from the outset and this was just another example of their incompetence and lack of judgement. My own approach would have yielded results more quickly. Perhaps," he added, meeting the President's eyes, "it would even have obviated the need to detonate that device in the Yellowstone system."

The mention of Yellowstone sent a small shock down Kinghorn's spine.

"I think we're beyond that now Herbert," he said coldly. "Why don't you tell me what it is you are suggesting we do?"

"President, we're at a crisis point. If we don't reach a solution in a matter of weeks it will be too late. These people are just blundering around. We should replace them as a matter of urgency."

"Replace them?" the President said, standing up and gripping the sides of his desk. "Replace them? Are you out of your mind?" His voice had risen to an angry growl, and Kramer shrank in his chair.

"It's because of Ferris and McKinley that we found out about this problem in the first place. It's because of them that any of us are alive today. It's because of them that we have a hope in hell of beating this thing!"

"Mr. President, I'm simply…" began Kramer.

"No, Herbert, I won't listen to any more. You've done nothing but second guess these people the whole way through without coming up with a single solution yourself and I'm sick and tired of your dissension. You will remain in your post to oversee the success of this project. After that I'll be expecting your resignation on my desk. Is that clear?"

"Sir…"

"Is that clear?" he roared.

"Yes, Mr. President," Kramer said weakly.

Kinghorn's voice dropped. "Good. Now get the hell out of my office."

Kramer got unsteadily to his feet and left without another word.

Silvia and Matt gave Alain Laroche the required sequences on Tuesday night, as promised. Laroche's team launched into action immediately and they had the construct by the end of the week. The success of the combined biological teams wasn't the kind of thing that could be kept quiet in a closed community of scientists. Word got around and there was a buzz of excitement as they made their way towards the lecture theatre. The last four Friday meetings had been dominated by depressing reports from the groups monitoring ammonia levels. They badly needed some good news and at last Maggie could provide it. Terry turned the weekly meeting over to her and she lost no time in asking Silvia Mussini to come to the microphone.

Silvia showed a schematic of the plasmid Zak had used. She explained how it produced a factor that switched on ammonia production and outlined how they'd identified the site responsible. Turning that site off would, she explained, neutralize completely the effect of Zak's plasmid. And then, almost casually, she showed them the sequence data for the construct they'd designed to do the job, which Alain had already incorporated into a plasmid.

It was what they'd been waiting for. The theatre broke into uproar. Everyone was on their feet. Silvia smiled and returned gracefully to her seat. Maggie went to the microphone and after allowing a little time raised a hand. The noise faded and people took their seats again.

She grinned and spoke into the microphone: "There's more."

In seconds everyone was sitting in an expectant hush.

"All right," she said. "At last we have a plasmid that can switch off the production of ammonia. But as you know, that isn't enough. The rogue organisms are already widespread. To overtake them we have to make sure that the organism we use to introduce our plasmid has a selective advantage. That advantage is resistance to infection by a phage. Dr. Kolesnikov and Dr. Gupta have been selecting the phage that will do the job. Sergei?"

Sergei took the podium. A rare smile lightened his normally thunderous countenance.

"There is large number of phages. We need one which spread quickly and kill host. Also we prefer one which is already in ocean, so is not absolutely new to ecosystem. This bring down choice to a few. I like to thank Rajiv Gupta who do this with us."

Maggie glanced at Rajiv, who was nodding his head and smiling. It had worked out even better than she'd anticipated.

Sergei had only one slide.

"Here is."

It was an electron micrograph of the phage: a head, a stalk, and some long filaments. Sergei left the podium to applause.

"And Rajiv…?" she said.

Rajiv Gupta went to the microphone.

"I am speaking here not only for myself but also for Pieter van der Rijt and Ulrich Lunsdorfer and their teams. You know that we are needing to put our plasmid into an organism, and this organism must be resistant to the phage. Pieter and Ulrich grew the candidate cyanobacteria, Sergei provided the phage, and we worked on the resistance. I don't think you want to know the Latin name for this species, but here is a photograph that we took under the microscope. We think this is a very good organism for us, and it is most resistant to the phage Sergei just showed you."

He sat down to further applause.

"So," Maggie summarized, "thanks to the exceptional work of our teams we now have all of the major elements that we need: the phage, the organism, and the plasmid. The next step will be to insert the plasmid into the organism and grow it on. Then we'll see how our engineered organism and the phage cope when they're put up against the ammonia organisms in the laboratory. After that we can test it in the field. If all goes well we'll arrange for quantity production. Terry, anything you want to add?"

Terry joined her at the podium. "I'd just like to say how impressed we all are with the brilliant job you people have done. This project could have taken years, and you've solved all the major problems in just a few months. God knows there's little time left: ammonia levels in the stratosphere are climbing fast. But it seems to me this could be a turning point. For the first time since Maggie Ferris and I discovered these organisms and realized what they could do, defeating them no longer seems totally out of the question. Let's keep up the good work and thanks to all of you."

He started to clap and everyone joined in.

There was a burst of excited conversation and a rattle of folding seats as the staff got up. They left the theatre in high spirits.

Few of them noticed that Kramer was not present.

CHAPTER 64

The following Thursday the leaders of all the biological groups got together in Maggie's room. Pieter van der Rijt and Ulrich Lunsdorfer had just concluded the laboratory testing of the new organism and phage combination against a culture of the ammonia organisms. They had all seen the results and the atmosphere in the room was subdued.

Maggie started the discussion. "Let's take it stage by stage. Our plasmid works, right?"

Silvia nodded. "There is no question about it. It switches off ammonia production completely."

"Okay, and the phage works."

Sergei and Rajiv nodded vigorously, and Rajiv answered: "It is most effective. And it does not kill our own organism."

"So are we getting plasmid exchange?"

Pieter replied. "The evidence says we are. What is not so certain is the efficiency."

"Should we run more tests, Pieter? Perhaps on a larger scale?"

He shook his head. "Maggie, you know it is very difficult to reproduce a natural environment in the lab – there are too many variables. Out there in the oceans there could be a completely different mix of organisms, there will be differences in temperature, light, the effects of currents and surface action, and so on. We could be successful in the lab and fail under real conditions, or fail in the lab when actually it would have been successful outside. I think we should test it in the field."

Ulrich lifted a hand. "I think this, too."

Matt spoke up. "We should go for it. We could spend weeks trying to sort things out in the lab. If the field test doesn't work, we can always try again."

Silvia asked: "Maggie, how long would it take to set up a field test?"

"Well, the idea would be to drop our organism into the ocean at a defined location, leave it for twelve hours or so, then collect samples at intervals of ten nautical miles in the direction of the surface currents. All that could be done in a couple of days. We'll need to organize fresh supplies of ordinary ice and dry ice out there beforehand, but that's not a problem. I think it all depends on how long it would take to grow up enough organism to do the test. Pieter?"

Pieter and Ulrich conferred briefly in Dutch. Pieter turned to Maggie.

"We think about a week."

Silvia said, "What I have in my mind is, there are other sequences we can use and other vectors. We could be working on those while the preparations and the field test are in progress. This way we are not wasting time."

Alain nodded. "I think this is an excellent idea. If the field test is not a success, we are ready with the next organism. We field test again, and we continue like this until we succeed. It is the most practical way."

Maggie looked around the room. "Do you all agree with that?"

There was a chorus of assent.

"All right," she said slowly. "In that case we have a problem. When it looked like we were getting close to the point of doing a field trial I saw Dr. Kramer about it. He is absolutely opposed to our carrying one out. He says it's too risky."

When the buzz of consternation had died down, Matt asked: "Then how in hell are we supposed to test it?"

"He wants to give it to the US Navy."

"Oh, fucking marvellous. I can just see it now: a bunch of fucking Navy SEALs careering over the ocean with our equipment in tow, taking samples at sixty knots. That's all we need."

"There is much you can learn just by being there," Ulrich said. "You cannot tell this to the Navy."

Pieter was frowning deeply. "Also who takes the samples must know how to store them properly, otherwise they are no use to us."

Maggie sighed. "Exactly what I said. He wouldn't shift. And he wouldn't even approve a Naval expedition unless we had a convincing demonstration of success in the lab."

"This is not sensible," Silvia said. "We would waste a lot of time."

They all nodded.

"The guy's an idiot," Matt said. "Can't we get round this some way?"

They all looked at Maggie.

"I think we can," she said quietly. "Say nothing at the meeting tomorrow. Nobody must know."

A couple of weeks ago he'd have strolled right into Maggie's office to have a chat, but things were more delicate now. He hesitated at the threshold.

"Got a minute, Maggie?"

She looked up. "Come in, Terry."

He entered the office and leaned against a bookshelf, his hands in his pockets.

"It's Friday. I was wondering if you had anything new you wanted to report at the meeting."

"Well, we can tell them we've completed the preliminary tests. We put our cyanobacteria and the phage up against an excess of the ammonia organism. It seems to work."

"But that's tremendous news!"

"Don't get too excited; we're not sure about its capacity to grow and how efficiently it will exchange the plasmid into the ammonia organisms. We can't test it reliably in the lab – there's a whole bunch of variables we couldn't account for. We've decided the only way to do it is in the field."

He frowned. "It's early days for that, isn't it?"

"I don't think so. If it works we've saved valuable time."

She turned to the map pinned to her notice board. "We'll use the hot spot north-east of Bermuda – the one you and I sampled; we know there's a good concentration in that area so it should give us a definitive result. We'll have to grow up more organism and phage for the trial, of course. Pieter and Ulrich think it'll take another week for them to put enough together. Then we'll empty a canister full about here," she tapped the map, "and collect samples along the direction of the ocean current."

"How will you take the samples?"

"Oh, from a surface vessel, of course."

"I see. Who's going?"

"Postgraduates and postdocs, mostly – the heads of teams will have to stay here. Rob Guillemain's very keen; he's a postdoc in Matt Oakley's team. Sara Tennant – she works with Silvia Mussini. Jos Wentink from the Dutch group; they're the cyanobacteria experts and he's had a lot of experience of ocean sampling. And Sonia Yudin from Sergei's group. And me, of course."

He straightened up, launching his weight off the bookshelf.

"You?"

"Yes, I'm going too."

"You can't..."

"Oh, and why not?"

He licked his lips. It was hard not to be too obvious. "We... your teams. They depend on your leadership. You can't leave them just like that."

"Of course I can! They know perfectly well what to do. They'll be making other plasmids and putting them in other cyanobacteria species in case this combination doesn't work. They don't need me for that."

"But what about the algal mats? They're absolutely loaded with ammonia organisms; they've been there longer than anywhere else in the world!"

"We'll be taking respirator masks."

He looked at her and for the moment he was lost for words. Then:

"What did Kramer say about this?"

"Kramer is a fool. He wants us to waste time doing lab tests that will almost certainly be totally invalid. And if it does come to field testing he thinks the Navy should do it. He was extremely unpleasant about it."

His mouth set as he balanced Kramer's position with his own dislike of the man.

"Look, Maggie, I've got little enough time for Kramer, but have you considered the possibility that he may be right in this instance?"

Her voice acquired a tone of exasperated patience. "No, he is not right and on no account are you to tell him what we're doing. And this is not for the meeting, either. Look, Terry, I've discussed this with all my group leaders and we're of one mind. Ammonia levels are high again – I don't have to tell you that. We need to get to the solution by the shortest possible route and this is it. I'm not asking for your permission; I'm just letting you know what's going to happen, that's all."

He turned away from her and raised a hand to his head. Then he whirled round.

"You're talking as if this was a… a tourist excursion! Can't you see the risks involved? You know you're essential to this whole operation. How can you contemplate putting your own life on the line at this crucial stage?"

"Don't be so dramatic, Terry. For a start, I don't think it is dangerous. But if it is, then that's all the more reason for me to go. First quality of a leader, isn't it – never ask your people to do what you're not prepared to do yourself? That team needs to have someone senior in charge and I'm the one person the researchers here can most easily do without. In any case," she continued, her voice dropping to a more conversational level, "I want to be there. It's the culmination of a lot of hard work. I have to see the result myself. And if it's not successful I want to know first-hand what went wrong. Then when I get back we can discuss how to put things right."

She fixed him with her dark eyes and her manner softened ever so slightly.

"It's kind of you to show concern, Terry, but you may as well give up. You won't dissuade me. I'm going and that's final."

His mouth tightened. He turned and left the office without another word.

For a climatologist John Gilchrist was curiously resistant to the dictates of the weather. He had long, floppy hair, thick-rimmed glasses, and he wore a tweed jacket, Fair Isle pullover, and corduroy trousers all year round. As it happened, his outfit was not altogether inappropriate at this moment. The air was cooler than ever, but the incessant drumming of rain on the windows had ceased, and although the paving stones still shone black in the feeble daylight, the gutters were no longer turbulent rivers, and even the puddles on the lawns had begun to drain away. Nevertheless if, by some miracle, the skies had cleared, and the warm Florida sun once again sent its healing rays into this blighted landscape, John Gilchrist would still have turned up wearing the same familiarly odd attire. Aside from the absence of a pipe, he was a caricature of a British boffin from a 1950s science fiction movie.

There was, however, nothing 1950s about Gilchrist's work. His team spent a good deal of their time downloading visual and infra-red images from meteorological satellites, using them to track the distribution of ash and to monitor weather systems. Gilchrist could read these images like no other.

"Hello, Terry."

"How are things, John?"

"Depends where you're living, chap. You know what we're finding? Things are definitely cooling down faster in northern latitudes – it's only October but up there it's like the depths of winter. It's starting to cause problems." He pointed to the computer screen. "See all this? We've got cool air masses moving south-eastward across Canada and the northern US and these are mixing with warmer moisture-laden air coming up from the Gulf of Mexico. In the St. Lawrence valley the warm air's ridden up over the cool air as usual. So Montreal's got an ice storm."

"Have you talked to anyone up there?" Terry asked.

"Yes, we've had radio contact."

"So how bad is it this time?

"It's lasted two days so far, but the precipitation's very heavy and the ice is building up fast. It's already reached a thickness of seventy millimetres in places. The power lines are holding at the moment but they're watching them carefully."

"Is it going to sit there much longer?"

"I don't think so. You see, Terry, there's such a lot happening out in the Atlantic it's got to shift within the next few days. The interesting thing is the way it's spreading. It's already more extensive than anything we've seen before. It started in Montreal but I think it'll affect a much bigger area than that before it finally moves off."

Terry nodded thoughtfully. He knew to his cost the consequences of thinking in global terms. It was easy to be detached when you were looking at satellite views. You had to force yourself to think about conditions on the ground. Montreal would be like a ghost town right now: ice on the roads, ice on the railways, ice on the runways – nothing would be able to move in or out. Temperatures would be sub-zero. The hospitals would be filling with the homeless and people suffering from broken bones and hypothermia. Trees and telephone poles would be collapsing under the unaccustomed weight. And always, in the background, there was that sinister accumulation on the power lines, the eight big arteries supplying the teeming city with hydroelectricity from the north. If the system moved on soon the ice would melt and things would return to normal. But if it were stable for too long the steel transmission towers would eventually crumple, pulling each other down in a shower of dying sparks, and the city could lose all power.

"Of course," John added. "When it does move off, that's when things start to get really lively."

Terry looked at him.

"What do you mean?"

"Well, those cold air masses are being driven to the south-east. Right now the pattern that's causing the inversion over the St. Lawrence is holding them back. But when it moves out of the way there'll be nothing to stop them. They'll push the mixing zone further south and out into the Atlantic. Heavy precipitation, rain, hail, thunderstorms. And these systems tend to intensify as they move out from the coast."

"John, do you have some up-to-date satellite pictures of that area?"

"Yes, of course. I'll get them up."

Terry watched the screen as the views loaded. Ash and ammonia crystals in the atmosphere obscured the view to some extent, but there were no major circulations.

"No hurricanes in prospect," he murmured.

"No," John replied. "As I said, the problems will be coming from the west."

"Where are we talking about?"

"Over the Gulf Stream, along here."

His finger moved from left to right, tracing a line across the screen. Terry stiffened.

"And when?"

He relaxed. "Hard to say for sure. But on previous form, probably towards the end of the coming week."

"Okay, thanks, John."

He went back to his office and sat down behind his desk.

Maggie had said they needed another week to grow up the new organism so there was no way they could carry out the field testing in the coming week.

It was just as well.

The line traced by John Gilchrist's finger had gone directly through their sampling route.

An hour after Terry left Maggie's office she looked up to see Pieter van der Rijt standing in the doorway.

"Hello, Pieter, come in." She waved him to a chair. "Is there a problem?"

"No, not a problem. I just thought I would tell you what Ulrich and I have been doing."

"Yes, go on."

"Well, we have borrowed some culture equipment from Sergei so now we have four times more capacity for growing up the organism. And we have made some improvements in the growth conditions. It grows now much faster. We do not need so long any more. I think by Sunday we should have enough organism and phage to carry out the field trial."

"Sunday? That's wonderful! That means we can do the field test during the coming week. Thank you, Pieter. I'll make the arrangements right away and tell the others. We'll fly out on Monday."

CHAPTER 65

The young woman who knocked on the open door to Terry's office on Monday afternoon was wearing a quilted jacket, wool hat, scarf, and gloves, and her cheeks were flushed.

"Can I help you?"

"Dr. McKinley?"

"Yes."

"I'm Gemma Sullivan, Mr. Milner's secretary. He wonders if you could drop by."

"Sam Milner? What – now?"

"Yes, he has an important phone message for you."

"I'll come back with you," he said.

On the way out he grabbed his overcoat, which he'd hung on the back of the door, putting it on as he followed her down the corridor. As they emerged from the building Gemma tucked her nose and mouth into her scarf. By British standards it wasn't that cold but he turned up the collar of his coat just the same. They walked over to the campus building that was evidently being used by the FBI.

Gemma took him to Milner's office.

"Hi, Terry." Sam got to his feet to shake hands, throwing a playful pat at Terry's shoulder at the same time. "Good to see you, man. Kind of chilly out there, isn't it?"

Terry grinned at him. "It is a bit." He folded down the collar and took off the overcoat. "What's up, Sam?"

"Eddie Dominguez wanted to talk to you. It has to do with the Zak Gould murder trial."

For the moment Terry was nonplussed. With everything that had been happening, he had completely forgotten that normal life would be trying to continue outside of the Institute. It seemed utterly bizarre. Well over a million people had died, and if the teams didn't come up with a working solution there'd soon be millions more. But two people had committed murder so they had to go on trial.

"I suppose I should call him back. Can I do it here?"

"Sure, no problem."

Milner punched in the number, spoke briefly, then passed the handset to Terry.

The familiar voice said, "Terry?"

"Hi, Eddie. How's the weather up there?"

"Oh, we got about four feet of very dirty snow but we're coping. Listen, Terry, the State's prosecuting those two upstanding citizens we brought in. The trial court suddenly had a slot come available so we grabbed it. We're good and ready: we got the evidence but you're a key witness. Sorry about the short notice, but we need you in court."

"Well, I'd like to help you out, Eddie, but we're doing some important work here. I'm afraid I can't get away right now."

"Terry… I'm sorry, buddy, you don't have a choice. The court's issued you with a subpoena. While they were working out a way of getting it to you I just thought I'd make the invitation a bit more friendly."

Terry heaved an exasperated sigh. "When?"

"Do you think you could get up here in time for tomorrow? Counsel would like to present your evidence then."

Terry hesitated. "I don't know. I suppose so."

"See, we got a real watertight case against Charles Edward Morrissey – he was the big guy who killed Zak and the young cop. Of course, Morrissey's mouthpiece will try to say that he shot the cop in self-defence and he only shot Zak by accident because he was struggling with you – "

"What?"

"Don't worry – we'll nail him. But that's why we need you on the stand."

"What about the other one, the prizefighter?"

"David Ramsay. Yeah – we need you for that too. So, you wanna make your flight arrangements? Let me know your ETA and I'll see someone meets you at Logan. And we'll book you into a hotel."

He sighed. "Okay, Eddie. See you soon."

"Sure thing. 'Bye."

He clicked off the phone, then looked at Milner.

"Sam, I've been served with a damned subpoena for the trial of those two thugs in Boston."

"Yeah, me too. It's the defense attorney. Eddie tells me he's a royal pain in the ass."

"Jesus, Sam, how small-minded can he get? Here we are, doing work of international importance, and all this guy wants to do is put a couple of murderers back on the street."

"That's his job, Terry. He has to defend his clients to the best of his ability."

"Isn't there some way I can get round it?"

"It would tie you up more than actually going there. Look, it may not be so bad as you think. It's an open and shut case; not even a crack lawyer could do much about it. We fly up, we fly back, is all. Because of the fuel situation they're only running three return flights a week now: Monday, Wednesday, and Friday." He looked at his watch. "I think we can still get on that Monday evening flight. I'll check the departure time with Gemma."

Milner went to the door and Terry heard a muffled conversation. He came back.

"Okay, we can just make it. I'll pick you up outside your residence in thirty minutes. That'll give us time to get to the airport and check in."

"I'd better get moving. I only need overnight stuff, don't I?"

"Two nights. We'll get back on Wednesday; Gemma is booking a couple of seats on the return flight right now – in case the court decides to let us off for good behaviour."

"All right. See you later."

Terry walked back to the Institute building feeling deeply frustrated. The public needed protection from those two, and they needed to be taken out of circulation. The trouble was that it took him out of circulation too, and at a rather crucial time.

Back in his office he shut down his computer, crammed a few papers into his briefcase and, after a quick look round, left.

He paused outside Maggie's office. The door was closed. He knocked and tried it, but it was locked. It was unusual but she was probably in one of the labs upstairs. There wasn't time to seek her out now.

He half-walked, half-ran to the hall of residence.

There was just one flight to Bermuda on Mondays and Maggie's team had arrived on it in the late afternoon. She had no difficulty securing accommodation for them at a hotel close to St. George's Harbour. When they'd settled in they got together in Maggie's room and sat round a coffee table.

"Have you got the calculations, Jos?" Maggie asked.

In answer, Jos Wentink produced a print-out of a chart in which Bermuda was the only land mass, just visible in the bottom left-hand corner. He spread it on the table and pointed to a pencilled cross.

"This is where we must put our organism," he said. "33 degrees 19 minutes north, 64 degrees 3 minutes west. It is about 80 nautical miles north-west of here."

"Right," Maggie said. "So the current will take it into the area I told you about, where we know the ammonia organisms are concentrated."

"That is right. I think we should leave it for ten hours. In that time it cannot travel faster than the surface current, so it will not go more than forty nautical miles. We begin to sample forty miles out along the direction of the current, before it has arrived. That is here." He pointed to another cross. "Then we take samples on the way back to the starting point. This way we see if it is working and how far it has spread."

"Timing?"

"We should do all the sampling in daylight. I suggest we are at the furthest point at one o'clock in the afternoon."

Maggie thought about the duration of her previous trip with Terry, back in May. "That means we need to leave harbour at about seven a.m. So our organism has to be put into the sea at three o'clock in the morning!"

Jos shrugged. "This part does not need daylight but we will be a long time without sleep."

She looked around at the others. "All right, look, here's what we'll do. Only one person needs to go out to actually dump the stuff. That'll be me."

They started to protest, but she held up a hand.

"No, it makes sense. I'll leave at eleven p.m. and come back at seven a.m. to pick up the rest of you. Then the schedule is as Jos said. But everyone has to be ready at the harbour, with the sampling gear and chests, at seven."

"When are you going to get some sleep, Maggie?" Rob asked.

"Don't worry; I may be able to snatch a little on the trip out and back. Yes, Sonia?"

"What about the respirator masks?"

"Yes, we mustn't forget them. I'll take the box with me; then we can be sure they're on board. In any case, I may need them myself."

"Maggie, where do we get the ice and dry ice?" Sara asked.

"The Bermuda Institute of Ocean Sciences. It's too late to go up there today; I'll organize it tomorrow morning. But first I'll be going down to the harbour to charter a boat." She put her hand on the chart. "Can I take this, Jos?"

"Yes, of course, it's for you."

"Good. I know just the person I want for this trip."

CHAPTER 66

The court room wasn't overheated but even so Milner was dabbing a handkerchief at his forehead as he regained his seat next to Terry. The trial had proceeded to time, and the two of them were giving evidence this morning.

The Clerk called Dr. Terence McKinley to the witness stand and Terry stood.

"Watch that defense counsel," Sam hissed, as Terry passed. "He's poison."

Terry hardly needed to be told. Forensic evidence had already been presented to confirm that the bullet that killed Zak had come from Charles Morrissey's pistol. But as Eddie Dominguez had guessed, the Defense case was that Morrissey had not intended to fire the fatal shot. Terry was the only one who could refute that argument.

As soon as he'd been sworn in, Denise Chadwick, Counsel for the Prosecution, opened with a question that gave him the scope he needed.

"Dr. McKinley, would you please describe in your own words what happened on the morning in question?"

Terry gave a clear account of the events up to the time the police reinforcements entered the room. In the back of his mind he was still wondering what traps Morrissey's lawyers had been preparing for him. He heard the words "your witness" and the Counsel for the Defense stepped forward.

Paul McAdam was short and somewhat overweight, with a self-consciously oratorical style. He led smoothly up to his main theme and began to pace in front of the jury while continuing to throw questions over his shoulder. Terry recognized the calculated rudeness and was determined not to rise to it.

"I put it to you that by grabbing the defendant's hand you caused the pistol to fire."

"That's just not true. The defendant managed to squeeze off two shots before I intervened."

"You accept, don't you, that no one apart from you saw those shots being fired?"

"Yes. Everyone else was focused on Dr. Gould."

A smoothness entered the man's voice.

"Dr. McKinley, I am not blaming you for intervening, and I am not suggesting that you intended it to happen, but it is entirely possible, is it not, that by grappling with the defendant you actually caused the firearm to be discharged?"

"No, it isn't possible. Both shots were fired before I took hold of him."

"May I ask how you come to be so qualified in the martial arts?"

"I took up Judo when I was at school. I rose to Black Belt, first Dan, during my undergraduate days at university."

"I see. As a black belt, then, you would know a good deal about the vulnerability of the human body. Tell me, Dr. McKinley, did you intend to dislocate the defendant's shoulder when you attacked him?"

"No, sir, I meant to break his arm."

This raised a murmur of laughter and the judge frowned and slapped his hand on the desk.

"So, Dr. McKinley," Counsel continued, "it would be fair to characterize you as a violent man."

Out of the corner of his eye, Terry saw Denise Chadwick half-rise to object, but he responded quickly:

"Only when someone's taking pot shots at my friends."

She smiled and sat down.

"Let us turn to the evidence in the case of Mr. Ramsay. You claim, do you not, that you were attacked by Mr. Ramsay?"

"I don't have to claim it. The others witnessed it."

"And yet, Dr. McKinley, when the police reinforcements entered the room they testified that Mr. Ramsay was being restrained most painfully by you in some kind of arm lock."

"That's right."

"Isn't there a contradiction here, Dr. McKinley?"

"None at all. He attacked me and I restrained him."

"No more questions."

Ms. Chadwick asked if she could put a supplementary question.

"Dr. McKinley, you were violently assaulted by the defendant Mr. Ramsay, and this left you severely bruised and beaten about the face and body. In the end you were able to use your considerable skills to immobilize your opponent. But suppose, like the unfortunate Dr. Grant Challoner, you did not have those skills. Would a sustained beating like that have been sufficient to kill a man?"

"Objection. Counsel is asking for an opinion, an opinion which the witness is not qualified to give."

"Counsellor?"

"On the contrary, your honour, Counsel for the Defense has already established that the witness is admirably qualified to provide an answer."

"I'll allow the question."

Terry took a deep breath. "I'm young and reasonably fit, but I found that short encounter with the defendant very punishing. In my view, a sustained attack of that intensity could well have proved fatal to an older man such as Dr. Challoner."

"No further questions."

"Thank you, Dr. McKinley. You may stand down."

St. George's Harbour had looked very different the last time Maggie was here. She recalled the intense blue-green of the water, the brilliant blue sky, the arriving cruise liners and the sails of the turning yachts. Now the sky was a uniform grey, the sea was the colour of pewter, and sky and sea merged in the distance without any apparent horizon. A solitary fishing boat made its way out of the harbour, the throb of the engine carrying across the water. There was no warmth in the sun and Maggie was glad of her windproof jacket as she lowered her head into a keen onshore breeze.

She suspected that Max Gibson would never be far away from his beloved boat. Sure enough as she went down the quay to *Cleaver II* she saw his battered white cap moving around near the wheelhouse. He looked up as she called his name and hurried over.

"I bet you didn't expect to see me again," she laughed.

He pumped her hand. "Well, well, well, you after findin' some more weed?"

"Sort of. Max. I'd like to charter your boat for two months."

His eyebrows lifted. She could imagine what that meant to him. Even during the normal season business would seldom be that good. Right now there was no tourism at all, even in season.

"Two months?"

"Yes, the people I work for want the boat available during that time. But you'll only have to make a few trips. There'll be some long days, that's all."

He frowned. "And weed?"

"Possibly, yes. But I have the respirator masks, and we'll be sure to use them this time."

He nodded. "Okay."

"Great. I'd like to show you the route. Is there somewhere we can get out of this wind?"

He pointed and they walked to the office on the quay.

While the girl at the desk was preparing the paperwork for an unprecedented two-month charter, he led Maggie through to the small room behind, where he spread the chart out on a table and studied the schedule she'd written down for him. The girl called through the open door:

"Ma'am, is that two months from today – Tuesday?"

"Yes, please. From today."

Max looked up at her. "So you wanna go out tonight?"

"Yes, is that okay?'

He shrugged. "An' we leave again soon as we get back?"

"Yes. We'll take the rest of the team and equipment on board at seven tomorrow morning. You won't get much sleep, I'm afraid."

He grinned, the teeth an unexpected show of white in that weather-beaten face. "Won' be the first time."

"Ma'am, I need your signature here."

"Okay," she called. They stood up.

"I best be gettin' back," Max said.

She shook his hand. "I'll see you at eleven tonight."

The waitress came by with a insulated jug.

"Would you gentlemen like some more coffee?"

Terry, Milner, and Dominguez shook their heads.

Dominguez said, "I'll take the bill now, miss."

"Be right with you."

"You don't have to pick up the tab, Eddie," Milner protested.

"It's mine – least I can do after you guys came all the way up here."

"Do you think they'll need to recall us, Eddie?" Terry asked.

"I don't think so. Take Charlie. See, if it was only Zak he shot there'd be just a shadow of doubt – you know, about whether he really intended to, or whether the pistol went off in the struggle. It was Terry's word against his. Of course, Terry's the more reliable witness but that doesn't always count if the jury has a bit of sympathy with the plaintiff. The young cop, that's different. Remember when I went out to fetch him? He was dead on the doorstep and his sidearm was still in the holster. That means Charlie shot him in cold blood. Courts don't like people shooting cops, especially in cold blood."

"I see. Shooting scientists is all right, but shooting cops is a serious business."

"Nah, you know what I mean. Scientists don't go out putting their lives on the line for the benefit of the public." Then he laughed, reaching across the table to punch Terry's shoulder. "At least, usually they don't."

"And Ramsay?"

"Yeah, I can't see him getting off. He made such a mess of Challoner there had to be evidence to place him at the crime scene and there was: forensic took spots of Challoner's blood off his clothes and his trainers so we know he was at the crime scene. The post mortem was pretty clear about the cause of death and from the way he lammed into you there's no doubt about who was responsible. It may not be first degree murder, but it sure as hell won't be manslaughter. And then you've got the fact that the two were working together. It would be hard even for that Defense Counsel to convince a jury that one of them was just an innocent bystander."

"That means we can fly back tomorrow, as planned," Terry said.

"Should be fine."

The waitress brought a small plastic folder to the table. Dominguez shot her a smile.

"I'll deal with this at the desk on the way out," he said.

The waitress said "Sure thing, have a nice day," and went away. Dominguez turned back to them.

"So, much as I enjoy seeing you guys I don't think there'll be any call for you to come up here again."

"We got off lightly," Milner said to Terry. "Sometimes you're hanging around forever with these cases."

"Just as well," Terry replied. "I have to get back. Besides, I've decided I don't like court rooms."

"Me neither," Milner agreed. He stretched. "Well, shall we make a move?"

They all got up. Dominguez selected a bill from his wallet and left it for the waitress. They waited for him at the reception desk, then moved to the glass entrance doors.

"Thanks for dinner, Eddie," said Milner. "Damn, looks like it's raining."

Terry opened the door and the air entered his lungs like a knife. Milner was about to follow when Terry grabbed him by the arm.

"Hang on," he said.

A couple emerged behind them, found that they were in the way, and pushed roughly past. The man stepped onto the pavement, slipped, and fell heavily.

"Omigosh, are you all right, honey?" the woman screeched.

He picked himself up cursing and rubbing his hip. "I guess. Watch the ice. Dammit, I didn't think it was that cold."

He limped away with his partner clutching his arm. Their breath escaped in short white trails that lingered in the air behind them.

At that moment a bus came around the corner and began to slide. They were close enough to see the driver battling with the steering wheel. Eventually it came to a stop almost broadside on, the back wheels resting against the kerb. They saw him turn to the passengers. He was saying something and shaking his head. The passengers were shouting back at him, evidently unhappy about something. The driver got out, grabbed at a handle as his feet almost went out from under him, then walked away.

"He wasn't prepared to take the risk," observed Dominguez. "Can't blame him. Those people will sue at the drop of a hat if there's an accident."

Milner looked curiously at Terry. "How did you know?"

"I didn't. I just sensed something was wrong. This street was buzzing with traffic and pedestrians when we went in. Look at it now."

Milner glanced up and down and nodded. "Jeez, and I thought it was only rain."

"It is rain. But it's supercooled. Turns to ice the moment it hits something."

"No shit. Where are you parked, Eddie?"

"Back in your hotel garage. Fortunately I've got an all-wheel drive but they can still go sideways."

Terry said, "This stuff's like glass. I suggest we link arms to walk back. Six legs are better than two."

Milner let him take his arm. "People will think we're gay," he said.

"Let them. Better that than break a leg."

At eleven o'clock the quayside was deserted. Maggie stood for a moment, looking out across the pool. The only sounds were the soft lapping of waves against the concrete walls and the boats creaking and knocking gently in their moorings. There was no moonlight and the water would have been invisible but for the runs of silvered ripples where it was caught in the lights from the quayside. Beyond the lights the blackness was impenetrable. The cool air sent a small shiver through her body.

Her footsteps echoed loudly as she boarded the boat. In the weak, yellowish illumination of the wheelhouse she saw Max lift a hand in greeting. He gestured at the smaller man with him.

"This here's Casey Brown. He'll be crewin' this trip. Casey knows these waters better'n anyone, even me."

Casey Brown grinned and touched two fingers to a wool hat that looked as if it had seldom left his head. Like Max he was wearing a roll-neck pullover two sizes too large, and his jeans disappeared into seamen's boots. In this light it was impossible to tell how old he was.

"All set?"

She nodded.

Casey didn't need to be told. He vaulted onto the hull and ran down the edge like a cat along a fence. She could see him detaching ropes from cleats, winding them into neat coils and hanging them on posts on the quay. Then he jumped back into the boat.

Max stepped into the wheelhouse, twisted a key in a panel in front of him, and pressed two large red buttons. The twin motors spluttered into life, shattering the silence of the pool. He flicked a couple of switches and the beams of two powerful spotlights probed the darkness ahead. Then, with the wheel in one hand and the levers in the other, he eased them away from the quay.

Maggie settled herself down in a corner of the cabin and watched the lights of the town and the quay receding. Some minutes later the increased motion of the boat told her they'd left the harbour. Max extinguished the spotlights and advanced the throttles. Waves splashed against the hull in a recurrent rhythm. Her eyelids grew heavy.

She awoke with a jerk, unaware of having fallen asleep. The engine note had dropped to an idle. Max's features were thrown into relief by the weak illumination coming from the instrument panel.

"On the button," he said, pointing – presumably at the GPS.

She got up, stretched, rubbed her eyes and gave her head a little shake. Then she checked her watch. It was ten to three.

She opened a wooden chest, painted grey with red stripes. Inside were the respirator masks, and with them the precious canister of the new organism. She lifted it out and went to the rear deck to wait for the precise moment.

In the darkness the sounds and smells of the night were magnified. The deck rocked gently under her feet, the motors puttered, and the water smacked against the hull. Then her nostrils twitched and she stiffened. It was faint, but there was no mistaking it.

Ammonia.

Should they put on the masks? She checked her watch again. Three o'clock.

Let's get this over with.

She unscrewed the cap, swirled the canister and emptied the contents over the side into the black, unseen water.

CHAPTER 67

"Ice storms," said Milner. "I heard about them, I seen pictures on television, but I never been stuck in one before. Why did it have to happen now?"

He and Terry had more or less finished breakfast, but they sat by the window, sipping coffee and staring disconsolately at the dim, deserted street.

Terry pushed his cup away. "John Gilchrist showed me this weather system last Friday. The ice storm was sitting on Montreal then. It was big but I had no idea it would affect us. Either it's spread all the way to Boston or it's in the process of moving off to the south or south-east. My hope is that it's moving."

"Because it won't last so long?"

"Not just that. A day or two after this little lot moves off it's going to set up severe storm conditions in the Atlantic. Maggie's planning to carry out some field trials in that area next week. I'd feel much better about it if the whole system had passed through by then."

Milner sighed. "Yeah. Well, so much for flying back today. I phoned Logan this morning. Still nothing happening."

"I'm not surprised. Far too dangerous for anything to land with the runways all iced up."

"What about helicopters? They don't need runways. They could fly us to an ice-free airport. Somewhere like T.F. Green in Rhode Island."

"Not in freezing rain they couldn't. It would ice up the rotors inside a minute. What did you do about the flights?"

"They rebooked us on the next scheduled service."

"That's Friday, isn't it?"

"Yeah." Milner craned his neck to look up again at the sky. He was almost talking to himself. "Day after tomorrow. Maybe it'll clear by then."

"Sam, even if the conditions change now the airport may not be functioning as soon as that. And the next flight isn't till Monday. Aren't there any alternatives?"

He got up.

"I'll go see. If I find something I'll phone your room. Otherwise we'll meet in the bar later."

It was still dark as *Cleaver II* entered the calm water of the harbour. Maggie stood in the wheelhouse, straining to see if her people were in place. A thin mist curled off the water, writhed in the spotlight beams, and formed haloes around the quayside lights. As the boat inched up to the quay the team came into view: shadowy figures standing there on the jetty, huddled in their padded jackets and windproof trousers. Max cut the engines. It was five to seven.

Sara Tennant called out: "All right, Maggie?"

"Yes, fine. Do you want to hand that down?"

Maggie took a large bag from her and carried it to the cabin. Rob Guillemain and Jos Wentink picked up an insulated chest between them. There was another chest on the jetty next to them.

"Casey," Max said, "you wanna give the youngsters a hand with those chests? They go here."

He pointed underneath the wooden bench that ran around the sides of the cabin.

With Casey's help Jos and Rob got the chest on board and went back for the second one. Sara Tennant and Sonia Yudin came up behind with the rest of the sampling gear. They were all on board.

"Okay, people," Maggie said. "Make yourselves comfortable. We've got a six-hour trip ahead of us."

Casey was already casting off. He jumped back into the boat and shouted to Max: "All clear."

Maggie said: "Max? You know where we're going, don't you? The furthest point. Then we'll take samples on the way back to where we dumped the stuff this morning."

He nodded and started the engines, and *Cleaver II* nosed out of the harbour again.

A blush was just beginning to spread into the eastern sky.

Terry returned to his room and stood there for several minutes, at a loss as to what to do next. He hadn't brought his lap top with him because it had data and programs on it that would have posed security issues. The streets were far too icy to risk venturing outside. He went back to the ground floor where there was a bookshop and newsstand, bought copies of the *New York Times*, *Washington Post*, and *Chicago Tribune*, and took them up to his room. There was little else he could do for the moment except settle down with Wednesday's papers.

There were many pages on the situation in the north-west, the articles frequently illustrated with the same syndicated photographs. An enterprising pilot had overflown Yellowstone and taken photos of the thirty-mile-wide crater. Much of it was obscured by smoke and ash, and there were no houses or other recognizable features to give it scale, but it had evidently remodelled not only the whole of Yellowstone Park but part of the Lake, too. This was brought home even more forcibly by the *Washington Post*, which had superimposed a dotted outline of the previous boundaries. The scars were seen in the surrounding areas, too; the explosion had sent out a shock wave over a huge radius, leaving trees scattered like matchsticks. It reminded Terry of the eruption of Mount St. Helens in 1980, except the volume of ejecta would have been at least three thousand times greater.

The towns were a picture of devastation. He had to force himself to read the accounts. Along the path of the surges no one had survived; those who weren't incinerated were asphyxiated. Above the dark grey surface that marked the new ground level, bodies were still being removed from the upper floors of buildings and taken away for quick burial; recovering those incarcerated in the solidified ash and mud would no doubt continue for years. The main humanitarian effort focused on the luckier ones who'd avoided the pyroclastic flows but were now totally cut off. Special trauma centres and supply dumps had been set up in neighbouring states. Cargo planes continued to make drops, and helicopters ferried in rescue teams and took out the sick and injured, but their efforts looked puny in relation to the size of the problem. The priority on the ground was to clear roads and runways so that the whole operation could be scaled up.

The articles were interspersed with personal tales of survival and heroism, and accounts of the less savoury activities of people who'd sought to exploit the situation.

When he'd turned the last page he felt empty. He got up and paced around the room.

The decision was the President's; the responsibility was mine. I'll have to live with this for the rest of my life.

He pulled up short and clenched his fists. It wasn't sensible to think in those terms. The important thing was to focus not on the million or so who may have died but on the seven billion it could yet save. He turned back and looked at the papers scattered over the sofa.

God, Maggie, I hope your solution works. Because if it doesn't, we did all this for nothing.

The steady note of *Cleaver II*'s engines dropped. Maggie looked at her watch. They couldn't be there yet, there was more than an hour to go. She got to her feet. Max was peering ahead and Casey had his head round the side of the cabin.

"What is it, Max?"

He pointed and her heart sank. It was an area of apparent calm ahead. She knew what that meant because she'd seen it before. Weed.

"Okay, everyone," she shouted. "Respirators on."

Rob was standing behind her. "I can't smell anything, Maggie."

"Rob, by the time you smell it, it'll be too late. Just put the bloody thing on."

For the next few minutes they busied themselves taking the masks out of the chest and fitting them to one another. It was something they'd practised, but Casey and Max needed a little help. When they'd finished Maggie inspected the result.

In spite of the mask, Casey had managed to get his woolly hat back on, to richly comic effect. Even Max was wearing his white cap. She was grateful for these touches because in other ways the group had taken on a sinister look, like a germ warfare exercise.

Their attention returned to the weed mat. Max was shaking his head, his voice muffled by the mask. "I been sailing these waters for many a year, and I never seen weed this far south."

A shout came from Casey. He was up on the bulwark, gesticulating.

"Max, quick, hard to starboard."

Max gunned the throttles differentially just as a brown mass washed by. It was a couple of metres across, with trailing arms, like some bizarre sea monster. Jos was quite excited.

"Look at the brown colour, Maggie. It could be a different species. Let me take a sample."

Maggie looked at Max. He tilted his head. "We'll go slow but I don't wanna stop them screws turnin'."

"Okay, Jos, but be quick."

Jos opened the equipment bag and fitted a filter and a bottle to the sampling drogue. He aimed, then tossed it out and handlined it in. Sara was standing by.

"Polycarbonate tube, Sara," Jos said.

"Here you are."

"No, just hold it. I will pour the sample, you cap it. Okay, now the jar."

Sara unsealed a jar and Jos removed the filter from the sampling drogue and dropped it in. The filter had been a fine white gauze when they'd assembled the drogue. Now it was a greenish brown.

"I will label this one, you label that one. Good, you can freeze that one now."

Sara walked forward to the cabin area, put on some thick gloves and opened one of the two insulated chests. A white mist billowed out. She tucked the polycarbonate tube well down into the dry ice, closed the lid, and pulled down the latch. Freezing the seawater to minus eighty degrees would arrest any chemical reactions until they got the sample back to the laboratory.

The jar containing the loaded filter went into the second chest. This one contained conventional ice, which would help to preserve the internal structure of the cyanobacteria without actually freezing them.

Jos looked up. "Okay, Maggie."

She nodded and paused to look at Casey, who was hanging over the bulwark, staring into the water. Then he did the same on the other side of the boat. He seemed quite agitated.

She followed Max's gaze out to the big weed mat. "Can you go around it, Max?"

"Could try, but..." He showed her the chart Jos had prepared. "Where you wanna get to is here. To be safe we need to go here, then here. No way we can make it by one o'clock."

The rest of the team were looking on. Casey came over to join them.

"Lot o' weed in this water all aroun', mon. Could be fouled already. Wouldn't go anywhere now if I was you."

Max's expression was grim. "This stoff stick to the hull," he explained. "It can slide off any time and wrap itself round the screws."

Casey touched her arm for emphasis, his eyes wide. "We seen it happen."

Maggie took a deep breath. "All right, I've heard enough. We're going back."

There was a chorus of protest from the postdocs.

She held up a hand. "I'm not taking chances with people's lives."

"What about the test?" Rob asked.

"We'll talk it over tonight."

Milner was already in the bar when Terry went down to meet up with him.

"That okay?" He pushed a glass across to him. The brown tinge suggested there was probably some scotch amongst the rocks.

"Thanks. Any joy?"

Milner shook his head. "Can't go by train: rails are still iced up. Any case the rolling stock's all over the place; it'll take days to get schedules back to normal."

"Can we rent a car and drive down?"

"Checked that, too. Trouble is, you'd never make it out of this area without an all-wheel drive. I made a few calls to local rental companies and there's been a run on them; they're clean out. Looks like we have to wait till Friday for the flight."

"Great, another whole day of this to look forward to." Terry sighed. "I am so bloody sick of hanging around up here. You know, I've been working non-stop since we moved to Florida. Now suddenly I'm twiddling my thumbs."

"Yeah, and I'm getting kind of tired of watching old movies." He drained his glass and stood up. "Get you another?"

"Yeah, why not? No ice this time."

Milner grinned. "Brits like their beer warm, too. Right?"

"Right."

Terry dropped into a leather bench seat while Milner got the drinks. His mind wandered to the Institute. Maggie would be wondering what had happened to him. He could get a message to her via Milner's secretary, but they hadn't been following each other's movements closely of late. She'd probably assume he'd gone on one of the sampling flights.

A shadow crossed his mind. Where had she been when he went to find her? He dismissed the thought. She was probably making preliminary preparations for the field trip. There was no way they could go out this week.

After they unloaded the boat Maggie phoned the Institute of Ocean Sciences. A technician drove down in one of their few vehicles and collected the chests of ice and dry ice. He agreed to place the samples in temporary storage. Then the team returned to the hotel and came up to Maggie's room. Maggie was desperately tired, but morale was low and she knew they needed to decide on a new strategy as soon as possible.

"It was sheer bad luck," she said. "Max stopped well short of that weed mat but we didn't realize how much there was floating around in the water. It was too dangerous to go on. In any case we couldn't make the far point by one o'clock so we wouldn't have been able to time the spread."

"Can we go out tomorrow?" Rob asked.

"I'm afraid not. It's going to take them all day to clean off any weed that's still clinging to the boat. It will have to be Friday."

"What will we do?"

'Well, we won't be able to see how fast it's spreading but we can still find out if it's working. Jos and I had a quick word about it on the way back. Jos?"

Jos produced a copy of his chart and laid it on the table. He pointed. "The current should have carried our organism through this area. We know now we cannot go there because of the weed. But if it is working it should spread like this." He made a wedge shape with his hands, expanding from the pencilled cross, the point where Maggie had emptied the canister. "So if we approach the area from the south we should be able to take samples before we reach the weed mats."

Maggie saw the others nodding. "Okay, then," she said, "that's the plan. We still want to do all the sampling in daylight so we may as well stick to the same schedule as today. Right now I need some sleep. Free time tomorrow, except for picking up the chests from the Institute in the evening. And let's be ready on the jetty on Friday morning at seven o'clock."

Milner came back with a glass in each hand. He paused and jerked his head towards the window.

"Hey, Terry. Look behind you. It's getting worse."

Terry got up and looked out of the window. It was snowing.

He came back to Milner.

"Not worse, Sam. The opposite. Snow confirms it. This system's on the move."

CHAPTER 68

It was shortly before seven on Friday morning when Maggie led the team through the darkness down to the quay. The four postdocs were unusually quiet, no doubt coping – as she was – with the shock of emerging from a warm bed into the biting cold of the morning. As they approached *Cleaver II* she saw Max Gibson's white cap moving around in the dimly lit wheelhouse. Casey was standing on the jetty ready to help them board the sampling equipment and chests. Max came over.

"Weather forecast said rain on the way," he said.

"We've got waterproofs; I think we can put up with a little rain. How bad is it likely to be?"

"Normally I'd-a taken one look at the sky last evenin' and told you. But this stoff in the air from the volcano, it make the sky grey all-a time. And fonny things been happenin' to the weather all over. Could be nothin'; could turn out rough. Hard to say."

Maggie bit her lip. She didn't want to take unnecessary risks but this really would be their last chance this trip. Ocean currents were not that predictable on a local scale and in another day or so a negative result could mean either that the organism wasn't working or that it had been washed into an entirely different area. They'd return no wiser than when they came out.

"Max, we really have to go today. What do you think?"

"Oh, I can take you, no problem. Things get real bad we have to come back, tha's all."

"Great. Do you still have the chart?"

He did. She indicated the route that Jos had suggested. "I'd like to take samples between here and here."

He studied it carefully then straightened up. "Okay. We c'n leave whenever you say."

The others were waiting on the afterdeck. She went over to them.

"How are you getting on?"

"All done," Rob answered.

"What about the respirator masks?"

Rob pointed to the painted wooden chest, grey with red stripes, which had been tucked beneath the benching. Alongside it were the chests with the ice and dry ice and the bag with the sampling equipment.

"Good." She turned. "All right, then, ready when you are, Max."

They stood on the open afterdeck, handlining in the last few metres.

"Have you got it?" Maggie called to Rob.

He lifted the drogue into the boat. "Yep."

They were one hundred nautical miles out and Sara was helping Rob take the first sample. She put the polycarbonate tube in the dry ice and closed the chest.

"Have you got the filter, Rob?"

"Sonia's got it."

Sonia passed her the filter and she transferred it to a jar, which she placed in the other chest. Maggie checked the latches on both chests and straightened up.

"Max?"

He was leaning with his back to the wheelhouse, watching the proceedings, his soulful brown eyes with the bloodshot whites roving from one member of the team to another.

"We all through?"

"Yes, we're done here. Stop in ten miles and we'll take another sample."

He looked up at the sky.

"Weather seems to be holdin'."

"Let's hope it lasts."

Half an hour later, Max throttled back the engines, then cut them, and the team went into action again. The moves were getting familiar now and the second sample was quickly on board. They were in the middle of the wedge shape that Jos had described on Wednesday evening.

"How are we off for dry ice?" Maggie asked Sonia.

"There's still plenty. It's only gone down an inch or so."

"Good. All right, Max."

The others exchanged grins as she turned back to them, rubbing her hands together. In a couple of hours or so the rest of the samples would be in the chests and they could return to port. Things were going smoothly at last.

The engine note rose, drowning any attempt at conversation, and they contented themselves with watching the grey ocean speed past. Before long Max was slowing the boat for the approach to the third sampling site. Maggie frowned and looked at her watch.

There should be several hours of daylight left. Why was it getting so dark?

Max cut the engines and emerged with Casey. They stood there, stiff and alert, squinting at the horizon. Maggie gave them an uneasy glance before following Rob and Jos, who were preparing to take the sample. She lurched as she went because a fresh breeze was coming off the sea and the deck was beginning to rock. The sky grew darker and the line sawed back and forth endlessly in the black water as Jos hauled it in. Eventually the drogue surfaced, got sucked back again and then came free. Rob helped Jos to transfer the sample filter to a jar, then staggered back to place it in the sample chest.

In the distance lightning flickered through the clouds.

"Okay, get the waterproofs on," Max commanded. "It's blowin' up fast."

Casey hinged open one seat, which formed the lid of the locker, and handed out the clothing. Maggie pulled on the waterproof trousers, fastened the jacket and put her life jacket back on over the top. Then, moving awkwardly in the stiff, bulky clothing, and with the deck now heaving under her, she retrieved the sampling gear. As she returned, Rob pointed at the empty locker. He had to shout over the growing noise of the wind.

"Maggie? We could probably get one of the sample chests in there."

She stopped where she was, feet planted wide.

"Good idea," she shouted. "Casey? Could you give Rob a hand?"

She watched the two of them manoeuvring the chest. Behind her the wind flowed out in gusts strong enough to tear white foam from the tips of the waves and stream it at her back, thundering on the waterproof fabric and forcing her to duck into her collar. As soon as the chest was stowed she put the rest of the sampling gear in the locker alongside it, tightened the drawstrings on her hood and stumbled over to sit down with the others. The gusts had now consolidated into a howling gale. It was so loud, so enveloping, that Maggie felt as if the sound of it must be generated inside her own head. The waves swelled higher and ran in excited surges, slapping heavily against the bucking hull, hauling back and running again with redoubled force, like an army retreating, mustering, and renewing its attack on an implacable foe.

A few minutes later the hail started. The rear deck danced with balls of ice that ricocheted off every surface and rattled deafeningly on the windows and roof of the cabin. Then the hail turned to rain. They hunched close together, holding the benches tightly, faces averted from the stinging drops that were flying in through the open back of the cabin.

Max struggled to keep *Cleaver II* pointing into a sea that was now cresting twenty to thirty feet high. The vessel rode down the slopes, shuddered as it was struck by intersecting waves, and climbed slowly back up again. Casey stood next to him handling the levers, throttling back quickly as the boat tipped and remained poised with the screws clear of the water before they descended into another trough. The noise was thunderous, the cabin drenched repeatedly with volumes of sea water that descended like blows from a giant hammer. The rear deck was awash and the water rolled in up to their ankles as the boat tilted. Sara and Rob were vomiting over themselves, incapable of moving.

A huge wave broke over the side of the boat and swamped the deck; water rushed in and the equipment chests were lifted and dragged back. Maggie saw one of the chests containing the precious samples receding across the deck. She hurled herself at it – and slid away with her arms still wrapped around it. Jos leaped up and grabbed her life jacket. The water drained back, then another huge wave dropped down from the opposite direction. Now both of them were in danger of going overboard. Sonia, and even Rob and Sara, staggered forward to help; Sara managed to grab Jos's ankles and for a moment they were all floundering in a welter of foam and water. Then the deck lifted clear again and they crawled, spluttering, back into the relative safety of the cabin.

Maggie used the trembling fingers of both hands to wipe strands of soaking hair off her face. Her eyes burned from the seawater, saltier here than anywhere else in the Atlantic. She shook her head to clear her vision and realized the others weren't with her. She got up quickly. Rob and Jos were coming back along the deck, pulling someone between them.

Sonia!

They hauled her up and sat her on the bench. Her eyes were flickering.

Another wave crashed against the cabin windows.

"What happened?" Maggie shouted to them.

"I don't know," Rob answered. "Seems like she slid the length of the deck. There's a winch back there. I think she banged her head it. Knocked her out."

Sonia groaned and rubbed her temple.

Maggie bent over her. "Sonia, are you okay?"

"Yes, I think so. God, that hurts!"

Maggie grimaced, then turned to the others. "Did we save the samples?"

Jos shook his head. "Sorry," he shouted. "Only the ones we put in the locker. The rest have gone."

Sonia murmured something.

"What was that, Sonia?" Maggie asked.

"I was trying to save the other one. But we lost that, too."

"Which one?"

"The painted one with the respirator masks."

The vessel continued to screw and pitch violently. Max was managing to maintain the heading, but they were making no forward progress. Each time the waves lifted the boat they carried it further back.

There was an excited exchange between Casey and Max. Maggie turned to see what was the matter and her blood ran cold.

Coming into view behind them, rocking on the mountainous waters, was a broad, dense blanket of weed.

CHAPTER 69

To Terry's dismay their Friday flights were cancelled as well and they had to rebook yet again for the following Monday.

Crews had worked throughout the weekend to clear the major runways and de-ice the aircraft, and by the time he and Milner checked in at Logan Airport flights were arriving and leaving in quick succession. There was, however, still a backlog to clear. They were scheduled to leave at nine o'clock; the plane took off at two-thirty in the afternoon. They were relieved just to be on their way.

Milner had left his car at the airport. He drove them back to the campus and dropped Terry off at the Institute. Terry waved goodbye and went in. He dumped the bag in his office and went to find Maggie.

The door to her office was closed. He frowned, knocked and tried the handle but it was locked. He turned for the stairs.

Silvia Mussini was in her lab on the second floor.

"Hi Silvia, I got stuck in Boston. Have you seen Maggie?"

"No, none of them are back yet."

He blinked.

"Back from where?"

"From the field trial. It must have taken longer than they thought."

Alarm drilled out along his veins. "When did they leave?"

"Last Monday. Maggie went with Jos, Sonia, Rob, and Sara. They should have been back by now."

His jaw went slack. "I thought they weren't going till *this* week!"

"Pieter and Ulrich managed to make enough organism so they brought the trial forward."

He took a deep breath, nodded to her, and made for the stairs.

He went straight to Kramer's office, knocked on the door, and went in without waiting for a response. He ignored the look of affront on Kramer's face.

"Dr. Kramer, did you know that Dr. Ferris went out to conduct a field trial in Bermuda waters?"

"I was aware of something of the sort, yes."

"And were you also aware that there were potential storm conditions in that area?"

"No, but really Dr. McKinley, this is none of my concern."

"It isn't? Five staff go missing from this Institute and it isn't your concern?"

"Dr. McKinley, I can't be responsible for someone who ignores good advice. I told your colleague that it was premature to conduct ocean trials without convincing laboratory evidence. I also considered such trials far too dangerous for anything but a skilled Navy team." He gave Terry a glacial smile. "It would seem I have been proven right."

There was the merest instant of blank silence, then Terry lunged forward, grabbed the astonished man by the tie and lifted him bodily halfway across the desk. He remained suspended there, squirming helplessly on Terry's fist, his face an inch from Terry's own.

"You really don't get it, do you? She's out there trying to save the lives of every man, woman, and child on the planet, including yours, you *pompous, self-satisfied little shit!*"

The tie bit deeply into Kramer's skinny neck; a purple flush rose into his pallid face, and his eyes bulged. Terry shook his head in disgust and threw him back into his chair. He left him there, spreadeagled like a rag doll, and stormed out without closing the door.

He went quickly to his own office.

It wasn't hard to guess which boat Maggie had chartered and he got the number from the contacts list on his lap top.

Milner looked up in concern as he came in.

"Terry?"

"Maggie did carry out those field trials last week, Sam, and they haven't come back. Could I use your phone?"

"Sure, help yourself."

The girl who took the call was guarded.

"Are you family?" she asked.

He swallowed hard. "This is Dr. McKinley," he said. "I'm a close scientific colleague of Dr. Ferris. Please tell me what's happened."

There was a pause, then the girl said:

"I'm sorry, sir. A real bad storm came through here. It blew up suddenly. Did an awful lot of damage."

"Dr. Ferris should have returned by now."

"I know. They were caught in the storm, see. Last time we spoke to Cap'n Gibson he said it was drivin' them backwards into the weed mats. We been tryin' to make radio contact with them ever since."

Something fluttered inside Terry's stomach. He forced himself to think rationally.

"Does the Maritime Operations Centre know?"

"Oh yes, sir. We told them."

"And?"

"They can't handle Search and Rescue that far out. Normally they ask an incoming vessel to divert, but there's nothin' due. No tourist industry now, you see – because of the volcano – we just gettin' the occasional tanker and container ship. Bermuda Harbour Radio got a message through to United States Coast Guard. We been trying to raise the Coast Guard ourselves since this morning but they're busy all-a time. Must be a lot of emergencies, right now, with the storm an' all."

"Right. I'll speak to them. Which station would that be?"

"The air station at Elizabeth City, North Carolina."

"Got it. Thanks for your help."

"You welcome. Please don' worry, sir. Max Gibson is a ver' experienced cap'n. I'm sure he can handle it."

"I'm sure. Thanks again."

He was breathing hard as he clicked off the phone. Milner raised his eyebrows.

"Just what I was afraid of, Sam. A big storm ripped through there. Maggie and the team were out in it. When they last called in they were being driven back into the weed mats. And now they can't be contacted at all. Sam, you've done a bit of sailing. What does a captain do in a situation like that?"

Milner screwed up his eyes. "It's a tough call. If he leaves the motors on he risks fouling them up in the weed. But if he cuts them the wind will turn him sideways and there's a real risk of capsizing."

"Even if they didn't capsize," said Terry, "they're stranded in one of the most poisonous places on the planet. That weed is one great mass of ammonia organisms. A group of holiday-makers got trapped in it and every one of them died."

"Maggie must have known that beforehand, though. Did she take respirators?"

"Yes, thank God. But they could be suffering from exposure or dehydration. I've got to get them out of there. The US Coast Guard seems to be the best bet. Who's the top man?"

Milner thought for a minute before answering, "the Commandant. The Coast Guard's a branch of the military, but the Commandant reports direct to the Secretary for Homeland Security."

"James Brierley?"

"Yes, do you know him?"

Terry didn't like to say he'd been introduced as they were about to enter the Oval Office.

"We've met. Where do I find him?"

James Brierley's desk was the counterpart of his own immaculate appearance. Pens and pencils were neatly aligned, the pad was square, the telephone at precisely forty-five degrees. Terry found him more daunting to speak to than the President, although he was no less helpful.

"The best thing," Brierley said as he returned to his room, where he'd left Terry sitting at the side of his desk, "would be for you to speak to Captain Andrew Boyd personally. He's in command of Air Station Elizabeth City. I've paved the way for you. My secretary can get him on a private line, you can take it in her office. She also has a map and a list of other Coast Guard stations. You may want to look those over first."

"Excellent. Thank you very much, sir. I appreciate your help."

"Not at all, Dr. McKinley. I know how much the President values your services. Good luck and let me know if there's anything else I can do."

The voice on the line said, "Boyd."

"Captain Boyd, this is Dr. McKinley. I – "

"Ah, Dr. McKinley. I was expecting your call. Right, missing vessel *Cleaver II* out of Bermuda. ASEC logged a call from Maritime Operations Centre last Friday at 1530 hours. Shortly after that we received a 406 MHz distress beacon with a position plotting 100 nautical miles north-east of Bermuda..."

His heart missed a beat. "Sorry, can I stop you there? A distress beacon? Does that mean they've capsized?"

Boyd sounded like he didn't enjoy being interrupted.

"No, it doesn't have to mean that. Category I EPIRBs – that's Emergency Position Indicating Radio Beacons, doctor – are released automatically at a depth of three to ten feet, it's true, but they can also be activated manually. Category II beacons are only activated manually."

"You've no way of knowing which sort it was?"

"No. Shall I go on?"

"Yes, sorry."

"Weather on scene was very severe so we couldn't do anything at that time. At first light things had improved enough to send a C-130 Hercules to the distress position. Crew sighted a vessel which appeared to be trapped in a large weed mat. The vessel released signal flares."

Terry's spirits lifted.

"So they hadn't capsized?"

"It's a fair assumption," the Captain remarked drily. "At that point we would normally send out a rescue crew in an HH-60 Jayhawk."

That, Terry knew, was Coast Guard's standard long-range helicopter.

"So why didn't you?"

Terry thought he detected a sigh.

"Sir, you have to appreciate what's been happening here. We have a crisis situation in a huge area of the north-west United States because of the eruption at Yellowstone. They need every helicopter they can get, especially long-range helicopters. They've requisitioned Jayhawks from wherever they can get them. All the Coast Guard Air Stations are down to just one, and that includes ours. The storm on Friday created emergencies up and down this coast. We've been running missions with that machine continuously for twenty-four hours. It did a valiant job but now it's grounded for technical reasons. We're working as hard as we can to make it airworthy but there are problems getting the engine parts. Until they come there's nothing we can do."

Terry's shoulders sagged, weighed down by an enormous burden of guilt. The supervolcano had been his idea. It had killed maybe a million people and it had come between him and Maggie. Now it had put her life on the line.

It made no difference what she thought of him: he simply had to get her back.

He pulled himself up. The situation was absurd.

"What about other stations, can't they lend you a bloody helicopter?"

"With the best will in the world, no. They have to be able to respond to emergencies themselves and they're all down to one craft. They're facing the same problems as we are."

Problems. All you're giving me is problems. I want solutions.

"Captain Boyd, the people on that boat are doing work of international importance and they've been marooned out there on the open ocean for more than three days. They're risking their lives for us. It is absolutely vital that we get them out."

The Captain's slow reply carried an edge.

"Let me tell you something, doctor. When you're conducting Search and Rescue operations, you don't make value judgements about who's worth saving and who isn't. We treat VIPs the same as drug traffickers."

Terry lifted his eyes to the ceiling.

"I appreciate that. But when it comes to priorities I know who I'd put higher on the list."

"I can assure you this mission has top priority. It's not a matter of pride for this service when people are left stranded like that. But what can I do about it? I've explained the situation. I don't have an operational helicopter. I did ask central command for a cutter to be dispatched to St. George –"

"How long's that going to take?"

"Depends where it's coming from. Twenty-four hours?"

"Not good enough – at this stage a few minutes could make the difference between life and death." Terry took a deep breath. "All right, Captain, how's this for a plan? When we finish this conversation I'll speak to the commanding officer at Coast Guard Clearwater in Florida. If I drive down immediately with a police escort I can be on his doorstep in the early hours. We'll fly their Jayhawk to you at Air Station Elizabeth City and refuel. By first light tomorrow we can be ready to leave. You can decide between you who's going to crew it to Bermuda, your people or theirs. We'll base ourselves at Fort George and conduct the Search and Rescue operation from there."

There was a pause, then an uncomfortable laugh.

"Can we be realistic for a moment, sir? Clearwater aren't going to part up with their one and only operational Jayhawk. Like I said, they've got to be ready for emergencies of their own. I've been asked to help you, doctor, and I'm being as cooperative as I can, but what you're suggesting just isn't feasible."

"Well, what would make it feasible? A directive from the Commandant?"

He could almost hear the man swallow.

"Ah, the Commandant delegates responsibility for maritime safety to the command at the nearest station. Only we know what the situation is on the ground."

"All right, then. How about a directive from the Secretary of Homeland Security? Or the President of the United States?"

Another silence. Then:

"You're not serious."

"I'm deadly serious."

"You can go as high as that?"

"You'd better believe it. I'll see you tomorrow. Early."

CHAPTER 70

The Jayhawk flew low over the water, making full use of ground effect, the steady thud of the rotors muffled by the headphones in Terry's helmet.

After his phone calls they were on standby at Clearwater. When he got there they quickly kitted him out in the dark blue US Coast Guard battle dress. The rotors were turning even before he added the high-vis vest and ran doubled over to the waiting craft. As soon as he climbed in a crew member swapped his Coast Guard baseball cap for a yellow flight helmet, made sure he was strapped in, and they were airborne. The sky was beginning to pale as they landed at Elizabeth City. They didn't stay long. There was a brief stop at St. George to refuel again and now, at last, they were flying in search mode.

The pilot's voice crackled through the headphones.

"Okay, we're approaching target zone."

Terry listened to the muttered exchanges in the cockpit.

"These are the coordinates ASEC gave us. I don't see a goddamned thing."

"The boat was caught in a weed mat. Could have drifted some."

"Or sunk. Anything on the emergency frequency?"

"Nope. Better set up a search pattern."

Terry bit his lip and waited, straining to hear more, but there was only the noise of the rotors, rising periodically as they turned for another pass.

Minutes went by.

"There."

"I see a fishing boat, where's the weed?"

"Let's take a closer look."

The cabin tilted as they turned and Terry, his face up against the window, leaned hard into the restraint of the belt to see more. A fishing vessel passed below them. White, modern. Two people on deck gave them a wave.

Terry moved the stalk of the microphone and spoke.

"That's not it."

"Who says so?"

"I say so. I've been on the bloody boat and that's not it."

An audible sigh. "Okay, resume pattern."

Ten more minutes passed.

Then:

"Over there. See?" And louder, "Okay, we have a visual."

The Jayhawk banked and circled and Terry caught his first glimpse of the stranded vessel. It was as if some giant hand had drawn a line through it. On one side was open ocean, the white-tipped waves grey beneath the ash-laden sky. On the other side was a gently undulating greenish-brown mat of weed. The boat seemed to be stuck fast, rocking fore and aft in the waves.

The pilots again.

"Any sign of life?"

"Not that I can see."

His heart was pounding. The boat had been marooned here for more than three days. What on earth were they going to find?

The helicopter slowed overhead, tipped back gently and hovered. The door opened and the cabin filled with noise. One of the crew had already attached his harness to a line and he was quickly out and descending to the afterdeck of the boat many feet below them.

Terry ventured forward, impatient for a better view but another crewman shouted, "Stand back!"

It seemed like an age went by. Then they began to winch up the line and the yellow crewman's helmet appeared. He was clasping what looked like armful of bedding.

They hauled it in and placed it carefully in a seat; the layers fell away and a head lolled back, trailing long brown hair. It was Sara. As Terry fastened her seat belt he examined her face carefully. It looked thin and pinched but she was alive – just. He placed a bottle of water in her cold, damp hands, helped her to raise it shakily to her lips. Some leaked down the side of her mouth but she managed to swallow a sip, eyes closed.

"Sara…?"

There was no response. She couldn't hear him over all the racket.

The crewman had gone down again.

Next to come up was Jos. He looked a little better than Sara.

Terry's mind was racing.

Where was Maggie?

His hopes rose as the winch rotated again but this time it was Rob they brought in. If anything Rob's condition was worse than Sara's. Terry buckled him in and tried to get him to take some water but he was too weak and exhausted to respond.

"How many more?" the co-pilot shouted.

"Two more. But we've got two dead down there: one male, one female."

Terry's heart dropped like a lift.

"You're sure?"

"Hundred per cent."

"We're not taking any chances. Leave the bodies behind. The cutter will pick them up when it tows the boat in."

Terry's mind raced. "We can't leave anyone…" he began, but couldn't finish. What if Maggie's was one of the bodies? He couldn't let them leave her. His heart was pounding in his chest as the crew-man dropped again towards the boat.

Terry could hardly breathe. Every second that passed seemed like an hour.

The crew-man's yellow helmet appeared in the doorway again. It swung to and fro, then the harness rotated and he caught a glimpse of the body strapped into it. The hair looked dark. Too dark? His heart shot into his throat. Not too dark. Dark curls peeping from underneath the hood of a jacket.

"Maggie," he breathed.

They pulled her in and he took her straight into his arms. What he accepted was a dead weight with no sign of movement. He set her down on a seat and cupped her cheek in his hand; it was cold. His momentary relief was pushed aside by fresh needles of terror, which prickled inside his chest. Then the eyebrows twitched, set into a frown, and she blinked. A distant light entered her eyes as she peered under his helmet. Her mouth moved. He couldn't hear her above the thrash of the rotor but he knew she'd said his name.

He nodded. "Yes, it's Terry. Don't worry, Maggie. It's over now."

"Get her strapped in," commanded the other crew member.

Terry did as he asked. He found it hard not to weep with relief as he fastened the seat belt and allowed himself to look into those dark, wondering eyes before returning to help with the last man. But this time the winchman came up alone.

"Captain refuses to come up," he said. "Says he'll stay with the boat till the cutter comes. Give me a ration pack and some water; that'll keep him going."

Moments later they shut the cabin door, snuffing out much of the noise. Then the engine note rose and the helicopter swung in a wide arc, heading for St. George.

The team occupied four adjacent beds on a ward in the King Edward Memorial Hospital. Maggie reclined on soft pillows, her arms resting on the sheets. Taped to her left arm was the tubing from an intravenous drip. She smiled wanly at Terry, who was sitting at the bedside.

"The doc says you're all rehydrating nicely," he said. "You ran it close, though."

She nodded. "Max had some emergency supplies but they didn't go far. We were dreadfully hungry but the real problem was water."

"How did you manage?"

"Well fortunately we had one chest of samples left. That was Rob's doing – he had the bright idea of putting it into an empty locker. The samples were on ice and when the ice melted we had just enough to keep us going. It tasted terrible but at least we're alive."

She paused, glancing at the three other beds, and tears came to her eyes.

"Sonia?" said Terry gently.

"It was when we lost the samples. She tried to grab one of the chests and she got washed down the deck and banged her head." She met his eyes. "We didn't realize it was so serious. She seemed all right for a while. Then she was complaining about headaches, and then she was drowsy so we let her sleep. We had no idea she was dying until it was too late. The doctor told me it was a subdural haematoma. Only prompt surgery could have saved her. If only I hadn't…"

"You mustn't blame yourself, Maggie. It was a tragic accident. It wasn't your fault."

She sighed and wiped her eyes. "And then there was Casey. Poor man. He passed away the night before last. We didn't hear a thing but when the sun came up Max suddenly cried out and we saw him holding Casey in his arms."

"They were old friends?"

"He'd known him all his life. He told me it was Casey who took him out on his first trip when he was barely into his teens. The man was only ever happy at sea so he let him crew for him from time to time, out of friendship. I gather he was in his late seventies, although he didn't look it. I suppose the physiological stress was just too much for him. Max put him next to Sonia and covered both the bodies in a tarpaulin. No one said anything but I think we were all wondering who'd be next."

"You knew help would be on the way, though."

"Well, yes, but the question was, when? We had no idea we'd have to hold out so long. An aircraft came over on the first morning, a big four-engine job. I could see the US Coast Guard markings. Max fired a signal flare so we knew they hadn't missed us. We expected to be rescued later that day but they never came back. We couldn't understand why. I still can't."

"It's a long story."

"Well?"

"Later, maybe. You know, things might have been worse. It wasn't a big boat. You could easily have capsized in that storm."

"Max was amazing. He didn't cut the engines until we were right in the weed; after that it more or less held us in the right orientation. The boat still screwed a lot, though. Rob and Sara were terribly seasick – that's why they were more dehydrated than the rest of us. I tried to give them extra rations of water but to be honest there was barely enough for any of us."

They were both silent for a while. Then, in a low voice, she said:

"I made a mess of things."

"The conditions were exceptional. You couldn't have anticipated it."

"No, I don't mean the storm. I mean I made a mess of us. I put up fences. I never really meant to. And you were so good. You were there for me when I needed you most." Tears welled up again. "Terry, I've been so unhappy without you."

He leaned forward to take her face in his hands and gently brushed the tears from the thick, wet lashes.

"You're safe, and I'm here. Nothing else really matters, does it?"

She took his hand, kissed his fingertips, and held it to her cheek. She was smiling through the tears. Slowly he sat back, letting his fingers trail lightly down her cheek and along the line of her jaw to her chin.

He could say nothing more; his throat was too tight. They sat in silence, contemplating each other, fingers entwined, their hands resting on the crisp, white sheet.

Somewhere a door opened and they heard voices, the metallic rattle of a trolley, the abrupt hiss of a curtain being drawn. She shifted slightly in the bed.

"I hope Max is all right," she said.

"The cutter should have got to him by now and I expect they'll have a medic on hand. They'll tow the boat into harbour. Your samples will still be on board – if they're any use to you by then."

"Oh, they should be. The ice was only a precaution – a lucky one for us, as it turned out. But we still have the samples from the other trip, the one we did on Wednesday. The people at the Institute of Ocean Sciences have been great: they supplied us with dry ice and put the first lot of samples in a chest freezer for safekeeping, so those should be fine. Jos and Sara and Rob will be itching to get the analyses done. Not that it matters now."

Coming from her, the last was such an uncharacteristic statement that it took Terry by surprise.

"Because you're safe, you mean?" he asked.

"No, because we're alive." A look of realization entered her eyes. "Of course! You don't know, do you?"

"Don't know what?"

"That we lost the respirators."

He almost stood up. "What?"

"Yes. A couple of big waves swept them overboard with the rest of the samples. That was the chest Sonia was trying to save."

"You had… no respirators?"

"That's right. We were stuck in the worst concentration of ammonia organisms in the world and we survived!"

"But how…?"

"Don't you see? The trial worked! It's the only explanation! Jos said the weed floating on the surface was a funny colour. He thought it might be a different species but it wasn't a different species – it was dead! The phage must have killed loads of it. Down below us the cyanobacteria were green – we managed to capture some strands after the storm passed – so that was living and it still didn't produce ammonia. We know that for certain, because otherwise we wouldn't be here to tell the tale."

He sat back and shook his head.

"My God, you were even closer to death than I thought. Normally I don't believe in luck but you've certainly had a fair share of it."

"It wasn't luck," she remonstrated, with a small lift of her chin. "It was the work of a very talented team." Then she grinned at him. "You know what this means, don't you? No organism could spread as fast as that by growth alone. It must be swapping in the plasmid really efficiently and it's doing it under real conditions. We can check the samples but there's no need to hold things up: we'll go into mass production right away. It's been a long time coming, but this is it: we did it."

EPILOGUE

It seemed like half of Washington was there. Maggie and Terry circulated discreetly, arm in arm, enjoying the atmosphere. Although they'd come to the White House several times they'd never been in these wonderful reception rooms.

"The First Lady must have had an army of cleaners through here," she whispered to Terry, flicking her eyes up to the glittering chandeliers. She and Terry had a constant battle with the fine dust that penetrated their Washington apartment.

They scanned the guests. A few they knew: Robert Cabot, Elaine Zanuck, Richard Pevensey, Noel Harrison, all with their spouses. Chris Walmesley came over and introduced his wife and they chatted for a while.

There was one person they were relieved not to see, although they hadn't expected him to be there. Herbert Kramer had left the Institute immediately after the confrontation with Terry, taking his administrative staff with him. His departure had attracted little comment, and their contribution was not missed.

Marie Kinghorn came bustling past, saw them, and stopped.

"Well, hello, you two. Glad you could make it! Good trip back?"

"Very good, thanks," Terry replied.

"Thank you so much for inviting us," Maggie added.

"Oh, but you simply had to be here. Now have fun. I must buzz. Will you excuse me?"

"Of course."

A tray of drinks came by, borne by a white-gloved waiter. Terry helped himself to a glass of champagne while Maggie took a Buck's Fizz.

They sipped their drinks and looked around the room. A smile came to Maggie's lips and she gave Terry a gentle nudge.

"Remember when we got the invitation?"

It was the last week of their honeymoon, and they were spending it at her parents' villa in Portugal.

A thin veil of ash still hung in the sky but the sun was beginning to show through more strongly, and it was warm enough to have lunch on the terrace. The wooden table was already crowded with dishes: freshly baked bread, salads, big tomatoes, roasted peppers, artichokes, olives, and grilled sardines in oil. Maggie set out plates, knives, and forks, then wandered over to the wrought-iron balcony, where Terry and her father were enjoying a glass of white wine together, looking out over the vineyard to the fluted terra cotta roofs of the village below.

Terry held his glass out to her. It was frosted with condensation.

"Here, try this, Mags."

She took a sip.

"Mmm. That's lovely. Is it local?"

"It is, yes," Roger answered. "Made by a cooperative. Not last year, of course – there wasn't enough sun to ripen the grapes. Things may be better this year."

"Did you buy the vineyards separately?"

"Oh no, they came with the villa. I was retiring, and Eleanor suffers with her chest, so we thought it would be a good idea to move out here. To start with I thought I might sell the vineyards off but it seemed a shame to split the property up. As it happens it's worked out rather well. Our neighbour's a member of the cooperative. He tends the vines and arranges the picking. When the skies clear properly we may even turn a small profit. Could be a useful supplement to my pension."

Eleanor emerged from the house. "Lunch is ready. Do you want iced coffee or are you going to continue with the wine?"

"Both," Roger said, unhesitatingly.

"All right. Go on, you get started."

She went back into the house. Terry started to cut the bread and Maggie and Roger helped themselves to the salad. A few moments later Eleanor emerged from the house with a jug of iced coffee.

"Here you are. The post just came. I brought it with me."

She sat down and fanned quickly through the envelopes. Then she paused, holding one up.

"There's one here for you, dears. American stamp. Good gracious, the envelope has 'White House' on it. It can't be that 'White House' can it?"

Maggie suppressed a smile. "We'll have to see, won't we?"

"It's addressed to Dr. and Mrs. McKinley. How did they know where you were?"

"Pretty well everyone knew we were coming here, Mum. Come on now, hand over."

Eleanor passed the letter to her daughter, making no attempt to hide her curiosity. She raised a hand to fluff up her grey curls as she waited and Terry suppressed a smile at the familiar gesture.

Maggie opened the envelope and scanned the card she found inside. She read it out. "'The President and First Lady request the company of Dr. Terence McKinley and Mrs. (Dr.) Margaret McKinley at a levee at the White House to celebrate the restoration of the centre of government to Washington, D.C. Black tie.'" She turned it over. "Oh, isn't that nice: there's a personal note on the other side, scribbled by the President. 'I very much hope that you, as principal architects of our recent success, will be able to join us. Best wishes on your recent betrothal and every good wish for the future. Yours, Harry.'"

Eleanor's mouth was open.

Roger said, "Here, let me see that."

He read the invitation, exchanged wondering glances with his wife, and said slowly, "What the devil have the pair of you been up to?"

The guests milled around. A continuous procession of trays of canapes appeared and receded amongst them. Maggie managed to pick up two vol-au-vents and handed one to Terry.

"I wish we could have told them what it was really about," she said.

"They were satisfied to know it was some sort of government job. They're terribly proud of you."

"And of you."

James Brierley came by. The woman with him was as tall and slender as he was, expensively dressed and with a tautness to her features that suggested the attentions of a plastic surgeon. There were those who referred to such women as "Washington wives".

"Ah, Dr. and Mrs.!" Brierley said. "Let me introduce my wife, Kendra. Kendra this is Dr. and Mrs. McKinley. Would you believe, these two have just been on honeymoon in Portugal."

"Oh, how lovely!" she exclaimed in a slow Southern drawl. "We were in Portugal a few years back, weren't we James? It was simply gorgeous." She suddenly looked deeply worried. "How are things there?"

"It's still beautiful, Mrs. Brierley," Terry reassured her.

"Oh, and you're from Eng-er-land!" she exclaimed. "What are you doing in here in Washington?"

Her husband looked vaguely discomforted.

Terry said cheerily, "I'm with NASA. I'm Deputy Director of the Exoplanets and Stellar Astrophysics Laboratory. And Maggie's at NIH. She heads up a molecular biology lab."

"Really?" Kendra's voice swooped down two octaves. "How

fascinating!"

She continued to look from one to the other with wide blue eyes.

"Terry," James Brierley interrupted. "I think the President is trying to attract your attention."

"Oh. Would you excuse me for a moment?"

"Well surely," Kendra Brierley said, linking her arm with Maggie's. "We'll take good care of your lady wife. Come with me, dear. There are some people you simply *have* to meet."

The President put his hand on Terry's shoulder and guided him over to a quiet corner.

"So many people around, haven't had a chance to talk to you," he said.

"I understand, Sir," Terry said. "It's a grand occasion."

"Yeah." The President surveyed the party as if confirming the fact for himself. "I figured we needed a bit of a morale booster." He turned back to Terry. "Of course, we billed it as a celebration of our return to Washington. There's only a handful of people in this room who know the real reason."

"Down to target levels for atmospheric ammonia – yes, we had a little celebration of our own when we got that news."

"Great job, great job. Let's drink to it."

They touched their wine glasses.

"Sorry about Herbert Kramer. I guess you and Maggie didn't get on too well with him."

"Let's just say we would find life perfectly tolerable if we never clapped eyes on the man again."

The President sighed. "Bad choice on my part. He'd given me some sound advice in the past but I guess he was out of his depth on this one. I accepted his resignation and he took early retirement. I offered the Directorship to Chris Walmesley."

"You couldn't do better than that."

"Yeah, unfortunately he wouldn't take it. Prefers to be closer to what he calls 'real science.'" Terry grinned. "But he'll be available to advise me informally from time to time."

He took a small sip from his glass and surveyed the room expansively.

"So, Terry, somehow we all came through this nightmare. Tell me something. When you look back on it in years to come, what's the part that'll give you the greatest satisfaction?"

Terry thought for a moment, looking down into his glass, swirling the wine slowly. He tried to think of alternatives but for some reason his mind kept returning to the same scene.

"It may sound silly."

"Go on."

"Well, there's a little village in Wales with a lovely trout river running through it. It has a kind of special significance for me. I used to go there with a fly rod every year if I could. Unfortunately it was ruined by the ammonia organism. I love to think of the insects and the birds and the fish – all the wildlife – gradually returning. And one day I'll go back too and it'll be just as I remembered it when I was an excited teenager clambering down that bank for the very first time."

Even as he said it he realized what a long way he'd travelled from that river, that little Welsh village, that former life. The President nodded slowly. "Sounds idyllic. You should make that trip." He looked around him but there was no one within earshot. He lowered his voice. "You know, Terry, I still ask myself whether we had to do it – Yellowstone, I mean…" his voice trailed off.

"So do I, Sir", replied Terry. "Every day."

"And what's your answer?"

Terry paused, then answered. "I remind myself that it was many more weeks before we could actually start spraying. That it took another five months to get the levels right down worldwide. That without the eruption, none of us would have survived."

The President sighed and said, "I guess." Then he leaned closer. "You know, my friend, in any other situation I'd award you and Maggie the Presidential Medal of Freedom. But you're in an unenviable position. You saved the world – and no one must ever know."

Terry flushed.

"We all played our part, Sir. You included."

The President slapped Terry's shoulder. "You Brits!" he laughed. "Always the diplomats. Not that the whole world is particularly grateful, I might add. Oh no, they want to know what we're going to do about all the mats of dead algae washing up everywhere. Thailand, for example. You know, before we started, Bangkok had some of the worst white smogs anywhere – they killed tens of thousands. Now the sun's beginning to peep through and the tourists are coming back and the Thai government's complaining their beautiful sandy beaches are being spoiled by brown algae. They say it's the spraying we did on the ocean. Of course, they're dead right about that part."

"You should tell them to scrape it up and put it on their fields. It's stacked full of nitrogen."

"Hey, that's a great idea..."

"Excuse me, Mr. President..."

The President's Secretary was standing there.

"Yes, what is it, Sarah?"

"You're wanted for the press photos, Sir."

"Back to the grindstone, eh? Ah well, see you later, Terry."

Terry raised a hand in farewell.

"Thanks for rescuing me," Maggie said, as they strolled together down a palatial corridor.

"I thought you'd probably had enough."

"She's very friendly but she is a bit overpowering. And he's so reserved, too. I can't understand it."

"They say opposites attract."

She looked at him. "Are we so different, then?"

"I don't know. I suppose we are. But you need something in common too. I'm sure they have shared interests. Theatre, friends, charities – I bet she's a terrific fund-raiser."

"Probably."

"There you are, then. He can get on quietly with his job while she gives them both a reputation for caring about the less advantaged. Perfect match. And at the same time she keeps tabs for him on Georgetown society, who's sleeping with who, and..."

"Terry!"

"I'm serious. Could be important in his job."

"You're getting very cynical, Terry McKinley. I think you've spent too much time around politicians. Talking of which: what did the President want?"

"Oh, he just wanted to thank us both for saving the world."

"Ha, that was nice of him, but we couldn't have done it without his support."

"That's more or less what I told him." The noise of conversation receded behind them. He tilted his head in that direction. "They certainly know how to throw a party."

"Yes..."

He caught the hesitation and stopped to look at her.

"You all right?"

"Yes… well, no."

"What is it?"

She sighed. "Oh, here we are congratulating ourselves on ridding the world of that organism and getting the atmospheric ammonia down again. I just have an uneasy feeling about it."

"Why?"

"Terry, the whole of mankind was at risk and nearly two million people died. Why? Because a powerful man who knew nothing about science refused to accept advice from people who did. Is that a unique circumstance, never to be repeated?"

He shrugged. "I suppose not. Of course some people are quite capable of doing something like that deliberately."

"Yes, but the point is, they don't have to be enemies of humanity, they may be just focused on the science or the commercial possibilities. They may even have good intentions, like Zak Gould. All it takes is one person who doesn't see the full ramifications – or prefers to close his eyes to them – and something like this could happen all over again."

He was silent for a while. Then he said:

"We'll just have to be vigilant, won't we?"

"Yes, we will. We all will."